Collected Stories and Sketches: 1
Photographed On The Brain

Etching by William Strang, 1898

R.B. Cunninghame Graham

Collected Stories and Sketches

Volume 1

Photographed On The Brain

Edited by Alan MacGillivray and John C. McIntyre

Kennedy & Boyd
an imprint of
Zeticula
57 St Vincent Crescent
Glasgow
G3 8NQ
Scotland
http://www.kennedyandboyd.co.uk
admin@kennedyandboyd.co.uk

Notes on the District of Menteith originally published in 1895
Father Archangel of Scotland originally published in 1896
The Ipané originally published in 1899
This edition copyright © Zeticula 2011
Frontispiece from *Etchings of William Strang* by Frank Newbolt, Newnes, 1907.

Contributors:
R. B. Cunninghame Graham: The Life and The Writings
© Alan MacGillivray 2011
Introduction to Notes on the District of Menteith
© Alan MacGillivray 2011
Introduction to Father Archangel of Scotland © John C. McIntyre 2011
Introduction to The Ipané © Alan MacGillivray 2011
Beyond English: Graham's Use of Foreign Languages in Father Archangel of Scotland, and Other Essays © John C. McIntyre 2011
R. B. Cunninghame Graham's "Aurora La Cujiñi": An Exploration
© John C. McIntyre 2011
Cover photograph © Matthew Hoelscher 2011
Cover design by Felicity Wild
Book design by Catherine E. Smith

ISBN 978-1-84921-100-0

"…a sort of record of a dream, dreamed upon pampas and on prairies, sleeping upon a saddle under the southern stars, or galloping across the plains in the hot sun, photographed in youth upon the writer's brain…"

The Ipané, "The Lazo"

Contents

Preface to the Collection   ix
Robert Bontine Cunninghame Graham: *(AMacG)*
    The Life   xi
    The Writings   xvii
Note to Volume 1   xxiii

Notes on the District of Menteith, for Tourists and Others   1
    Introduction (AMacG)   3

Father Archangel of Scotland, and Other Essays   67
    Introduction (JCMcI)   69

The Ipané   185
    Introduction (AMacG)   187

Appendices   305

Beyond English: Graham's Use of Foreign Languages in *Father Archangel of Scotland, and Other Essays (JCMcI)*   307

"Aurora La Cujiñi: A Realistic Sketch in Seville" — R. B. Cunninghame Graham's "Aurora La Cujiñi": An Exploration *(JCMcI)*   313

Index of Stories in Volume 1   327

Preface to the Collection

Robert Bontine Cunninghame Graham first came to public attention as a Radical Liberal Member of Parliament in the 1880s, when he was in his thirties. The apparent contradiction between his Scottish aristocratic family background and his vigorous attachment to the causes of Socialism, the Labour movement, anti-Imperialism and Scottish Home Rule ensured that he remained a controversial figure for many years right up to his death in the 1930s. Through his father's family of Cunninghame Graham, descended from King Robert II of Scotland and the Earls of Menteith, he had a strong territorial connection with the West of Scotland. On his mother's side, he had significant Hispanic ties through his Spanish grandmother and a naval grandfather who took part in the South American Wars of Liberation. His own world-wide travels, particularly in the Americas, Spain and North Africa, and his amazingly wide circle of friends and acquaintances in many countries and different walks of life gave him a cosmopolitan breadth of experience and a depth of insight into human nature and behaviour that would be the envy of any writer.

And it is as a writer that we now have primarily to remember Graham. His lasting political monuments are the Labour Party and the Scottish National Party, both of which he was deeply involved in founding. Yet he has to share that credit with others. His literary works are his alone. He wrote books of history, travel and biography which were extensively researched but very personal in tone, so that, although highly readable, they might not easily withstand the objective scrutiny of modern scholarship. Rather it is in his favoured literary forms of the short story, sketch and meditative essay, forms often tending to merge into one another, that Graham excels. Over forty years, between 1896 and 1936, he published fourteen collections of such short pieces, ranging over many subjects and lands. With such a wealth of life experience behind him, Graham did not have to dig deep for inspiration. Probably no other Scottish writer of any age brings such a knowledge and awareness of life's diversity to the endeavour of literary creation. However, the quality of his achievement has not as yet been fully assessed. One reason is not hard to find. There has never yet been a proper bringing together of Graham's separate collections into a manageable edition to provide the essential tools for critical study. Consequently literary attention has never been really focused on him, something for which the climate of twentieth-century Scottish, and British, critical fashion is partly responsible. Neither the Modernist movement nor the Scottish Renaissance seems to be an appropriate pigeonhole for Graham to inhabit. He has instead had to suffer the consequences of being too readily stereotyped. Perhaps entranced by the glamour of his apparent flamboyant persona of 'Don Roberto', the Spanish hidalgo, the Argentine gaucho, the Scottish laird, the horseman — adventurer, a succession of editors have republished incomplete collections of stories and sketches selected more to reinforce an image of Graham as larger-than-life legend rather than as the serious literary man he worked hard to be.

The purpose of this series is to make Graham's literary corpus available in a convenient format to modern readers as he originally intended it. Each collection of stories is kept intact, and they appear in chronological order with Graham's own footnotes, and retaining his personal idiosyncrasies and eccentricities of language and style. It is not the intention of the editors to make magisterial judgements of quality or to present a fully annotated critical edition of the stories. These purposes would go far beyond the bounds of this series in space and time, and must remain as tasks for future scholars. We merely hope that a new generation of general readers will discover Graham's short stories and sketches to be interesting and stimulating for their own sake and in their own right, diverse and revealing of a strong and generally sympathetic personality, a richly-stocked original mind and an ironic, realistic yet sensitive observer of the amazing variety of life in a very wide world.

Alan MacGillivray
John C. McIntyre

Robert Bontine Cunninghame Graham

The Life

Robert Bontine Cunninghame Graham belonged to the old-established family of Cunninghame Graham, which had its ancestral territory in the District of Menteith lying between Stirling and Loch Lomond. The family had at one time held the earldom of Menteith and could trace its ancestry back to King Robert II of Scotland in the fourteenth century. The title had been dormant since the seventeenth century, and the Cunninghame Grahams showed no real interest in reviving it. In fact, Graham passed his childhood officially bearing the surname of Bontine, because, during his youth, owing to a strange legal quirk relating to the entailing of estates and conditions of inheritance, the name 'Graham' could only be borne by Robert's grandfather who held the main Graham estate of Gartmore. Robert's father, William, an army officer, had to take another family surname, Bontine, until he inherited Gartmore in 1863. As a young man thereafter, Robert does not seem to have bothered which name he used, and when he in his turn inherited Gartmore, he kept Bontine as a middle name.

Graham was born in London in 1852. His half-Spanish mother preferred the social life of London, while his father had his responsibilities as a Scottish landowner. Accordingly, Graham's boyhood years were spent moving between the south of England and the family's Scottish houses at Gartmore in Menteith, Ardoch in Dunbartonshire and Finlaystone in Renfrewshire. Before going to preparatory school, he spent a lot of time with his Spanish grandmother, Doña Catalina, at her home in the Isle of Wight and accompanied her to Spain on a number of visits. This was his introduction to the Spanish way of life and the Spanish language, in which he became proficient. At the age of eleven he went to a prep school in Warwickshire, before going to Harrow public school for two years. He apparently disliked Harrow intensely and in 1866 was taken from it and sent to a Brussels private school which was much more to his taste. It was during his year there that he learned French and had instruction in fencing. After a year in Brussels, Graham's formal education ended and he spent the next two years until he was seventeen between his homes in Britain and his grandmother's family in Spain, developing along the way his passion for horses and his considerable riding skills.

Graham's adult life began when in 1870, with the support and financial encouragement of his parents, he took ship from Liverpool by way of Corunna and Lisbon for Argentina. The primary motivation was to make money by learning the business of ranching and going into partnership on a Scottish-owned estancia, or ranch. This was seen as a necessity, given that the Graham family had fallen into serious financial difficulties. Graham's father, Major William Bontine, had sunk into madness, the final consequence of a severe head injury in a riding accident, and had engaged in wild speculation with the family assets. Consequently, the estates were encumbered with debts and the Major's affairs had been placed under the supervision of an agent of the Court of Session. As the eldest of three sons, Robert had to find his own fortune and eventually pay off his father's debts. Much of his travelling in the following decades, both alone and later with his wife, Gabriela, had the search for profitable business openings at its heart.

Between 1870 and 1877, Graham undertook three ventures in South America. The ranching on the first visit came to nothing, although, being already an accomplished horseman and speaker of Spanish, he very quickly adapted to the life of the gauchos, or cowboys. He also observed at first hand some of the violence and anarchy of the early 1870s in Argentina and Uruguay; he contracted and recovered from typhus; and finally he undertook an overland horse-droving venture before returning to Britain in 1872. The following year he returned to South America, this time to Paraguay with a view to obtaining concessions for cultivating and selling the yerba mate plant, the source of the widely drunk mate infusion. In his search for possible plantation sites, Graham rode deep into the interior and came across the surviving traces of the original seventeenth and eighteenth century Jesuit settlements, the subject, many years later, for one of his best books. He had little success in his efforts and returned to Britain in 1874. After a couple of years travelling, mainly in Europe, but also to Iceland and down the coast of West Africa, Graham set out again, this time with a business partner, bound for Uruguay, where he contemplated ranching but actually set up in the horse trading business, buying horses in Uruguay with a view to driving them into Brazil to be sold to the Brazilian army. This (again) unsuccessful adventure was later described in the novella, "Cruz Alta"

(1900). Graham again returned to Britain and took up residence at his mother's house in London, becoming a familiar man about town and a frequenter of Mrs Bontine's literary and artistic salon, where he began to develop his wide circle of friends and acquaintances in the literary and cultural fields. It was his experiences in South America in the 1870s that formed his passion for the continent and directed so much of his later literary work. Out of this came the appellation of 'Don Roberto', which is now inescapably part of his personal and literary image.

Paris was another of Graham's favourite places, and it was there in 1878 that he met the woman whom he very rapidly made his wife, much to the apparent hostile concern of his family, particularly his mother. The mystery and (probably deliberate) uncertainty surrounding the circumstances of his marriage cry out for proper research among surviving family documents. One can only sketch in the few known facts and legends. Graham met a young woman who was known as Gabriela de la Balmondière. By one account she had been born in Chile with a father of French descent and a Spanish mother. She had been orphaned and brought up in Paris by an aunt, who may or may not have had her educated in a convent. By another account, she was making a living in Paris as an actress.

After a brief acquaintanceship, she and Graham lived together before coming to London and being married in a registry office in October, 1878, without family approval. In time everybody came to accept her as an exotic new member of the family, although there seems to have been some mutual hostility for several years between her and Graham's mother. It was not until the 1980s that the discovery of Gabriela's birth certificate showed that she was in fact English, the daughter of a Yorkshire doctor, and her real name was Caroline, or Carrie, Horsfall. Why Graham, and indeed the whole Graham family, should have gone on through the whole of his and her lives, and beyond, sustaining this myth of Gabriela's origins invites speculations of several kinds that may never be resolved.

After a few months of marriage, Robert and Gabriela set out for the New World, first to New Orleans, and then to Texas with the intention of going into the mule-breeding business. Over the next two years they earned a precarious living by various means both in Texas and Mexico, until the final disaster when a Texas ranch newly acquired by Graham and a business partner was raided and destroyed by Apaches. The Grahams finally returned to Britain in 1881 with substantial debts, and lived quietly in Spain and Hampshire. The death of Graham's father in 1883, however, meant that Robert finally inherited the main family estate of Gartmore with all its debts and problems, and had to live the life of a Scottish laird with all its local and social responsibilities.

The restrictions placed upon Graham by his new role could not confine such a restless spirit for long, and in 1885 he stood unsuccessfully for Parliament as a Liberal. The following year he was elected the MP for North-West Lanark, the beginning of an active and highly-coloured political career that continued in one form or another for the rest of his life. He spent only six years actually in Parliament, a period in which he soon revealed himself as more a Socialist than a Liberal, espousing a number of Radical causes and becoming deeply involved and influential in the early years of the Labour movement, being, along with Keir Hardie, one of the co-founders of the Labour Party. The high point of his time in Parliament was when he was arrested and committed to prison, accused of assaulting a policeman during the 'Bloody Sunday' demonstration in Trafalgar Square on 13th November, 1887. From his maiden speech onwards, he wrote and spoke out forcefully on behalf of Labour causes and finally in 1892 stood unsuccessfully for Parliament directly as a Labour candidate. Even out of Parliament Graham continued to be active politically. Although he gradually ceased to be a leading figure in the new Labour Party, his new-found talent as a polemical journalist, in great demand in the serious papers and journals of the day, enabled him to remain in the public eye with his concern about social conditions and his unfashionable anti-Imperial attitudes. He was opposed to the Boer Wars, as he was also to the new imperialism of the USA, shown during the Spanish-American War of 1898, which affronted his strong attachment to Spain and Latin America. His commitment to Scottish Home Rule led him in his later years to find a new role as a founder of the Scottish National Party.

After leaving Parliament in 1892, Graham and his wife were free to travel more frequently, sometimes together but more often pursuing their diverging interests apart, and always on the look-out for possibilities of improving their finances. Spain and Morocco were the main areas of their travel. Graham also began to diversify in his new-found interest in writing into the prolific production of travel books and collections of short stories and sketches. Yet nothing could stave off for ever the inevitable consequences of his father's irresponsibility. The debt-ridden estate of Gartmore had eventually to be sold, and the Grahams settled for financial security on the smaller family estate of Ardoch on the northern side of the Firth of Clyde. Even so, a worse blow was to befall Graham. Gabriela had never been physically strong and was prone to pleurisy (not helped by her chain-smoking habit). She died in 1906 on the way back from one of her many visits to the drier warmth of Spain. Her marriage with Robert of more than a quarter of a century had been childless, but they were a close couple and Robert missed her greatly.

As his life advanced into late middle age and old age through the new century, Graham developed his writing with more collections of short stories and works of biography centred on Mexican and South American history. His astonishingly wide circle of friends in all fields of society and his continuing political activities kept him close to the centre of society and often in the public gaze. At the outbreak of the First World War, though he had been critical of the warmongering attitudes that had marked the years from 1910 to 1914, Graham, at the age of 62, volunteered for service and was charged with two missions to South America, one in 1914-15 to Uruguay to buy horses for the Army, and the second to Colombia in 1916-17 to obtain beef supplies. The first mission enabled him to recapture some of the excitement of his early years on horseback in South America, although it made him desperately sad as a horse-lover to think of the dreadful fate awaiting the animals he bought. The second mission turned out to be unsuccessful, owing to a lack of shipping.

After the war, Graham continued to travel, now more for relaxation and for the sake of his health. He had a new close companion and friend, a wealthy widow, Mrs Elizabeth ('Toppie') Dummett, whose artistic salon in London he frequented and who travelled with him on most of his journeys. Back in Scotland, Graham continued to spend summers at Ardoch, and was well known round the Glasgow and Scottish literary scene, as well as being involved in Scottish political controversy. Among his literary friends were the poet Hugh MacDiarmid (C.M.Grieve) and the novelist and journalist, Neil Munro. Graham made a point of attending the dedication of a memorial to Munro in the summer of 1935. Graham was then eighty-three years old. A few months later, Graham set out on what he probably knew would be his last journey, back to Argentina, the scene of his first youthful adventures. In Buenos Aires, he contracted bronchitis and then pneumonia, and after a few days he died. His funeral in Buenos Aires was a large public occasion attended by the Argentine President, with two horses belonging to Graham's friend,

Aimé Tschiffely, the horseman-adventurer, accompanying the coffin as symbols of Don Roberto's attachment to the gaucho culture that had been such an influence on his life and philosophy.

Robert Bontine Cunninghame Graham is buried near his wife Gabriela in the family burial place at the Augustinian Priory on the little island of Inchmahome in the Lake of Menteith. A memorial to him is now placed near the former family mansion of Gartmore.

The Writings

It may not be too much of an exaggeration to say that the greatest blessing bestowed upon Robert Bontine Cunninghame Graham in his boyhood years was an incomplete formal education. Two years at prep school, two years at Harrow and one 'finishing' year in Brussels gave him little of the classical education deemed essential for the well-born Victorian gentleman. Instead he reached the age of eighteen with considerable fluency in Spanish and French, and an undoubted acquired love of reading gained from the books in the libraries of his family's Scottish houses and his mother's house in London. His extensive (if difficult to decipher) letters home to his mother from abroad make this latter fact clear. The proficiency in Spanish and French gave him immediate entry into two major literatures of the modern world in addition to English, a more bankable asset for the modern writer-to-be than any familiarity with the classical writings of Greece and Rome.

It is conventional to ascribe the beginnings of Graham's writing career to the period after he left Parliament and was settled back in Gartmore, in the last decade of the century. However, the habit of writing had undoubtedly been acquired by him over many years preceding, when he was writing long letters home about his experiences in the Americas, and, later on, writing speeches and articles as part of his work as a strongly involved and committed Radical Liberal Member of Parliament.

Nevertheless, we can only begin to speak of Graham as a true writer when in the years after 1890 he began to publish both fiction and non-fiction on a regular basis. Probably beginning with an essay, "The Horses of the Pampas", contributed to the monthly magazine, *Time*, in 1890, Graham went on to write extensively for the *Saturday Review* and other periodicals. There were essays, sketches and short stories, and, later, books of travel and history. Graham's confidence in himself as a writer can be seen to grow during this period, especially when he acquired the literary and critical friendship of the publisher, Edward Garnett.

What makes Graham very different in his writing from any other late Victorian upper-class traveller and man of action is his conscious awareness and absorption of the realistic spirit and literary techniques of contemporary European writers. His main subjects initially are his beloved South America and Spain, as filtered through his personal experiences as a younger man, and aspects of life in Britain, perhaps especially Scotland. Yet he describes these with, in the main, a detached unsentimental insight gained from his reading of the short stories and sketches of Guy de Maupassant and Ivan Turgenev. Equally, after reading *La Pampa*, a set of vignettes of gaucho life written in French by Alfred Ébélot, on the recommendation of his close friend, W.H. Hudson, he came to see how his memories of life among the gauchos could be structured into short tales blending close detailed observation and brief narrative. Yet it would not be true to think of Graham as always being a totally controlled and dispassionate writer. There is both fire and anger in those of his pieces that set out to confront rampant and racist imperialism, social injustice and cruelty directed against helpless human or animal targets.

There is perhaps a tentative quality about Graham's first two books. *Notes on the District of Menteith* (1895) is a highly personal short guidebook to the part of Scotland he knew at first hand surrounding the ancestral home. It almost seems to be a practice for the real thing, before going out into the territory of the big book. Similarly, *Father Archangel of Scotland, and Other Essays* (1896) is an initial attempt at the short story collection, in which Graham shares the contents with his wife, Gabriela.

Graham's first true full-length book conceived as a single narrative is his account of personal experiences in Morocco, *Mogreb-El-Acksa* (1898). The book, whose title translates as 'Morocco the Most Holy', deals in the main with Graham's time there in the later months of 1897. Paradoxically, for a man who travelled so extensively throughout his long life, it is one of the only two real travel books that Graham ever wrote. The other is *Cartagena and the Banks of the Sinú* (1920), which arose out of Graham's mission to Colombia in 1916-17. It is clear that he came to see his experiences in the wider world primarily as a fertile and energising source for fiction.

Between 1899 and 1936, Graham published thirteen collections of sketches and short stories. Generally, his approach for these collections was to bring together stories and short pieces of a rather heterogeneous nature, with settings ranging from his favourite locales of South America and Spain, and increasingly North Africa, to Scotland, London, Paris and more distant parts of the globe. Some of the stories are crafted narratives; others may be little more than detailed descriptions of life and manners with a minimum of narrative, or even personal essays on a range of diverse topics. Although his tone is mostly detached and often ironic, the persona of the writer is never far away and at times Graham's partialities emerge clearly through the text.

The first two collections, *The Ipané* (1899) and *Thirteen Stories* (1900), give the impression of being the most diverse, partly because of the throwaway nature of their titles. 'Ipané' is merely the name of an old river boat that appears in the title story of the first collection. The book has a random quality about it with no sense of a central thread behind the choices.

Thirteen Stories, as a title, suggests an equal randomness. Indeed the main story in the collection is in fact a novella, "Cruz Alta", which takes up fully a third of the length of the book on its own, the other stories being very diverse in their settings and themes. However, the collections that follow in the years before and during the First World War have titles that seem to show a more directed thinking by Graham about their central thrust or themes. *Success* (1902) and *Progress, and Other Sketches* (1905) imply an inspirational quality. *His People* follows in 1906, and *Faith* (1909), *Hope* (1910) and *Charity* (1912) seem to be linked as a group within Graham's mind. *A Hatchment* (1913) and *Brought Forward* (1916) bring to an end the first cycle of Graham's fictional output. Thereafter, there is a gap of eleven years before the final late collections, *Redeemed, and Other Sketches* (1927), *Writ in Sand* (1932) and *Mirages* (1936), the titles of which seem to suggest a disengagement from the serious business of life. And yet perhaps too much weight can be attached to the titles of these works. In all of them, the stories are equally varied and exotic in their sources, and Graham never lets himself be pinned down by a reader's or critic's desire to pigeonhole him as a fiction writer on a particular subject or theme.

It is in his historical writing that Graham does reveal himself as having a specific interest and purpose. Beginning in 1901, he published a sequence of works, mostly biographical, dealing with aspects of South American history from the time of the sixteenth-century Conquistadors right down to his own lifetime. For the writing of these books, he undertook extensive research into the original source documents, a labour in which his knowledge of Spanish proved to be invaluable. The largest group of historical biographies deals with prominent figures in the conquest of

South America by the Spaniards. *Hernando de Soto* (1903), *Bernal Diaz del Castillo* (1915), *The Conquest of New Granada* (1922), *The Conquest of the River Plate* (1924), and *Pedro de Valdivia* (1926) show his interest in most areas of Latin America, not merely his own beloved Argentina. Indeed, his travel book, *Cartagena and the Banks of the Sinú* (1920), includes a sketch of the history of Colombia from the Conquest onwards. In that same year Graham also published his biography of the Brazilian religious revolutionary leader of the 1890s, Antonio Conselheiro, under the title, *A Brazilian Mystic*. Two biographies of later figures in South American history are *Jose Antonio Paez* (1929), dealing with one of the heroes of the liberation of Venezuela from Spain in the 1820s, and *Portrait of a Dictator: Francisco Solano Lopez* (1933), about the leader of Paraguay through the disastrous Triple Alliance War of the 1860s. How popular these books about a continent and culture little-known in Britain could ever be is questionable. In writing them, Graham was undoubtedly trying to counteract the contemporary craze for writings about the British Empire, an institution about which he held distinctly unfashionable views. Probably the most enduring of his historical works has turned out to be *A Vanished Arcadia; Being Some Account of the Jesuits in Paraguay, 1607 to 1767* (1901), for reasons more to do with its later cinematic connections than any historical appeal. A historical biography of more personal significance to Graham was *Doughty Deeds* (1925), an account of the life of Graham's own direct eighteenth-century ancestor and namesake, Robert Graham of Gartmore.

Graham's wife, Gabriela, had literary aspirations of her own and published a number of works, frequently infused by the deep religious feeling that developed as she grew older. Her main work was a two-volume biography of Saint Teresa, to which she devoted years of travel and research. Graham clearly played a major role in encouraging her in her writing, and helped in its publication. He had collaborated with her in *Father Archangel of Scotland, and Other Essays* (1896). After her death in 1906, he arranged for the posthumous publication of a new edition of *Santa Teresa* (1907), her poems in 1908, and a new collection of her shorter writings, *The Christ of Toro and Other Stories* (1908).

This survey has touched on all the books that Graham published in his lifetime. Selections have been made by some of his many admirers from his considerable output of short stories and sketches, usually focusing on specific subject areas of his work, such as South America, Scotland or his passion for horses. One unfortunate effect of this may have been to stereotype Graham as a particular kind of writer, an exotic breed who sits uncomfortably in a literary climate dominated by the Modernists of the earlier twentieth century. The extravagant larger-than-life image that has built up about him has perhaps skewed our perceptions of his writing, which is more European in its sensibility than British Edwardian or Georgian. Paradoxically, despite his class origins and cosmopolitan experience, Graham can also often seem to be closer in tone and outlook to twentieth-century Scottish writers like George Douglas Brown, Hugh MacDiarmid or Lewis Grassic Gibbon, writers whose work he almost certainly knew well. There is a great deal of scholarly work waiting to be done on Graham as a Scottish writer, not least the unquantifiable task of bringing into print the large body of his articles, journalism and letters that have never been properly investigated. The full canon of his work has still to be established. Until that is done, it is not possible to make any true assessment of the literary significance of Robert Bontine Cunninghame Graham.

Alan MacGillivray

Note to Volume 1

The works by R.B. Cunninghame Graham in this volume were published between 1895 and 1899. *Notes on the District of Menteith* (1895), while not a collection of stories, is included because it was Graham's first book, a brief survey of the district of Scotland around Graham's house and ancestral estate of Gartmore. In a sense, it is the physical, social and historical landscape seen from the windows of his own home. *Father Archangel of Scotland, and Other Essays* (1896) is a collection of essays and sketches from the hands of both Robert and his wife Gabriela, their only joint literary venture. *The Ipané* (1899) is Graham's first true collection of his own short stories and sketches, although he had already published a travel book, *Mogreb-Al-Acksa* (1898), about his experiences in Morocco.

Alan MacGillivray
John C. McIntyre

Notes on the District of Menteith, for Tourists and Others

R. B. Cunninghame Graham

Introduction

By the end of 1892, Robert Cunninghame Graham was out of Parliament, having been defeated in the Glasgow Camlachie constituency when he imprudently stood as a Labour candidate. With his new-found freedom from the burden of Westminster politics, Graham did much travelling, particularly in Spain and Morocco, and involved himself fully in the early activities of the newly-founded Labour Party. When at home in his crumbling mansion of Gartmore, surrounded by the damp lands of Menteith, he fought a constant financial battle through the 1890s to keep the family estate going. It was eventually a lost cause and in 1900 Gartmore was sold.

Graham felt the loss of the family seat keenly, and it is said that he took considerable pains to avoid having to gaze upon it again. The district of Menteith was always close to his heart, and along with Gartmore it constantly appears in his imaginative writing of later years. As the impulse to write gradually took hold of him, it is no surprise that his first important subject for a book was Menteith as revealed in its topography, history and traditions. *Notes on the District of Menteith, for Tourists and Others* was published in August 1895, being reprinted in the same year and going through a number of editions in the years that followed.

Graham dedicated the book to a local character, a poacher, identified as Mr Wilkie of Balfron, nicknamed 'Trootie', a man whom he sees as representing a way of life that is fast disappearing before the relentless march of industry and the modern world, and to whom he devotes a significant section of one of the later chapters. Graham is already signalling one of his principal writing preoccupations — the inevitability of change and the sadness that attends it. In his 'Preface to the Disingenuous Reader', however, Graham does not touch upon this topic. He utters the conventional excuses of the writer for imposing on discriminating readers, and for any errors that may be detected in his treatment of the subject. He identifies his reasons for writing the guidebook as being a mixture of the need to fill hours of idleness and to prove his affection for the area. In his first reason, Graham is himself disingenuous for idleness was not one of his problems; in the second reason, he was being truly honest. In an eccentric, erratic and still rather amateurish style, Graham expresses a love for his ancestral land and its people, mixed at times with a degree of exasperation and critical dissatisfaction that he has not yet learned to control as a professional writer. Perhaps the stylistic feature that gives the *Notes* a unifying tone is Graham's regular use of witty irony in his comments on his family history and the traditional lore of the Menteith district. Overall, the *Notes* come across as a very personal book, in which Graham can be seen beginning to learn his authorial trade.

Notes on the District of Menteith is a very short book, only six chapters in length. The first chapter, 'Descriptive', deals with the location and physical nature of the area, but also includes some historical information. This is followed by three chapters dealing more specifically with the history of Menteith, focusing particularly on the Earldom and the families that held it, particularly Graham's own ancestors and forerunners. 'Historical' traces the history of Menteith from the earliest records down to the mid-fourteenth century. 'Some Reflections on the Incontinence of Kings' continues the history to the later seventeenth century, and 'Atavism' comes down to the end of the Earldom in the eighteenth century. The chapters, 'Traditional' and 'Pantheistic', are concerned with memorable local events and characters and the beliefs and superstitions of the district. There is a rather wayward quality about Graham's chapter titles, as if they were afterthoughts lightly decided on when he set about dividing up his collected notes and anecdotes and observations into a conventional structure of distinct sections. It is as if he is not taking the notion of structure and development entirely seriously.

The most obvious clue to his lack of serious attention to such matters is the fact that, while the first edition of 1895 carries the main title of *Notes on the District of Menteith, for Tourists and Others*, the start of the main text at Chapter 1 is prefixed by a different title, 'Shadows of Menteith'. Was this how Graham actually saw his book? Not as a guidebook, as which it may be said to be seriously deficient compared with the kind of guidebook we now expect, but as a kind of meditation on the shadowy transitory nature of human life in a particular landscape. This view of the book would anchor it firmly within the context of Graham's later collections of stories and sketches, where, as a recurring theme, he is recalling and reimagining a world which has largely passed, is still changing and will inevitably give way entirely to a newer less congenial order. The broken whisky bottles and empty sardine cans left as dangerous litter by the tourists in Menteith prefigure the enclosed and commercialised South American pampas that Graham regretfully sees replacing the free seas of grass that he knew in his youth. The description of the book as notes for tourists seems to run quite counter to the spirit of Graham's writing, which might more convincingly be described as an attempt to place the small district of Menteith, part of a small nation, in a wider context through his frequent reaching out by example and parallel reference to a wider international setting. Because of Graham's own earlier experience, this setting is usually Spanish or Hispano-American. The shadows of Menteith are shadows shared with many other places.

The final paragraphs of the Notes are perhaps very relevant to this view of the book. "The motley elements which went to make the history of Menteith are gone and buried, but their shadows still remain ... Life is a dream, they say, but dreams have their awakening. A shadow, when it passes over the bents so brown, across the heather, and steals into the corries of the hills, returns no more. Only a reflection of the clouds, you say. Well, if it is so, is not life only a reflection of the past? ... Could we but see a shadow of the future, and compare it with the shadows of the past, why then, indeed, we might know something of Menteith and other districts where the shadows play, coming, like life, from nowhere, and returning into nothing."

There is a strong emphasis on the shadowy nature of reality and life, and undoubtedly this is Graham's final word on all that pertains to the place of humanity within the hills and mosses of his native heath. It might have been expressed with more clarity. However, Graham found that clarity of expression as his writing developed, and the ironical realism of so many of the stories and sketches that later flowed from his pen amply compensates for the fumbling beginnings of his craft in this slight but always entertaining prentice work.

Alan MacGillivray

Loch Achray

A & C. BLACK, LONDON.

I dedicate this little work to Mr. Wilkie, of Balfron, known to the world as "Trootie." This I do because, being himself a shadow of the time before the railway snorted across our moors, he should know most of the shadows as they come and go over the district. Already the shadow of St. Rollox's chimney, so to speak, reaches almost to Inverness, and in the time to come there will be no place for such as "Trootie."

DISTRICT OF MENTEITH.

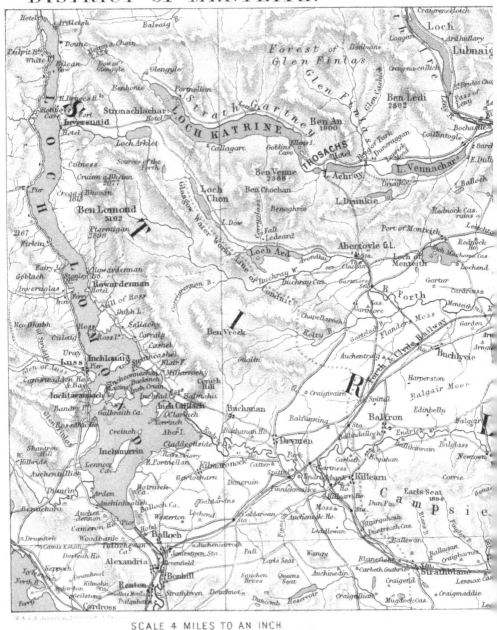

SCALE 4 MILES TO AN INCH.

0   1   2   3   4   5   6   7   8   9   10

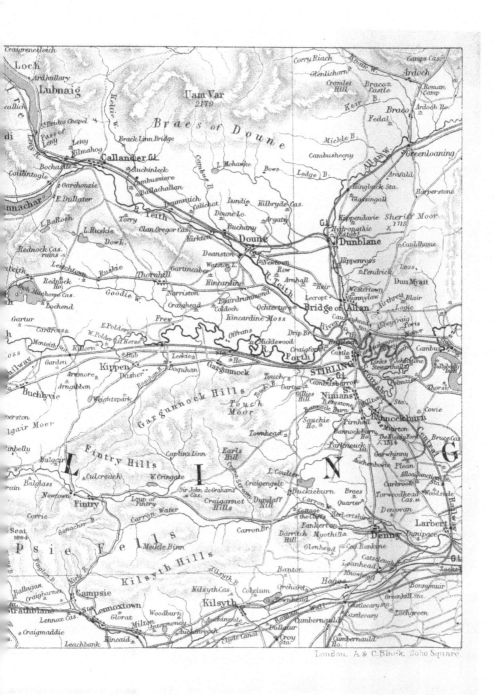

Contents

Preface to the Disingenuous Reader   13

SHADOWS OF MENTEITH

I. Descriptive   15

II. Historical   23

III. Some Reflections on the Incontinence of Kings   29

IV. Atavism   41

V. Traditional   51

VI. Pantheistic   61

Preface to the Disingenuous Reader

There must be many such in the world, that is if reading is the least like other forms of business. Therefore I address myself to you, O Disingenuous Reader, believing as I do in the wisdom, taste, and rectitude of majorities, and I take it that amongst readers you are in the majority. If, therefore, the greatest number of readers be disingenuous, it follows as a political sequence that the manner of their reading is the right manner. Your majority can make black white and right wrong, in fact often does so.

Now the man who writes a book, even such an unambitious one as the present booklet, likes to have the majority on his side, for certain reasons. Moreover, he who writes a book acts usually as a horse-dealer does in assigning his reason for parting with the animal he is selling. That is, the writer commonly conceals his reason for writing, or at best puts forth some plea so transparent that by it no one is deceived. And touching my object, I will declare it later, that is, if circumstances render it expedient for me so to do. Suffice it to say that it was not penned for the general benefit of mankind, nor, as far as I know, to increase knowledge, either scientific or theological.

Least of all did I labour and struggle with the evil generation of copyists and others, who make our mystery a weariness of the flesh, as Chaucer setteth forth, to enunciate some great truth which I had discovered. If in my peregrinations about the region of Menteith I had lighted on any such matter, I should have kept it to myself, thus ensuring to it at least one believer. It is commonly the case that when a man writes an account of any district that the natives are enchanted, if in his descriptions there is anything that they can comprehend, or have ever heard before related.

The casual writer, too, if he can detect a printer's error, or an inaccuracy of statement, writes to a newspaper and rejoices most consumedly. Therefore, in descriptions of any district, it is not infrequent that a writer pleases where he did not look to have given pleasure. Some have (it is asserted) entertained angels unawares. What I have set down I have set down half in idleness and half out of that affection which is common to man and trees for the soil in which they have been for ages rooted. What I have set down in error, O Disingenuous Reader, put down, I pray, not to any malice of afore- or after-thought, but rather to the innate devilry of typewriters, barratry of mariners, the act of God, or any of those causes to which mankind is prone to attribute their own errors. Vale.

R. B. Cunninghame Graham

SHADOWS OF MENTEITH

1. Descriptive

With a general idea of the configuration of the district of Menteith; also a digression as to whether religious belief may not modify the human countenance; and other matters connected with other things

Menteith has always seemed to me a shadowy district. On the one side the shadows of the Grampians stretch towards the Campsies; the shadows of the Campsies at times stretch to the Grampians. On a summer evening often only a little belt of tawny heather or bright green moss is left in the sunlight; all the intervening space is bathed in shadow. The Flanders Moss has been a sea, tradition says, and those sworn enemies, the science of the study and the science of outdoor observation, seem to corroborate one another in confirming the tradition. The sea, it is said, once washed round the rocks at the foot of Stirling Castle, and extended to the "Clach nan Lunn" (the Stone of the Wave), on the Easter Hill of Gartmore; so, at least, the iron ring in the aforementioned stone was accounted for. The Clach nan Lunn is gone, broken up by an otherwise unenterprising farmer. The sea is gone, and in its place the low flat moss remains; but still the shadow of the sea seems to hang over it, and the sea-gulls hover screaming about it, as if the moss might change to waves once more. Reminiscences of a mysterious and stormy past still cling to the district. Nearly every hill and strath has had its battles between the Grahams and the McGregors. Highlander and Lowlander fought in the lonely glens or on the stony hills, or drank together in the aqua-vitae houses in the times of their precarious peace.

Monk the Restorer led his more or less merry men through the Pass of Aberfoyle. He addressed a letter to the Earl of Airth desiring him to order the cutting down of the woods of Miltown and Glessart in Aberfoyle, "whiche are grete shelters to the rebelles and mossers."* Said letter dated from Cardross House.

---

*Paper in Gartmore Charter-chest.

In the same Pass of Aberfoyle the Earl of Glencairn and Graham of Duchray defeated a party of my Lord Protector's soldiers. Graham of Duchray, no doubt, fought all the better because the Cromwellians had burnt his house the night before the action, in order to show him that it was unwise to attach too much importance to mere houses built with hands.

Robert the Bruce visited the Priory of Inchcolme in 1310, in one of the brief intervals of rest in the battle of his life, though he had visited the island twice before, once as an adventurer, and once on his way from Rathlin Island to the North. In this third visit he granted a charter to the monks of Aberbrothock, dated "apud Insulam Sancti Colmoci." Montrose must have known the district from end to end, and probably acquired his knowledge of the Highlanders in his youth, as boys on the frontiers of America learn the habits of the Indians.

Knox, as far as history informs us, never deaved the inhabitants of the stewartry with any of his clavers, though Claverhouse now and then deaved them to some extent by reason of his knocks.

The latter worthy corresponded much with the Earl of Menteith, and on one occasion compliments him thus: "I rejoice to hear you have now taken my trade of my hande, that you are becom a terror to the godly."* This was on the occasion of the Earl having exerted himself against the Covenanters.

He also tells him that he knows "that feue have toyld so muche for honour as I have don, though it has been my misfortune to atteene but a small shear."† Of glory certainly he did "atteene his shear," but honour, if it means money — and I think that is the way we estimate the commodity at the present time — like most of the name of Graham, he never succeeded in "atteening" much.

Rob Roy himself was a sort of unofficial local Chancellor of the Exchequer, and did his work so thoroughly that not a single case exists of conscience money ever having been paid into the treasury at Craig Royston.

His blessed Majesty Charles, first of the name, was pleased to stop at Milling Farm, on the Lake of Menteith, and take his "poor dejeune"; also to borrow certain moneys from the Earl of Menteith — said moneys still unpaid, though his pious son, the ever-blessed Rowley, at Portend

---

* Letter from Claverhouse quoted in "Red Book of Menteith".
†Ibid.

Farm (close to Milling), was pleased to "heerby promise on the word off ane prince to sie it faithfullie payed whenever we fynde occasioune."* Occasioune has not arisen as yet, but hope springs eternal in the human breast.

On the island of the wood-locked lake Augustine monks dwelt for centuries. Their memories still cling to the ruined church and monastery. One whole year of the troubled life of Mary Queen of Scots was passed as a child on the same islet. She, too, has left memories which hang about her little garden, girt with box-trees, as the scent of rose-leaves kept in a china bowl still lingers though the leaves have mouldered into dust.

In the mountain fastnesses near Aberfoyle many of those who fled from Culloden found refuge, thus bringing the Middle Ages, so to speak, almost to yesterday.

So it is, to me at least, that the district seems a "shadowy one," for memories are the shadows of men's lives.

Dr. Johnson could not be got to believe that the most disturbed districts of the Highlands were those which bordered on the Lowlands. Still, it is very easy for any one who stands on the Loch Katrine road from Aberfoyle, and looks back over the district of Menteith, to see why this was the case. The Grampians, running down at this point into a rich and fertile district, formed a secure retreat for the Highlanders, both to make their sallies from and to return to, with their booty.

The interior of a savage country is always quieter than its frontier, for in the interior the peculiar social constitution of the people is always in more perfect order, and few countries ever live in a state of constant warfare. The Highlands, though, were not a savage country, but, on the contrary, an old civilised country, of a peculiar kind of civilisation.

Much the same state of things must have existed there two centuries ago as exist to-day in Tripoli and Morocco and in Afghanistan — a regular polity, of an antiquated sort, and not a society like that of some of the frontiers of America, which may be compared to a sort of kaleidoscope of human atoms looked at through the hind sights of a Winchester rifle. Perhaps no district of the Highland frontier was so typically a borderland as the district of Menteith; perhaps at no one point in all Scotland is the dividing line between Celt and Saxon more distinct in the nomenclature, language, and configuration of the two countries. Till

---

*Warrant by Charles II in favour of William Earl of Airth.

a short time ago — for sixty or seventy years is a short time in the history of a country — the habits of the people were as distinct as they are today in Spain and Portugal on their respective sides of the Minho. At Tuy, in Galicia, though a portentous international iron bridge spans the river, the separation between those peoples is as complete as in the days when a clumsy boat, rowed by five Portuguese women, took the traveller over the stream, as when the writer first crossed on his way from Santiago de Compostela to Oporto, or as in the Middle Ages. The Spaniards still talk of the villainy of those Portuguese, and whilst cheating the stranger with the utmost imperturbability themselves, warn him, philanthropically, to beware of the dishonesty of the Portuguese in Valença. A similar sharp demarcation is to be observed at Salvatierra and Monzon, which look at one another across the same river with as charitable feelings as those with which the Free Church minister gazes at the manse of the Establishment in a modern Scottish village.

If this is the case amongst people who are identical in origin with the Galicians and the Portuguese, how much more must it have been between the Saxon Lowlander and the Highlander in the days when it was a practical saying that "the Forth bridles the wild Highlandman." Even to-day, though convention has lent a thin varnish of hypocrisy to manners, the old feeling of antagonism is not dead, and occasionally is very noticeable at ploughing matches, Highland games, and other public festivities. In Menteith, which the American traveller whirls through in the railway without time to realize that he is passing into as different a country in a few minutes as it takes hours to do in going from one State to another of the American Union, the long antagonism of race has left its results in many ways. On the lowland side of the Forth the countryman is a "bodach," a heavy and excellent being, but uninteresting unless seen through the spectacles of a patriotic novelist. You cannot find a decent shepherd amongst them; they know too much ever to remember their sheep.

Education is a splendid thing for engineers, county councillors, and waiters; it makes them fit to bear their crosses and to impose others on the general public, but it spoils a shepherd. A shepherd is born, rarely made, and the native Highlander has generally a genius for the business.

In the flat district of Menteith the countryman is too anxious to raise and improve himself. Who ever heard either of a shepherd or a poet anxious to do either the one or the other? Throughout Menteith, though poets are as scarce as in most other parts of the world, you can find many valuable shepherds. This, no doubt, arises from the proximity of the Highlands and the mixture of blood. The good (Highland) shepherd does not give his life for his sheep, or for anything else, with the possible exception of whisky; but he fulfils at least as useful a function in the State as the minor poet, and in this respect, therefore, Menteith is at least on an equality with Grub Street. The people (that is, those of the old stock) seem to me to have preserved more of the characteristics of a fighting race than those of almost any other district of Scotland.

Not that they are quarrelsome more than good citizens should be, but a rooted dislike to any continuous occupation is very noticeable amongst them. This is said to be the case with all those races descended from ancestors who have been constantly engaged in war.

The climate of the western portion of Menteith is mild and humid; the snow rarely lies long in winter, nor does the sun shine overmuch in summer; and much of the country is not far above the sea-level. Whether on account of the constant rain, or from the virulence of the religious beliefs of the natives, it is uncertain, but travellers have remarked that in few parts of Scotland are the faces of the people so much lined and scarred. "A wet cloak ill laid up," or "the new map together with the augmentation of the Indies," are apt descriptions of many of their countenances. Ethnologists have not remarked if the features of the inhabitants of Strathglass in Inverness-shire, or those districts of Aberdeenshire which have remained Catholic, are as repellent as those of the inhabitants of the more essentially Protestant cantons of Scotland; and the testimony of theologians on such a matter would be doubtful. If Buckle is correct in his theory that the minds and even the bodies of men are moulded by the aspect of the country in which they live, the inhabitants of Menteith might well be rough, for most of the land they live in is a mass of hillocks and hummocks, broken up by little pools intersected with rushing streams, hirsute with heather, the fields stony as those of Palestine, the whole country bounded by mountains to the north and huge flat mosses to the south.

As the lantern of Maracaibo dominates the sea of the same name, Ben Lomond dominates the land — a sort of Scottish Vesuvius, never wholly without a cloud-cap. You cannot move a step that it does not tower over you. In winter, a vast white sugar-loaf; in summer, a prismatic cone of yellow and amethyst and opaline lights; in spring, a grey, gloomy, stony pile of rocks; in autumn, a weather indicator: for when the mist curls down its sides, and hangs in heavy wreaths from its double summit, "it has to rain"; as the Spaniards say of Jabalcuz, in the Vega of Granada, "ha de llover aunque Dios no quiera." In fact, the characteristic and chief feature of the district — a very nose upon its face. Ben Ledi and Ben Venue the minor lights or heights; Ben Voil in the distance, peeping over the shoulder of Ben Lawers; Ben More, Craig Vadh, the Gualan (the Shoulder in Gaelic); the Ochils and the Campsies, with the rock of Stirling, and sometimes a faint blue line of the hills in Fife. In the far Highlands rise Ben Nevis, Ben Voilich, Schehallion, and many another, which have done Sir Walter Scott good yeoman service. A kind of sea of moss and heath, a bristly country (Trossachs is said to mean the bristled land), shut in by hills on every side. Sometimes, indeed, so broken is the ground that one wonders if the "riders of Menteith" that history talks of were mortal riders, or a sort of Walkuren sacred to the Valhalla of the district. Menteith, like other regions of Scotland and of England, is losing fast all the remaining characteristics of the past. The old-fashioned Scotch is going rapidly, giving place to a hideous jargon between the East End of Glasgow and that of London. No doubt in times to come pure English will be spoken from St. Michael's Mount to John o' Groat's; but in the meantime, sometimes, one longs for decent Cornish or Scottish, if people will be talking. Hardly an old tradition really lives (apart from books) in the memories of the people. Scarcely a dozen real old types, even faintly approaching to those which Scott and Galt delighted in, remain, and they as few and far between as trees in hedges. Surely but steadily the thing called civilisation (see Edward Carpenter for its "Cause and Cure") has covered up most of the remaining high lights of the old world with its dark grey pall. Certain it is at present the effect is not a pleasant still less a pretty one. A world of people each so like his brother that his wife can only differentiate him by the buttons on his ulster is not a cheering sight, but in the future, it may be, we shall get the type again, and see less of the man run like a candle out of a mould.

Gone are the Augustinian monks who built the stately island church. Out of the ruined chancel grows a plane-tree, which is almost ripe. In the branches rooks have built their nests, and make as cheerful matins as perhaps the monks themselves. The giant chestnuts, grown, as tradition says, from chestnuts brought from Rome, are all stag-headed. Ospreys used to build in them in the memory of those still living. Gone are the riders of Menteith (if they ever existed); the ruggers and the reivers are at one with those they harried. The Grahams and McGregors, the spearmen and the jackmen, the hunters and the hawkers, the livers by their spurs, the luckless Earls of Menteith and their retainers, are buried and forgotten, and the tourist cracks his biscuit and his jest over their tombs.

Gaelic is gone, or only just remembered by the elder generation, yet it gave the names to all the burns and glens and lochs; names curious and descriptive, like the names the Indians give to places in America. It may be, when all are numbered, Ben Number One, Loch Number Two, and so on, that even Gaelic will become a thing to be regretted. What is most to be deplored is that the ancient Scottish courtesy of manner has gone too, and given place to the "transition manners" which make every man inferior to his neighbour. The old-time Scottish kindliness is said to linger still, but where deponent sayeth not. Where stood the Highland cottage thatched with heather and roof kept on with birchen poles and stones, and gardened with house-leek and corydalis, now stand the hideous slate-roofed cottages, properly sanitated, and hideous enough to spean a bairn. From the beginning of the world children have drawn the design of the latter dwelling upon their slate. Over the Fingalian path, where once the redshank trotted on his Highland garron, the bicyclist, the incarnation of the age, looks to a sign-post and sees, "This hill is dangerous."

The Grahams and the McGregors have, it is to be hoped, dropped their long enmity in the world or worlds where they have gone to. Their names, once so numerous in the stewartry of Menteith, seem almost to have disappeared out of the land. The days are changed from the times when an Earl of Menteith entered into a league against "all but the kinge and those of the name of Grahame." Perhaps it is as well they are gone, for they were always (like Jeshurun) mighty prone to kick, though commonly not waxing very fat. It is good that all should change, for novelty is grateful to mankind; besides, it paves the way to the happy time when all shall sit, apparelled in one livery, at little tables, drinking some kind of not too diuretic "table water" approved by the County Council, and reading expurgated Bibles.

The lake from the east

The Hotel Pier and Steam Launch

II. Historical

Containing some reflections on ancient history in general; also some account of Gilchrist, the first Earl of Menteith, and of how certain English adventurers, for the bettering of their private fortunes, intermarried with certain Scottish ladies; and of other things which may be profitable to the student in local history

History of any kind is generally written for one of two objects: either to falsify some set of political events or to show the writer's erudition. As regards the first of these objects, the present writer believes that to endeavour to falsify political events is a work of supererogation. In regard to the second, this little sketch is abundant proof of his complete innocence.

Ancient Highland families often kept a "Leabhar dearg" (*Anglice*, Red Book), in which they set down what seemed remarkable to them. The unfortunate thing is, that what seemed remarkable to them is generally uninteresting to the modern reader; that which the modern reader would have been infinitely obliged to them for recording was to them commonplace. What they chiefly chronicled were the accounts of fights, of murders, of sudden deaths, marriages, and apparitions of saints and goblins. What we should have desired to hear of would have been the account of the fashions of their clothes and arms, the amount of half-raw meat, or quantity of bowls of porridge, they consumed in a day; if women had rights amongst them, and of what kind they were; and as to whether there were any other amusements at night except the somewhat monotonous pastime of sitting listening to the bards chanting the praises of Fingal and his heroes. Even the bards at times must have been somewhat flat, for in such a climate the difficulty of keeping the Clairseagh at English concert pitch must have been almost insuperable. It is, perhaps, as interesting to read in Barbour's "Bruce"* that "crackes

---

*Book XIV, line 168.

of warre," i.e. cannons, were first seen at such a battle, as to learn the style and title of all the knights killed or taken prisoners at the battle in question.

From the earliest ages Menteith was one of the five great districts into which Scotland was divided. Its ancient history, down to the creation of the earldom in the twelfth century, was as shadowy and indefinite as that of most parts of Scotland at the time. For what, after all, is the knowledge of the fact that a man's name was appended to a charter in the twelfth or thirteenth century of avail to the general public? Early history of almost any kind is as fragmentary reading as is a railway guide, and about as illusory and fallacious. In neither case does one ever seem to be able to get anywhere. The history of Menteith formed no exception, and even the few deeds of violence which relieve the eternal monotony of subscribing charters are not sufficiently authenticated to induce much repulsion towards their shadowy perpetrators.

One Gilchrist was the first Earl, but nothing is known of him except that he existed. In this respect he has a decided advantage over some historical personages. On Gilchrist, at any rate, the burden of proof does not lie, as on some other characters in history, for he is mentioned as one of the witnesses to a charter by Malcolm IV to the Abbey of Scone, granted in the eleventh year of his reign, 1164, under the style and title of Gillecrist Comes de Menteith. It is not stated in what manner Earl Gilchrist witnessed the charter, but it seems not unlikely, belonging to the category (as he probably did) of "Knightes, Lordes, and other worthy men who can litel Latin," that he placed a modest cross after his name in the usual style of the ancient Scottish nobility.

McGregor Stirling says, in his book on the Priory of Inchmahome, that the earliest spelling of the name Menteith is found in Appendix I to James's "Essay of the Antiquities of Scotland," and that there it is written "Meneted." In a charter dated 1234 it is spelt "Mynteth." There was a noble freedom about ancient spelling which added much to the interest of many sciences, notably to geography.

No reliable derivation of the word has ever been presented to me, but it is not unlikely a compound of the word Teith, as that river runs through the earldom. The Highlanders called the Teith the Taich, and applied the name also to the whole district, as the word Menteith is said to be unknown to them. They also called it the "warm river," on account of the high wooded ground through which lies much of its course.

From the twelfth century down to the middle of the seventeenth century, the usual monotonous course of villainy, which characterised all Scottish history both of that epoch and of later times, went on with unfailing regularity.

In the time of James III the town of Port of Menteith was erected into a burgh or barony by a charter which bears the date of 8th February 1466.

The forests in Menteith were at that time one of the favourite hunting resorts of the Scottish Court. Scotland enjoyed Home Rule in those days, and the blessing of a national parliament, with the pleasure of knowing that the taxes were wasted in Edinburgh instead of in London. It is doubtful if the forests alluded to in the old charters were really woods, or only grounds set apart for hunting. Certainly at the present day Menteith is entirely bare of natural woods, with the exception of oak and birch coppices which fringe the streams and sometimes jut out into the fields, forming peninsulas of wood, and at other times enclosing little open spaces of ground in a complete circle. In 1538, in the "Lord Treasurer's Account" (see "History of the Forest of Glenfinlas"), there is an entry for payment of a horse "whiche was slaine tursand the kinge's venisoune out of Glenfinlas, at the kinge's command and precept." How the horse was "slaine" is not set down; but as even a king would hardly (by command and precept) enjoin his foresters to pile venison on a horse till its back was broken, it seems probable that some McGregor may have shot him out of pure delight in life. The king had to provide himself for his hunting as if he had been going into the Pan Handle of Texas, for another item occurs in the treasurer's accounts, "to fee twa careage horsis, to turse the king's bed, and uther graithe to the hunting."

It seems probable that the regal taste in venerie descended sometimes to a species of battue. For the entry: "Pro expenses per eundem Willelmum factis, tempore venationis in floresta de Glenfyngask, et per importatione (sic) bestiarum ferarum Domino Regi." "Importatione" is significant, and may have served as a precedent for the Master of the Buckhounds. How pleasant Latin, written in the above style, becomes, and how comprehensible to any one gifted with an adequate knowledge of the Scottish tongue!

One may suppose, and supposition is most lawful in history, especially in Scottish history, that the whole earldom was continually involved in broils with its Highland neighbours. Norman barons seem to have visited the district periodically, as when Sir Edward Hastings was ordered into

Scotland by Edward I in 1298. He came to assist in the conquest of Scotland, and promptly married the heiress of Menteith, Lady Isabella de Comyn, and signed himself afterwards Edward Hastings Comes de Menteith, with considerable prolixity.* Even before that, in 1273, a futile Englishman, Sir John Russell, married a widowed countess of Menteith. Her relations considered the match an ignoble one, but the countess secured the advantage of a residence in the comparatively milder climate of England, where she died and was buried. This family of Russell has subsequently been mentioned occasionally in English history, but since then has never again intruded into Menteith.

It is a humiliating fact to have to set down, and greatly to the discredit of democracy, that the only shred of interest in the dreary annals of treachery, arson, and murder which go to make up the history of Menteith, attaches to the Earls themselves and their adventures. Indeed, in reference to the early history of Menteith there is such a plethora of hard dry facts that little human interest can be extracted from them. It is certain, indeed, that Edward III of England, with that cheerful disregard of justice which was one of his attributes, and unquestionably goes far to make up his greatness in the eyes of historians, executed an Earl of Menteith, who was taken prisoner with King David at Durham in 1346, on the paltry plea that he had once sworn fealty to himself, as if an oath more or less was ever a hindrance to a patriot.

This Earl of Menteith, Sir John Graham, the ninth earl, seems to have been a man of courage and sense, and had his advice been followed at the battle of Durham, to charge the English archers on their flanks, the disaster might have been averted. Wynton, occasionally a severe critic of the Scottish nobility, makes him exclaim to the king: "Gettes me but men ane hundred on hors wyth me to go, and all your archyrs skayle sail I." Quite naturally, his advice was disregarded, and the king was taken prisoner and his army routed. When, though, have not kings, in common with deaf adders, been famous for stopping their ears to the words of wise counsel?

In the case of kings it may be that the exigencies of their position often forced them to appear more foolish than they really were, though the necessity is not often apparent.

---

*See Sir William Fraser's "Red Book of Menteith".

Why an adder which was born deaf should put itself to further trouble in the matter remains a mystery. The various families of Menteith, Stewart and Grahame, who held the earldom at various times, their Murdochs, Morices, and Malises succeeding one another, produced some stout phlebotomists and now and then a mediocre statesman. But fortune never seemed to smile upon them. Unfortunate people have always been the very sheet-anchors of historians. They have furnished them with reams of "copy," with matter for infinite digression, and without digression all histories would be as lethal as that of Guicciardini's.

THE PORT CHURCH AND THE HOTEL

THE PORT CHURCH

III. Some Reflections on the Incontinence of Kings

Treating of the redness of the blood; the fortunes of William, seventh Earl of Menteith; of the incontinence of a king, and other things; the slaughter of Lord Kilpont; and how the body of Stewart of Ardvoirlich was "shoughed" at the Point of Coilmore

The misfortunes which from the beginning of their history had always pursued the holders of the title of Menteith, so thickened in the reign of Charles I that they eventually overwhelmed the earls entirely.

In countries like England and Scotland, where there is no idea of abstract dignity or essential worth in any one who does not keep a carriage, the position of a poor peer has always been most painful. Many a bill for a suit of armour from Milan, or an overdue account from Toledo for swords, must have disturbed the slumbers of the Earls of Menteith from the days of David Earl of Stratherne downwards.

Still they were a cheerful as well as an unfortunate race, not apparently humourists, but of a sanguine temperament. When they were exiled, or forfeited, or forced to attend parliaments, or scour the country in pursuit of "phanatickes" or "Hielande rogues," it was all one to them; they relied on their descent from a royal prince, and fought manfully against the dreary climate of their native land and the assaults of their own and the king's enemies.

At the age of forty-eight we find William, eighth Earl of Menteith, writing to the Marquis of Montrose from the "Yle of Menteith," under date of 4th January 1680, "Ther is nothing on earth I love so well as to be in a just war for my King and Prince."

A mighty pretty sentiment, and one that does his lordship's loyalty much credit. Most of us even now would like to be engaged in a just war (if we could be sure of one) for our king and prince, especially if these last were subjected to danger, or sufficiently interesting to raise enthusiasm. The expression of the wish was natural enough in one whose grandfather had boasted that his blood was redder than the king's, and who only wanted a sharp sword, as a contemporary nobleman observed, to make his boast a valid one. Sharp swords (and even axes) have often been excellent instruments of service, as the king in question, Charles the Martyr, was destined to discover. To have blood redder than a king's, that is, genealogically, not chemically, is of itself a capital crime; but that it was a fact appears extremely likely.

It is with considerable pain that I have to refer to anything that might in any way seem to be an aspersion on the morality of one of our Scottish kings. Personal morality has always been the strong point of our Scottish Sovereigns. It is hinted amongst those not of the blood royal, that personal chastity — the "Lacha ye trupos," as the gipsies call it — is not so keenly valued as Captain Cook found it to be in the Marquesas Islands, but this a prudent writer may well leave to the attention of statesmen. Hence a sin (if it was a sin) committed so long ago is well-nigh purified by the lapse of ages. It may be subject for debate if indeed any sin, when or how committed, is so great as that of him who comments on and by that means spreads it.

Robert II, the first prince of the house of Stewart, succeeded to the throne of Scotland in 1371. Had it not been for the bad example set by him, Scotland might still have been a moral nation. It is related of him that previous to his accession he bore the title of Earl of Stratherne, given to him by his uncle, David II.

In early life, the miserable Robert had formed a connection (so the historians describe his horrid action) with Elizabeth, daughter of Sir Allan Muir of Rowallan, by whom he had John, afterwards Robert III, Robert Duke of Albany and Earl of Fife and Menteith, and Alexander Lord of Badenoch. In 1347 he obtained a Papal dispensation for his marriage with the said Elizabeth, which marriage, says Fordun (an arch-liar on occasion), took place in 1349. By this it will be observed how relatively milder the superstition of the Seven Hills was, at least in 1349, than the tyranny of Geneva became under the inquisitors Calvin and Knox. Had the superstition of either of these last-named worthies been in force, the poor king had assuredly done penance in the face of some congregation of his loyal subjects.

Not content with what had passed, in 1356 the king married Euphemia, daughter of the Earl of Ross. As he again obtained a Papal dispensation for his rash act, he would seem to have been incorrigible. Willingly I would draw a veil over him and his papally dispensed wives, but the duties of a historian are to be impartial — that is to say, impartial to the failings of kings. As to their virtues, they demand to be more carefully distorted before the public can bear to look on them. From this second marriage (or connection) there were two sons, David and Walter. Walter disappears in the obscurity of the earldom of Caithness and dukedom of Atholl. David, afterwards Earl of Stratherne, was the progenitor of the Earls of Menteith. Buchanan, a despicable fellow, in spite of his latinity, with Bower and Boethius, asserts that Robert III and the other children of Elizabeth Muir were not only born before marriage, but that the marriage of their parents did not take place till the death of Euphemia Ross.

This raises the curious point for theologians, that whereas the Pope had given already one dispensation, if he gave a second in the lifetime of the first wife, either he was not infallible or that in this particular case he was infallible, but did not choose to exercise infallibility. The impression, however, that the children of Elizabeth Muir, from whom the Stewarts were descended, were illegitimate, existed strongly in Scotland even to the time of Charles I, and hence the unlucky boast of the Earl of Menteith about the redness of his blood induced the ruin of his family. Nowadays, if we were certain that all the Stewarts had been illegitimate from the fourteenth century, it would only be another title to our esteem and affection. In those times people thought differently, and to Charles the Martyr the idea must have been peculiarly repellent. As kingship was a matter of divine right, it will be readily perceived that to stand for several hundred years between the Deity and His Anointed was a thing not to be lightly contemplated by men of tender conscience.

Comparatively uninteresting persons the Earls of Menteith seem to have been up to the birth of William the seventh earl — that is to say those of the name of Graham.

They were born with unfailing regularity, were returned heirs of their fathers at the proper time, married, hunted, fished, administered injustice after their kind, and died, and their place knew them no more. From Malise Graham, in 1427, through Alexander, William, John, to William the seventh earl, Johns and Williams succeeded one another as passively as keys upon a plane-tree in the recurring autumns of its existence. Some of them attended parliaments and courts, but their most frequent occupation (at least that has come down to us) was the signing and witnessing of charters. In this latter occupation they seem to have at least equalled in diligence other noblemen of their time and standing. True it is that William, the third Earl, contrived to get himself killed in 1543 by the Tutor of Appin. It still remains a moot point as to whether the credit of the action is to be put down to the slayer or the slain. Jamieson's portrait of the seventh Earl shows us a man of a different stamp. Long hair, small ruff, with quilted doublet and pointed beard, he looks the type of the novelist's "unlucky nobleman." One divines at once that such a man, however red his blood, never was made for success; he looks too honourable. If, as the proverb says, profit and honour go not in one bag, the like may be extended to success. Whether painted by Jamieson, Titian, or Velasquez, the successful man proclaims himself in spite of the artist. Not that Velasquez ever softened the acerbities of success, or left out a single mean line or a wrinkle even of the features of a king. Still success, like drink, is sure to mar a face. The price that is paid for it is sure to leave its mark.

It appears the seventh Earl was born in 1589. The author of the "Red Book of Menteith" remarks that "from comparative obscurity he rose with great rapidity to be the most influential nobleman in his country." His fall, however, was even more rapid. Had he been but an ordinary successful courtling of the Villiers stamp, perhaps he would have been as utterly uninteresting as many of the favourites of the pious but mendacious Charles. Early in life we find him inspecting his charter-chests in the Isle of Talla, and noting down, amongst other things, "that the original chartar of the erldome of Mentheith with tua ither greit evidentis, are in ane litell coffer bandet with brass."

This seems a curious statement, as modern writers on the subject are agreed that the original charter of the earldom of Menteith never existed, or that, if it did, it was destroyed at a period anterior to that at which the Earl is of opinion that he saw it. In cases such as these, the modern writer, with his modern instances, is sure to be more worthy of belief than the mediæval chronicler. For, strange as it may appear, it is almost always proved to demonstration that when a personage in history sets down that he has seen a certain thing, your modern commentator is always sure to prove the thing was never within the range of the ancient's vision. At times a doubt arises whether any one who was born before the present century was not an idiot. Be that as it may, it is a dangerous thing for noblemen who lack advancement to pore too much on ancient documents. Your ancient document, with its crabbed characters, its crumpled edges, soft yellow paper or parchment, and its ponderous seal, is always so explicit. It seems to say so much and says so little, just like your modern politician. Poring upon his charters, Earl William took it into his head to redeem his family estates, which kings and others had filched away from him. So in 1619 he redeemed the lands of Dunmore from Grissel Stirling, in 1624 the lands of Rednock, and so on. So far, so good. It is a commendable enough thing for a nobleman to do to extend his boundaries at his neighbours' expense.

In 1621 he was appointed justiciar over Menteith. Theft, reset of theft, and pykrie were most common at the time in the district. In more modern times, pykrie is rarer, but still exists.* Again we find him incidentally mentioned by James I in a letter to the Earl of Mar, in which his Majesty bespeaks "some of those dogges they calle terrieres, and in Scotlande earth dogges." It appears the Earl of Menteith was the possessor of some, "whiche are bothe stoute, good for killers, and will stay longe in the grunde." Little by little he became a Privy Councillor, and a Commissioner of the Exchequer, and Justice General of Scotland. It is not set down if in his office he continued to pursue "reset of theft and pykrie," but probably not, as pykrie, if I apprehend the matter rightly, is sometimes to be observed even in Privy Councillors.

In 1628 he received a yearly pension of £500. In those days pensions were cheaper to the nation than at present, for they were rarely paid when granted; a very commendable practice. The unpaid pension is a burden that a nation can stand to the tune of millions. No one is hurt except the hypothetical receiver, and he, if he has really performed a public service, is only paid in the same coin by the public as he would be paid in private by those he had obliged. In poor Earl William's case the pension was an especially barren honour, as it seems he had expended at least £500 in providing robes for the judges of the circuit courts at his own expense. Not contented with searching his "littel brass-banded coffer" in the Isle of Talla, the Earl must needs go and search the national archives. In these, in 1629, he found the documents which caused his ruin. Most modest-minded men — and Scotsmen are proverbially modest — will shrink from making public the frailties of a Scottish king, even though the frailties had been committed ages ago.

Earl William must needs obtain two charters of Robert II of the earldom of Stratherne to his son David. Now, as we know that this same Robert was the very king who could never marry a wife without a Papal

---

*Writers on legal matters leave us in some doubt as to the nature of "pykrie," but the balance of their opinion seems to suggest the supposition that it was a method of conveyancing.

dispensation, the importance of that action at once appears. If William Earl of Menteith was really the heir of David Earl of Stratherne, and if the mother of the said Earl was the only lawful wife of the King (Robert II), it was at once patent that William also should have been the King of England in place of Charles, who really was an interloper. Perish the thought; up to that time no one had called the title of King Charles in question. Indeed it was not politic to do so, Charles was a man so eminently kingly. Who sat so well and quietly to Vandyke? Who rode more stately on a cream-coloured horse from Naples or from Cordoba? Who looked so melancholy? Who lied so circumstantially, or worshipped God more piously, than Charles, in the three kingdoms? Under these circumstances it would have been worse than a crime, almost, in fact, an error in good breeding, to supplant him. It is not alleged in any of the kingly attributes set down above that William, seventh Earl of Menteith, surpassed the King. It is not, indeed, apparent that he wished to supplant him in anything. In fact, his conduct proves him to the last a loyal courtier. It may be that his blood was redder than the King's; but even if it was, another Papal dispensation would doubtless have reinstated matters (and molecules) in their proper position. The search for papers in the "Yle of Menteith," and subsequent search in the national register, resulted in the Earl laying claim to the earldom of Stratherne, which had been taken from Malise Graham, first Earl of Menteith, by James I. The Earl, as direct heir-male of the Countess Euphemia of Stratherne, who married Sir Patrick Graham of Kincardine, without doubt was rightful claimant to the title of Stratherne. Sir Thomas Hope, the King's Advocate, advised him to place a renunciation of the lands of Stratherne in the King's hands, which he did. After the usual legal formalities customary in such cases, the King was graciously pleased to accept of the lands of Stratherne, which did not apparently belong to the Earl. But when were kings, or any son of man, averse to graciously accepting that which cost them nothing? In return, the King granted a sum of £3000 to be paid to the Earl. Needless to say, he never got a penny of it, and both the King's conscience and the national exchequer were salved and comforted. In July, 1631, the King by patent ratified and approved to the Earl the title of Earl of Stratherne. Other grants of money were also adjudged to him; but payment did not wait on adjudication. Later on he obtained the lands of Airth, and reached the culminating point of his short-lived prosperity. At this time he was the first nobleman in Scotland, rich in honours and in hypothetical grants of money.

But, as not unfrequently happens, a lawyer was the cause of his downfall. Sir John Scot of Scotstarvet, director of Chancery, and author of the pamphlet, "The Staggering Ystate of Scots Statesmen," was the instrument. Either in the account he presented for services in the claim to the title of Stratherne his costs had been taxed, or the Earl had objected to paying for letters the Director of Chancery had never written, or something of a like nature had occurred. Anyhow, from a friend he became a bitter enemy. We find him, with the Earls of Tullibardine and Seaforth, preparing a memorial to the King, which contained six reasons why the Earl of Menteith should not be allowed to remain also Earl of Stratherne.

All, of course, was grist to Scotstarvet's mill. Whether he prepared memorials for or against the Earl, he was always paid to draw them up. The reasons were certainly ingenious, notably the first, which referred vaguely to the Papal dispensations, and suggested that in case of public commotion the descendants of Euphemia Ross might claim the crown. Of course people exist foolish enough to claim crowns; but Sir John Scot overlooked the fact that Charles, as head of the Church, was as capable as a pope to issue a dispensation declaring himself legitimately descended from whoever he chose, and also the worthy Director of Chancery omitted to inquire into the descent of the brewer of Huntingdon, a claimant to the crown more to be feared than all the nobility of Scotland.

The six suggestions having revived the sleeping jealousy which lies at most men's hearts, and most of all at the hearts of kings, the usual commission of inquiry, composed chiefly of accusers, was instituted to examine into the matter. Even in the stupid farce called Justice that we to-day are so familiar with, such buffoonery would not be tolerated as that which seems to have taken place. Question and answer, as in a modern conversation-book, was the form the clowning took.

That staggering statesman, Scot of Scotstarvet, after several conundrums, proposed the following masterpiece of legal cynicism: "Is it not boldness that the said Earle should have served himself heir of blood to David, Earl of Stratherne, eldest lawfull son of the first marriage to King Robert II, whereby he is put in degree of blood equall to his Majestie? It is answered in our judgment, the boldness seems too great."

The King is said to have complained he never could love a man without some one pulling him from his arms. This from the beginning has been the pathetic fate of kings, that they could never have a friend; but even a king need hardly have been moved to give up a friend by foolery of the calibre of the questions of Scot of Scotstarvet. On the top of this Sir Robert Dalyell reported to the king that the Earl had said "he had the reddest blood in Scotland." Prince Rupert was a chemist, and could have reported (after phlebotomy) scientifically upon the matter.

However, this course seems to have been neglected, and the unlucky Earl was stripped of all his dignities, ruined in estate, confined to a castle in the North, and, worst of all, a pantomimic title, the earldom of Airth, was forced upon him. Earl of Menteith had a fine rolling sound about it. Earls of Menteith had been more or less incompetent generals and statesmen for two hundred years. The title of Stratherne was royal, though carrying with it misfortune. Airth no one in his senses could care about. And the unlucky Earl seems to have used it semi-furtively, in the way that a brave general or admiral, who is made Lord Tooting or Viscount Hoxton, uses his epithet of opprobrium in modern times. Back to Airth Castle the unlucky man repaired, and then his creditors fell on him like coyotes fall upon a lean bull-buffalo in America; at least in the way they used to do in the days when buffalo existed. After his creditors appeared his friends to buy his property at half its value, as the tried and trusty friend is wont to do in times of trouble. The King, too, promised him money on hearing of his distress, but the money is included in the sums the payment of which one rather hopes for (like Sir Thomas More) than looks to see realised. Strangely, the only one of the Earl's friends who stood to him in evil fortune and purchased none of his estate was a lawyer, the Lord Advocate, Sir Thomas Hope. It almost seems he must have been of an inferior legal mind, the case is so extraordinary.

In Menteith the Earl seems to have devoted his time to field sports, as befits a country gentleman, for in 1636 he received a letter from Charles I thanking him for the capture by his son, Lord Kilpont, of a Highland rogue, John Roy McGregor. The King assured him that this was the best way of regaining his favour, by doing him services. It would seem that had a king insulted most men by offering to make them Earl of Airth, or Camlachie, Tooting, or Bishopbriggs, that it had been more natural to have joined with honest John Roy McGregor to try and catch the king rather than hand the poor Highland rascal over to the kindly gallows of the town of Crieff.

Tastes have always strangely differed in mankind, and that which is intolerable to a bagman, a courtier seems to relish. Little by little the Earl regained the royal favour. In 1639 the sycophantic Scottish nobility almost to a man subscribed to the Covenant. The Earl and his son

Kilpont refused to do so, not being good men of business.

From the days of Edward I of England, who was a man if not a patriot, the nobility of Scotland have always been the slaves either of English kings or Scottish priests. At the present time, as kings and priests have had to some extent their day, and as the Scottish noble must have a master, he has put his neck under the yoke of the London tailor and is happy. Instead, therefore, of joining the Highland and Covenanting rogues, the Earl preferred to try and win back royal favour, and in 1639 he was again appointed a Privy Councillor. The Earl and Lord Kilpont were made lieutenants of Stirlingshire, to raise forces against the Covenanters.

In his son John, Lord Kilpont, the unlucky Earl might have found some one to raise the fortunes of his house. It appeared that the man whose fate furnished Sir Walter Scott with the theme of one of his most enchanting novels was destined to play a brilliant part. He married the Lady Mary Keith, daughter of William Earl Marischal, and received as her dowry thirty thousand pounds Scots. Though the pound Scots is certainly inferior to the pound sterling, I fancy that the Lady Mary's dowry surpassed in value the probably hypothetical one thousand merks a year with which the Earl of Menteith proposed to endow the wife of his son. The Lord Kilpont employed himself with credit in various matters in Scotland, and was appointed one of the Committee of War for Perthshire, under the Marquis of Montrose. His death by the hand of Stewart of Ardvoilich at Collace, in Montrose's camp, extinguished all his father's hopes and broke his heart.

The author of the "Red Book of Menteith," quoting from a paper furnished to him by a member of the Ardvoilich family, says: "It was a hard life the Major (Ardvoilich) led after that he had slain Lord Kilpont, even though he had the Government with him." This is not so surprising to us moderns, who have seen Major Le Caron, the favoured agent of the Government of both sides of politics, pass not exactly a peaceful life. "There was (sic) many powerful families that were kin to the Menteiths, specially the Graems, and they were all at feud with him." It is said that even after he was dead "his followers daurna tak his body so far east as Dundura for fear of the Graems," so they just "shoughed" it at the point of Coilmore, whence it was exhumed and placed afterwards in the old chapel. A charming picture of the time. It is pleasing to reflect that even the Government could not protect Ardvoilich.

The "shoughing"* of the body is very graphic, and the word should be incorporated into the English language by Act of Parliament. So the last ray of hope went out for the unlucky Earl of Menteith, and the remainder of the voyage of his life was bound in shallows and in miseries. Little by little he lost his lands, and his creditors became clamorous. The King at one time asked that £7000 should be paid to him "out of the first and readiest of the Customs." Furthermore, he said to the Lords of the Treasury, "we recommend this seriouslie unto you and expect your performance thereoff." However, the debt was not paid, and King Charles, in 1651, again acknowledged the debt, and promised, "on the word of a prince, to see it faithfully paid whenever he found occasion." This, indeed, is the true way to pay old debts, and reminds the writer that he has seen the legend, "Hoy no se fia mañana si," [*sic* = mañana tampoco] written over the counter of many a "pulperia" in the River Plate.

In 1650 the Earl created his "cusin," Sir William Graham of Gartmore, his lieutenant for calling and convening "our kind freendis, tenants, cotters and hinds betwix Achyll and the foot of Lochard." A ragged regiment Sir William Graham must have found himself at the head of; but then Coventry is not situated "betwix Achyll and the foot of Lochard." The Cromwellians seem to have added to his afflictions by "totallie burning and weisting the paroch of Aberfoyll, which wes stocked with hys steilbowe corne." After the loss of the King's favour and his son's death, the petty miseries of a man struggling against a load of debt seem to have broken down even his hopeful spirit, for in a paper in the Buchanan Charter-chest he describes himself "as much decayed and worne."

In l661, Campbell of Glenorchy was unable to visit him at his castle in Inch Talla, by "reason of the ice." The ice, too, was settling round his heart, and in the same year he died, worn out with grief and debt, and leaving to his heir a heritage of troubles. Thus ended, in a little island in a little lake, the life of one who at one time was the first peer of Scotland, high in favour with the King, fawned on by courtiers, but at the last without a friend, without an occupation but to chew the cud of bitter recollection and watch the wavelets breaking on the pebbles of Arnmaak, or listen to the cawing of the rooks in the stag-headed chestnuts of Inchmahome.

---

*Saxons, and the unlucky folk who live south of the Tweed, may like to learn that to "shough" means to place a plant temporarily in the ground.

THE HOTEL LAWN

INCHTALLA

THE RUINS, INCHMAHOME

THE BELFRY, INCHMAHOME

IV. Atavism

Showing how misfortunes are often hereditary, and relating the death of the
Beggar Earl of Menteith

It is said that the evil that men do lives after them, and this saying may
be extended to the follies of mankind. It is quite likely that had William,
the seventh Earl of Menteith, attended to business at home, stringing up
McGregors and McFarlanes when occasion offered, and refrained from
going to Court to seek for titles, that his grandson William, the eighth
and last Earl of Menteith, would not have passed through the thirty
years purgatory of poverty that he endured. Certain it is that the house
of Menteith with him fell into complete decadence. He does not seem
to have been a foolish man, at least not more foolish than many other
noblemen of his or of our own time. Wicked he certainly was not, for
has not Holy Writ itself informed us that the wicked commonly flourish
like green bay-trees? From first to last evil fortune, debts, ill health and
ill assorted wives, made his life a misery.

In 1661 he succeeded to the title. Like a wise Scotch nobleman he
determined to travel "furth of Scotland" at once. This seems to have
been the one prudent resolution of his life. Fate, however, laid him
by the heels fast with the ague in London at the "Signe of the Blacke
Swan" in the Strand. Thus the Earl never swam in a gondola, visited
Rome, Amsterdam, Brussels, Paris, or any of the capitals where noble
youth of the period were wont to repair to improve their minds and
to perfect themselves in fencing. Not that the district of Menteith has
not produced some notable swordsmen, "tall fellows of their hands," as
Dugald Ciar Mohr, Rob Roy, Henry Cunningham of Boquhan, and
Captain McLachlan of Auchentroig, who fought at Minden, are there
to testify. A tradition lingers that Andrea de Ferrara once made swords
at Auchray. The aforesaid Andrea is reputed to have plied his trade in
so many parts of Scotland that he must either have been in constant
motion, which would soon have rendered his industry precarious, or he

must have lived about a hundred years, or his residences have become as migratory as the birthplaces of Homer or Mr Gladstone.

Failing in his object of foreign travel, the Earl seems to have addressed himself to the illusory pursuit of the money owing to his family by the Crown. A good "ganging plea" has been the ruin of many a Scotch proprietor, but a ganging plea against the Crown is an unusual opportunity even for a nobleman. The Earl availed himself of it to the full. As in the country where he was born he must have had plenty of the Bible, it is almost a wonder he did not remember the allusions to the promises of princes which it contains.

In 1661 we find him at the Court of Whitehall asking for the "ffifty thousande pounds [whether sterling or Scottish is not stated] due untoe your petitioner's grandfather. And your petitioner shall ever pray." Perhaps is praying still. What faith it must have required to have petitioned the ever-blessed Charles by the grace of God! In 1663 he married his sister Elizabeth to Sir William Graham of Gartmore.

In 1677 he writes to David, second Earl of Wemyss, that he was "warpt in a laberinth of almost a never-ending trouble." His orthography also seems to have been a little "warpt" even for the times in which he wrote. The trouble was undoubted, for it appears he was "on everie syde perplext by to pressing creditors, and in conseene this term of Martinmas they wil get no monyes, tho' they should tak my life." Life is the last thing a creditor ever wishes to take. The Earl need have been under no apprehension. Then came marriage, often as bad as creditors or worse. However, death is said to relieve a man of both. About this time he married one Anna Hewes, who, as the author of the "Red Book of Menteith" observes, was probably an English lady. From her he was divorced. But his creditors had taken him for better or for worse, and again we find him complaining against their "unreasonablenesse." His second wife was Katherine Bruce, daughter of Bruce of Blairhall. She could not stand the croaking of the frogs in the lake under the Castle of Talla, and betook herself to Edinburgh. The droning of the bagpipes in the hall and the croaking of the frogs under her bedroom window might have been a valid plea or pleas for Anna Hewes to take herself from the company of her sweet lord.

For Katherine Bruce, however, the case stands differently, and as a Scottish gentlewoman she ought to have been proof against all kinds of national music.

In those days few things strike one more vividly than the fact that lawyers and a "wee bit writing" were the very essence of the people's lives. Scotland has always been the home of lawyers, and the people only took their necks from underneath the yoke of the priests and friars to place them just as fairly under that of the ministers and attorneys. Still, in these degenerate days, a man would not deliberately enter into a duly signed and witnessed contract with his own wife, as the Earl did, and set forth that "he shall have full freedom and libertie to goe about his affairs to Edinburgh, or any place elsewhere theranent." A latchkey would be cheaper.

This omnipresence of the scrivener and his intrusion into daily life was not confined to Scotland. During the conquest of America not a ship sailed or expedition started into the wilderness without its lawyer, and that in the face of an edict by Charles V that neither solicitors nor advocates (procuradores ó abogados) shall pass to the Indies. In 1541 Francisco de Orellana, in a boat with forty-seven companions, descending the then unnavigated Amazon, gives up his command, is elected again by his forty-seven followers, with different powers, writes down the same in a ragged bit of paper, in a contemporary legal hand signs it, and the forty-seven soldiers also sign, in various styles of characters, resembling crossbow arrowheads, lance points, and other hands of write peculiar to the age. The document reposes at Seville in the archives of the Indies.*

Luckily to-day men do not make contracts with their wives as to their personal liberty, though, no doubt, we shall return to that as things progress.

"Riding the Parliament" was one of the chief recreations of a self-respecting Scottish nobleman of the seventeenth century, a custom as honoured in the observance as the breach. Surely if a man chances to be a peer, one of the duties of his condition is to appear in public, that is, if he be a personable peer. Stuck upon a horse in cotton velvet-gown, with an ermine hood and coronet, the mob could tell who was and who was not a gentle man. To-day, when the possession of an Albert chain decides the question, the examination almost approaches that undergone by thieves and politicians at a police court. The Earl of Menteith was one of those who never shrank from any public duty, however painful.

---

*It has been recently published by Don José Medina, at the cost of the Duke of Tsaerclaes de Tilly.

So in 1687 I find him writing to the Marquis of Montrose, asking him to get some earl's robes for him, as "our aine was destroyed in the Einglish tyme." Many and manifold have been the outrages on Scotland by our ancient enemies of England. In times gone by they hanged us and they harried us, they quartered and they drew us. In more modern days they have usurped our kilts, and forced their speech upon us, making the modern Scottish jargon a sort of linsey-woolsey of a thing got betwixt Whitechapel and Cowcaddens. Never, though, as far as I have read, except on this occasion, did they palter with the garments of a belted earl. In after times they abolished the Scottish Parliament, and in their dastardly attempt to prevent a Scottish nobleman attending I see but the precursor to their subsequent villainy. So urgent was the earl that on the same day he writes again to the Marquis, "to provide and get the lene from some earle, their robs, fite mantle, and vellvat coates, and all things that belongs to Parliament robs. I will heave four footmen in livra. Last tyme when I reid the Parliament I carried the scepter and I had the lene of the decesed Erle of Lothian's robes, but perhaps this Erle will reid himself."* There is something pathetic in the way the poverty-stricken and disillusioned man recalls how, in happier days, he bore the sceptre. How the deceased Earl of Lothian was to ride even to a Parliament passes the mind of man to imagine; not that a dead rider is a thing unknown.

Once between Villaguay and Nogoyá, in Entre Rios, the writer of this brief chronicle came, in a little clearing of the great forest of Montiel, on two brothers, one living and one dead, jogging at the "trotecito" on their horses. The living brother, a fine young Gaucho, upright and swaying with his horse, like only a Gaucho, the dead one just as upright, tied in his saddle to two sticks. The object of the journey to bury the deceased in consecrated ground at Gualeguay. Vayan con Dios Caballeros.

Horses were another cross in the life of the unlucky eighth Earl of Menteith. In the same letter in which he asks for "the robs," he asks for the loan of "a peaceable horse." The horrors of attending Parliament must have been intensified when a man's horse was not peaceable. Of all the costumes for riding an unquiet horse in, a peer's robes must have been the most ill-advised. Again, in 1678, the Earl writes excusing himself for not going to Perth to attend a militia meeting from want of a horse. "Though I was leader for one horse within the parish of Aberfoyle, and although I gott never my localitie for the horse, butt was given to others,

---

*"Red Book of Menteith," from papers in Gartmore and Buchanan Charter-chests.

yet notwithstanding for all that, I will sett my horse to the rendivouse." Clear composition is not necessary to a peer, but we would like to know what the above meant to the Earl, and why he never "gott a localitie" for the horse.

In 1688 the Earl writes to the Marquis of Montrose, informing him that he has apprehended some men engaged in harbouring the murderers of Archbishop Sharpe, and narrowly missed laying hands on Balfour and Hackston of Rathillet. His zeal for the Government was reported to the King, who promised (as per usual) to remember him on "a fitt occasioun."

Parliament never ceased from troubling the Earl, as it now does the nation, for the minister of the Port of Menteith signs a certificate as to his unfitness to attend in the year 1689.

The chief thought as death approaches an unfortunate man is generally how to entail the property which has cursed his life upon some innocent successor. Earl William was no exception to the rule. In 1688 he writes to his "unkle," Sir James Graham, as to the marriage of the daughter of Sir James with some one on whom the earldom could be conferred. A smart captain of horse, and a most personable man, as his picture at Glamis Castle testifies, "myne own cousing, the Laird of Claverus," first occurred to him. He, writes the Earl, "is a person exceeding weell accomplished as any I know with natur gifts ... and hes a free extent of good payable rent near by Dundee."

If "natur gifts" are to be a handsome man and a fine horseman, certainly Claverhouse was well endowed; and as to "payable rent," it is exceedingly likely that few tenants would have cared to get into arrears with such a landlord. Sir James, however (no doubt a whey-faced Whig), refused the alliance.

The young lady married a Captain Rawdon, son of an unknown baronet, Sir George Rawdon, and lost the opportunity of being the wife of the most brilliant Scotchman of the age.

In reading the letters of Claverhouse to the Earl, one is almost tempted to believe that there may be some truth in the aphorism, "le style c'est l'homme," so very like they are to what one imagines the writer. "Asseur yourself," he says in one, "if ever ther be baricades in Glescw* again, you shall not want a call, and my Lord I bespeak ane imployement with you, which is to be your lieutenant generall, and I will asseur you we will

---

*Glescw for Glasgow is quite a Cavalier's spelling.

make the world talk of us." It is probable, indeed, the world would have talked, but only of the "lieutenant generall." By the letters Claverhouse seems to have been at least as good a diplomatist as he was a soldier. The way in which he flatters the poor old Earl in his letters from the Court, shows he could have made his fortune had he chosen to be as dishonest as most men of his time, or of our own.

The marriage with Claverhouse having fallen through, and another projected match with the Marquis of Montrose having been a failure, despair seems to have settled on the unlucky Earl. The earldom he wished to leave to the Marquis of Montrose, but the King objected, and Claverhouse tried hard to get the Earl to leave the title to him; but death was soon to set him free from all of them.

In 1694 he died, after a life of struggling with debts and troubles and misfortunes from his birth. His personal estate went to his nephew, Sir John Graham of Gartmore, but it proved chiefly a heritage of debts. So in misfortune expired the earldom of Menteith, one of the most illustrious titles of Scotland.

Round certain names there seems a halo of ill-luck. Often it makes the owners of the names more sympathetic to us, as a golden nimbus in a picture by the Ferrara school often redeems the angular features of an early Italian saint. At other times, especially when joined with poverty, it makes the victim almost ridiculous. Justice, divine or human, always presses hardest on the unfortunate, and the Earls of Menteith seem to have been criminal enough in some way known to Providence. Courage they had as an inheritance of race, and often showed it, but to little or no account. Ability was shown by several of them, but it availed them nothing. Possessions and titles were showered upon them, but they neither profited by nor kept them. Little by little all their broad acres made themselves wings, till at the last, of all the earldoms of Menteith, Airth, and Stratherne, only the little island in the reedy pine-girt lake was left, and there, in the grey peel-tower facing to Ben Dhearg, the last Earl died. Even his burial-place is not well known, though in his will he gave directions to "my nevoy" Sir John Graham "to cause ane exquisite and cunning measone erect two statues of fyne hewen stone for anself and for me deerest spouse Dame Catherine Bruce."

The statues were never erected, or, if erected, have mouldered away like the Earl; or, may be, some Presbyterian has taken them for saints, and being angry that poor mortals should have any to pray for us, has made away with them.

A lower depth of misery had to be touched by one who called himself Earl of Menteith. In 1744, when the peers of Scotland were proceeding to engage in the degrading ceremony of stamping a Scottish nobleman as inferior to a peer of England by election, the name Menteith was answered to by a thin, cadaverous-looking youth, who informed the assembled mummers that he was the Earl of Menteith by right of birth and of descent, and was at present studying medicine in Edinburgh. From that moment till his death, although warned to desist by the House of Lords, he never dropped his claim.

For a year or two he regularly attended at all elections of a Scottish peer, but at last seemed to have become disgusted, perhaps at the whole undignified proceeding, and used to retire from Edinburgh before the day of the election. Gradually he sank into obscurity, and little by little into mendicancy, and at last sustained himself by begging from house to house, under the title of the "Beggar Earl."

In 1747 he published a pamphlet, now become most rare and hard to meet with, entitled, "The Fatal Consequences of Discord, or a Political Address to the Noble and Rich Families of Great Britain." In the title of the tract are contained several propositions, such as, "That there can be no true unity without true religion and virtue," a proposition excellent in itself and difficult to controvert, and which places its enunciator on about the same intellectual footing as the member of the "National Convention" in Paris during the "Terror" who rose to demand "l'arrestation des coquins et des lâches."

Ever since honest men have mixed in matters political they have always seen at once that "true unity is impossible without religion and virtue," but, unfortunately, the difficulty as yet has been the want of any one to arrest "les coquins et les lâches."

The pamphleteer also sets forth "that the multiplicity of laws is as great a sign of the corruption of a State as the diversity of medicines is of the distemper of the body." Had not the pamphlet been dedicated to the Prince of Wales, "our only hope of a Protestant succession," I had almost come to the conclusion the writer had been an Anarchist.

After much of Alexander (he of Macedon), of Philip, Aristippus, and the proper quotation on Government by Aristotle, he concludes by saying: "May virtue then flourish in this island and appear to the Englishmen [no word of Scotland] to be somewhat more than a little pork with a variety of sauce." The end is rather enigmatical, for virtue seems to be flourishing enough, even in England, where sauces never vary. And as to pork, virtue is not so fickle as to dissever it from apple-sauce.

"The whole by the Right Honble. Earl of Menteith, Stratherne, and Airth, Lord Kilpont and Baron Gartmore." As the last title never existed, it shows the writer of the pamphlet was not entirely without imagination.

Pamphleteering does not seem to have raised his fortunes, for by degrees even his beggar's wallet seems to have grown empty, and last scene of all, some neighbours near Bonhill, in Dumbartonshire, came on the body of the Beggar Earl by the roadside.

So, like a cadger's pony, passed away one who without doubt had in his veins the blood of a king of Scotland, and whose ancestors had been the proudest in the land. Perhaps the Beggar Earl, in his poverty and wanderings, was not much more unhappy than his ancestors, bowed down with all the cares of State. One wonders, seeing who he was, he did not join Charles Edward Stewart and march to Derby. At least he could have suffered on Tower Hill, and shown a Beggar Earl could meet his fate as bravely as the most duly coroneted.

Considering that his family had all been great upholders of the Stewarts, the "Protestant succession" and the Beggar Earl seem strangely ill assorted. What could it matter to him if they mumbled a mass, or dinged the very "harricles" out of the bible, and garred the stour flee about the Chapel Royal, after the fashion of Geneva. Still, all the thousand ills which wait on poverty, and take away its dignity and pathos, ofttimes rendering it ridiculous; the miseries of a wandering beggar's life, the hope deferred, the insolence of fools, and the last night by the roadside dyke in Bonhill parish may have been as keen a martyrdom to bear as the shorter and sharper, though more glorious one, he might have met on Tower Hill.

THE WEST DOORWAY OF THE PRIORY

THE CHAPTER HOUSE

QUEEN MARY'S BOWER FROM NUN'S HILL

QUEEN MARY'S BOWER

V. Traditional

Of things and others; on the infrequency of types in modern life; with all about "Trootie"

Painstaking historians not a few have laboured both in and out of their vocations to preserve the memory of all most notable within Menteith and the surrounding districts. Graham of Duchray, the Rev. Mr. Kirk of Aberfoyle, "who went to his own herde" in 1692, the Rev. Patrick Graham, also of Aberfoyle, Sir Walter Scott, the Rev. Mr. Mc Gregor Stirling, Sir William Fraser, and others, including Mr. Dunn, have written of the antiquities and legends. Of later years, Mr. Andrew Lang has enriched our literature with one of his most successful flights in minor poetry, in memory of Mr. Kirk, the astral vicar of Aberfoyle. Each in his own particular style after their kind have done brave things for themselves and their district.

Few have been so Homeric as Graham of Duchray in his account of Lord Glencairn's expedition, of which he was "an eye- and also an ear-witness." Pleasant in these days of prosing to record a history beginning thus: "The Earl of Glencairn went from his own house of Finleston in the beginning of the month of August, 1653, to Lochearn, where several of the clans did meet him."

Pretty to read, too, the combat on horseback, as befitted cavaliers, between Sir George Monro and the Lord Glencairn, and to learn how, at the first blow, my lord disabled Sir George's bridle-hand, and when the combat was resumed on foot my lord did strike him such blows on the forehead as caused the blood to trickle into his eyes and blind him; and to hear that my lord evidently intended to "mak siccar," as his lordship's valet, one John White, struck up his lordship's hand, exclaiming, "You have enough of him, my lord; you have got the better of him."

A presuming and impertinent fellow this same John White, and it does one good to hear that my lord turned on him and "struck him a great blow on the shoulder." In fact a case of the most proper infliction of "your right strappado," and an example of what comes to those who interfere between two gentlemen taking the air of a morning upon Dornoch Links.

Duelling seems to have been more severely punished in those days on occasion, than we generally believed, for a second combat having arisen (also on Dornoch Links) between two gentlemen called Lindsay and Livingstone, on account of their having taken different sides in the quarrel between Lord Glencairn and Sir George Monro, the victor, Lindsay, who had slain his foe, was executed at Dornoch Cross. "The Earl of Glencairn was troubled at this gentleman's death; but all must be done, forsooth, to please Sir George."

Execution was a summary affair in Graham of Duchray's time, for a trifling Englishman, masquerading as Captain Gordon, but whose real name proved to be Portugus (sic), was also executed later on for some breach of duty. "Portugus" seems doubtful as an English name; but when have Southrons kept even to probability in dealing with Scotsmen?

After the incident of the pseudo-Portugus, Graham of Duchray relates how Lord Glencairn's expedition laid siege to the Laird of Lethen's house, and lost five men. "The general being incensed at this, ordered the soldiers to pull down several stacks of corn, with which he filled the court and gates of the house, which being set on fire, he judged the smoke would stifle them, the wind blowing it into the house; but it took not the effect that he expected."

Graham does not inform us if this incident "troubled Lord Glencairn," but briefly finishes by saying, "we departed and burnt all Lethen's land." A military incident told in a military fashion for soldiers, quite in the manner of the French in Algeria or the English in Zululand. The narrative finishes abruptly, after describing the terms the Earl of Glencairn made for his followers with General Monk, with the announcement that "this happened on the 4th day of September, 1654. The Earl of Glencairn that same night crossed the water and came to his own house of Finlaystone." The narrative reminds one of the account of the conquest of Mexico by Bernal Diaz del Castillo, though Graham of Duchray lacked the power of description which makes the history of the stouthearted, simple-minded Governor of the city of Santiago de Guatemala such a charming book.

Antiquarians have commented on and disagreed about the origin and name of one of our natural curiosities, the Flanders Moss. Some have it it once formed part of the *Sylva Caledonica*. Others, again, derive its name from a supposititious Danish word, "Flynders," said by themselves to signify a flat. Antiquarians are such a joy to a community that it is perhaps a work of supererogation to look too closely into their assertions.

The Moss is still amongst us, and Nimmo, in his "History of Stirlingshire," declares the ancient name was the Tilly Moss, and instances the survival of the name in the local Sessentilly.

Baad nan Sassenach (the Englishman's wood), near the Miltown of Aberfoyle, is duly celebrated in local chronicles, and the slaughter, or murder, for he was said to be shot by a non-combatant, of the luckless Sassenach in the times of Cromwell.

Tobanareal, the spring where the Tutor of Appin slew the Earl of Menteith, or is said to have slain him, on the road to Glenny, has also had its chroniclers and commentators. The old Fingalian path that the Appin men must have followed as it leads past the spring still exists, a whitish trail through the heather and bracken left by the deerskin mocassins of centuries, and perpetuated by the hobnailed boots of the rustics of to-day. Few traverse it nowadays, though in its time many a "creagh" must have been driven from the "Laich" to the hills of Appin, past the decayed old house of Glenny.

Few of the present generation know the "Tyepers" or the "Red Path," and fewer still the wild track which leads out of Glen Finlas, past the Alte Glen Mean* into Balquhidder. Rob Roy must have known it blindfold by day and night, as it is difficult to see how cattle could have been more quickly driven into Balquhidder than by that path. A shepherd now and then, or a strolling beggar, can tell the names of the old tracks and paths which frequently crossed the hills from strath to strath. To-day the keeper, the only man except the shepherd who ever uses those forgotten ways, knows them but as the "short cut to so and so." Of cartridges and bores of guns he is learned, but knows as little of the history of the past as the Spanish peasant, who attributes anything older than his father's time to the all-constructing Moors.

The sportsmen, who gambol like skirt-dancers at a music-hall, dressed in the parti-coloured petticoats they believe the clansmen wore, euphemiously call all wells the "Luncheon Well," all stones and rocks the "Telescope Rock" and "Game Bag Stone," inventing as complete and homogeneous a phraseology as if the district of Menteith were situated in Deaf Smith County, Texas. No one can blame them, for Gaelic is not an easy tongue, and an acquaintance with it hard to acquire for many reasons, one of which is the extreme reluctance of the talented

---

*Alte Glen Mean; in English, the waterfall in the glen of the roe.

possessors of it to condescend to base particulars. Who has not asked a Highlander what such and such a name portends and not been answered, "Och, it is just a Gaelic word whatever!" An excellent explanation, full and satisfying enough to those proud beings who "have the Gaelic," but strangely unsubstantial to the mere Sassenach.

It might have puzzled even Professor Blackie, who between Greek and Gaelic was never at a loss to construct a derivation for most Scottish names, to disentangle the confusion into which many of the names of places have fallen into in the Menteith district. Naturally, as Gaelic became forgotten, the pronunciation of the names became a matter of personal convenience rather than etymology, and as in Spain, where the Arabic names have often been mangled beyond recognition, the Gaelic words in Menteith have suffered a sad Lowland change. Never shall I forget the efforts of a grave Arab to preserve his gravity before a restored Arabic inscription in a Spanish church. It appeared the verse of the Koran had been written upside down, and several letters wrongly made, so that the inscription assigned some attributes to God which even a true believer could with difficulty reconcile to his belief. Whether a Gaelic scholar would encounter a cryptogamic joke in some of our local names I know not, or even if joking is recognised in Gaelic, but I am certain that names like " Critilvean," "Polybaglot," and others, would puzzle most philologists.

One site of a clan battle none of the historians I have mentioned seem to have dealt with. At Craig Vadh, above the slate quarry of Aberfoyle, on the ridge where the old Loch Katrine road just loses Menteith from sight, are ten or fifteen long-shaped cairns. Here tradition has it that a band of foragers from Lochaber were overtaken by the men of Lennox and Menteith, and a fierce fight ensued. The cairns are where the dead men's bodies were found; their graves a little farther down the hill, buried in fern and bracken, marked by grey stones.

As for burial places, folk are hard to please. Some like your quiet corner, under a yew-tree, close to some Norman church in England. A quiet resting place enough it makes too, with the parson's pony (or the intruding donkey of the Nonconformist) cropping the long lush grass above one. Pleasant to come to in the summer evenings, when swifts flit to and fro like ghosts, and cockchafers hum in the leafy trees, are these same country churchyards in England.

In spite of the natural beauty of the land, in spite of faith sufficient to turn all Scotland into a pampa, what is it makes a Scottish churchyard so different? It may be that the knowledge that the sleepers' souls are all in torment — for none could possibly have escaped the penalties so liberally dispensed to them in life in church — renders one apprehensive. Again, the absence of "affliction sore" upon the tombstones may make the graves less homelike, but still the fact remains, our national churchyard is not inviting to the world-worn traveller. Again, there are some who think your three square yards of canvas and your lump of lead, with the Union Jack, and "therefore we commit this body to the deep," the fittest burial for man. Still, for the men who lie so quietly on the green slope under Craig Vadh I fancy no other resting-place would seem as pleasant. What if the tourist passes, in the diurnal coach, within a quarter of a mile? What if the cockney (oblivious of the fact that Rob Roy's well is really under Craig Vadh) descends to slake his whisky and his thirst at a spurious fountain, made with hands, hard by the turnpike road? All this, and how the world is changed, they can know nothing of, or how to-day tall fellows are slaughtered in different fashion from that in which they died. For all I know, the times in which they lived were better than the times we know; perhaps were worse. At any rate, wolves roamed the hills, as the name Craig Vadh would seem to show. Around the desolate Loch Reoichte, perhaps, the Caledonian bull has fed, the wild boar harboured; and yet the ground was more secure than nowadays, for fewer perils from broken whisky-bottles and sardine-tins lurked in the heather. And how shall sardine-tins offend? Are they not, after all, a sign, natural and visible, of the spirit of the age, and did not Providence place them (most likely) in our path to show us something? What if we cannot see it, and only cut our feet upon the bottles or jagged tins? No doubt the cross, which, seen in the sky, converted Constantine, was there before; and many another Roman general was not so much a deep-dyed pagan as merely unobservant.

Hard by Craig Vadh is the desolate hill tarn known as Loch Reoichte. In the district there are many of these curious black hill lochs, generally in peaty hollows, with water black as jet, peopled with little muddy trout, and often overgrown with water-lilies.

Each has its legend, as in duty bound. Loch McAn Righ, close to the Lake of Menteith, is sacred to the memory of a king's son who, in the days when princes of the blood-royal perambulated the world at a loose end and unattended, almost lost his life whilst chasing the wild deer, by his horse bogging down with him. Tradition hath it that one Betty or Betsy, for there is room for doubt which of the forms of the name the maiden bore, extracted him, like a royal cork, from the mud and saved his life. The field is known as Achnaveity, said by Gaelic-speaking men to mean the field of Betty. Tradition is in error in having woven no romance about the King of Scotland's son and Betty, but then how seldom tradition, on the whole, misses its opportunities in matters of the sort. Anyhow, near by the field is the "laroch" of the chapel of Arnchly, one of the four chapels connected with the monastery of Inchmahome, so possibly the nearness of the sacred edifice prevented scandal making free with the Prince's or Betty's name.

Other little lochs preserve their legend, as the Loch at Duchray Castle, said to be unfathomable, and the Tinkers' Loch (Loch an Cheird), above the hills of Aberfoyle, in which the mysterious water-bull of the Highland legends was said to dwell. Amongst them all for desolate beauty Loch Reoichte stands first.* In winter it may well be called the frozen loch, standing as it does in a sort of cup on the top of a hill. In summer clouds of midges hang over its sullen waters. Standing by it is the only place in the district where one sometimes fancies he can conjure up what a Highlander of two hundred years ago was like.

It does not want much effort of imagination to see the Lowlander, the hard-featured, commonplace "stipulosus vernaculus," as Bower described Henry Smith of Perth, over whom Sir Walter has thrown such a glamour of romance. Whether in a rusty morrion and jacks, clothed in a "stan o' black," or in the fearsome "defroque" (no English word expresses the crassness of his appearance) that he wears to-day, the Lowlander must have always been the same. Where shall we find anything like the Highlander of the old chronicles in Scotland of to-day? Not in the gillie of the shooting-lodges, insolent and servile at the same time; not in the crofter or the cotter, for it is well known the bone and sinew of the Highland clans are to be looked for rather in Canada or Georgia than in Scotland.

Still, standing by Loch Reoichte, it sometimes seems one can call up a sort of Indian, lithe and agile, yet lazy and indolent when off the warpath, stealing through the heather with his silent deerskin shoes, looking at nothing, yet seeing everything, as men who spend their lives in the open air engaged in war or hunting are wont to do.

Types have become infrequent in Menteith, as in the other districts of Scotland. The author of the "Scotch Hairst Kirn," printed in 1821, and

*Reoichte means frozen in Gaelic.

descriptive of a harvest-home at the farm of Ledard by Aberfoyle, might search the country in vain for such a character as "Bauldy McRosat," or "Will Shore," and return like Diogenes after his search through the Athenian Stock Exchange. Were it not for "Trootie" we might almost say the type of semi-mendicant, of whom Sir Walter has so many specimens, had ceased to exist. "Trootie," however, saves us from the reproach. In the dark ages he was said to have been a weaver "aboot Balfron." This statement I put forth, whilst not believing it, for all it may be worth.

Weavers (*vide* the works of Barrie and others) have mostly been superior-minded persons who were taken up with politics, theology, and other matters which do not go far to help to keep a family. Writers of talent have told us of how the virtues banished from cities still lurk amongst the brethren of their craft. One thing I cannot think it possible they have done, that is, produced a fisher. Fishers of men may be they have put forth, but that kind mostly fish for their own hand, and "Trootie" in that respect is blameless. It may be that his father or some degenerate scion of his family plied the base shuttle in fashion tame and mechanical. "Trootie" himself, I'll swear, has never soiled his hands with honest toil, that honest toil we talk so much about and all avoid. Nature turns out a perfect fly-fisher but very seldom.

Your "pêcheur à la ligne" swarms in the suburbs of our cities, and has his villa. His faith is great, his cuticle is pachydermatous, turning off jokes and midges as a tapir's hide turns off an Indian's spear in Paraguay. Who has not seen and silently despised your fisher with a float?

On the much-painted upper reaches of the Thames, along the quays in Paris, they sit in rows, like penguins on a beach. The very fishes know them, and eat their ground bait in a condescending way. Their faith is great, as great as a Theosophist's, and just as practical. One wonders at them, but would not care to imitate their mode of life. Your fly-fisher is of a different race. His toil is not productive, as a general rule, but then his daily business takes him into pleasant places. He knows the reaches of the river under the alders, where the water eddies round the stones and where the big fish lie. Not that he catches any of them.

He knows the stepping-stones, can tell of perils in crossing them in the great spate, and does so. The stump the dipper sits upon, for all the world exactly like a judge upon the bench, and just as wise of face, the fly-fisher can point to. Where from the reeds the heron rises of a misty morning, or where the whistling mallard settles with a splash in the gloaming of the day, he knows. The kingfisher flashing through the sunlight like a bit of the tropics gone astray in northern latitudes, the fly-fisher has marked. Something there is of peril in the very exercise and mystery of his craft, at least to the eyes and clothing. So that, take him for all in all, the fisher with the fly to the manner born is not a man you meet with every day.

Nature alone can make him, and, like most of her best products, she turns them out with parsimony. "Trootie," I take it, fly-fished from his earliest youth. Like Indians I have seen, who could take a tired horse and somehow make him gallop when no one else could make him move, "Trootie" appears to have the instinct of the fisher. Let others fish with all the best appurtenances of fishing-tackle makers, and toil all day and yet catch nothing, let "Trootie" pass and fish the selfsame water, with a rod with as many splicings as Petrucchio's bridle, and fly like a piece of a moulting feather broom, and ten to one he fills a basket. Withal not proud of his success, but taking it as something sent from heaven and marketable.

It was on a summer evening I first saw "Trootie," waddling like a Narragansett pacer up the avenue. At first sight nothing about him showed the intrinsic merit of the man. No one could call him handsome or majestic in appearance. Had Edie Ochiltree risen from his grave and stood beside him, your halfpenny had certainly not gone to "Trootie," that is if personal appearance had influenced your judgment. A little shilpet, feckless-looking body, dressed in a sort of moss-trout coloured and much patched coat of various shades of troutiness and stages of decay; summer and winter a grey woollen comforter resembling a stocking, such as farmers used to wear in the dark ages, round his throat; his "cadie," for I cannot call it hat, a cross between a beehive and a pudding bag, and girt about with casts of fuzzy home-made flies; over his shoulders a dilapidated fishing-basket, always well stuffed with trout; for freedom and convenience in working, his toes protruding through his boots, which looked as if they were chosen on a dunghill; his walk a sort of shuffle, such as fishers often use, and seem to take a pride in.

Apparently the man was older than the rocks; no one can say with certainty they ever saw him younger than sixty. A pleasant age enough to be born at, sixty is, if one was born quite free from rheumatism. Love over, and the taste for speculation and adventure on the wane, avarice but just beginning, with the prospect of a healthy, untroubled life till eighty, and then oblivion of life's troubles, with the usual mendacious epitaph. However, "Trootie," if he was not fashed by love, except perhaps of "speerits," and if in his case avarice was a thing illusory, yet had his cross, and it was rheumatism. He thought it was contracted sleeping by the banks of streams, in order to get to business early in the morning, after a glass or two at night. Perhaps it was the sleeping by the streams, perhaps the glasses overnight; at any rate, the rheumatism was "sort o' fashous," and he appeared to think it a special instance of the malevolence of Providence in dealing with His fishers.

His conversation, if I recollect it rightly, was entirely of his craft, and ran on fishes and fishing, fishes caught and basketed, but more on fishes lost. A tale he had of fishing in the Tinkers' Loch alone amongst the hills. There it appears he hooked a monster early in the morning after sleeping beside the loch. Visions came to him of fame and even wealth if the monster could be landed. The "paragraph" in the local paper of "that veteran sportsman, Mr. Wilkie (better known as 'Trootie')," was all set up and ready in his mind's eye; the monster, duly stuffed, was in a case in the window of the fishing-tackle maker's shop, when see, the cursed luck that always hovers o'er a fisher! Just at the bank, "I had almost grippit him; he gaed a wallop wi' his tail," and then "Trootie" can mind no more until next morning, when he woke beside the loch feeling stiff and "sair forfouchten." The devil of it is that from that day to this he is not sure if he passed one or two nights sleeping by the Tinkers' Loch.

Like Lear, his children were not worthy of him, for none of them were fishers, but took up trades and followed settled occupations in a prosaic fashion. This caused him grief, but drew forth no astonishment, for he would moralise upon the hardness of the fisher's lot, and how the lairds of his youth would often give a guinea for the fish (worth eightpence at the most) that I had purchased most unwillingly for half-a-crown.

Let him fish on, if he still lives to fish — for, for a year or two I have missed him from his usual haunts — let him fish on, before the County Council sends an inspector to see that fishers all wear goloshes and chest-protectors, and none use rods exceeding eighteen feet in length, or contravene the bye-laws.

A man like "Trootie" in a country such as ours, where all endeavour to make money and to rise in the world by shoving others down, ought to be kept (perhaps he is) by national subscription, as an example of how even a Scotchman may revert to the ways of his uncivilised progenitors. As far as it concerns me, all I hope is that his shadow on the bank may never dwindle; and if his personality was somewhat snuffy and his talk like that of other fishers, not always quite exact in detail, much can be excused in one who left deliberately the gross delights of sleeping in a bed and meals three times a day ("aboot Balfron") to fish laborious days.

VI. Pantheistic

Setting forth some particulars of two Menteith worthies, with something of Sith Bruachs, and some remarks on shadows

One of the most characteristic of the few remaining types of the past was certainly Hugh Graham, of the Port of Menteith. Those who do vainly (like the Pelagians) think that good manners and courtesy imply servility ought to have known Hugh Graham. Personally I am not certain if he knew with any accuracy the situation of the Seychelle Islands, or could have told one much of the binomial theorem. What I do know is that he retained in a great measure the ancient Highland manners. Oh, how refreshing those ancient Highland manners were, starting as they did from a different basis from our modern method of deportment! Strange as it may appear, Hugh Graham, although a boatman, considered himself, and was, a gentleman, and being one himself, he treated all humanity in the same style. The modern fashion, which implies that every one is not a gentleman, leaves a different feeling on the recipient of their flavour. Not that most probably they are not better than the older style, in the same way that a bicycle is better than a horse; but then the style is different. All the legends of the district were known to Hugh, who, of course, "had Gaelic," and seemed to have personally assisted at most events of importance in Scottish history for the past two hundred years. That is the way in which a man who has the traditions should take himself — as he grows older and contemporaries die, always to antedate his birth each year a year or two, so that at last he comes to have really lived with those he talks about.

Only by living with people do we really get to know them (not always even then); and if a man makes it his daily duty to talk of Claverhouse, John Knox, Rob Roy, and other men of violence in days gone by, he gets by degrees to think he knew them all. With what an air of truthfulness old Hugh would tell the story of "Malise and the Roeskin Purse."*

---

*McGregor Stirling preserves this story in his "History of the Priory of Inchmahome," now become a somewhat rare book.

One saw the Earl of Menteith laid up in lavender in Edinburgh; one saw the faithful Malise arrive on foot, bringing relief, and when the door was opened accept the halfpenny the owner of the house bestowed on him, struck with his miserable appearance. Then the Earl appeared upon the scene, and chid his follower in Gaelic for accepting alms; and Malise answered, "Och ay, my lord, but I would cheerfully have been accepting every penny the honest gentleman had in his possession." Instinctively the listener divined that Hugh had borne the purse, or been at least a listener to the dialogue, either in person or in some previous incarnation. A sportsman, too, was Hugh, having walked to Ayrshire to attend the tournament at Eglinton, of which he had a store of reminiscences. Other envious old Highlanders, when Hugh, at ninety years of age, used to go "east to the Port" to fetch his cow at nights, were wont to say, "Ay, Hugh was gey and souple for his years, but then Hugh never wrocht ony in his youth." If this was so I honour him the more, for he who can live to ninety without having "wrocht ony," and be, as Hugh was, free from guile and property, is a man to be admired.

Scotland at one time must have been full of men like Hugh. They fought at Bannockburn, at the Harlaw, were at the Sheriffmuir, went with the Chevalier to Derby, and suffered after Culloden, taking the losing side on all occasions with unerring accuracy. Commonly in every battle the winner commands respect, the vanquished has our love; and so it may be that, whilst the men like Hugh have gone down hopelessly before the men of single and double entry, still a corner of our hearts is kept for those who fought, not against their mere conquerors, but time itself.

Of the small gentry who in times past furnished so many perfect types, those who produced the "gash Garscadden," and that fine old laird who thought there might be "wale of wigs upon the Stockie Muir," McLachlan of Auchentroig was about the last survival. Sprung from one of the oldest families in the district — his ancestors had been at Bannockburn, his grandfather at Minden — he occupied a place that no one fills today. Keen at a bargain, yet always loser by it; active in the affairs of others, forgetful of his own; his face as red as the great bottles in a chemist's window, he seemed a tower of strength, and yet was delicate. A sort of link between the gentry and farmers; with the first by choice a farmer, with the latter a gentleman; esteemed, yet overreached by all mankind, as lovers of a bargain often are, the laird of Auchentroig was an instance of the survival of the unfittest — that is, the unfittest for modern life. Had he been born a little earlier, he had been content to ride his Highland garron over his estate and keep his health, and midden at the door, till eighty. As it was, his lot was cast in times too hard and uncongenial; so, like a wise man, finding the chimney of his house always a-smoking, he left the house, and also left the world the poorer by the extinction of a type.

The gradual decay of the English yeomanry is often deplored by writers and historians; few seem to take into consideration that the Scottish yeomanry is quite extinct. The Laird of Auchentroig was the last specimen of his class — at least in the district. With him expired the last of a family whose ancestors were present at almost every battle famous in Scottish history.

The little foursquare, grey stone house,* with its courtyard and its "crowsteps," the coat of arms with its entablature let into the wall over the entrance door, the door itself studded with iron nails, and curiously wrought-iron pendant, serving for knocker and for handle, and which, tradition says, endured a siege from no less a commander than Rob Roy himself, the giant ash trees opposite the house, are now the only relics of the McLachlans, for, after all, what is the tombstone in the churchyard of Drymen? One reads "Hic Jacet," has just time to start a-moralising, and then to catch a train.

History informs us that the Romans once ruled the greater part of Scotland, and one wonders sometimes, looking at the Roman camp, or the camp which some call Roman, others Pictish or Caledonian, at Gartfarran, why they came so far. The little camp, with its ditch now dry and fringed with hazels and with rowans, and through which runs a road, making it so like the camp where Marmion fought the spectre knight that I fancy that Sir Walter had Gartfarran in his mind's eye when he described it, is pleasant enough to go to on a summer day and sit and ponder in.

What an abode of horror it must have been to the unfortunate centurion, say from Naples, stranded in a marsh far from the world, in a climate of the roughest, and blocked on every side by painted savages! No doubt there was a sense of glory in being (except the camp of Ardoch) the farthest outpost of articulate-speaking man in the known world, but even that could scarcely have made up for the lack of news

---

*The house still stands, and can be examined with pleasure by those who take no interest in modern improvements.

from Rome. Although the building spirit of the age has left intact (as yet) the Fairy Hill at Aberfoyle, still for some time past, in fact since the time of the Rev. Mr. Kirk, that eminent pastor "amongst the Scoto-Irish of Aberfoyle," we have no information of the Daoine Shi. Yet the existence of a veritable and historic Sith Bruach is a thing to be envied by the inhabitants of less favoured regions. It profits little whether the Daoine Shi were really fairies or merely "Peghts," as some folk say. With all due deference to Andrew Lang, to the Rev. Mr. Kirk, and to the members of the Psychical Research Society, I opine for the theory of the "Peghts."

Sanchoniathon, Apollonius Rhodius, and Diodorus Siculus, with other well-known and deeply studied writers, such as Silius Italicus, Albertus Magnus, and Mr. Stead, may be against me, still I cleave to the "Peghts." "Singular little folk and terribly strong" is the description given of them by an ancient writer. Besides, in almost every country of the world there are traditions of a former pigmy race having trod the ground where now the giant inhabitants of the land disport themselves. So flattering to the vanity of the present inhabitants and so like the habit of mankind. All those who have gone before us were pigmies, that is proved to demonstration. Solomon never wrapped up a foolish thought in finer-sounding words than when he said that the dead lion was not the equal of the living dog.

Ten times more philosophical was the unknown elector of the State of Illinois, who always voted at the Presidential election for Henry Clay, on the plea that if it were impossible to get an honest living statesman he preferred a man like Clay, who had been honest when he was alive. So I stick firmly to the "Peghts," and not entirely because I have seen the interior of the Sith Bruach called the Peghts' House in the moss near Coldoch, but because a fairy is a thing that a true Scotsman should not tolerate. What value can possibly attach to fairies, upon 'Change? They are never quoted except by foolish and unpractical men who deal in poetry, in folk-lore, history, and other exercises of the imagination. That which we do not see, cannot exist, else why should Providence have given us the power of sight?

In the Laguna called Yberá in Corrientes there exists a wondrous island. From the days when Hulderico Schmidel and Alvar Nuñez first sailed upon the waters of the Parana, the tradition has existed that the inhabitants of that island were pigmies. No one has seen them, and though to-day in the city of Corrientes, some fifty miles from the shores of the great Laguna, the inhabitants enjoy the blessing of electric light, municipal government, the delights of bicycles, the income-tax, as well as a revolution every three months, the mystery is still unsolved.

In matters of this sort it is well to premise a little sometimes, like the ancient Scottish lady who, having stated that the apples grown in Scotland were the finest in the world, added a rider to her statement and said, "I maun premise I like my apples sour." Therefore I must premise the Laguna Yberá is nearly three hundred miles in length, and the interior a thicket of canes and "camaloté," through which no Christian (he who is not an Indian is an *ex-officio* Christian in those countries) has ever passed. Some of the more imaginative Christians of Corrientes assert there are no pigmies in the islands in the lake at all, and quote the Holy Scriptures, and cite the "Witch of Endor" and other portions of Holy Writ, all just as apposite, to show that fairies are the dwellers in the hidden recesses of the cane-brakes of Yberá. Fairies or pigmies, it matters little which they are, whether in Corrientes or Aberfoyle.

Good Mr. Kirk, the "painful preacher," is gone, as his son says, to "his own herd," and is said to dwell in the centre of the Fairy Hill. Better that there he stays; and if he has learned wisdom, he will never venture out again. A man might easy travel far and fare much worse than have his dwelling in the Fairy Hill.

Of pigmies in the world there will always be a plenteous supply, but fairies tend to become less common, even in Menteith. I do not mean to say a fairy is of necessity a being opposed to progress. When wire fences first were used in Scotland some thirty years or so ago, horses turned out to grass in pastures generally ran into them and maimed themselves. The more sagacious horse of modern times rarely or ever does so, but takes them into regular account with the other foolish devices contrived by man to stop his grazing at his pleasure. All in good time the fairies will get accustomed to changed conditions, and dance as merrily upon the girders of a railway bridge as formerly upon the grass and tussocks. The motley elements which went to make the history of Menteith are gone and buried, but their shadows still remain. The Earls of Menteith, from Gillechrist to the Beggar Earl, the fairies, the Rev. Mr. Kirk, Rob Roy, the monks of Inchmahome, the Romans, Peghts, the Caledonian cattle, with the wolves, John Graham of Claverhouse and Mary Queen of Scots, have left Menteith for ever, but the shadow of their passage still remains; at least I see it.

Life is a dream, they say, but dreams have their awakening. A shadow, when it passes over the bents so brown, across the heather, and steals into the corries of the hills, returns no more. Only a reflection of the clouds, you say. Well, if it is so, is not life only a reflection of the past?

Could we but see a shadow of the future, and compare it with the shadows of the past, why then, indeed, we might know something of Menteith and other districts where the shadows play, coming, like life, from nowhere, and returning into nothing.

Father Archangel of Scotland,
and Other Essays

G. Cunninghame Graham

and R.B. Cunninghame Graham

Introduction

Father Archangel of Scotland, and Other Essays (1896) contains thirteen pieces, nine by Graham and four by his wife Gabriela. Graham's nine pieces include four pairs of sketches: two on tensions between the Protestant and Catholic faiths; two on the Jesuit missions in the colonial territory that would become Paraguay; two on Moorish life in North Africa; and two on the horses and cowboys of the River Plate area. With Gabriela contributing items two, ten, eleven and twelve on aspects of sixteenth-century Spain and remote, traditional corners of Spain, Graham closes off the collection with a visit to the burial-place of General Sir John Moore in north-western Spain.

By 1896 Graham already had a colourful reputation: a Scottish gentleman, fine horseman and speaker of Spanish; a cowboy in South America; husband to Gabriela, said by Graham's family at the time to be a half-French, half-Chilean poetess; failed cattle-rancher in Texas; fencing-master in Mexico City; failed gold-hunter in Spain; a radical Member of Parliament for the Liberal Party, fine orator and castigator of British imperialism, capitalism and its abuse of workers; a prisoner for six weeks in Pentonville; a traveller seeking to reach a forbidden city in Morocco; author of a handbook on his local region of Menteith in Scotland (1895); an early Socialist; and writer of articles in newspapers and magazines of the 1890s, some of them repeated here in this collection.

What evidence is there in *Father Archangel of Scotland, and Other Essays* of the emergence or crystallisation of a distinctive literary voice?

"Father Archangel of Scotland", the title piece, is long — some 41 pages in the first edition. Graham's other eight pieces total 120 pages, averaging 15 pages each (around 3,000 words), closer to the scale he will generally favour in later collections.

In five pages of introduction Graham in first person voice reports being in a small town "today fallen into decay" on Spain's northern meseta: his eye and pen will often be drawn to old decaying buildings. He is comfortable wandering round a Hispanic town, bargaining successfully in a local shop for a small, old book in Spanish — the biography by Fray (Brother/Friar) Francisco de Ajofrín of one George Leslie of Aberdeenshire, published in 1737. Graham gives ample details of his source text, including its previous editions in various languages.

Admitting lack of enthusiasm in matters religious, Graham is drawn to "religious enterprises pursued under disadvantageous circumstances — such, for instance, as that of the attempt to convert Jews, Scotchmen, and Mahommedans". 'Scotchmen' set between the two major faiths strikes a sardonic note. Graham — a Scotchman — does not accept the common perception that only Calvinists were persecuted in Scotland. George Leslie/Father Archangel tried and failed to bring Calvinist Scotland back to Catholicism, and Graham is drawn to his "sturdy failure".

Though the introduction seems to meander, Graham actually presents as an experienced traveller and a fluent speaker of Spanish well able to digest and re-work with due seriousness an obscure eighteenth-century biography. He is a man of critical and independent mind, willing to challenge prevailing beliefs, sceptical of religion, well-informed on Scottish history and culture, mockingly witty and interested in people who fail in their enterprises and lives. Whereas Montaigne developed his *persona* over several essays and years, the 43-year-old Graham in a first collection of sketches whose title includes '[...] and Other Essays' seems to emerge fully formed: speaker of other tongues, well-travelled, combative and fearless, interested in discoursing intelligently, provocatively and humorously on human behaviour.

Graham's re-worked life of George Leslie occupies the remaining 36 pages. Graham could opt for a straightforward third-person summary of Ajofrín's text. Instead, he injects his version with regular doses of his own strong personal opinions. Brought up a Scottish Calvinist, George Leslie became a Catholic, a Capuchin friar, a highly-regarded preacher in Italy and court preacher to Queen Maria de Medici in France. Sent as a missionary to his homeland, he converted his mother, his family and thousands of Scots. Expelled from anti-Catholic England, he helped fight the typhus epidemic in Italy before eventually returning to Britain where he had many more dramatic adventures before dying — not hanged and disembowelled at Glasgow Cross like the Jesuit John Ogilvie in 1615 — but of fever in 1637.

Graham's reworking of Ajofrín's text is done at a vigorous pace. His insight into the Scottish Calvinist mind-set is sharp: George's mother hears of her son's conversion and "cuts him off with a pound Scots, declaring that no Catholic shall sing the mass at her lug." Graham just as sharply shows the tensions in an England officially anti-Catholic when George/Father Archangel and his brother Henry are imprisoned as spies and then liberated by King Charles I, against the dispositions of the king's own edicts. Graham offers final pathos: Father Archangel, "a simple-minded friar who did his duty as he thought he saw it, and did it for itself and not for honour or reward or hope of heaven, nor yet for fear of hell", is buried at night, dressed in his Capuchin habit, "in a wild and secret place in the hills".

Graham's pieces occasionally carry challenging titles, as in 'De Heretico Comburendo' (Latin, meaning 'Concerning the Heretic to be Burned'). This piece again opens in northern Spain, in Valladolid, once the capital of the country but "now a dull, decaying town". Valladolid's two Catholic seminaries for foreigners — a Scots College and an English College — are proof that "we too were persecutors". Light-hearted in commenting upon Scotsmen, Graham in serious mode sees little difference between the actions of the Spanish Duke of Alva against the Dutch Protestants and Elizabeth of England's treatment of Catholics. Graham waspishly contends that "[...] the Spanish butcheries ceased with the sixteenth century. Ours have continued almost to the present day" — against natives in Tasmania, Australia and New Zealand. Less waspishly he even-handedly recognises that "if freedom has been won by martyrdom", the Catholic victims of persecution are martyrs as much as the Protestants who perished at Smithfield or upon the moors of Galloway. In this sketch Graham's background knowledge, not openly paraded, again seems broad and deep. The title refers to the edict of 1401 issued by the Catholic King of England Henry IV against any use (post-Wyclif) of an English translation of the Bible. In Spain Graham knows that Valladolid locals mispronounce the Spanish word for Scotsmen, that Columbus died and Cervantes lived close by the Scots College and that church interiors in the Churriguera style can seem "a sea of gilded gingerbread". An apparent dilettante, Graham seems quite the master of this material — physical, religious, linguistic and cultural.

"In the Tarumensian Woods" and "A Jesuit" reflect upon the Jesuit presence in the area now occupied by eastern Paraguay. The Jesuits from 1607 onwards gathered large numbers of Indians into thirty towns or missions where they taught the Indians Spanish, crafts and Christianity. Graham grounds this sketch on a record left by one unnamed Jesuit who around 1756 was stationed in San Joaquín, in the tarumá forest: 'tarumá' generates 'Tarumensian'. This priest, having brought into the settlement an old woman, her three peccary pigs, her daughter and her son, all healthy, then saw the three forest people die. For Graham the Jesuit becomes "the good and worthy muddlehead". According to Graham, when the Spaniards in Paraguay wanted the eighty to a hundred thousand Mission Indians as slaves for their plantations, Jesuit resistance led to the authorities expelling the Order — whereupon the mission system collapsed. For Graham "[…] the Jesuits did much good, mixed with some folly […]". His humorous parting shot against the Jesuit of San Joaquín is that "he did not tell us if town life proved fatal to the three little peccaries". Here, Graham, while acknowledging the worthy motives of the "kindly, honest, simple-minded" chronicler (echoes of Father Archangel), hints that his well-intentioned treatment of the Indians may have been physically fatal to them. Graham's ideas will be seen in much more detailed and developed form in the 294 pages of his *A Vanished Arcadia, being some account of the Jesuits in Paraguay 1607 to 1767* (1901).

"A Jesuit" opens with an unassuming priest stepping onto a steamboat making its way north up the River Paraná from Argentina towards Paraguay and inland Brazil. Four pages are given over to describing the monumental natural environment, the steamer's crew and very mixed bag of passengers. The priest, carrying only a newspaper wrapped round his supply of tobacco, soon "wound himself into our hearts".

Beyond Asunción, "[…] where all traces of civilisation are left behind", he told of working in a secret mission station amongst the fierce Guasarapo Indians — till the Indians killed all the priests but himself. Back in Buenos Aires he telegraphed Rome for instructions and was told: "Return". Graham cleverly blends the steamboat's slow progress through a fascinating riverscape with the priest's quiet growth in moral stature in the eyes of crew and passengers. In Graham's final image, the priest, experienced in the area, aware of the dangers, obedient and committed to his missionary calling, "walked into the forest". No drumrolls are heard, but Graham — who may privately think that this Jesuit priest re-entering a South American 'Heart of Darkness' is sure to be killed — yet clearly sees the man as at least heroic, perhaps a worthy successor to his martyred fellow Jesuits — and to the Capuchin Father Archangel.

In "Ras Doura", a village on the Atlantic coast of Morocco, Graham witnesses an Arab funeral: he admits to "a sort of interest in a funeral myself". Over eleven pages he describes the village and its residents in confident detail. The last three pages focus on the burial preparations. From his tent outside the village Graham hears the Arab wail signalling grief for the man killed when crushed by his horse. He reports the body wrapped in a sheet, strapped to a board, tied on to an old grey mare and taken off for burial. Echoing the little peccaries in "In the Tarumensian Woods", the final image is of another animal, the mare's foal — "an unconscious mourner". Graham's evocation of the place and its people is full and convincing: the dead man's feet "sticking out stiffly in the pathetic and half-comic way that dead feet have". Running alongside the costumbrist detail is a personal voice exuding scepticism, relativism and mocking, sometimes caustic humour — on ever-open mosques and locked Christian churches; on women's rights under the Koran and those claimed by English women; on self-proclaimed great horsemen of different regions being outshone by an Icelander on his little pony. He ventures that "a man of no profession of faith [...] may enter paradise when clergymen lie howling" and that the Arab wail — "something outside humanity" — sounds just as doleful from the lips of a professional mourner. This sketch is a good example of Graham's mixture of fluent realistic depiction of a foreign place and his free-ranging expression of acerbic personal opinion.

"El Babor", like "Ras Doura", has an initial statement of the theme, a long scene-setting and a final shorter illustration of the theme. Though the East feels horror of the industrialised West, Western machinery might help prevent awful misery and starvation. Graham delivers a fluent description of a generic Moroccan coastal town, outside whose walls is a new steam-driven corn-mill: local Arabic speakers render the Spanish 'vapor' (steam) as 'babor'. Graham is in this sketch interestingly ambivalent. He knows of the horrors of life then in North Africa: "[...] the flies rise in their myriads from a dead horse or camel, and settle in the corners of the beggars' eyes". So he allows that Western technology may be able to alleviate much pain and misery in Arab lands.

Yet the steam-mill is "as hideous as if in England or Massachusetts": in a witty borrowing from Burns, the steam-mill is as transfixingly repulsive as the louse Burns spotted on the lady's bonnet in church. Graham admits to his own almost Oriental awe in the face of anything mechanical, and — told by an Arab of a French colonial execution by guillotine — remarks sarcastically: "I agreed that French philanthropy could go no further". He has reservations about the industrial system.

And his presentation of the Catalán steam-mill owner is a rollicking caricature. The Catalán feels rabidly superior to the Arabs, complains — in the supposed tradition of money-minded Cataláns — about the low return on his capital and sees nothing amiss in men working twelve hours a day and women fourteen. Graham — co-author as a Member of Parliament of a report on the vile working conditions of nail-makers and chain-makers in English factories — sees the Arabs shifting heavy sacks in ninety degrees of heat: they work thus only because the Catalán has advanced them money. Graham suggests to them that perhaps they need to think about work in a more Western way, yet — such is his empathy — allows them to express their considerable hostility to the alien machine and to the way it now dominates their previously agreeable lives. This first attempt to bring Western technology and working methods to the East is not reassuring.

"The Horses of the Pampas", defined by Graham as "rambling and incoherent reminiscences", delivers a sometimes quite technical commentary on the Pampa horse. In this first pampa exercise in book form, Graham recalls life in the 'desert' when the pampa horse was "part of me". Just as in the 1820s the North American plains, thought unfit for (white) human habitation, were labelled 'The Great American Desert', so too for long the pampa was thought an unproductive wilderness.

Pampa horses resemble those of the south of Spain, though different food, climate and surroundings have created a special type. The small-statured pampa horse is valued for endurance and strength: it favours the slow gallop and the jogtrot. For Graham its origins lie in Córdoba in Spain and beyond Córdoba, in the Arab Barbary horse, with which it shares five lumbar vertebrae rather than the usual six. Arabs and Gauchos share riding gear and styles and many superstitions about colourations, though unlike the Arabs the Gauchos love piebalds and mount from the near (left) side. Images to be repeated in future sketches include the tinkling brass of the bell-mare leading a herd; Gaucho skill in mounting effortlessly; Gauchos never pushing the foot fully into the stirrup; the ability to fall well at full gallop; and a Gaucho child's wake. Earlier sketches in this collection had hinted at the contrast between a 'before' that was better and a 'now' that is worse. Here Graham bitterly regrets that "[...] hideous civilisation" will replace this world of horses — "tender-hearted, hospitable, nomad creatures" — and their Gauchos.

"A Vanishing Race" opens where "The Horses of the Pampas" closed. Civilisation has no place for the Gauchos: they are doomed to disappear.

The Gaucho — a mixture of Indian and Spaniard — is so rare by 1896 that Graham — faced with approaching "universal ugliness" — feels obliged to record the main features of their vanishing world, at the same time laying down the foundation of his many future pampa-based sketches. Gauchos as a social type emerged fifty years after the Conquest in the early 1600s. In the first decades of independent Argentina and Uruguay major political figures often came from Gaucho backgrounds (though usually from the landowning class). Gauchos were influential during the Rosas dictatorship (1833-1852) and were still significant in Graham's time in the 1870s. Graham highlights four special types of Gaucho: the 'Idler Gaucho', still a nomad; the skilled tracker; the Gaucho poor and unable to work because he has no horses; and the miscreant Gaucho condemned to military service — in the infantry. Ordinary Gauchos, often owning many horses taken at will from the millions on the open range, debated endlessly about horse brands. Gauchos hated their cousins, the wild Indians who terrorised the frontier for 300 years. Lawless Gauchos, however, could take refuge in the 'Inside Land' — Indian Territory. Gauchos loved the narrative protest poem, *Martín Fierro* (1872; 1879) by José Hernández, which reflected their way of life and its values.

The Gaucho at most shared a simple hut with his companion and his children. His weapons were the throwing weapon (the *boleadoras*) and the long knife. Consuming little milk or vegetables, he enjoyed meat, tobacco and rum. He hated all Europeans, especially Spaniards. He could kill with utter indifference. Interestingly, Graham does not mention here the Gaucho's move from nomad to fixed ranch-hand, the mass immigration, improved cattle breeds, townships, fencing, railways and refrigeration techniques that transformed the old pampa: Graham again blames 'civilisation'. As its "hideous pall of gloom and hypocrisy" descends on the pampa, Graham's final two short exclamations in Spanish might read better as one unit: "What woe has come upon my pampa!" Nostalgia and regret for his fast-disappearing Gaucho Arcadia are palpable, and will recur in his many future sketches based on pampa life.

Gabriela's four Spanish-based sketches are well worth consideration. In "A Will", the second piece in the book, Gabriela finds an old will in Ávila in northern Spain: this device echoes Graham's re-working of an old biography and a Jesuit Mission log. Gabriela's will-maker, Francisco de Salcedo, was clearly a gentleman of means. His wife was also wealthy.

After his wife's death, he became a priest and a Jesuit. Known as "The Holy Gentleman", he gave good counsel to all, including to the young Saint Teresa. In his will, dated 7th April 1579, he gave away his wealth to a long list of beneficiaries. Gabriela's translation of sections of the will allows the dead man to speak in his own voice as "[…] the bounteous master and chivalrous gentleman who […] once paced through Ávila, solemn, stately, and kindly". Gabriela, making no reference to Spain's national or international problems, uses the will to suggest the almost flawless goodness of one sixteenth-century Spanish Catholic gentleman — the very opposite of any 'black legend' of Hispanic capacity for evil-doing.

Both "Yuste" and "La Vera de Plasencia" revolve around the figure of Charles I of Spain and Holy Roman Emperor (1500-1558). In "Yuste", Gabriela and her muleteer travel through remote western Spain to the gates of the 'convento' of Yuste: 'convento' in Spanish can be 'monastery' or 'convent'. Charles abdicated in 1555 and retired there. Gabriela and muleteer visit this modest "palace", where virtually all is decay and they are "invaded by an immense sadness". This sketch is in part a character study and in part an evocation of a place momentarily important in Spanish history. Gabriela shows good skill in describing the natural environment, the medieval village of Cuacos and the atmosphere of decay and neglect in the old monastery. From her readings she delivers striking details: locals stealing the Emperor's favourite cherries; the ailing Emperor feebly mounting his old blind pony; and Philip IV's words on seeing his ancestor's body delivered to the Escorial. Gabriela, disliking the "vulgar greed of the sightseer", reports tourists stripping pieces off the empty coffin, an American offering to buy it and the coffin being slung high above the floor for safety. The whole is a meditation on a remote place made melancholy twice over — by the death of a great king and then by long-term decay and neglect.

In "La Vera de Plasencia" Gabriela sees this isolated area in northern Cáceres province as becoming — a little strangely — the haven of rest for the King-Emperor after his abdication. Gabriela enjoys reaching a town in La Vera area at nightfall, joining the travellers in the inn and watching typical village activities in the square at dawn. Gabriela, affected strangely by La Vera's loveliness and loneliness, uses 'picturesque' four times to highlight its special quality. She warns that development will destroy La Vera, will cost the locals their real happiness and freedom and will turn the rich landscape into a melancholy plain. Charles's courtyard will see a Bible pedlar with a strange accent — a reference possibly to George Borrow, author of *The Bible in Spain* (1843) — and the installation of a coin-operated cigarette machine. Gabriela's hostility to change and modernity is as entrenched as Graham's. In keeping with her vision of an ancient Spain, Gabriela occasionally uses older English forms of speech, as in 'cresset' and 'I am fain to say'. As happens with Graham over several sketches, there is here a touch of repetition — the imperial cherries and the blind or one-eyed pony — and the two sub-headings are hardly needed.

In "The Batuecas", Gabriela reviews a trip to "the strangest, wildest, most forgotten corner of Spain", a dreamlike place different from the now tame reality of the inn where she writes as she waits for the coach. At Las Batuecas, the most famous Carmelite monastery in Spain, her party visited its dependencies, disconsolately noting things left by the monks when they were forced to abandon their home as a result of the Disentailment Laws of 1835-1837. She climbed up to one of many little hermitages in the surrounding heights. In the evening a goatherd corralled his herds nearby. Talk in the kitchen with half-inarticulate locals induced an "inexplicable sadness". She recalls that a noble lady with an illicit page lover first discovered these solitudes. Even before retiring, her mind was imagining shadowy figures outside the building. Counting mules' hoofs as she tried to sleep, a stern gigantic brother loomed over her: she started awake to the sound of rain. After a simple breakfast her party left. In this neo-Romantic sketch, Gabriela handles well the surface detail needed to describe the beautiful countryside, her muleteers and the locals in wayside inn, medieval villages and monastery. Her repeated use, however, of variations of 'strange' as well as 'fantastic', 'curious', 'dreamlike', 'fairy-like', 'fancy', 'enchantment', 'fascination' and 'fantasies' show her striving anxiously — a little desperately, perhaps — to convey the powerful impact that this journey and this place have had upon her imagination.

Gabriela in 1894 had published a two-volume study of the life and times of Saint Teresa (1515-1582) and the reform of the Spanish religious orders. In these four sketches, probably derived from her research readings and travels, she seeks to present a positive image of old-style Spain.

"In a Garden", by Graham, completes the collection with a gentle — almost slight — meditation before a grave where the reader learns less about the dead person than about Graham's sensibility. The image of a dead soldier resting in a garden appeals to Graham — if only for the garden. Graham describes the main features of La Coruña in north-western Spain before finding his way to where Sir John Moore, killed in 1809 in battle with the French, lies buried in a half-Italian garden that is "Spanish, purely Spanish, in neglect". Curiously he makes no mention of the fact that Moore had been a fellow Scot. The discovery that a local Spanish boy had been told by his father that the grave is that of "the French general" leads Graham to reflect that "So pass fame, honour, glory, even remembrance. All is vanity [...] all except your gardens by the sea".

Graham's final piece seems almost Gabriela-esque in its meditative air, but his other eight sketches in this collection — spread over settings in Scotland and England, Spain, North Africa, Paraguay and Argentina — show good understanding of the scenarios chosen and an alert, combative and opinionated intelligence. They also reveal in Graham an ability to convey the appearance of his settings while exploring particularly the tensions between an older world and system of values and a newer and harsher world emerging to challenge and displace the old. With *Father Archangel of Scotland, and Other Essays*, Graham firmly established many of his characteristic themes, in the *persona* and voice that would inspire thirteen further collections of sketches and tales.

John C. McIntyre

Contents

To The Respectable Public   81
I. Father Archangel of Scotland   83
II. A Will   101
III. De Heretico Comburendo   111
IV. In The Tarumensian Woods   117
V. A Jesuit   129
VI. Ras Doura   135
VII. El Babor   141
VIII. The Horses Of The Pampas   149
IX. A Vanishing Race   157
X. Yuste   165
XI. The Batuecas   171
XII. La Vera De Plasencia   177
XIII. In A Garden   181

'To The Respectable Public'

Why the adjective 'respectable' should be applied to the public rather than 'gullible,' 'adipose,' or 'flatulent,' I am unable to determine. Taken in bulk, the public is prone to eat and drink more than is good for it, either in its corporate or individual capacity. No reasoning being will maintain that its taste in art, literature, gastronomy, or politics is worth a moment's serious consideration. Its knowledge of 'knurr and spell,' or 'numismatics' is apt to be deficient. Still I presume it is respectable if only as the final court, to which all actors, politicians, mountebanks, physicians, lawyers, writers, whether of trifling articles like these or ponderous volumes destined to repose amid the dust of libraries, come for its decision.

Let it therefore be respectable because every professor, whether of ground or lofty tumbling, in arts, literature, sciences, or veterinary surgery, by its opinion must live and have his being.

Therefore a preface is a thing quite indispensable.

Now in these latter days your preface has fallen into considerable neglect. It may be that the public has no time to spare from the perusal of the share lists to devote to prefaces. It may be that the art, like that of chiromancy, Roman glass, Byzantine mosaics, and the proper knowledge of heraldry, venery, and other things conducive to a liberal education, has been lost. It may be that advertisements have killed the preface. Perhaps the lack of noble patrons to whom to address oneself has caused its ruin. Who in cold blood could call upon a School Board Duke for his protection? The man would be pursuing (his electors) at a meeting, or perchance passing the post-office employés in review.

Prefaces and advertisements are either compliments of one another or else sworn adversaries, I don't know which. In former times the author had to do much of his own advertisement, therefore in his preface he gave a taste of what was in his book, or, if not that, of what was in himself. To-day, no matter how bad the book may be itself, the preface is almost certain to exceed it. Which latter case, for all I know, may point the moral to this little volume.

The articles which follow were all written without reference to one another. Therefore it is not unlikely that they resemble a crowd of people at a railway junction, all rushing to and fro, without connection save only of the labels on their luggage. Still in one thing there is a 'nexus' (not of cash), for all the articles treat chiefly of Spain or Spanish America. Both Spain and South America are little written of in England. Neither of the two are capable of being dealt with in the modern spirit. Neither in Spain nor Spanish America do men think, act, or look at things — men, actions, and events — in the way of England. Therefore they must be wrong. Nothing can interest any one but what he knows, and that is why so little interests most of us. Nothing is true to nature but the ways of Brixton, Belgravia, Scotch provincial towns, or French Bohemia duly emasculated. Except of course the sorrows of ladies with too few, or else a plethora, of husbands, or the woes of scrofulous young men a prey to folly, drink, or syphilis. With all these subjects neither of the humble folk who now address you is fit to deal; perhaps from lack of opportunity, experience, or from want of due imagination. And most unfortunately neither of them can command a dialect in which to wrap their platitudes, so that they must go forth to a harsh world, unveiled in Irish, Welsh, Manx, Somerset, or even in that all-sufficient cloak of kailyard Scotch spoken by no one under heaven, which of late has plagued us. Perchance the unavoidable admixture of Spanish morals may serve as an excuse, and cause the writings to be sufficiently unintelligible to be appreciated. If not, but only this excuse remains, as the Spanish proverb says, "That wheresoever dwells the heart, there also lives the speech." *Hasta despues,*

R. B. Cunninghame Graham

Thanks are due to the proprietors of the *Nineteenth Century*, the *Saturday Review*, the *World*, *Pall Mall Gazette*, and the *Daily Graphic* for permission to republish such articles as have appeared in their pages.

I. Father Archangel of Scotland

Medina del Rio Seco, though an interesting old Castilian town, remarkable for having been at one time a sort of Nijni-Novgorod, today fallen into decay, and left to shepherds to pen their flocks in at night, with all its former commerce reduced to three or four of those strange little shops full of nothing useful, and other articles which only a Spaniard can possibly want, and only he on credit, is not exactly a cheerful place to be long detained in.

After looking about the broad sandy streets, and wondering where the town ends and the country begins; after sitting down in turn on all the cracked plaster seats in the Plaza, and sauntering into the chemists' shops, the general lounge and news mart of a Spanish town; after having seen the diligence, with three miserable mules and an apocalyptic horse, start without passengers for nowhere, with as much noise as usually accompanies the arrival of an excursion train at Euston, one feels that the excitements of the place are exhausted, and that one must go and buy something or fall asleep.

Turning into the local curiosity shop — in the smallest town in Spain there is often an 'antiquario'— I took up one of those little volumes all so common in Spain, bound in sheepskin, lettered on the back with a pen, fastened by string loops, with little shells forming the buttons, and printed in a type as faint and dusty as that on the outside of a cigar-box. After a sharp half-hour's bargain, in which the 'antiquario' and myself exhausted much rhetoric, protested we were both going to be ruined many times, and made many well-simulated pretences of leaving one another in anger, I prevailed on him to abate his first demand of twenty dollars, dollar by dollar, till the little volume became mine for a peseta. I did not want the book at all, but merely wished to 'pass,' or, as the Spaniards say, 'make,' time. Distinguishing as I do, with some difficulty, a semi-Pelagian from a Neo-Platonist, and being absolutely unconcerned as to the number of angels that might (but did not) stand on the point of a needle, and seldom feeling sufficiently in the frame of mind to cope with books on spiritual matters, it was with a chastened joy I found I had purchased the life of a Capuchin friar.

Still, though matters of an ultramundane nature often leave me without enthusiasm, I have always been interested in religious enterprises pursued under disadvantageous circumstances — such, for instance, as that of the attempt to convert Jews, Scotchmen, and Mahommedans. I fancy that the faith required to pursue such enterprises, if rightly exerted, might move not only a mountain but whole chains of mountains like the Andes or Himalayas; and the attempt to preach Catholicism in Scotland had always seemed to me one of the most desperate of these theological filibustering expeditions.

The book I had acquired with so much eloquence and a peseta treated precisely of such an adventure; pursued, moreover, in the wilds of Aberdeenshire, and in the reign of Charles of blessed memory.

It is an erroneous opinion, held by many, that all those who have suffered for religion in Scotland have been Calvinists. That this is not the case is made manifest in the admirable and astonishing *Life of Father Archangel of Scotland* — called in the world George Leslie — by Fray Francisco de Ajofrin, Doctor of Theology, Chronicler of the Holy Province of the Capuchins of the two Castilles, Commissary of the Holy Congregation for propagating the faith in North America and the missions of Thibet; the whole written in very choice Castillian, with the necessary licences, and published at Madrid in 1737 at the office of Antonio Fernandez. Not that this is the first time this *Admirable and Astonishing Life* has been published, for it was given to the world in Tuscan by Don Juan Bautista Rinuci, Bishop of Fermo; again in French, by the learned Father Francis Beccault, and printed in Paris in 1664; then in Portuguese, by Fray Cristobal Almeida, of the Order of Augustinians, and preacher to the King of Portugal, printed at Lisbon in 1667; once again in Italian, under the title of *Il Cappucino Scozzese*, in Brescia, in the year 1736. The first notice I can find of it, however, is by Fray Basilio de Teruel, printed in Madrid in 1659.

Notwithstanding this wealth of editions, it seems to me probable that not one Scotchman in ten thousand ever so much as heard of any one of them, and, for all I can see, the errors of Calvin (and many others) flourish as luxuriantly in that country as if Father Archangel had never lived.

My edition procured from the antiquary in the Plaza of Medina del Rio Seco is dedicated to the 'Most Illustrious Lord Don Manuel

Maria Pablo Antonio Arizun y Orcasitas, Marquis of Iturbieta, etc.,' and contains the usual praise of his perhaps hypothetical virtues.

I find that George Leslie was born (no date) in Aberdon or Aberden, 'car l'un et l'autre se disent.' All historians and geographers who have written of this city, such as Bauldrand, Echard, and Moreri (though Moreri is not so reliable as the other two), unite in praising its beauty. His parents were Count James Leslie and Juana Selvia. As to Juana, I suppose that to be the Spanish for Jean; but Selvia is, I confess, too hard for me; but there are many things besides these, mentioned by Solomon, which to me are in the same category; Selvia as a Scotch surname is amongst them. They were Calvinists, the dominant sect in these lugubrious and mountainous provinces. Padre Axofrin draws no comparison as Buckle has done between the religion and the configuration of the country.

His father having left the errors of his life and of Calvinism when George was eight years old, his mother determined to send him to Paris to pursue his studies; so with a competent tutor, of much learning and experience, though a bitter Calvinist, George starts for France. Amongst other things on his departure, she enjoins him not to let the heresies of Paptists obscure the precious jewel of his Calvinistic faith. See him, then, at eight years old, arrived with his noble following in Paris, and established in a house fit for one of his condition. Imagine him pursuing his studies, as Ajofrin says, 'like even noble youths have to do'; first in the obscure paths of grammar, then rising to the awful contemplation of the Humanities.

We have on good authority that death, and division, and marriage make barren our lives; but in George's case it was neither of these, but friendship with another boy. This most astonishing, if not admirable, specimen of a boy is pained to find George's mind obfuscated with the darkness of Calvinism. I recognised a boy in this at once. It is so like boys I have known, and if I had been blindfolded and asked who was pained about the state of George's mind in all the city of Paris, I should unhesitatingly have said — a boy. This boy, when the tutor was away, took occasion, as boys will do, to turn the conversation on religious subjects, but very cautiously (*con disimulo*). Such a portentous boy could only be of noble extraction, and his father the Count, thinking of course the occasion opportune to save a soul and mark a sheep, invites the unsuspecting George to spend his holidays with his son.

Well grounded in the Calvinistic faith as we may well imagine such a youth as George to have been, still the battle was too unequal, and little by little he falls away; little by little he forgets his mother and her teachings, perhaps forgets with pleasure the two hours' Calvinistic sermons in a church composed of equal measures of barn and windmill.

Slowly the Romish poison filters in, and the recollections of home and remembrance of the singing at divine service, only comparable to the 'indiscriminate slaughter of multitudinous swine,' grows fainter in his ears.

Naturally, near the Count's house there lived a venerable ecclesiastic, who, by his sophistry and knowledge of the Gospel, gives the last push to his tottering faith, and George becomes a Catholic; but secretly, for the venerable priest informs him that Holy Scripture* says 'that it is good to conceal the sacrament of the Great King.' And who was George to set himself up against Tobit?

The tutor, who, as we may remember, was a man of experience, begins to smell a rat, and, being troubled in his mind, determines to 'mak' sikkar,' and says George must accompany him to divine worship *à la Calvin*.

At 'Xarentan,' near Paris, was the University of the *perfidious Calvin* (el perfido Calvino), and hither the tutor was accustomed to repair when he wanted to hear the right doctrine and wile away an hour or two. George, though, with greater spirit than discretion — obviously forgetting that it is good to conceal the sacrament of the Great King — refuses to accompany him, and says somewhat rudely (for we should respect the opinions of others when we have no power to hand the holders of them over to the proper authorities) that he had no mind to go to Xarentan to listen to the ravings of Calvin, for he was a Catholic. Now, if we were not speaking of a grave case of conscience, I should say that here was a pretty kettle of fish. Argument entirely failing as per usual, George's mother is communicated with, who, after running through the gamut of tears, reproaches, and threats, finally cuts him off with a pound Scots, declaring that no Catholic shall sing the mass at her lug.

Poor George, finding himself, so to speak, 'marooned' in Paris, is glad to take up with the father of the ingenious boy theologian, and with him is sent to Italy to make the grand tour. Arrived at Rome, he meets the celebrated Father Joyeuse, once a marshal and a peer of France, and now a Capuchin.

Whilst the quondam disputatious theologic boy, now turned a gallant, trifles away his time at fencing-schools, at palaces, and picture-galleries,

---

*Tobit, xii, 71.

or learns, perhaps, *l'arte de biondeggiar i capelli* from some fair Venetian, George, as a Scotchman, passes his time in studying metaphysics with Father Joyeuse. The shrewd ex-soldier friar sees in George a man prepared to suffer all things for the Church, and so persuades him not to try the wicked world at all (as he himself was tired of it), and George becomes a Capuchin in the well-known convent of Camerino.

Says Padre Ajofrin, 'The "navigations of America" have taught all Europe that the hardest trial the constitution of a man can bear is to pass the equinoctial line; further, in this change a man loses the heavens he has been born under. He who passes the equinoctial line of religion changes not only his heavens but his very pole-star.' This will at once commend itself, if not to the perception, at least to the attention of the careful reader. 'After this change the difference of *meum* and *tuum* is buried in the world.' I myself have even observed this phenomenon in regard to *meum* and *tuum* without any perceptible equinoctial line either in physics or religion having been passed at all.

Naturally the world, his religion, and *meum* and *tuum* being changed, the only thing left for George to change was his name, and he accordingly becomes Father Archangel, and as such I shall refer to him in future.

How the characteristics of nationality come out in any great crisis of a man's life! A Spaniard would have become a missionary in Japan, a Frenchman an Abbé in Paris, in George's circumstances. He, as a Scotchman, naturally turns to what is most natural to him, and becomes known all over Italy as the Scotch preacher. Take notice, of course, that the modern five-per-cent hypocritical shop-keeping Scotchman was unknown, so that the Scotchmen of that day, mostly warriors or theologians, were as different from the modern Scots as they were from Laplanders.

All this time, though, in Aberdon his mother is having a black time (*la pena negra*) on his account, thinks George a lost soul, and, not knowing Italian, would be incapable of appreciating his sermons and therefore of consoling herself for his lapse from Calvinism, with that keen enjoyment of pulpit eloquence which makes Scottish life so truly admirable. What a strange unknown land Italy must have seemed to the good lady in Aberdon! The Pope was there, the person she had no doubt heard described every Sunday of her life as Antichrist, and Antichrist is such a mouth-filling word, and seems to mean so much, as often happens with words which really mean so very little.

In the midst of her doubts and fears, a gentleman fresh from the grand tour in Italy happens to visit Aberdon and tells her George is living in

Italy, turned a Capuchin, and settled in the Marches of Ancona.

Fancy the mother's joy! George is not dead, only a heretic! And which of all the mothers one knows (even a Calvinistic mother) would not rather have her son alive, though steeped in all the heresies of Manichee or Gnostic, than orthodox and dead? She has another son called Henry, reared in the paths of strictest orthodoxy, to whom Popery and all its works are as the Scarlet Woman of Babylon, and to whom a church having, as we say, *Scotice*, 'a kist of whistles' in it is more repellent than a temple of Baal Peor. Him she sends to fetch her lamb straying in the Marches of Ancona. Arrived in Italy, he seeks the court of Don Francisco de la Rovere, Duke of Urbino.

How the gawky Aberdonian youth impressed the Italians of Urbino we know not — perhaps, as the wealthy lad from Tennessee or Queensland does the Parisian to-day. His Latin, freckles, possible red hair, and cheek-bones fit for hat-pegs, his aggressive Protestantism, must all have afforded subject for mirth and wonder in the Italian court. At Urbino he meets his brother, who by this time must have become quite civilised although a Capuchin. Like true Aberdonians, they fall immediately to theological debate. 'What an agreeable spectacle this must be to God, to angels, and to men (observes our author), to see two brothers, one a Catholic, the other a Calvinist, disputing on their faiths!' This may be so, of course, but still I think it would not have struck me in that light; but then, as the Spaniards say, 'there are tastes that merit sticks.'

Victory, as in duty bound (for we do not possess Henry's account of the debate), inclined to the side of Archangel and against the champion of the doctrines of *el perfido Calvino*; worsted in argument before the whole court of Urbino, Henry expressed his willingness to become a Catholic. One thing, though, disturbs him — will he be obliged to give up his rank and position, and never see his mother again?

Archangel, though, had not wasted his time in the Convent of Camerino, and I rather suspect that Suarez and Molina had something to do in the preparation of those admirable sermons for which he was so justly admired. He at once answers, 'Having found truth does not take away from you the joys of home, and the right to enjoy the legitimate pleasures (golf and curling) of Aberdeen; riches are not against the divine law (oh! Archangel!); rather can you buy heaven with them' — though in what manner heaven is to be purchased, Archangel omits to inform us and Henry. Then comes the official reception into the Catholic Church, and the great banquet at the court of Urbino before Henry starts for

Scotland, the Duke with his own hands, on bidding him farewell, hanging round his neck a splendid gold chain and crucifix set with Balas rubies.

Having gone out for wool and come back shorn, poor Henry must have had an unpleasant journey from Urbino back to London. Here he seems to have had some qualms, if not of conscience yet of fear. Perhaps he was uneasy when he speculated on the lengths to which a Calvinistic lioness robbed by Antichrist of both her cubs could go. So he indites a letter saying he has had good health in Italy and will soon be home. His mother, all anxiety to hear of George Archangel, was astonished, for she knew that Henry was as hardy as a wolf or Highland bull and never had an ache or pain in all his life.

However, home he had to get, and in a Dutch smack (*urca Olandesa*) he sails for Aberdeen. The mother rushes out with 'Where is George?' Henry, poor fellow, begins a sort of guide-book story of his travels, the people he has met — Duke of Urbino and nobles of the court — what a fine preacher her George is, how ladies do their hair in Venice, and generally comports himself in a manner which inclines me to believe the Italian proverb, 'Inglese Italianato diavolo Incarnato,' has some foundation in it.

All this shuffling on his part raises suspicions in his mother's mind she cannot explain. Is George dead? Or is he come, and waiting in Aberdeen? Is Henry married to a daughter of Antichrist, or has he fallen amongst St. Nicholas's clerks and lost his 'siller'? So after dark she steals into his room to search his luggage and his pockets like a mother in a play to see if any unconsidered trifle, as a letter from a fair Venician, a note of hand, or undertaker's bill, is there to solve the mystery. As luck would have it, the first thing she lights upon is the gold crucifix and chain given by the Duke to Henry on his departure from Urbino.

Alarums and excursions faintly shadow forth what happened at this sight. Here was indeed the abomination of desolation spoken of (I think) by Daniel, set up in a Protestant household with a vengeance. One can but deeply sympathise with the outraged lady when the shocking sight of the counterfeit presentment, done in gold of the founder of the faith she doubtless thought she held, fell on her vision.

One wonders, with the power of pit and gallows at her disposal, that she was so mild, for after many tears and scoldings Henry is only banished to the castle of Monomusco. This time it seems to me Moreri (though, as we remember, not always to be depended on) is right in placing Monomusco two leagues from Aberdon. How admirable are the works of God! (says Padre Axofrin) — one brother in Scotland praying for the conversion of that wild and ignorant land, and the other preaching in Italy; for all the time Archangel preaches away as if nothing unusual had happened in his family.

The scene now shifts to Paris, where it seems either that there is a dearth of preachers or that Maria de Medici, the Queen, cannot sleep easily in church during Parisian sermons, for she sends to Italy for a new court preacher... The choice falls on *il Cappuccino Scozzese*, our Archangel, and he goes to Paris, there to preach before the Queen. What he preached about, his text, and length of sermon (an important matter) we are not told, but only learn that he becomes the rage there. In fact, if the Madeleine had but been built he must have preached there every Sunday to the *plus haute gomme*.

Whilst he is in Paris gathering his laurels or the vegetable, whatever it may be folk give to preachers, Gregory the Fifteenth (the Antichrist of the day) determines on a mission to those *partes infidelium*, England and Scotland, and names Archangel head of it.

In the happy days of Charles the First, a Catholic, especially a priest or friar, was contraband in England, and to get him smuggled across the Channel took far more trouble than to-day it does to introduce a library of Tauchnitz novels.

At that time as at present, ours was the land of freedom for the man with a balance at his banker's, and all society was open to him who went to church.

To enter the enchanted island (land of the free, etc.) for a Catholic meant disguise. The greatest chance to pass the religious custom-house was in the Spanish Embassy, and, as at the present time, the Spanish Embassy, speaking 'Christian' and no other tongue always requiring an interpreter, Archangel, as possessing the English language, although filtered, as we may suppose, through the medium of Aberdeen, in that capacity accompanies it.

With some repugnance he puts on a rich velvet suit guarded with gold, a hat with plumes, and rapier; but, says Padre Ajofrin, to appease the irritation of his conscience (nothing is mentioned of the epidermis), underneath his velvet suit he wore a shirt of horse-hair.

In his purse he had a store of gold (pieces of eight), but counted it as mud — perhaps because he had been a friar so long without it he had forgotten that at times it is more useful than a breviary.

Arrived in London — the author does not tell us where he stayed or what he did there — he meets a Scottish cavalier. A Scottish cavalier — how strange it sounds to-day, when one so often sees a Scotchman, a being dressed in black broadcloth, a sort of cross between a huckster and a preacher! Still in those days the species Scottish cavalier must have existed, and one meets Archangel and tells him what is going on in Aberdon, and, not knowing him, of his own wicked and foolish courses, how he has been a curse to all his friends, and generally speaks to him as our friends discuss us in our absence.

The cavalier tells him of his mother's sorrow at his apostasy and of his brother's exile to Monomusco. Wishing to see his brother, Archangel writes to Monomusco, and Henry, under pretence of a hunting party, slips away and travels to London. Meeting his brother, ruffling as a gallant in the Spanish Embassy, and not dressed as a friar, Henry salutes him, in a fashion that if we were not treating of Aberdonians might be called chaff, and asks him if the sword he wears is to convert their mother with.

The Spanish ambassador (perhaps Gondomar), being recalled to Paris, behaves as every Spanish ambassador did in those days, and presents Archangel with a fine Spanish horse. How they always had them, so to speak about them, to give as presents, has always been a mystery to me, when transit was so difficult.

The brothers arrange to visit Aberdeen. The night before the journey Archangel spends in prayer, and with morning (perhaps for warmth) puts on a second horsehair shirt.

On the journey, so great is his humility, or so intense his terror of the Spanish horse, that, for greater self-abasement, or to arrive more quickly at his destination, or to avoid abrasion of the cuticle, or for some other reason I cannot fathom, he walks on foot, only mounting, to save appearances, when a traveller appears upon the road. In twenty-two days (considered a fast passage then) he arrives in Aberdeen, and writes to his mother to say a gentleman wishes to see her who has known her son in Italy. His mother, not knowing him, receives him ceremoniously, and his two brothers usher him to a room, where, notwithstanding that it is August, the cold is so intense that a great fire is blazing. Here one gets a document, so to speak, that makes one confident that the scene passes in Aberdeen. Exquisite wine and good beer are served to him, but Padre Ajofrin says nothing of that whisky for which I feel sure Archangel's soul was longing.

At dinner in the great hall he sees people grown old whom he remembered young, as must also have happened to the Prodigal Son when *he* returned from his Marches of Ancona from amongst the swine, and the other people he consorted with. What, though, strikes him to the heart, both as a Catholic and an economist, is to see seated at the table a heretic preacher, and to remark that not only was the perfidious Calvinist making havoc amongst the pease brose and the cockie-leekie, but to learn that he received three hundred ducats for preaching heresy. One can well see that Archangel thought that if there was preaching to do he could do it as well, and perhaps at as reasonable a figure, as the son of Belial he saw battening at his mother's table.

Long conversations ensue between Archangel and his mother and brother, and to the latter he gives the Spanish horse, perhaps being secretly rather glad to get rid of him and to be able to walk comfortably on foot in his hair shirt.

One thing leads to another, till at last his mother overhears him ask a servant why the old pigeon-house had been removed, and, on asking him how he knew there was a pigeon-house, perceives his trouble, feels sure it is her son, and they fall sobbing into each other's arms, as has been the way of mothers and sons since the beginning, and probably will be till the end of the human comedy.

Naturally, there is more joy over the son who has returned from Italy than over the ninety and nine who have remained in the wilderness of Aberdeen, and his mother freely forgives him, for all she has done, including the cutting him off at nine or ten years old with an unnegotiable pound Scots. It is agreed that religion shall not be mentioned between them — as fatuous a bargain as for a Unionist and a Gladstonian to agree not to mention Ireland during a sea passage.

Archangel, not being able to talk religion at home, sets about preaching and converting the country-people in the vicinity of Monomusco. Notwithstanding the extreme stoniness of the soil, as one would have thought, he makes, according to Padre Axofrin, such progress that he converts more than three thousand. During his peregrinations he is astonished, as well he might be, at the climate of Aberdeen, but reflects that Scotland is to the north even of England, and that the rivers Esk and Solway and the mountains of 'Eschevoit' separate it from that country, and hence apparently the cold — for your mountain is a plaguy non-conductor of heat.

Seeing, though, is believing, and his mother, seeing the 3000 or 300 (for what is a cipher after all, as I have so often reflected in reading history, sacred and profane?), thinks there is something in Archangel's faith, and proposes a theological debate between her son and the Calvinist domestic preacher. In his double capacity of theologian and Aberdonian, naturally, the prospect of a debate delights Archangel, for he knows his power, snuffs the battle from afar, and prepares to say ha-ha amongst the syllogisms. The Calvinist does not seem to have been so confident, for he rejoins, rather pertinently as it strikes me, 'that the faith needed not always to be debated on, and that if the lady was sure of being saved what more did she require?'

Archangel's mother, though, whilst wishing to see him defeated and converted, not unnaturally wished to see her son display his learning even in a bad cause, so the debate begins.

From the outset, success inclines so strongly to Archangel, that one almost inclines to believe the whole affair a put-up job, if we were not so sure of the absolute *bona fides* of the mother. From the first, the luckless Calvinist goes down like wheat before a sickle, or as the moral man propounded in a Scotch sermon only to be demolished by the propounder. Archangel demands on what the faith of Calvin is grounded, and the futile Calvinist rejoins, 'On the Church of Geneva.' Archangel sees his opening and triumphantly demands, 'Is the Church of Geneva mentioned in the Bible?' The Calvinist (I cannot help wishing that reporters had been present and that we had the debate *in extenso*) incautiously, as it appears to me, rejoins that he thinks it is, and promises to find the passage in four-and-twenty hours. This is the first passage in this *Admirable and Astonishing Life* which raises some doubt in my mind as to the absolute truthfulness of the compiler, for I have known Calvinists ignorant of the binomial theorem, or of the principles of perspective or politeness, but rarely one who did not know the Bible as a stockbroker knows his share list or a mariner his compass.

However, this particular Calvinist passes the watches of the night in fruitlessly searching the Scriptures. Archangel, on the other hand, passes the night in prayer — though why I cannot imagine, as he must have known that he had a dead sure thing without the need of prayer. In the morning the Geneva champion says he has not had time enough, and that if he may get a friend..., but that he on his part would like to know (here my doubts begin again) where the Church of Rome is to be found in Holy Writ. Archangel calls for a Bible, though I am sure he need not have done so, as the castle was most likely stuffed with them, and he only had to put out his hand and take up the first book he saw. Those of my readers who are Calvinists, and know their Bibles, will at once see that Archangel finds his text in the Epistle to the Romans. On this the somewhat inconsequent preacher rallies, and, being worsted in Scripture history, rejoins that in his opinion the Church of Rome and the Scarlet Lady are convertible terms. Archangel eventually demolishes him by pointing to the long list of martyrs, and asking if any one had ever died for Calvinism. The preacher, who seems to have been as ignorant of the history of his sect as of the Bible, and not, apparently, thinking Servetus good enough to cite as a Calvinist martyr, entirely peters out, and remains as confused as a monkey (*corrido como una mona*).

The poor man, after being worsted in debate, having had the mortification of seeing his patroness avow herself converted to Catholicism, and above all having lost his salary, flies, not to Geneva, as we might reasonably suppose, or to St. Andrews, but to Erastian England, where he takes service in the household of an Anglican bishop. After this, the whole family is converted to Catholicism, having been able to comprehend at once the directness of the reasoning that if one Church is mentioned in the Bible and the other is not, the doctrines of the one mentioned are bound to be the right ones, or else why should the Church have been mentioned at all? Edicts having come out against the Catholics (Charles of blessed memory was very free and impartial with his edicts), Archangel takes refuge in England — on the principle, perhaps, that the nearer the king the less likely was the edict to be put in force. On his way to England, luckily for him without the Spanish horse, he runs many dangers, once nearly falling into the clutches of his old friend the Calvinist preacher, who, in the train of the bishop he has fled to, is proceeding to London. Archangel hides in a wood, but his servant is taken, and in his baggage is found a chalice, which, according to the universal custom of Calvinists and Anglicans, the bishop and the ex-chaplain drink out of till at last they 'fall into the detestable vice of drunkenness.'

Arrived in London, his mother writes that all her property has been confiscated, so Archangel sends to the Guardian of the Capuchins (*el Guardian de los Capuchinos*) in Paris, to get the Queen of France to intercede with the English king, which she does, and the property is restored. He once more returns to Aberdeen; but by this time, having doubtless become a well-known figure on the northern road, disguises himself as a hawker and visits his mother, whom he finds in a cottage, not knowing that her property has been restored. The neighbours, finding it impossible to stand more of Archangel's preaching, seize on him and send him by ship to England. On the voyage he reflects on the condition of Scotland, given over to the terrible plague of Calvinism — a plague, though, which seems to have endured long after Archangel's time.

From London he is removed to Rome, and on arriving there finds that Italy too is suffering from a terrible plague, but of a less persistent nature perhaps than the one affecting Scotland, being merely an outbreak of typhus fever. This happens in the year 1630, the solitary date, except that of Archangel's death, in the whole book. After his services in this plague honours descend upon Archangel, and he is made Guardian of the Convent of Monte Gorgio in the diocese of Fermo, and, according to the Padre Axofrin, close to the river of Lethe.

Some loadstone or other, though, always seems to draw him to Scotland, for after a year's residence at Monte Gorgio he starts once more for that benighted land, this time at the head of a Catholic mission. At Cales (Calais) he meets the rest of the mission, and takes ship with them in a vessel of which the captain happens to be a Catholic. In spite of the captain's Catholicism a storm arises, as in fact it always seems to have done when Archangel put out to sea. Though 'disguised as a gentleman' (and therefore perhaps as easily recognisable through his disguise as many who assume that character in more modern times) the passengers discover he is a friar, and, in order to appease the Moloch they apparently adored, wished to throw him in the sea to calm the tempest, thinking, it seems, that Catholic friars are specially obnoxious to the elements and to Moloch. The Catholic captain speaks to the passengers, and offers to be thrown overboard instead of Archangel. From this we may judge that the *odium theologicum* had not made so much way at sea as on shore, for I believe the offer must have been dictated by the sailor and not the Catholic in the captain, and that a Protestant or Mahommedan captain would probably have done the same. This offer being refused, and the crew and passengers being occupied, as is customary in such cases, in casting lots for the privilege of not being thrown overboard, the vessel strikes on a rock, and, breaking into two halves, the after part with the captain and crew is lost, and Archangel and some of the mission and passengers are cast on shore. A shepherd informs the forlorn band that they have been thrown on the 'Isle of Wicht,' and that the well-known city of San Calpino is near at hand. Well as I am used to English names written phonetically in Spanish, and recognising in an instant, as I do, Whitehall masquerading as 'Quitvall,' Frobisher as 'Ofrisba,' Drake as 'El Draque,' and Westminster as 'Questmonster,' I confess that I can neither recognise nor identify this San Calpino. However, at this unknown town they in due course arrive, and Archangel, for reasons known to himself but not divulged to a perhaps too curious public, takes the name of Selviano, after his mother's family name of Selvia, which, I confess, leaves me in the same position of agnosticism as does San Calpino.

Whilst taking their ease in the San Calpino inn they hear the King is at 'Neopurt,' not far off, and Archangel meets a young Scotch gentleman, who I saw at once must be his brother Edward. Such proves to be the fact, in spite of Archangel's own obtuseness, which delayed the recognition for some hours. They are mutually astonished at meeting one another in the Isle of White, so far removed from either Italy or Aberdeen, and in a place, as Edward well says, and as I myself have often reflected in that island, which is on the road to nowhere. Here Archangel hears of his mother's death, and the restitution of the family property.

Arrived at 'Neopurt,' they leave their cloaks and swords in the inn, and go out to view the fortification. It appears at that epoch that in Newport there was a celebrated tower said to be impregnable. Edward, who, like most Scotchmen, had seen far better towers at home, began to scoff at it and to point out how easily with a few gentlemen of Aberdeen he could carry it at point of pike, and whilst discoursing of mamelons and ravelines and of the 'leaguer of Strigonium' is overheard and arrested for a spy. As the author well observes, 'the greatest injustices are always executed with the greatest exactitude' (he might have added also with the greatest promptitude), and Archangel and his brother are taken before the governor, and by him cast into prison. The King, hearing of their arrest, sends for them to interrogate them himself — though I confess I do not recognise the methods of Charles of blessed memory in this proceeding. With great show of probability, when we remember that we have been told that an edict had been specially promulgated against the Catholics, and that Archangel was named in it — or perhaps, indeed, it was to show how little he cared, through his divine right, for his own edict — Charles, on recognising Archangel, whom he had known when interpreter to the Spanish Embassy, immediately liberates him and his brother. Of the rest of the passengers (and perhaps quite properly) we hear no more, and of this I care but little, except about the fate of the Catholic captain, and on this point, alas! the author is inexorable.

After some days at the court of 'Neopurt' Archangel starts again for Aberdeen, sailing from the well-known port of Viklen, which is still waiting for its Columbus as far as I am concerned, for neither Cabot, Ponce de Leon, Juan de la Cosa, or any of those Spanish navigators who showed us the world, seem to have visited it.

Here I may remark that, after a careful perusal of his life, I have come to the conclusion that there was no port of Europe in which, if Archangel found himself stranded, he did not instantly find a ship just sailing for Aberdeen; hence, I imagine, the trade of Aberdeen was vastly more considerable in the days of Charles the First than it is at present, as, indeed, seems not unlikely.

Arrived once more in Monomusco's halls, he throws himself into mission work with as much alacrity as if it had been the heart of Africa, and the place becoming once more too hot for him, he retreats to Edinburgh, the capital of Scotland, remarkable for having been the birthplace of Alexandro de Ales.

In Edinburgh one Baron Daltay (el Baron de Daltay), for whose name I have unsuccessfully searched in Nisbet's Heraldry, lies sick to death, and, being a Protestant, not unnaturally wishes to confess to a Catholic priest before his end. His friend Baron Balguay (whom Douglas's Peerage is powerless to assist me in identifying) brings in Archangel.

The Protestants, who seem to have been always on the alert for cases such as these (which happened frequently), rush into the house to kill Archangel, who only saves his life by jumping from a window. Balked of their victim, they fall (like theologians) on poor Baron Balguay and purge him of his heresy with their skeenes.

The author says a skeene (*esquin*) is like an Albacete knife, and indeed it may be, for one is straight and one is crooked. Then, to free the land from Catholics, they kill the son, aged ten, who, as the father was a Protestant, most likely was one too; but when did ever theologians, when killing was to be done, haggle at trifles of that nature?

Having seen enough of Edinburgh and of the way they argued religious differences there, Archangel, disguised as a physician, goes to the province of Esterling, and there at once sets to convert the sound and heal the sick.

Throughout the book these little indications show that Archangel was a simple-minded honest fellow, doing what he thought his duty at all hazards. This, to my mind, appears so novel that I do not doubt it happened three hundred years ago. Though Padre Ajofrin never quotes a single word Archangel says, I fancy I can see him just as plainly as if, in the modern fashion, he had spoken pages and never done a thing worth doing.

The cures he effected were quite wonderful, the author says, and then somewhat enigmatically observes he is unaware if Archangel had ever studied medicine. The fact he cured at all induces me to believe that perhaps he had but little previous knowledge. But be that as it may, the doctors of Esterling (all trades-unionists) look on his practising with great disfavour. Whether they thought him wanting in a knowledge of pathology, or that a Catholic had no right to doctor Protestants, does not appear, but anyhow they forced him to leave Esterling and retire to Aberdon. Hardly arrived there, a royal messenger summons him to London, but whether to answer for his tampering with the faith of Aberdon, or to ascertain whether he held a foreign medical degree, remains uncertain. Archangel, ever ready for a journey, starts at once, and at Torfechan, on the borders of the kingdom we are told, stays at an inn, in which he meets a nobleman, Baron de Cluni, an Englishman (*sic*), whom he converts, with all his retinue. Just about to start for London, he is taken ill with a fever, gets worse, and ends his journey and the journey of his life in 1637.

By night the Catholics of the retinue of the Baron, with a priest who happened to be in the neighbourhood disguised, carry the body, dressed in the Capuchin habit, and bury it in a wild and desert place in the hills, far from the dwellings of mankind. They mark the grave with a simple slab of slate, and water it with blood disguised in tears (*sangre disimulada en lagrimas*).

Thus ends, says Padre Ajofrin, the life of him who in the world was called George Leslie (Jorge Lesleo), born to much honours, wealth, and titles, and in religion known as Father Archangel, and who passed his life in poverty, in journeyings, and in good works. From it we may learn, remarks the author, obedience, truthfulness, humility, and holy caution, and how ingenious is charity in God's saints. They may be so, though for 'ingenious charity' somehow one seems not to be much 'enthused.'

What I discern is that Archangel was a simple-minded friar who did his duty as he thought he saw it, and did it for itself and not for honour or reward or hope of heaven, nor yet for fear of hell. I care but little that 'this servant of the Lord' published a book divided in two parts and titled 'De Potestate Pontificis Romani,' and which the learned and ingenious Wadingo cites, or if he had written nothing; I like him for his life of sturdy failure.

Possibly in England and in Scotland, far from the dwellings of mankind, on hill and moor, there sleep under rough slates many who like Archangel struggled manfully to stop the march of time and bring back yesterday. Well, peace be with them. To me those lonely burial-places now forgotten, so silent, buried in mist and lost on hill, fit graves for those who fail, mean more than all the pomps of alabaster with due mendacious epitaph in church or synagogue.

Now that Aberdeenshire is free from his assaults, and could we find it in Torfechan, over his deserted grave, even the Calvinist, I take it, would not refrain from saying with Padre Ajofrin, when thinking of the simple-minded Capuchin, 'Pretiosa in conspectu Domini est mors sanctorum ejus.'

R. B. C. G.

II. A Will

Before me is a thin quarto volume bound in vellum, stained and yellow by the ages during which it has lain unmolested in the archives of Avila. It is tied together with strings of parchment. On loosing them one finds a manuscript written in characters strange, twisted, picturesque, enigmatical to all but those who have made a long study of deciphering old handwritings. It is a will, and unlike modern wills, gives us some clue to the character, throws across the centuries some shadow of the living figure of whose last wishes it is the guardian. A will, every clause of which is a duty performed, an act of charity or of justice, every disposition of which was thought out carefully and slowly, as if the conveying of each individual item to paper was to be an everlasting burden or a relief to the conscience of the testator in the inevitable blank beyond the tomb. A will that cost long hours of prayer before the shrines of many churches, much unwearying consultation with confessors, Jesuits, and others, much pondering over the construction of every phrase before the 'notary public.' Master Gaspar or Blas, or whatever his name was who gave it its definitive form, stamped on it his notarial seal and rubrica*, in testimony of its truth and his own fidelity.

And as one reads it, it seems as if a window opened into the past and the figure of the old Castilian gentleman who loved, fought, suffered, and struggled, over three centuries ago, shapes itself firmly out of the shadowy dimness and takes definite form and outline.

The precise date of his birth is unknown. The date of his death is undecipherable on the grey slab under which he lies in the Discalced Carmelite Church of Avila, 'which,' he says in this same will, not without some pride and intimate satisfaction, 'I myself built at my own expense.'

The details of his life are few and vague. He was a gentleman of means. His possessions lay scattered in the hills and plains of Avila.

---

*Rubrica, i.e. rubric, is the flourish at the end of a signature. Without the rubrica the signature was not valid in law. Hence the saying, 'Mas reale rubrica que firma.'

In the little rugged village of Colillas, that looks about a handbreadth off in the clear searching air and is three leagues; in Serranillos, the rough mountain hamlet at the head of the pass between Avila and Estremadura; at Muñosancho, at Xemerandura, and in other places now difficult to identify he owned yugadas* of land, *pan de trigo y pan terciado*, producing wheat and other crops in succession. Besides his scattered territorial possessions, his cornfields, flax-fields, and villages, his woods and pasture-grounds, he owned in spite of piety many a productive mortgage over the entailed estates of others.

Many a time before religion weaned him from material interests, he rode out of Avila, a black figure, his long cloak sweeping down over the horse's quarters, by the first light of day to visit them; many nights the stars twinkling over the battlements of the city welcomed him on his return. That he was a hard master to his labourers is impossible. That he was exact to the last farthing in his accounts with them is certain. But it was the exactitude that is followed by generosity. All these possessions small and great, calculated to the last yugada of ground, to the last fanega† of grain, are scheduled in his will. But then he was only the steward, and had to render an accurate reckoning. Had it not been so, what of his nieces, nuns in the Convent of Sta. Maria, to whom he leaves 12 ducats a piece, besides paying down their dower to the convent? What of the Benedictine Monastery, to which certain possessions of his wife's had belonged, and which must now return to Holy Mother Church, unshorn of a tittle of their value? Kindly, formal, courteous, sweet of nature, and holy of life we know he was from contemporaneous testimony — so holy that he was known in Avila as the Holy Gentleman. His wife was Da. Mencia del Aguila, one of the noblest amongst the many noble families of Avila. She brought him possessions as extensive as his own. He and his wife as long as she lived worked hand in hand, and lightened the lives of many poor neighbours, — he too lightened various souls of their heavy burdens by his judicious counsels and soothing consolations. He was a familiar figure in all the convent locutories, and was beloved alike of saintly mother-prioresses and father-abbots. His household was tranquil, full of Christian kindliness and good-will: so says his nephew, who lived with him, — one amongst the many recipients of his large-hearted bounty, — in a book which has long ceased to exist.

---

*A yugada was as much as an ox could plough. In Scotland it was called an 'oxgangis.'
†A fanega is about a hundredweight.

At the head of it was a certain old housekeeper, a type which has disappeared with the simple patriarchal age it belonged to, the devoted friend rather than a servant in the house she ruled. A woman that her master and mistress treated with respect, and loved not as a dependent but as one belonging to them, whom even they never addressed without her title Sra. Ospedal, a woman so upright and Godfearing that when her master shall be lying dead in the bed he describes so minutely, she shall not be required to swear to, or give any account of the jewels, the silver, and other valuables under her charge, 'for,' says he, 'she is so good a Christian and of so fine a conscience, that whatever she will say will be the truth.'

On his wife's death he became a Jesuit and a priest. How long he laboured in the company of Jesus we do not know. The one date we can be certain of is the date of the will, signed on the 7th of April, the year of the birth of Jesus Christ 1579.

It begins not with possessions but with the soul. This writing of a will is a solemn moment to a Spaniard. It was with the black shadow of Death already shrouding his thoughts that he dictated the opening paragraph (for no notary could have evolved a note of such sincerity, earnestness, and belief).

'Jesus In Dei nomine, let it be to all who shall see this testamentary letter and last will a manifest and notorious thing, how I, Francisco de Salcedo, priest and native of this very noble city of Avila, minding me of death that it is a natural and certain thing, and the hour of it most uncertain, and considering how convenient a thing it is that I should settle what is necessary for my salvation in time, and dispone of the goods which our Lord has given me by His infinite mercy for His holy service; for this cause, believing as I believe in the most Holy Trinity, Father, Son, and Holy Spirit, three persons, and one only true God, and all the rest that Holy Mother Church holds, believes, and confesses, in which faith I protest I live and die as a Catholic and Christian, being, as I am, sound in body and in my right mind and natural understanding, I grant, and recognise by this present letter I am making, and order this my testament and last will to the service of God our Lord and His blessed mother in the following manner :—

'First, I commend my soul to God, our Lord Jesus Christ, who made and redeemed it with His precious blood, and my body to the earth of which it was made, and I order that when our Lord is pleased to take me from this present life my body be buried in the Church of Señor San Pablo, which is adjoining the Church of Señor San Josef of this city, which I made and built at my expense, from its beginning.'

As to the funeral, the honours, the mass, the wax, and the offering, these he remits to his legatees. But it pleases the old man, as he follows in spirit his own imaginary funeral procession through the silent streets of his native city, amidst the deep tolling of the cathedral bell and the bells of many monasteries and convents, to know that in the little Church of San Pablo the friends of his life — the good Master Daza, Gonzalo de Aranda, and Julian de Avila — shall say and sing their masses over the upturned face of him who was once their comrade. Nevertheless, so that all may be done seemly, fifty-two masses are to be said as speedily as possible for the repose of his soul in San Pablo, fifty masses each in the monastery churches of Sto. Tomás and San Francisco, and yet another fifty in the College of San Millán.

In the cathedral of Avila, nailed on one of the pillars, close to the west gateway, a little blue Talavera plaque still beseeches of the faithful alms for the wretched captives languishing in the Baths of Tunis or Tripoli. The need for it has gone, although the plaque remains. That blue and white plaque, today merely a relic of times gone by, was for Francisco de Salcedo a daily reminder of an obligation, and he leaves to the redemption of captives *lo acostumbrado*, the sum he had ever been accustomed to give. If he remembers forgotten captives in Tunis, his servitors in Avila are not forgotten. His clothes and shirts are to be distributed amongst them, and Sra. Ospedal is to dole them out as she thinks fit. Two ducats are to be given to the sons of Agustin, the son of Maria Diaz, 'for what I may owe him, if I owe him anything, and even if I do not.'

He sets apart a portion of his house, viz. the apartment presently occupied by the Sr. Pablo Xuarez, consisting of a room with its alcobas and two sleeping places over the corral, and a little cellar underneath opening into the zaguan for Mistress Ospedal, 'free of rent or any other thing, and no one shall be able to cast her out.' It is pathetic to see how tenderly solicitous he is about the little comforts of his old housekeeper. She is to open if she likes a door from the room to the zaguan*, but nevertheless she is still free to use the patio as before. There she is to live with her servants for all the days of her life, and over and above is to take

---

*Zaguan is the porch between the door and the patio (court). It is an Arabic word, which means 'covered.'

such jewels and furniture, to be chosen and pointed out by herself, as amount to the value of 12 ducats. Nor shall Mistress Ospedal be bullied and worried by scriveners or legatees. 'Neither the heir nor any other person shall require of her any account whatever, either of bread, or money, or silver, or valuables, or furniture, or anything else that she may have had or has under her charge until the day of my death; and when that shall take place she is to be believed on her word alone, and the usual oath is to be done away with, because I hold her for so good a Christian that one can trust her and her conscience, and I am certain she will keep nothing belonging to me or any one else.

'Ana, my servant, daughter of Maria Ceveca, besides 10 ducats, is to have the bed I sleep on, with its two mattresses, a blanket, and a coloured counterpane, and two sheets, two pillows, and another bed made of rope (*cordeles*).'

There is an old house in Avila, close to the Archbishop's Palace, in Salcedo's time the Jesuit College of San Gil. Both house and palace form part of the famous walls of Avila, which shows that they were in other times the fortified dwellings of the old conquistadores who wrested the city from the Moors, and whose proud duty it was to guard the ramparts. A half-defaced coat-of-arms hangs over the doorway which leads into the patio — the famous patio into which Sra. Ospedal was to have, in Scotch legal phraseology, 'free ish and entrance.' The patio is dank, grown over with straggling grass and trees. In the centre there is the well. A few indigent families now inhabit the dwelling of the old Castilian hidalgo, although, from the proverbial incuria of the Spanish character, it still retains traces of its ancient and more honourable uses. The last of the Salcedos, a little official in Madrid still draws its rents, but between him and his ancestor there is a great gulf fixed. As to its interior, it is only a convent that can give any adequate idea of its stateliness, its grave repose, and the dignity of the surroundings.

The brief clause in which he bequeaths his most valued belongings to the Church of San José shows what was its furniture. To it he bequeaths all his Flemish tapestries (*lienços de Flandes*) and images that he may leave; 'also all that is in the oratory that I have in my house, with its Spanish leather (*guardamecíes*), altar, and chests, and looking-glass, and all the rest I have, and which may be found within my said oratory on the day of my death; and moreover all the ornaments (*hornamento*), chalices, and chest in which is contained all the other things I have for saying and serving mass; and moreover three carpets that I have, so that all that may be the property of the said Church of San Pablo, and for its use and adornment; and moreover I bequeath it two French chairs (*sillas francesas*), so that they may remain in the said church for ever.'

Indeed a church was the only fitting place for such treasures to repose in, for the stately beauty of them may be dimly imagined in the dry enumeration signed by the notary public. There, where was his grave, it was most fitting that on great and solemn festivals, the Flemish tapestries should hang from the aisles, their gigantic figures lit up by the flickering flame of torches and wax tapers. It consoled him to know that the ornaments which had served him so long would have a still nobler use than in the oratory of a private house; that the *sillas francesas* would eternally abide, one on each side of the high altar, and that the Bishops of Avila, succeeding each other like shadows, would one and all make use of the gifts of his bounty.

I am glad to say that, perishable as are dead men's last wishes and comminations, the chairs still stand in the place allotted to them by the donor who died three centuries ago, and to-day is forgotten as he had never been in the Avila into which he had intertwined his life.

Indeed this same Discalced Convent of Avila, founded by one Teresa of Jesus, whom he had loved and comforted ever since, an introspective and wretched young nun in the Encarnacion, she had confided to him the agonies of her soul, was the object of the old man's dearest predilections. For the endowment 'dote,' building and repairs, lamp, and ornament of the Church of San Pablo, and for the maintenance of a sacristan to take care of the ornaments and things belonging to it, to keep it clean and swept and in good order, and to assist at the masses which shall be said in it, he leaves all his hereditaments and lands situated in Xemerandura, close to Hontiberos, with its houses and all belonging to it, consisting of over two yugadas of land, which produce 166 fanegas of grain, half wheat and half oats, so that they become the property of San Pablo for ever. From this fund is also to be provided the wax, wine, and consecrated wafers free of charge to all the priests who there said mass, and 1000 maravedises of annual salary to a priest who personally, and without committing the charge to any other person, shall bind himself to say, and shall say every week of the year, four masses in the Church of San Pablo for the souls of such as he may choose. Of the soul of the founder (himself) Salcedo, with a refinement of self-denial and a feeling closely approaching to heroism, makes no stipulation. In a parenthesis he adds softly and apologetically, like the humble and unworthy Christian he felt himself to be, 'I ask him of his charity to pray to God for me,' and without any trace of emphasis adds simply that his appointment is to be made in accordance with a paper which 'I and the nuns of San José have drawn up between us.'

Nor were these the only gifts to his favourite convent. To it he left his lands of La Nava, with all its woods, pasturages, and houses; to it he left his hamlets of La Colilla and Cortos. Not only so, but in an unhappy moment for the nuns and his heirs, — for his act involved a lawsuit which cost the contending parties more than the property was worth, and was only ended in 1849, when the government appropriated the whole of the territorial possessions owned by the religious bodies of Spain, — he wrested for their benefit the lands of Muñosancho from the entail under which he had succeeded to them.

But if the nuns receive benefits so great, they contract a debt no less great and onerous, — a debt which they are bound to pay so long as they and the convent remain in existence. For all time coming on the anniversary of his interment, or if it falls on some solemn festival within the octave of the same, they bind themselves and the generations after them to sing a mass for souls in purgatory.

'And I desire,' adds Salcedo solemnly, 'that this may not be postponed to any future obligation, but I charge it on their consciences that they keep and fulfil it in respect of the said estates which I leave them for that purpose, and as a charitable bequest.'

In Spanish convents an official register is kept, often dating back many centuries, in which every successive prioress enters the names of all who have given alms to or benefited the community. No matter whether it is the rich man's lands or the poor man's pence, there the names lie embedded side by side to all eternity. The community has contracted a solemn obligation to its benefactors, and to accomplish this is as much a part of the routine of their lives as the ordinary conventual discipline. It may be doubted, with so many donations to convents and monasteries, whether Salcedo had any heir.

But the man who remembers first of all his soul, and then his faith, and then his charity, does not forget his duty to posterity.

To Marcos de Salcedo, his nephew, youngest son of the licentiate Adrada, he leaves 30 fanegas of land *de pan de renta* in the confines of Picamixo for all the days of his life, after which it is to revert to the entail. To him also he leaves a mortgage of 30,000 maravedises over the property of Don Diego Mexia, which said mortgage also belongs to the entailed estate, and after his death shall revert to it again.

For a religious man like Salcedo, and at a time when the canonical law so strongly deprecated as sinful the possession of mortgages, he seems to have held a considerable number of them. For in the next breath he leaves to his nephew a second perpetual mortgage of 1050 maravedises, which is also entailed on his heirs. Perhaps, like the regular Castilian he was, he was of opinion that *todos los males con pan son menos*. To him also he leaves the old fortified house, which he describes as 'the principal houses where I dwell.'

There is a very curious clause relating to Marcos de Salcedo, which illustrates the spirit of the age in a very graphic manner. Item — 'I will that the whole of the said houses and the rest of the estates which in this my testament I bequeath to Marcos de Salcedo, the younger, which belong to the said entail, he shall enjoy and possess for his life only, and afterwards after his death, or if before it, he shall put *himself into religion* (become a monk); then Da. Maria de Salcedo, daughter of Agustin de la Serna, shall have and inherit them all, for herself and her heirs and successors.' Marcos de Salcedo *did* become a monk, and Agustin de la Serna succeeded to the entail.

This same entail had cost old Salcedo many uneasy hours in life, for it was the cause of a lawsuit between him and his nephew, the said Agustin de la Serna. It had been the cause of long whisperings in the confessional, of much consultation with learned Jesuits and others versed in canonical law, such as the Dr. Rueda, who was also in the most critical hours of her life the adviser of Sta. Teresa. Fancy a man now seeking legal advice from a Jesuit and a cathedral canon instead of that domestic tyrant, his family solicitor!

This lawsuit he transferred by his will to the nuns of San José, who, from his death until 1849 (when the convents were relieved by a careful and economical State of all their territorial possessions), were ever waging war, wordy and otherwise, with the despiteful and litigious heirs of entail. Let the old man die content, however, and peaceful, dreaming neither of past lawsuits nor future ones, satisfied that his last wishes shall be respected, and happy in the prospect of his own tranquil rest under the grey slab of San Pablo.

Imagination — that feeble picture-maker — may see the last impressive scene, may even strive to render it to others, and be partially successful. Still we are dealing with realities. There, in that quiet little plaza, shrouded today in green, are the doors of the house, now worm-eaten and shaking on their hinges, whence he passed out for the last time, surrounded by his fellow-townsmen, to his eternal resting-place within the walls of San José. The silent streets of the grey old town through which, escorted by all the stately and old-fashioned pomp of torch and candle, the dead Francisco de Salcedo was borne on that funeral day, to which he refers solemnly as 'the day of my burial,' although the life of the sixteenth century which then floated through them has left to us only the rumour of its passage, are but little changed.

Watch a funeral to-day in Avila. See the many-robed confraternities as they fall into procession around the bier, and the priests in their violet robes going before, chanting solemn and lugubrious responses. Listen to the bells tolling from the cathedral, echoing through space and arousing that sentiment which dwells in all of us — of the irrevocable and the past, and the quick passage of Humanity into Oblivion. As the dull thud of them strikes the ear, as earth upon the coffin, their sound is taken up by the tinkling response from monastery and convent tower.

The white coifed, mysterious figures who, hidden in the shadowy depths behind the grating bars, watch the old man's corpse as it lies in state for the space of one night and one day before the altar of their convent church, are the same now as then. Centuries have passed, but these strange communities conserve and revere all the footprints of the generations who trod the cloister floors before them.

Through the dusky aisles of San Millán, San Francisco, and San Gil those fifty masses each shall be sung with all due and mournful solicitude. San Francisco lies a heap of ruins at the outskirts of the town; San Millán has become a seminary, the Jesuit College of San Gil, the Bishops' Palace. Time has waved his transforming wand, and they are now mere memories. Still, there it all is, and it only wants a little touch to lift the veil, and amidst much that has changed, more that is Dead, and past memories still living, it only needs this old yellow will, three centuries old, for us to see a figure, very firmly and finely shaped, of the bounteous master and chivalrous gentleman who left Sra. Ospedal to mourn for him alone in the desolation of her old age, and once paced through Avila, solemn, stately, and kindly, as if he and his age were to be remembered there for ever.

G. C. G.

III. De Heretico Comburendo

Valladolid, from Belad el Walid — that is, in Arabic, the Land of Walid, once the capital of Spain, and now a dull, decaying town in Old Castille, on the Pisuerga.

Few places even in Spain recall more forcibly the past. On every side a plain stretching for miles, to the north the mountains dimly visible, on the south and east and west plains, and more plains.

No commerce, little traffic, few modern buildings except a court for the *pelota* (the national game of ball), to which the inhabitants draw your attention with pride as evidence of coming prosperity. Even the bull ring seems decaying. No bicycles, but few advertisements, and these chiefly of things that no one can have any use for.

Still, an air of ancient splendour hangs about the town. In the arcaded plazas many a heretic has purged his contempt by fire, and gone, perhaps to heaven, perhaps from fire to fire. In every street a ruined palace, at every turn a house in which lived some one known in history; an air that only having been a capital ever imparts. In the Plazuela del Ochavo, where the Emperor Charles V pardoned the Comuneros, still stands the house, with the window bars not yet repaired, where Philip II was baptized. The bars were cut to show the infant to the people.

Just the sort of town in which one might expect to find a Scottish and an English Catholic College. Philip, of pious memory (in Spain), founded them both. Perhaps his motives were political, perhaps religious. Who in England can judge of motives in Spain? As easily as a Spaniard can judge of morals in England. Climate, I take it, influences both, as it does judgments. Mary, in England 'bloody,' in Spain is 'pious.' Claverhouse, a fiend in Ayrshire, is a hero in the Highlands. Still we owe Philip gratitude for his two colleges, if only to remind us that we too were persecutors.

In a long rambling street the Scottish College stands. The natives (of the poorer sort) speak of the College as *el colegio de los Escorozeces*, giving the word an extra syllable, perhaps for euphony. Still they add they are good Christians, and this is the highest praise men of their kind in Spain can give.

Hard by the College Cervantes lived and wrote the second part of *Don Quixote*; close by Columbus died poor and brokenhearted; not far off dwelt Gondomar. A bit of Scotland lost in Castille, and yet a place no Scotsman (even a Presbyterian) should behold unmoved.

Many in Scotland are the tales of suffering and persecution that Protestants endured, but never does one hear of the tyranny that forced a Scottish Catholic to seek his education at Douay, Valladolid, and St. Omer. How many Scotsmen have heard of the Scoto-Spanish College? How many have visited it? Yet thoroughly to comprehend the faith sufficient to move mountains and extirpate humanity in man, which reigned in Scotland in times past, it must be visited. Much has the Odium Theologicum to answer for in Scotland and other lands. How admirable, when thinking of it, appears the simple faith of the savages of whom some traveller relates that of whatever faith the missionary was, into the hot stone oven straight he went.

Passing the ponderous door, set in a horse-shoe arch, the present melts away. On every side the past looks down on one. A flagged and vaulted corridor leads to a long refectory, with the table set, as in the 'Cena' of Leonardo, with bread, and jugs of rough Valencian pottery. Mary Queen of Scots looks through the gloaming from the wall; Semple of Semple (a pious founder) faces her. Out of every corner Scottish Jesuits of the past seem to appear. Across the passage seem to emerge the shades of Scottish priests, who in their lifetime had lurked in Scottish castle and Elizabethan manor-house, and occupied the secret chamber in the houses of the English and Scottish Catholics. At once the air of rest and quiet seems to suggest the College as a fitting place in which to rear up men to minister to scattered Catholic communities in Aberdeenshire, Lochaber, and Strathglass.

Scholars — some twenty, chiefly peasants' sons from Aberdeenshire; priests — three or four; lastly, the Rector. Only in *Redgauntlet* and in books of Jacobites does such a priest exist. I fancy the Rector of the Scottish Castilian College is the last surviving type. Scotissimus Scotorum, a Scot of Scots, tall, thin, and sinewy, a Highlander, a scholar and linguist, withal a gentleman, with the geniality that Presbyterianism seems to have crushed out of the modern Scotsman. In talking with him one seems to see what sort of men the Scotsmen of the past had been before the worship of the Bawbee and the Bible had altered them. Something quite unlike Scotland in the urbanity of the man; a sort of being, as it were, in community with the rest of Europe, instead of, as at present, condemned to fellowship with only Germans (High and Low), Dutchmen, and Scandinavians; people who, excellent no doubt, have nothing of the Slave or Latin interest about them. Just the kind of man who in old days was charged with missions by the Pope, 'the King of Spain,' or Mary Queen of Scots, to save the somewhat scabby, if faithful sheep who still remained in Scotland. If the world had only gone on right (or wrong) Father M'Donald had been enthroned at Edinburgh, at Brechin, or St. Andrews, 'a fayre prelate,' with cope and chasuble, crosier and ring of amethyst on his forefinger, with candle, bell and book, and power to curse the heretic and lift the finger in the attitude, so dear to bishops, of malediction. As it is, a Scoto-Spanish priest and gentleman speaking Castilian faintly tinged with Gaelic, and dinning education and religion into fledgling Scoto-Spanish or Hispano-Scottish priests.

Nature or fate is, very prodigal of men, not in the way of turning out many, fitted to excel in anything but cheapening bicycles, but in another fashion. When in a million a man is born fitted to rule the Church, lead men, or to direct a country, ten to one that fate or nature sets him to do that which the million others could have done as well as he, and leaves his task to fools.

Over the Scottish College hangs an air of Scotland, but not of Scotland of to-day, but of that older Scotland that was poor and furnished soldiers and adventurers to all the rest of Europe; that Scotland which vanished after Culloden, and has been replaced by factories and mines, progress and money, and an air of commonplace, exceeding all the world.

Not looking over carefully at the writing of St. Thomas of Aquinas, the autograph of Her of Avila, the relics (all authentic), the rich groined roof so finely arched, or even at the curious wooden flooring of the church, unique in Spain, I say farewell to my compatriots and out into the street, thanking my stars for the chance of having seen that which enabled me to reconstruct the Scotland of the past more vividly than by perusing libraries.

In the Calle Real de Don Sancho, as close to the Scottish College as Gretna is to Carlisle, stands the Colegio de los Ingleses. Founded, like the other, by Philip II, the English College was designed to commemorate the triumph of the Invincible Armada. The 'Invincible' is long dispersed; its sailors from Biscay and from Catalonia have left their bones on Achill and upon the Hebrides; all of it has disappeared with the exception of here and there a rusty anchor, but here and there a darker cheek in Galway or a brighter eye amongst the ponies of the coast. Had it succeeded, without doubt today we had all been Catholics, and the poor Catholic gentleman of Garstang, mentioned by Froude, had been relieved from the obligation of going on Sunday to 'take wine' with the vicar at the parish church. The College still remains, apparently unchanged since its foundation.

The work begun by Campion, Parsons, and their fellows, still goes on. The corridors through which they paced, reading their breviaries, remain identical. The pupils (more ruly, let us fain hope, than their predecessors, of whom the Jesuit fathers had to complain at Rome) still sit down in the self-same stone refectory.

In England how few remember the disgraceful page of history that the fantastic tortures and the martyrdoms of the Jesuits in the pictures hanging on the wall attest. Let them rest on, secure at least in one thing, that the torments that a hard world inflicts on their descendants defy the limner's power to put in pictures, even with a knowledge of perspective.

If the Scots College had an air of Scotland, so the English College has an air of prosperous England; but how unlike the other. The self-same architecture, the self-same iron-studded doors, the altars in the style of Churriguera in the chapels, where saints and angels float in a sea of gilded gingerbread, identical, but still an outward air and inward grace making them different, as Thurso is from Yeovil.

Why is it that the races English and Scotch have never really amalgamated? So close, so like, both wizened by the same east wind, tormented more or less by the same Sunday, and yet unlike, and so the colleges. St. George for Merrie England. No one in his wildest fits of patriotism ever talked of Merrie Scotland. Did Knox kill merriment, even as Macbeth did murder sleep? Loyal, abstemious, business-like, haggis-eating, tender, disagreeable, true, a Scotsman may be, but merry never.

An air of Oxford pervades the English College, all seems so prosperous, so old- established, and so English. The well-stocked library, with its rows of fine old Spanish, Latin, and English books clothed in white vellum, lettered on the backs in strange old-fashioned hands; the comfortable reading-desks and well-warmed room, all spoke of England. Not that there were not things unusual to be seen in English colleges. The pictures on the wall of English Catholics, martyred for conscience' sake by so-called freedom-loving Englishmen, gave a different note. These are particulars it pleases me to dwell on. Pleasant to slap one's chest and say,

'I am an Englishman;' to think that in my country every faith is free, from Christianity to Obi worship, free and untrammelled as long as it observes the laws of decency and of the Stock Exchange. It pleases me to think that if the cruel Duke of Alva racked and burnt and scourged the Protestants of Holland, Elizabeth of England was not a jot inferior to him in her dealings with English Catholics. Is it to be allowed that Catholics shall have the copyright of persecution? Perish the thought; Christians of all denominations have shown their love to one another by the rack and stake. Certain it is Pizarro and Cortes depopulated empires, but they at least imagined that their mission in the Indies (after the gold was found) was to convert the Indians. Besides, the Spanish butcheries ceased with the sixteenth century. Ours have continued almost to the present day. Where are the natives of Tasmania, the Australian blacks, the greater portion of the Maoris? Is it to be believed that we exterminated these men out of a desire to save their souls?

After the martyrs' pictures the chief glory of the place is the image of the Blessed Virgin richly carved in wood. Powerful in miracles (*muy milagrosa*) the people of the town affirm her, and why should any doubt it? During the sack of Cadiz the heathen soldiers (so runs the Spanish story) of the Count of Essex tore this Virgin from her shrine, and to display their Christian toleration hacked off her arm and drew it through the streets tied to a string. After the sack, and when the pagans had returned to England, what could an English College do better than show its faith by offering an asylum to the poor image maltreated by the English who in England denied the faith? So in procession they received her, with music, incense, and with acolytes, and placed her where she stands to-day, blackened with age, but comely and most miraculous.

Each name upon the lists on the refectory walls has had its tragedy. Tichbornes and Babingtons, Englefields and Catesbys, jostle one another. They set one thinking on the past, and on the way in which all history is written to suit the conscience of the conquerors. The world has always readily come out to greet the conqueror with trumpets and with flowers; but he has always had to conquer first. The names upon the walls are names of beaten men, and speak of causes long forgotten. Neither racks nor calumny can further harm them, and in their time they had their fill of both. Therefore I take it that without incurring *scandalum magnatum* a man may drop his literary tear upon their memory. At any rate, if freedom has been won by martyrdom, to the Campions, Garners, and the rest we owe as much as to the men who perished at Smithfield or upon the moors of Galloway. And if they did not snuffle through the nose, or take the names of Hebrew worthies, instead of calling themselves plain George or John, they were as truly martyrs, and their state, for all I know, as gracious.

So out into the deserted sandy street, between its *tapia* walls, to muse upon the colleges, and to reflect that had not stake and rack and red-hot pincers proved so efficacious, perchance the England of to-day had been as Catholic as Belgium.

R.B.C.G.

IV. In The Tarumensian Woods

Strange that reason should so often go astray, but that digestion should be unerring. So it is, though. The greatest minds have fallen into error. There is no recorded instance of even a congenital idiot having deceived his digestion. It may be, then, that after all reason is not the highest attribute of humanity.

Be that as it may, reason, in its eternal conflict with faith, seldom comes off so badly as when it encounters prejudice. So inveterate is prejudice and so shamefaced is reason, that one sometimes wonders whether faith and prejudice are not synonymous.

Few prejudices are so inveterate, and therefore on few questions is so little reason displayed, as on the subject of the Jesuits.

To be a member of the Society of Jesus conveys to many excellent people the impression that a sort of baccalaureate of lying, of chicanery, and of casuistry has been attained. It would seem that a Jesuit is a man perpetually, for no particular object, endeavouring to deceive the world, and even himself. Macchiavelli is his favourite author, Suarez his dearest study, and his political ideal that of Ezzelino da Romano, or Malatesta of Rimini. In history, when a king was murdered or dethroned, a queen poisoned, a conspiracy hatched, or a revolution attempted, the blame was thrown upon the Jesuits, with or without proof, in the same impartial way as it is now thrown upon the Anarchists. In both cases no doubt the desired result was attained, and a scapegoat acquired on which to lay the sins of others. Humanity dearly loves a scapegoat.

Nothing in all the Mosaic Dispensation appears to me to show more clearly the profound knowledge of the human heart possessed by its compiler than the institution of the sin-bearing quadruped. If the people were worth the sacrifice of the goat appears doubtful after a perusal of their history, and it might have been prudent, one would have thought, to hesitate before sacrificing the unoffending animal.

The Jesuits were said to be self-seekers in the Indies and schemers in Europe.

True, St. Francis Xavier was a Jesuit; and few, after reading his life, would accuse him of being a schemer or a self-seeker, and, after reading his hymn, I should imagine that the doubts of any one would be removed. Still, perhaps he was the exception that proved the rule; though how exceptions prove rules has not been vouchsafed to us at present.

By a curious fatality, not only Catholics and Protestants, but also freethinkers, were united against them, and their only defenders were Rousseau, Raynal, Mably, and Montesquieu. Even Felix de Azara, impartial as he was on most matters, and amiable, as his celebrated dedication to his History of Paraguay clearly shows him to have been, became a violent partisan when writing of the Jesuits. That in Paraguay, at all events, the Jesuits were not all self-seekers and plotters, that they accomplished much good, endured great perils and hardships, and were the only people whose mere presence did not bring mortality amongst the Indians, I hope to try to prove at some length at the proper time and place. Meanwhile I have to deal with the adventures of one particular Jesuit, a kindly, honest, simple-minded man, whose lot was thrown in strange places, and who fortunately has preserved for us a record of his undertakings.

On the eve of St. John, but without chronicling the year, except more or less (*año de 1756 mas o menos*), did he, so to speak, strike the Gospel trail from San Joaquin in Paraguay, accompanied by some Guaraní neophytes; but this demands a little explication.

In the last century the Jesuits had gathered most of the Guaraní Indians in Paraguay, and what has now become the Argentine province of Corrientes, into some thirty little towns or missions, known to the country people as *capillas* (chapels), and extending from Guayrá, near the cataract of the Paraná, to Yapeyú, on the Uruguay. On this somewhat stony vineyard they worked unceasingly, instilling not only theology, but some tincture of civilisation, into the Guaranís.

The Tobás, the Guaycurús, the Mocobíos, then as now roamed the swampy wilderness of the Gran Chaco, the Great Hunting Ground (Chaco in Guarani signifies a hunting-ground) of the remnant of the tribes who fled from Peru and Chile on the advance of Almagro and Pizarro, and from Bolivia and the Argentine Republic before Solís and the Mendozas, to wander in its recesses. In the little town of San Joaquin, called Tarumá by the Jesuits, on account of the forests of tarumá-trees which surrounded it, there dwelt the chronicler of the following little episode.

He was a member of the crafty, scheming Society of Jesus, it should be remembered, so that no doubt his writings had an esoteric meaning. From his youth he had been engaged in missionary work.

Like Moffat and like Livingstone, he burned with zeal to change the faith of men who had done him no previous injury, and, like them, having begun his labours, his humanity rose superior to his dogma. In those days no paragraphs in newspapers, no plaudits from a close-packed audience in Exeter Hall, at intervals of a year or two, no testimonials, no pious teas; nothing but drudgery amongst savages, but journeys, ridings by night and day, sleeping amongst swamps, fightings and preachings, and death at last of fever, or by Indian club or arrow.

For all reward, calumny and misconception, and a notice in the appendix of a book written by a member of the Society, in this wise:-

> Padre Julian Lizardi, a Biscayan, caught by the Chiriguanos,
> tied to a stake, and shot to death with arrows.
> Diego Herrera, pierced with a spear.
> Lucas Rodriguez, slain at the altar by the Mocobíos.
> Gaspar Osorio, killed and eaten by the Payaguás.

In those days a missionary, even a Jesuit, had to bear his cross; not that the missionary of to-day does not ascend his little Calvary, but still I fancy that the pebbles in the road are not so lumpy, and that the road itself is better fit for bicycles. Thrice had my Jesuit crossed the Pampas from Buenos Ayres to Mendoza, as he tells us. Often had he travelled amongst the Tobás and the Abipones; amongst the Guaycurús, 'most turbulent of heathen, who extract their eyelashes to better see the Christians, and to slay them; their bodies painted many colours; worshipping no gods, except, perhaps, their horses, with whom they are more truly of one flesh than with their wives.' In perils oftentimes amongst the Payaguás, 'those pirates of the Paraná, disdaining gods, destroying man, staining their faces with the juice of the caraguatá, a purple like that of Tyre; having a vulture's wing dependent from their ears; very hard of heart, and skilled in paddling a canoe, and striking fish with arrows, like themselves alone.'

Languages so hard as to appear impossible to Europeans, 'so do they snort and sneeze and cough their words,' had to be overcome; speaking both Guaraní and Mocobío, 'with the Latin and some touch of Greek and Hebrew.' Though brought up as a priest, he had become a horseman; riding with the Gauchos day and night, though, as he tells us, never quite so much at home upon a horse of Paraguay as on a horse of Europe; for it appears 'a horse of Paraguay' (and this I have observed myself, though not a Jesuit) 'is apt to shy and bound, and if the bridle be neglected, lift his head up in the air, and, arching his back, give with his rider (*dar con el ginete*) on the ground.'

Medio chapeton* el padre, as I think I see.

This was the sort of training a Jesuit missionary underwent in Paraguay, and for which it may be that Salamanca, Rome, Coimbra, or even Paris, fitted him but moderately.

San Joaquin itself could not have been a place of residence to be called luxurious. Like all the Jesuit missions in Paraguay, it must have been a little place built round a square, enclosing a bright green lawn; a kind of island lost in the sea of forest. A well-built church of stone in the Jesuit style of architecture, the college with its storerooms for hides and wool and maté. On each side the church a date palm, waving like a bulrush. A long low row of wooden houses, with deep verandahs, thatched with palm leaves. An air of calm and rest and melancholy over the place, a sort of feeling as if you had landed (and been left) in Juan Fernandez. Sun and more sun, heat and more heat, and a whitish vapour stealing at evening time over the woods, wrapping the town within its folds, and giving the bell of the Angelus a muffled sound.

In the daytime women, in white clothes, with baskets on their heads of maize and mandioca, hair like horses' tails cut square across the forehead and hanging down their backs, clustered like bees in the centre of the square, and chattered Guaraní in undertones, like Indians always use. The men in white duck trousers, barefooted, and with cloaks of red *bayéta*† lounged about, doubtless when the Jesuits were not looking; as they do today.

Before the houses, posts of heavy wood, to which from sunrise till sunset horses ready saddled stood fastened; horses which seemed to sleep, unless an unwary passer-by approached too near them, when they sprang back into life, snorting with terror, sat back upon their *jáquimas*, causing their owners to leave their maté, and to bound like cats to quiet them, with cries of 'Jesus', 'Ba eh picó' and other things less fitting to record, even in Guaraní. Outside the town the forest stretching into

---

*Chapeton is used by Spanish Americans for a new-comer, and by inference a bad horseman.

†*Bayéta* is a kind of fine baize.

distance. Forests of viraró, of urunday, tarumá, araguaý, and zamaú, of every strange and iron-hearted wood that Europe never hears of, even to-day. Trees which grow, and fall and rot, and spring up bound with lianas like thick cordage, and through which the bell-bird calls, the guacamayos flutter and tucanes dart; and where the spotted tiger creeps (that Jesuit of the jungle) beside some pool covered with leaves of the Victoria Regia.

The college itself, no doubt a cheerless place enough, dazzling with whitewash on the outside, and in the interior dark and heavy, with an aroma of tobacco-smoke to serve as incense. For furniture a *catre* of wood, with strips of hide for bedstraps, or a white cotton hammock swung from an iron ring let into the beams. A shelf or two of books, chiefly on medicine or engineering or architecture; for your Jesuit was doctor, music-master, architect, and sometimes military instructor to the community. Two or three chairs, roughly cut out of solid wood and seated with stamped leather in the Spanish style; a table or two, a porous water-jar; in the corner the padre's saddle on a trestle, and on a nail a gun; for at times a Jesuit *capilla* became a place to fight as well as pray in.

In the forests scattered families of Indians lived, remnants of tribes destroyed by small-pox or by wars; and it was the dream of every self-respecting, able-bodied Jesuit to find and mark these sheep wandering in the wilderness without a shepherd. What they underwent in hardships, lack of food, attacks of Indians, crossing swamps and rivers, by heat and cold, Guevara and Lozano, Ruiz Montoya and Father Dobrizhoffer, have set forth with pious pride, and more or less dog Latin.

News having come to San Joaquin that the trail of Indians had been crossed near to the town, he sallied forth, and having found and marked his sheep, compiled the following description, in which he tells, besides the story, what kind of man he was himself; and proves beyond a doubt that, following the words of Santa Teresa, he 'was only fit for God.'

On the eve of the Evangelist, Blessed St. John the Baptist, I took a guide and entered the Tarumensian woods accompanied by some neophytes. I crossed the Rio Empalado, and having carefully explored all the woods of the river Mondaý Miní, and discovering at length on the third day a human footstep, we tracked it to a little dwelling where an old woman with her son and daughter, a youth and maiden of fifteen and twenty years, were dwelling.

Being asked where the other Indians were to be found, the mother replied that no one dwelt in the woods but herself, her son and daughter, and that all the rest had died of small-pox.

Perceiving us doubtful as to the truth of this, the son said, 'You may believe my mother, for I have looked for a wife up and down these woods for leagues, but never met a human being.'

Nature had taught the young savage that it was not lawful to marry his sister.

I exhorted the mother to remove to my town, where she would be more comfortable.

She declared herself willing to do so, but there was one objection: 'I have,' she said, 'three peccaries which I have brought up. They follow us wherever we go, and I am afraid, if they are exposed to the sun in a dry plain, unshaded by trees, they will soon die.'

'Pray be no longer anxious,' I said; 'I shall treat these dear little animals with due kindness. Lakes, rivers, and marshes will always be at hand to cool your favourites.'

Here I detect the cloven foot for the first and last time in this worthy man's career, for round San Joaquin there are no rivers or lakes, and I fear his anxiety to mark the sheep rendered him careless of the little peccaries.

Induced by these promises, she set out with us, and reached the town on the first of January.

No date is given, but I fancy in San Joaquin time was what they had most to dispose of.

And now it will be proper to give an account of the dwelling of the mother and her children. Their hut consisted of the branches of the palm-tree and their drink of muddy water.

To this day the majority of huts in Paraguay are of palm-leaves, and, for the muddy water, it grits yet (in dreams) between my teeth.

Fruits, antas*, rabbits and birds, maize and mandioca were their food,

*Tapirs.

a cloth woven of the leaves of the caraguatá their bed and clothing. They delighted in honey, which abounds in the hollow trees. The smoke of tobacco the old woman inhaled day and night through a reed. The son constantly chewed tobacco-leaves. The youth wore a cloak of caraguatá*, reaching to the knees. The girl wore a short net by day, which she used as a hammock by night. This appearing to me too transparent, I gave her a cotton towel to cover her more effectually. The girl, folding up the towel, put it on her head; but at the desire of her mother wrapped herself in it. I gave the youth, too, some linen clothes to wrap himself in. Before putting on these he had climbed the trees, agile as a monkey, but his wrapper impeded him so that he could hardly move a step.

Whether my author thinks it an advantage that, of a happy climbing faun, he had made a being who could not move a step, I do not know. But 'all was conscience and tender heart' with him, for he observes immediately:

In such extreme need, in such penury, I found them, experiencing the rigours of the anchorites of old without discontent, vexation, or disease. The mother and son were tall and good-looking, but the daughter had so fine and elegant a countenance that a poet would have taken her for a nymph or dryad. She united a becoming cheerfulness with great courtesy, and did not seem at all alarmed at our arrival.

When one reads an account like this, and reflects that Cook, Cabeza de Vaca, de Bougainville, Columbus, and others, all unite in describing similar people; and when one has even seen them oneself, it seems a pity that villainous saltpetre should have been digged, more villainous whisky distilled, and that Bible peddling should have become a trade.

As this insulated family had no intercourse with any but themselves, their Guaraní was much corrupted. The youth had never seen a woman but his mother and his sister. The girl had seen no man but her brother,

*The Caraguatá is a plant of the Bromeliacæ. For all I know in the language of science (?), it may be 'hirsute,' 'imbricate,' and all the rest of the jargon called scientific. It resembles a pineapple in shape; only it is at least three times as large, and the inside of the leaves are bright red. It grows by the side of woods. It is used instead of hemp in Paraguay. The Indians of the Chaco called it chaguar.

her father having been torn to pieces by a tiger before she was born. Not to go unattended (*sin compañero*), she had a little parrot and a small monkey on her arm.

The new proselytes were quickly clothed in the town, and food supplied them.

L'ultimo lasso! de' *lor* giorni allegri.

I also took care that they should take frequent excursions to the woods to enjoy the shade and pleasant freshness of the trees, to which they had been used, for we found by experience that savages removed to towns often waste away from the change of food and air, and from the heat of the sun, accustomed as they have been to moist, shady, and cool groves. The same was the fate of the mother, son, and daughter.

One hardly knows whether to laugh or cry. Hamlet has put the folly of falling a-cursing in such a light that perhaps not to *raggionar* is best, but silently to pass.

A few months after their arrival they were afflicted with a heaviness and universal rheum (*reuma universal*), to which succeeded pains in the eyes and ears and deafness. Lowness of spirits and disgust to food at length wasted their strength to such a degree that an incurable consumption followed. After languishing some months the old mother, who had been properly instructed (one feels relieved) in the Christian religion and baptized, delivered up her spirit with a mind so calm, so acquiescent with the Divine will, that I cannot doubt but that she entered into a blessed immortality.

I would fain hope so too, so that at least the unhappy sufferer had some practical set-off against the clothes and baptism which were her apparent ruin.

The girl, who had entered the town full of health and beauty, soon lost all resemblance to herself. Enfeebled, withering by degrees like a flower, her bones hardly holding together, she followed her mother to the grave, and, if I be not deceived, to heaven.

Again I hope the good and worthy muddlehead was right in his conjecture, though there is no mention of baptism or religious instruction in this case.

The brother still surviving was attacked by the same malady, but being of a stronger constitution overcame it. The measles, which made great havoc in the town [another blessing in disguise], left him so confirmed in health that he seemed beyond danger. He was of a cheerful nature, went to church daily [*pobrecito*], learnt the doctrines of Christianity with diligence, was gentle and compliant to all, and in everything discovered marks of future excellence. Nevertheless, to put his perseverance to the proof, I thought best to delay his baptism. At this time a rich and Christian Indian [*un Indio rico y cristiano*], who at my request had received the catechumen into his house, came and said to me: 'Father (*pai*), our wood Indian is in perfect health of body, but is a little astray in mind. He makes no complaints, but says sleep has deserted him: his mother and sister appearing to him every night and saying, "Suffer thyself to be baptized." '

I wonder a little at this, when they knew how fatal baptism had proved in their own case.

'We shall return to take thee when thou dost not expect it.' This vision, he says, takes away his sleep. 'Tell him,' I answered, 'to be of good cheer, for that the melancholy remembrance of his mother and sister is the cause of his dreams, and they, as I think (O Pai Yponá, were you not certain then?), are gone to heaven, and have nothing more to do with this world.

A few days after the same Indian returned, giving the same account. Suspecting there was something in it, I hastened to the house, and found him sitting up in bed. On my asking for his health, he answered, 'I am well and free from pain,' but that he could not sleep, from the vision of his mother and sister telling him to be baptized, and saying they were ready for him. This he told me prevented him from getting any rest. I thought it probable that this was a mere dream, and worthy of neglect. Mindful, however, that dreams have often been Divine admonitions, and oracles of God, as appears from Holy Writ, it seemed advisable in a matter of such moment to consult the security and tranquillity of the catechumen. Being assured of his constancy and of his acquaintance with the chief heads of religion by previous interrogation [*interrogatorios previos*], I soon after baptized him by the name of Luis. This I did on the 23rd of June, the eve of St. John, about the hour of ten in the morning, by the sand clock.

On the evening of the same day, without a symptom of disease or apoplexy, he quietly expired.

This event, a fact well known to the whole town, and which I am ready to attest on oath, astonished every one.

I should have only looked on it as certain to occur after the fateful effects of the previous treatment (and *interrogatorios*) on the mother and sister.

I leave my reader to form his own opinion, but in my own mind I could never deem the circumstance merely accidental. I attributed it to the exceeding compassion of the Almighty that these three Indians were discovered by me in the recesses of the woods; that they so promptly complied with my exhortations to enter my town and embrace Christianity, and that they closed their lives after receiving baptism. The remembrance of my expeditions to the Empalado, though attended by many dangers and hardships, is still most grateful to my heart; insomuch as it proved highly fortunate to the three wood Indians, and advantageous to the Spaniards. These last having been certified by me that no more savages (*sic*) remained, collected many thousand pounds of yerba maté, from which they derived an amazing profit.

This much of the Guaraní town of Tarumá. If on this subject [says our pious author] I appear to have written too much, let the reader be told that I have passed over many remarkable things in silence.

The above history almost seems to show that there were Jesuits and Jesuits even in Paraguay.

Why has their rule, then, called forth such censure, and gained them such an evil reputation? Why have both Catholics and Protestants combined to write them down? It could not be their wealth in Paraguay, for at their expulsion, when all their colleges were ransacked, only a small sum was found. It could not be that the luxurious lives they led excited envy, for the little episode I have commented on is but one of many scattered through the lives of all of them, and recorded in various tongues from Latin to Guaraní. It may be that the viceroys feared an *imperium in imperio* in Paraguay; though how some thousands of such Indians as those who suffered baptism and death in the old priest's story could shake an empire is difficult to understand. It may have been that the Mission priests in Paraguay paid for the sins of Jesuit intriguers at the Courts of Europe. Theology does not, I think, reject vicarious punishment. Certain it is that mention of Paraguay and the Missions never fails to call forth talk of despotism and tyranny, and complaints of Indians turned to mere machines by the too paternal government of the Jesuits. This may have been so. It may have been that their scheme of government would not have satisfied Sir Thomas More, Karl Marx, or Plato. Still, there were then Indians to govern. Where are they now? Where are the thirty towns, the 80,000 or 100,000 inhabitants, the flocks and herds, the domestic cattle ('with wild ones innumerable'), spoken of in the report of the suppression of the Missions, by Buccarelli, Viceroy to Charles the Third?

Where are the well-built churches, and the happy simple folk who worshipped in them, believing all things?

Take horse from Itapua, ride through San Cosme, the Estero-Neembucú, or San Ignacio Miní, and look for Indians, look for churches, look for cattle, or any sign of agriculture; you will find all dead, gone, desolate, deserted, or fallen to ruin. Sleep in the deserted towns, and perhaps, as I did, camping in the plaza of La Trinidad alone, my horse tied to a tuft of grass beside me, you may see a tiger steal in the moonlight out of the deserted church, descend the steps, and glide into the forest.

Azara and Bonpland say that the communistic rule of the Society rendered the Indians thriftless and idle; though this is difficult to reconcile with their further statement that they were well-nigh worked to death. The Indians themselves were not aggrieved at communism; for, in their petition to the Viceroy at the expulsion of the Jesuits, they complain of 'liking not the fashion of living of the Spaniards, in which no man helps the other.' It may have been that the Spanish settlers in Paraguay wanted the Indians to slave for them in their plantations, and that the Jesuits withstood them. But when the ruin of an institution or of an individual is decreed, reasons are never wanting. The Jesuits in Europe may have deserved their fate. In Paraguay, in spite of writers none of whom saw the Missions under their rule, the Jesuits did much good, mixed with some folly, as is incidental to mankind.

If only on the principle that a living dog is of more value than a dead king, the policy of isolation the Jesuits pursued was not a bad one, for it left them at least Indians to govern. Be all this as it may, I have no doubt that many learned men, skilled in the Greek and Latin (but not in Guaraní), have written and will write of the Jesuits in Paraguay, and prove to demonstration that it is fruit for self-congratulation that the Indians of the Missions are free and non-existent. Still, I sometimes wish that I had seen the Missions full of Indians, and stocked with cattle, instead of desolate and fallen into decay. And for the amiable and apostolic priest who told the story of his labours in the Tarumensian wilds, and chronicled in execrable Spanish the discovery, death, and baptism of his three victims, I have only one complaint to make, and that is, that he did not tell us if town life proved fatal to the three little peccaries.

R. B. C. G.

V. A Jesuit

It was, I think, at the little port of the Esquina in Corrientes that he came on board. A priest at first sight, yet not quite similar to other priests, at least to those whose mission is only for mass and meat. A Spaniard, too, at first sight, with the clean-cut features of Old Castille, the bony hands that mark the man of action, and feet as square as boxes. Withal not commonplace, though unassuming, but with a look of that intensity of purpose which many saints have shared with bulldogs. All day the steamer had been running between the myriad islets of the Paraná. Sometimes it seemed impossible she could thread her way between the mass of floating *camalote* which clogged the channel. Now and then the branches of the tall Lapachos and Urundays swept the deck as the vessel hugged the shore. On every side a mass of vegetation, feathery palms, horny mimosas, giant cacti, and all knotted together with lianas like cordage of a ship, stretching from tree to tree. The river, an enormous yellow flood, flowing between high banks of rich alluvial soil ever slipping with a dull splash into the stream. On every side Nature overwhelming man and making him feel his littleness.

Such a scene as Hulderico Schmidel, Alvar Nuñez, or Solis may have gazed on, with the exception that now and then wild horses came into sight and snorted as the steamer passed; or a Gaucho, wilder than the horse he rode, with flowing hair and floating poncho, cantered along the plain where the banks were low, his *pingo* galloping like a piece of clockwork. In the slack water, under the lee of the islands, alligators lay like trunks of trees and basked. In the trees the monkeys and parrots chattered and howled, and *picaflores* flitted from flower to flower; and once between the islands a tiger appeared swimming in pursuit of some *carpinchos*. The air was full of the filmy white filaments like cobwebs which the north wind always brings with it in those countries, and which clung from every rope and piece of rigging, making the steamer look as if she had run through a cotton manufactory. In every cabin mosquitoes hummed and made life miserable.

On board the steamer everything was modern of the modern, but modern seen through a Spanish medium — no door would shut, no bolt would draw, and nothing made to slide would work; engines from Barrow-in-Furness, or from Greenock, but the brass-plate which set forth the place of their manufacture was so covered with patina as to leave the name a matter of conjecture. The captain was from Barcelona, and fully impressed with the importance of his native province and city; the crew, Italians and Spanish Basques; the pilot, a Correntino, equally at home in the saddle or in a schooner, and knowing every turn and bend of the river in the nineteen hundred miles from Buenos Ayres to Cuyabá. The passengers, chiefly Bolivians and Brazilians, hating one another, but indistinguishable to the undiscerning foreigner; an Argentine *tropero*, going to Corrientes; a Spanish merchant or two from Buenos Ayres; the ambulant troop of Italian opera singers, without which no river steamer in South America ever seems to leave a port; a gambler or two in pursuit of their daily avocation; some Paraguayans with innumerable children and servants, and birds in cages, all chattering in Guaraní, like the Christian Indians they are; some English business men, looking as business-like as if in London. On the lower deck a group of Gauchos with their *capataz*. Seated all day long they played at 'Truco' with cards as greasy as bits of hide, and so well marked upon the back that the anxiety of the dealer to conceal their faces seemed a work of supererogation. These were the only passengers who thoroughly enjoyed themselves. Lounging on the deck when tired of playing cards, or when tobacco failed or maté was unprocurable, they talked of horses and scratched their marks upon the deck, to the annoyance of the captain, with the points of their *facones*. Had the voyage endured a month they would not have complained, so long as meal-times came in regular succession and there was room to stretch their *recados* upon the deck at night to sleep. Mosquitoes troubled them not, and though they never seemed to look at anything, not a bend of the stream or a tree, still less a horse, escaped their observation. If there was a guitar procurable, they sang to it for hours in the moonlight, but in such quiet fashion as to disturb no one, least of all themselves. Their songs were chiefly of melancholy love affairs or of the prowess of famous horses. If the first-class passengers danced upon the deck at night, the Gauchos sauntered up and criticised them, as if they had been cattle at a *saladero*.

At the Esquina, the usual mild bustle of a South American riverine port was soon over. The captain of the port, after a full hour's waiting, rode leisurely to the pier, got off his horse, lighted his cigarette, and sauntered to his boat. The Italian boatmen were galvanised into a little life, and stood and grinned, and tried to look as if they were at Naples or at Genoa. After much talking of yellow fever and the perennial revolution, and inquiries if such and such a one had had his throat cut, the passengers surrendered themselves to be cheated by the boatmen and went ashore. As the vessel slid away and the little city baking like a white oven in the sun, with the Argentine flag with its bars of blue and white flapping against the flagstaff, and the horses tied to the *palenque* in front of the houses in the plaza, faded out of sight, our interest centred on the only passenger who had come aboard. Nobody knew him, and he did not seem to be a man of much importance. The stewards, observing that all his luggage consisted of a newspaper which he carried under his arm, turned from him with disdain. The traders and the gamblers saw he was not of them. Even the Gauchos looked a little scornful, and remarked that he was most probably a *maturango*. In their vocabulary *maturango*, meaning a bad rider, is the most contemptuous term of them all. Amongst them, a philosopher who touched his horse with his toe in mounting would have no acceptation. As for the itinerant opera company, even the basso (always the wit of an Italian opera troupe) had nothing to say about him.

Still, after a little time, and as the steamer skirted the city of Corrientes and entered the Paraguay, passing Humaitá with the church a ruin still from the time of the war, and left Curupaity behind her, passing into the regions of dense forests where the Bermejo and the Pilcomayo, after running through the Chaco, fall into the Paraguay, it was clear that the lonely passenger had become a favourite. Why, was not apparent at first sight. Certainly he knew the river better in some respects than the Correntino pilot, and could point out the various places where, in bygone times, such or such a missionary had met his fate by Indian spear or arrow. 'Just between that tuft of palms under the mountain in the distance, Father Julian Lizardi, a Biscayan, received his martyr's crown in 1735 at the hands of the Chiriguanás. Beside his body, pierced with arrows, was found his breviary open at the office for the dead, as if, poor soul, he had been trying to read his own funeral service. *In pace requiescat.* There, where you see the broken tower and ruined walls, the *tapera*, as they call it here in these countries, the Jesuits had a town amongst the Guaycurus. This was before the Philistines prevailed against them, and withdrew them from their work and light from the souls of the poor Indians.'

Thus discoursing and smoking cigarettes perpetually, for the newspaper contained nothing but paper and tobacco, he wound himself into our hearts. The traders swore by him; even the Englishmen, when he said he was a Jesuit, replied that they did not care, he was a damned good fellow, and he smiled, not understanding but seeing they were pleased. The Brazilians in the morning asked for his blessing on the sly, though all freethinkers when talking in the smoking-room. The opera troupe were his devoted slaves, and he used to sit and hear their grievances and settle their quarrels. Even the Gauchos, before they went ashore at Asuncion, chatted familiarly with him, and asked him if he knew the Pope, and told him of the 'deaths they owed,' and wondered if one of them who never was baptized and, therefore, had no saint, could go to heaven; to which he answered : 'Yes, my son, on All Saints' Day.'

We left Asuncion with its towers and houses hidden in orange gardens, and the great palace, in the style of Palladio, by the river's edge. Asuncion, the capital of the viceroyalty of Paraguay — in the Spanish times a territory about as large as Europe, and now a sleepy semi-Indian village, after having endured the three successive tyrannies of Francia and the two Lopez — looks over the Chaco at the great desert, still an unknown wilderness of swamps and forests. Then the river narrows and all traces of civilisation are left behind. Here the Jesuit, for all had now begun to call him nothing else, seemed to brighten up as if he expected something, and his stories of the Jesuits of old times became more frequent. Little by little his own history came out, for he was not communicative, at least about himself. Near the Laguna de los Xarayes it appeared that the Company of Jesus had secretly started a mission amongst the Guasarapos, and he was of it. Never since the days of the Jesuits' glory in America had any missionary been bold enough to make the experiment. Fernandez and Alvar Nuñez, in times past, had written of their fierceness and intractability. Nuflo de Chaves, the bold adventurer, who founded the town of Sta. Cruz de la Sierra, had met his death close to their territory. At long intervals they had been known to come to the mission of El Santo Corazon, or sometimes to wander even as far as that of Reyes in the district of the Moxos, while throughout the region of the upper Paraguay stories of their outrages and murders were rife. In the long hot nights, as the vessel drew near to Corumbá, the passengers would sit and listen to the tales the Jesuit told. Seated in a cane chair, dressed in rusty black, a jipijapa hat, nothing about him priestly but his breviary and *alzacuello*, without an atom of pose, he held us spellbound.

Even the Catalonian captain, nurtured to show his Liberalism by hating priests of all degrees, Catholic and Protestant, grew quite friendly with the 'little crow,' as he called him, and promised to put him ashore as near the mission as he could. 'Mission, Señor Captain! there is no mission, that is, now. I am the mission, that is, all that now remains of it.'

Such was the case, for it appeared that the Indians, either tired of missions or bored by preaching, or because they wished to kill a white man, had risen some months ago and burnt the church and buildings, killed the priests, with the exception of our passenger, and returned to wander in the forests. 'Those who are dead are now in glory,' our Jesuit observed, 'and the Indians will find some other pastors more successful, though none more self-devoted.' Every one on board the steamer protested, and the little man smiled as he informed us that he had escaped and made his way to a settlement, had gone to Buenos Ayres, whence he had telegraphed to Rome for orders, and the one word had come : 'Return.'

Next day, after much protestation from the captain, the steamer stopped at a sort of clearing in the forest, lowered a boat, and the Jesuit went ashore, his newspaper well filled with cigarettes. Stepping ashore, he stood for an instant, a little figure in rusty black, a midget against the giant trees, a speck against the giant vegetation. The steamer puffed and snorted, swung into the stream, the Jesuit waved his hand, took up his newspaper of cigarettes and, as the passengers and crew stood staring at him from the decks and rigging, walked into the forest.

R.B.C.G.

VI. Ras Doura

A funeral in fine weather has always seemed to me much more depressing than on the ordinary wet day which is generally associated with the function. It may be that the very rarity of a fine day in Great Britain makes it seem hard that the principal should be unable to enjoy it. Indeed there is a sort of feeling that the funeral cannot be a real one, in the same way as, on arriving at Naples, or any southern port on a fine day, one never fancies the people can die, or need suffer any hardships in life other than mosquitoes. Especially is this true of Northern Africa, where a violent death seems natural enough to all true believers; but a funeral with mourners, tears and sham tears, black clothes, strong drinks, and all the pomp and circumstance of ignoble woe, seems out of place; and when a Christian dies in Tunis or Morocco, it is as if the mourners were acting a comedy. It is said a funeral has a special attraction for all North Britons. Why this should be so I do not know. Certain it is that in this country a funeral is not an attractive ceremony. However, I suppose no man can ever quite be outside his nation, and I confess to a sort of interest in a funeral myself.

Between Larache and Rabat there is a chain of swampy lakes, haunted by ibises, flamingoes, and herons, and navigated by the natives in bales of bulrushes fastened into a sort of gondola with strips of hide. Just the sort of reedy swamp, with a white miasmatic vapour hanging over it, that used to be depicted in steel engravings in old books of African travels. The head of the chain of lakes is called Ras Doura. All along the lakes are little collections of huts — half village, half encampment — as if the Arabs who inhabit them were haunted with *saudades* (no English word renders the Portuguese *saudade*) of the desert from whence they come, and were afraid to lose their individuality by building in too permanent a fashion. In fact these recollections persist amongst them in a way to us quite unintelligible. Travelling one day between Fez and Tangier, I asked an Arab at an encampment where he and his people came from. 'From the Nile,' he answered. 'That seems far enough to journey,' I rejoined; 'when did you leave it?' Said he, with the air of one who states a commonplace, 'About six hundred years ago.'

All these villages are dreary places, situated on a strip of sandy soil between the Atlantic and the chain of lakes. Beyond the lakes are plains, on which graze horses, camels, goats, and sheep, tended by men who pass a life like that passed in Chaldea and Palestine by the authors of the Bible. In the distance are three sacred white domes, the tombs of saints. In Morocco every district has its saint's tomb, and the traveller asks his way from Sidi this to Sidi that, in the selfsame way as a tramp in rural England steers his course from the 'Chequers' to the 'Bells.' All round the three white tombs is a burial ground; for where a saint is buried your true believer likes to lay his bones. Women resort to them to gossip and to pray, and to implore the saint to grant them children who shall grow up horsemen and good men at spear and gun. Something about your Moorish cemetery appeals to me. Often it is a waste of lentisks, dwarf rhododendrons, and arbutus, with lilies and white cistus interspersed like stars in a half-cloudy night. Seldom there is a wall; and if there is one, it is generally built of *tapia* (sun-dried mud), crumbling, and with many breaches in it. If there is no wall, as is most usual, the cemetery lies open to all passers-by; on some of the graves rough slabs of stone without inscriptions stand up, others are quite flat, and some stuck edgeways in the ground. A goat or two, or a black curly lamb, is always grazing there, and paths in all directions cut it into patterns. It is not the place to ride across in the dark without a shiver, and yet, by a sort of attraction, you are sure to find yourself with a tired horse at night galloping amongst the graves on the outskirts of the town. There is nothing to do on such an occasion but give your horse his head, reflect that those whose graves you ride upon have been bold riders to a man, and trust in Allah.

The little village at Ras Doura looks like a colony of bees. Not that the people work an atom more than just to keep themselves from starving. In all Morocco no man can be found so foolish as to say he likes to work, far less to labour, except under the pressure of hunger or of his superiors. The likeness to a colony of bees is purely esoteric. The huts are circular on a sort of *fond de jupe* of wicker-work with rushes. They finish in a point, just like the beehives in an English cottage garden — I mean the kind before the patent wooden and glass inventions, which I feel quite sure the bees detest, came into vogue. The doors, for the convenience of keeping the huts dry, and for preventing hens, pigs, dogs, and other small mammalia from coming in, are placed about a yard above the ground, and measure but three feet in all in height, so that the spectacle of a fat muslin-swathed sherif struggling to emerge from one of them is comical enough. Round about every beehive stands a hedge of prickly bushes, cut by the women in autumn and left to dry. The Christian should not tie his horse to them or touch them, any more than he should fasten his reins to an area-railing or a knocker in England. In the centre of the village may be found a little square building thatched with reeds, resembling either a boathouse on Virginia Water or a crofter's cottage in Harris or Benbecula. This is the mosque where travellers sleep, and whence the call to prayer arises five times every day. Christians may no more enter it than if it were the Khutubieh at Marakish or Muley Edris at Fez. It is as sacred in its way as either of them. But though so sacred, yet it is homelike as a church in Iceland or in Spain; not that, as far as I know, wayfarers ever sleep in Spanish churches, although they do so to this day in churches in Iceland — of course at night, not at matins or at evensong. No one ever saw a mosque locked up so that the faithful could not enter it. By night and day the doors are open (in Morocco), and it always seems to me, after returning from there, that the Christian church with its padlock and its door seems churlish in comparison. Surely to the true believer, Christian or Mohammedan, the door of the sanctuary never should be closed.

Over the village rests an air of listless self-content — content that comes from the sun and the possession of a horse or two, tempered only by fleas, and the thought that the Basha may be expected at any moment. Yellow ulcerous dogs, that shrink before the stick descends, may be seen on every side, thin cows and mangy camels, and before the house almost certainly a horse, tied to a post as on the Pampas, blinking in the sun, with a high red saddle and a long gun hanging from the pommel. No inhabitant is much richer than his fellow, except perhaps the omnipresent sherif, without whose presence no village is complete. If all sherifs descend from Mohammed, his family must have been as reproductive as the families of the Norman knights who fought at Hastings, from whom all self-respecting Englishmen claim their descent. Still they fulfil a function in Morocco, being a sort of Levite class, in whom is vested the traditions of the race.

There is poverty, of course, in every Arab village, and plenty of it; but not the poverty we know in Europe, and which we talk about and ponder on, and use for purposes of politics or religion, and by means of which we think to save our souls. Often no one has enough to eat, but no one dies of hunger. The race, in spite of want of food, is famous for beauty; the men are active, tall, and strong, the women almond-eyed and swaying in their walk like 'oleanders by the water-courses when the south wind blows.' Marriage to an Arab villager is the key to the position. If he is married enough, his path is easy. One wife is poverty — only one pair of hands to work for you; two wives, a little better; three, respectability; four, the happy consummation arrived at when a man does nothing but mount his horse at evening time and canter to the saint's tomb, to chat and pray, join in the 'powder play,' or, better still, sit in his garden thinking of nothing. Women, of course, have rights according to the Koran, but of a different nature to those dreamed of by women who claim such things in England. Each class of right is, no doubt, the best for the country it arose in.

There is nothing in life to make existence either lively or unbearable in the village at Ras Doura. Hardly any politics, no news, but little scandal, no promiscuous visiting, as no one, not the Sultan himself, can enter any other person's house without his leave. Nothing but stealing women and horses, with gazelle-hunting and bustard-shooting, in the way of field-sports; and for their mental exercise, the practice, in all its details, of their religion. Strange as it may appear, in Morocco, and generally in the East, no ridicule attaches to the practice of one's faith. That which a man believes, he is not ashamed to do, even in public. Middle-aged men with beards dyed red with henna fall down and pray in public, and no one thinks them mad. They rise and talk of bullocks and of horses, of money and of women, the moment after, and no one thinks them hypocrites. In fact it is the fashion (just as in London or in Paris at the present time) to be religious. Your irreligious man, who does not pray at proper hours, omits to say Inshallah when he speaks of future things, who does not wash when washing is prescribed, and eats in Ramazan, is looked on as a *bourgeois*.

Still, even in Ras Doura, life has some excitements. At times the Zimouris issue from the forest of Mamora and drive off cattle in the night and carry away the girls. Then all the young men get to horse, and gallop to and fro, firing their guns, and swearing what they intend to do. Sometimes, of course, if the Zimouri *razzia* is a small one, they get their cattle or horses back, the girls more rarely; but in general, as when a cry of 'Stop thief!' echoes down a street, each passer-by is eager to repeat it, but leaves the thief alone. At other times the fighting is serious enough, and the fighters fight the better as they know the vanquished will receive no quarter.

Occasionally a Sultan dies, and then ensues a pleasant time of anarchy, in which, if you be young and own a horse and gun, you sally forth and join yourself to others of the proper sort, and slay, burn, ravish, and steal horses, in the selfsame way as these pastimes are so graphically described in the Old Testament. Then, too, there are the feasts, as the Mulud, the birthday of Mohammed, which corresponds to our Nativity. Close to Ras Doura is held the feast of Muley Busalham, the patron of the riders. There, mounted on their best, their *creditos*, as the Gauchos of the Pampas say, seated on saddles of white and green and eau de Nil coffee, with orange-coloured silks, with *haiks* and *selhams* flying in the air, the horsemen for miles around are trysted to 'play powder.' The 'powder play' (Lab el Barod) is the great diversion of all Eastern horsemen. Europeans think it foolish because they seldom try it themselves. In the same way, no doubt, a Maroqui would think a game of polo quite beneath contempt. To 'play the powder' on a fresh horse, amongst a mob of horsemen, on rough ground, to stand in the saddle and twist a heavy silver-mounted gun about one's head, wants practice. Only theologians are as intolerant as horsemen: 'no one can be saved but professors of my faith, but members of my church; and even of my church but few are certain of salvation.' In the same way, no men can ride but Mexicans, Australians, Cossacks, Englishmen, Arabs, Hungarians, and Gauchos, and if you belong to any of those peoples, few but you yourself have ever really mastered the higher branches of the mystery. Then comes along a blue-eyed, flaxen-haired native of Iceland, on his little pony, and flies across a field of jagged lava, and leaves you sore amazed; and so, perhaps, in the spiritual field, a man of no profession of faith, who never learnt a creed or a catechism, may enter paradise when clergymen lie howling.

Seated in my tent outside the village, watching the horses feed, and wondering if, after all, it was really worth while ever to return to England, I heard a wail. Like the Celtic *coronach* the Arab wail is something outside humanity. No jackal or coyote can produce a sound more dismal. It makes you sad at once, and yet sadness must be a kind of mental convention after all, for both the *coronach* and the Arab cry are just as doleful when they issue from the lips of a professional mourner. Fancy a mute at a funeral impressing one with sadness, or inducing thoughts of anything but gin and water. At the door of a little hut appeared a woman scarcely veiled, her hair streaming like a pony's tail. After her another, and then a group of children, all raising the same doleful cry. Then from the other beehives and huts came groups of women, to comfort and to wail in concert; in the midst the widow, with tears running down her cheeks, and striking her nails into her arms and breast. The night before a horse had fallen on her husband and killed him. The sorrow that is dumb is not for Arabs; the reserve of power we hear so much of, and which makes our grief, our joy, our eloquence, our acting seem so unreal to all except ourselves, is not for those who see the sun. 'Eyes of my soul, how lightly didst thou ride over the desert. True was thy aim at the enemies of the Prophet. Generous thou wast and noble. Protector of the poor, stay of the childless, father of the downtrodden. How shall I forget thee, life of my life!' Most likely the horseman had never ridden except to market on a stumbling, spavined horse, or fired a shot except at wild duck in his life; and as to being generous or noble, these are but merely terms of comparison. Still, in an epitaph (in Latin, so that the common people may not read it), even in England, you occasionally see apocryphal virtues set forth. Be that as it may, the tears, the grief, the utter self-annihilation were as touching as if the tears had filtered through a cambric, hemstitched pocket-handkerchief.

Burial in Morocco follows hard upon the heels of death. The climate makes waiting impossible, and as a coffin is seldom or never used, there is no reason for delay. Wrapped in a clean white *haik*, strapped to a board, the feet sticking out stiffly in the pathetic and half-comic way that dead feet have, the dead man's body was brought to his own door. Before the tent a flea-bitten old grey mare with a little foal was feeding. A ragged boy, with a piece of camel's-hair rope, went up and caught and saddled her, and then the body was strapped upon her back face upwards, the foal watching the proceedings most intently. The burst of lamentation broke out louder than before, the wife appearing distraught with grief, the children standing stupid with the effect of weeping. The women led the widow to the house, the men formed in procession, with one leading the mare in front.

They passed along the lakes, waded a stream, a horseman every now and then firing a shot, the mare looking round anxiously. As they rode across the hill and vanished out of sight, the little foal whinnied and galloped after them, an unconscious mourner.

R.B.C.G.

VII. El Babor

At times in the East, the horror of the West, with all its factories, its hurry and its smoke, its frauds and charities, and life rendered so complex with infinities of nothingnesses, falls out of recollection at the actual horror of what is present. Before one's eyes appear the mud, the dust, the heaps of garbage rotting in the sun; the scrofulous, the leprous folk seem, with the halt and maimed, to comprise mankind. The fleas, the lice, the dirt, the stench seem to be all-devouring. The ulcerous yellow dogs, who shrink away before the stick is even raised, give one a feeling of repulsion. On every side appears injustice, not alone the injustice that is coeval with life itself, but absolute injustice crying in the streets — no man regarding it; even perhaps applauding.

Then the thought arises if machinery were introduced things might amend. At least the wretched mules and donkeys might find their hell a little cooler. The camels might perhaps suffer less rope-galls, and generally resemble a little less decayed hair trunks; the women turning the stones to crush the corn be not so old at twenty, and when one was taken the other not so much inclined to cry, 'Why was I left to suffer?' At times one thinks so in despair, when the flies rise in their myriads from a dead horse or camel, and settle in the corners of the beggars' eyes, on the scald-heads of the children, or on the sores in the horses' backs. Then comes a vision of a neat steam-mill, with corrugated iron roof, and greasy honest engineer with a handful of cotton waste, wiping his face. His wife with figure like a yard of water, lank and elliptic in her cotton gown; the children with their flaxen heads, rude manners, and dirty noses; even the house with its furniture of two-carat mahogany, and ponderous Bible, falsely called a polyglot (always wide open for advertisement), become almost agreeable by comparison. Even at times when jogging across the sands, or ploughing through the mud, a railway with its dust and clatter, clinker in your eye, lost luggage, insolent ticket clerks, and offal sandwich at the so-called refreshment-room, appears a thing to be desired.

Thus moralising (and physical fatigue conduces to philosophy), it seems to stand to reason that if a man can do in a day that which it takes a horse three days, a camel a week, to do, that something, as well as time, is saved. Then comes the totting up of the pros and cons, the balancing of conjectures, so dear to fools and public men, one with another. If in one province grain is rotting in the fields and in another is worth five dollars the almud, and folk are starving, and yet the superfluity cannot repair the famine for cost of carriage, the railway would be a blessing. Let us, then, introduce it; let us have the switchback too, the bicycle, and turnip dibble, and all will prosper. What a reformer even the most conservative of Westerns is in the East, or anywhere, in fact, away from home! Not that in the East there is not much to reform, both in the temporal and the spiritual domain.

Mohammed, when he walked behind his camels, looking, no doubt, not very much unlike other Mohammeds of his and of our own time, and thinking of the time when somebody besides Ayesha would believe in him, never thought of saints or saints' tombs. Yet from Mecca to Agadhir, from Cairo to Candahar, the land is full of them. Perhaps the worship of St. Peter's, Eaton Square, might not seem ideal to the Syrian hegemonist. However, be that as it may, the name Mohammed is borne today by full three Arabs out of five. Where but in Spain do you find a Christian called Jesus? Familiarity, you say, ensures contempt. It may be so, but when the founder of a faith is not for ever in the faithful's mind or on his lips, the faith begins to languish. The real test of all religions is the material condition of the faithful. So, perhaps, Mohammed might just as well have driven his camels to the end, and never troubled himself about humanity. Idols are so consoling to the world.

Material condition of the faithful. What a base view! Is not the assurance that all mankind is damned except oneself and brother fetish worshipper enough? Well, that I leave to true believers, Mohammedan or otherwise. The difference between the kind who fardels bear and grunt and sweat under the burden of their lives appears to be a difference only of degree, whether the prophet is of Mecca or Jerusalem. If we in England shoot, when in the mood, a miner or two to encourage industry, in Morocco the Sultan eats up a whole village. The Christian works long hours, and is a bondsman to his trade, the Moor can never call his life his own; and so they ripe and rot respectively.

After a long day's march nothing is more impressive than suddenly to see the town you have begun to think is nonexistent appear before you.

Up it rises on a rocky hill, or on a cliff over the sea, like a town in the pages of a missal. On every side a waste of sand, a sea of grass, or wilderness of forest, and the town a thing apart, mysterious and wall-girt. Most Arab towns have a generic look to Western eyes, as I suppose Chemnitz and Blackpool would seem alike to Arabs. No blending of sky and houses, no cloud of smoke, no distant murmur, scarcely an indication that a town is near. Only the tracks which form the roads get broken and zigzag, in and out, like points at Clapham Junction; donkeys and camels wander about looking for grass or orange-peel, dogs, and more dogs, and then the road leads through the gardens.

A garden in the East is not exclusively a place for flowers, nor yet for slugs and gardeners, gravel and mowing-machines, but generally a sort of unkempt paradise, hedged in with aloes. An unkempt paradise of palms and orange-trees, figs and pomegranates, patches of canes all waving in the air like dulse in the slack-water on a beach, grass studded with lilies, clover, and narcissus, a *noria** in the middle, and at the entrance two inconsequent white gate-posts, with a broken bullock cart to serve as gate. Everywhere a sound of water running in little channels of cement. Still a garden, according to the Eastern tastes, and pleasant to come to of an evening, ambling on one's mule, and sit with a Koran open before one and not to read it, but doze till the hour of prayer.

Then the town with its walls and battlements, on which the chattering storks are sentinels, the steep approach, and the gate with its horseshoe arch — the whole standing against the sky as if cut out of cardboard. The embrasures for cannon in the walls grow green with moss and over-grown with lentisks, palmitos, and white alyssum, and through which peer carronades left by the Spaniards or the Portuguese in the times of their glory, with snakes carved round the touch-holes, and the legend, 'Viva España. Soy de un Dueño', and the date of the reign of the Catholic King of the time of their manufacture. The fortifications built by some Spanish Vauban of those days, with many bastions and ravelines and counterscarps and other marvels of the art, now become obsolete, and with the angles of the walls sharp as the bow of a torpedo-boat. All around, the moat now dry, and turned into a garden for cabbages,

---

Noria is the Arabic *hansah*, the wheel with earthenware jars on it, which, turned by a camel, woman, bullock, or donkey, brings up water in sufficient quantity for Spanish or Eastern wants.

pimientos, and berengenas*, though in its time a defence for the town against the infidel, as in the days when Don Sebastian's army took refuge in it after the battle at Alcazar el Kebir. Inside, the usual Arab streets, slippery with filth, strewn with intestines of sheep and fowls, with rotten eggs and fruit, and set with pebbles fitter to pave hell with than all the good intentions forgotten since the Deluge. Crowds of men in dusky white, with hoods like Capuchins. Merchants in little stalls, sitting, like josses in a temple, at the receipt of custom and never finding any, and yet just as contented as if they dealt in thousands. Men jostling past as if the fate of empires depended on their reaching the beach with their load of refuse in a given time. Camels pass by swaying like vessels at an anchorage. Blind men, lepers, and madmen, whom we seclude in madhouses (and parliaments) ostensibly to do them good, but really to spare our feelings the shock of seeing how little difference there is between us, roam the streets or sit serenely in the sun, hunting for lice. A square arcaded plaza where corn is sold, and where soft soap, oranges, and spices, and the futile things which form the staple of the commerce of the East, change hands. Houses white and red and chocolate, pale yellow, and light blue, with doors hermetically sealed, and of which the master carries the key (eight inches long) stuck in his waistband when he sallies forth to cheat or pray, give an air of unreality to everything. Under the arches, the merchant cheats his customer with false weights, and the customer imposes (when he can) bad copper money on the merchant by the sackful. All passes in full light of day, and neither is ashamed.

The mosque towers, slender like stalks of cat mace, rise into the clear sky. The Marsa (port) at which barges unload and towards which a stream of laden donkeys is always staggering, and where a sallow Maltese or Gibraltarian (Consul for all the nations under heaven) lounges and ticks off nothings in a note-book; then a tidal river with a bar harbour, where the ribs and keels of ships which once were pirate galleys from Sallee lie bleaching. An Arab town, in fact, just like another, with all its horrors to the ear and nose, and beauty to the eyes, but with a notable exception. Just outside the walls an open space of sand, where caravans have camped for centuries, a mangy plot of grass or two, on which women sell firewood, and where grave men walk up and down holding

---

*Berengena is the egg plant. It has always been a favourite vegetable with the Moors. Before the expulsion of the Moriscos from Spain, it was a saying in reference to the abundance of anything, 'As plentiful as *berengenas* in a Morisco's garden.'

each other's hands like little children. On one side a height looking down on a shipless sea, defended by a battery, in which the cannon lie rusty amongst the ruins of their carriages; and on the other side the notable exception. Hard by a little grove of fig-trees, an enterprising Spaniard has started a corn-mill, in its neat tin shed with corrugated iron roof, as hideous as if in England or Massachusetts. All day long the wheezy high (or low) pressure engine puffs, and sends a jet of steam into the air. It is the *babor*, such being the way the Spanish word '*vapor*' issues from Arab lips. As it puffs and wheezes the sun seems to die out, and an air of Hartlepool or Greenock overspreads the place. Like the creature Burns saw on the lady's bonnet in church, it fixes the attention upon itself — Arabs, camels, women in their shroud-like robes, Jewesses with unstable busts and hair like horses'-tails, dressed in the crudest of crude colours, and still not without attraction, grave riders on their fiery horses, with pasterns dyed with henna, pass and one does not see them. As in an exhibition, the Whistlers, Sargents, Laverys and Guthries pass unperceived, and one cannot tear oneself away from some outrage by a Royal Academician.

Machinery of every kind is awe-inspiring to the Oriental mind, from a watch to a phonograph all is 'Shaitanieh,' a devil's trick, a thing past comprehension. Even to some of us not born Orientals, the way a key turns in a lock, or how the sucker in a pump raises the water, is a thing which, like faith or baptism, we take on trust from our elders without inquiry. I remember (here 'I enter on the scene in person') talking with some Arabs of the villainy of governments, — the staple topic of conversation in lands where no one is so foolish as to think his rulers love him. A man took up his parable and said, 'In Algeria, I believe, the Government does really love the people.' All were incredulous, myself among the rest, or more than all the rest. 'I happened to be in Constantine,' he said, 'at the fête of the Republic.' How is it in a Republic they have no Sultan? . . .'On the first day there were the races, horses ran fleeter than gazelles, and on them were seated little English devil-boys, ugly as Ginûn, and dressed in parti-coloured clothes. In the evening there were fireworks, then a ballet, at which 200 Christian girls, each one well worth 500 dollars, danced with hardly any clothes on. Next day was best of all, for early in the morning the soldiers brought a man out into the public square, and then before us all they cut his head off with a machine.' I agreed that French philanthropy could go no further.

All things must begin slowly, and if a railway or a steam merry-go-round were not attainable, a corn-mill (or guillotine) was at least a step towards progress.

The owner of the mill, a Catalan from Reus, stood at the door. The kind of man able and willing to drive a nail into a wall with his head, or draw it with his teeth. His costume neat and civilised; trousers of bed-ticking, a dirty shirt held up at the wrist with elastic bands, a necktie with a pin of malachite, a greasy *boina** upon his head, and *alpargatas*† on his naked feet. Spitting through his teeth he said in the sweet dialect of Catalonia (I omit his garnishing): 'The Arabs are a lazy lot, liars and shirkers from their birth, and thievish as the mother of the devils. Here in this miserable place' (he came from Reus) 'I try to show the sons of dogs the way to progress and to civilisation. Mother of God! you would scarcely credit it, I cannot get the swine to work more than six hours a day. In Catalonia every man works twelve at least, and women work fourteen.' I ventured to remark that the climates were different, and the people, and then insinuated, 'Surely you make a lot of money?' 'Money, Barajo, not more than 7 per cent upon my capital, and what is that to live among such heathens?' Resignedly I looked into the mill.

The day was hot, the temperature some 90 in the shade. Inside the mill, in a cloud of flour and dust, sweat trickling down their naked shoulders, I saw some Arabs hurrying about feeding the hoppers and carrying sacks of flour. They told me (also with garnishing) that the Catalonian had advanced them money or they would not work another minute: capital and labour. 'Hurry,' they said, 'was made for devils in hell and not for men and true believers, and here we hurry all the time.' 'Only six hours a day, my friends,' I said, 'and Christians work ten hours and twelve, and pass their lives dreaming of an illusive eight-hours day.' 'Christians are sons of " ———— " ' — well, the word was not a pleasing one — 'little it matters to us how long they work, if they are fools enough.' 'Look, too,' I ventured, 'how fine the flour is ground, how quickly and how cleanly.' They answered, 'We eat none of it; before this mill was built sometimes we worked all day, but then we stopped at intervals and talked and smoked, and even slept; now all is changed, and this cursed "Babor" is our master, and while the wheels turn round we stand and minister.' 'Minister' was good, but still, if the men spoke truth, perhaps there is a

---

*Boina is the Basque cap.

†*Alpargatas* are sandals made of canvas, with hemp soles.

glory of the sun, another of the snow. It may be that a *haik* looks ugly patched with broadcloth. Not to generalise too much, and not forgetting that in Morocco there are no Factory Acts, no County Council, and no busybodies who, leaving their own affairs to ruin, rove like Don Quixote about the land to smooth out other people's wrinkles, still the first essay I saw of bringing Western methods to the East was not too reassuring.

R.B.C.G.

VIII. The Horses Of The Pampas

An Argentine friend of mine (old style) wrote to me the other day from Paris:-

> I know you will think me a barbarian [I did not], but this Paris, this exhibition, this hurrying to and fro, this Eiffel Tower which I had to go up, have bored me dreadfully.
>
> Strange, too, that on the Pampas, as I read Daudet, the Goncourts, and Zola, it seemed so interesting to me. Now, I would give it all for an hour's gallop in my own country.

It was perhaps this letter (on which my friend, to show his contempt of our civilisation, had affixed no stamp) that set me thinking of horses in general and of the horses of the Pampas in particular.

Thus thinking, the thoughts of the Eight Hours Bill on which you asked me to write became vaguer and dimmer. Therefore (a Scotchman must have his therefore) I send you these rambling and incoherent reminiscences of a life I have lived, of men I have known, and of horses that have been to me what horses never can be to a man who surveys them through the eyes of his stud groom.

Short-tailed, long-tailed, in cart or carriage, ridden by 'Arry or by Lord Henry, the horse of Europe (excepting always the coster's pony) delights me not, or very little. He seems to me a species of property, a sort of investment for capital, precarious sometimes, an unsatisfactory one too often.

Is he ill, his malady must be ministered to in the shape of beer to his groom; does he die, my equine investment is lost; I must try another.

On the Pampas it is different. He is part of me, I live on him, and with him; he forms my chiefest subject of conversation, he is my best friend, more constant far than man, and far exceeding woman.

What wonder, therefore, that my friend's letter brought back to me the broad plains, the countless herds of horses, the wild life, the camp fire, the thousand accidents that make life alike so fascinating and so fatiguing in the desert.

Most people know that there are great plains called Pampas. Books of travel more or less authentic have informed them that these are roamed over by countless herds of horses.

As to what these horses are like, where they come from, and if there are any special peculiarities that distinguish them from other horses, few have inquired.

It seems to me that there are certain differences between the horses of Spanish America and the horses of any other country.

That they should more or less resemble those of the south of Spain, from whence they came, is nothing to be wondered at. That special conditions of food, climate, and surroundings should have produced a special type, is nothing extraordinary.

What, then, are the general characteristics of these horses?

That which specially attracts the attention of all those who see them for the first time is the great differenwce to be observed betwixt them when in motion and at rest. Saddled with the *recado*, the American adaptation of the Moorish *enjalma*; the heavy bed on horseback, with its semi-Moorish trappings; standing patiently before the door of some Gaucho's house from morn till sunset, they appear the most indolent of the equine race. But let the owner of the house approach with his waving poncho, his ringing spurs, his heavy hide and silver-mounted whip, and his long, flying black hair; let him by that mysterious process, seemingly an action of the will, and known only to the Gaucho, transfer himself to their backs, without apparent physical exertion, and all is changed. The dull, blinking animal wakes into life, and in a few minutes his slow gallop, regular as clockwork, has made him and his half-savage rider a mere speck upon the horizon.

In a country where a good horse costs a Spanish ounce (£3:15s.) it is not wonderful that all can ride, and all ride well. In a country where if you see a man upon a plain, you are always certain that it will be a man on horseback; in a country where the great stock-owners count their *caballadas* by the thousand (Urquiza, the tyrant of Entre Rios, had about 180,000 horses), it is to be supposed that much equine lore, 'hoss sense' the Texans call it, has grown up. It is to be looked for that a special style of riding has arisen, as that what we in Europe think strange is there regarded as an ordinary occurrence of every-day life.

It would indeed be as impossible to measure the Pampas horse by the standard of an English horse as to measure a Gaucho by the standard of an ordinary city man. Each man and each animal must be estimated according to the work he is required to do. Putting aside cart horses and those employed in heavy draught, almost every horse in England, except the cab horse, is an object of luxury. He has a man to look after him, is fed regularly, is never called on to endure great fatigue, carry much weight, still less to resist the inclemency of the weather. He is valued for his speed, for his docility, or merely for his pecuniary value in the market. In the Pampas none of these things is of prime importance. We do not require great speed from our horses, we care nothing as to their docility, and their pecuniary value is small. What we do look for is endurance, easy paces, sobriety, and power of withstanding hunger and thirst. A horse that will carry a heavy man seventy miles is a good horse, one that can do ninety miles with the same weight is a better horse, and if he can repeat the performance two or three days in succession, he is the best, no matter if he be piebald, skewbald, one-eyed, cow-houghed, oyster-footed, or has as many blemishes as Petruchio's own mustang.

Talking with some Gauchos, seated on the gravel, one starlit night, before a fire of bones and dried thistles, the conversation fell as usual upon horses. After much of the respective merits of English and Argentine horses, after many of the legends as closely trenching on the supernatural as is befitting the dignity of horsemen in all countries, an ancient, shrivelled Gaucho turned to me with, 'How often do you feed your horses, Don Roberto, in England? Every day?' Thereupon, on being answered, he said, with the mingled sensitiveness and fatuity of the mixed race of Spanish and Indian, 'God knows, the Argentine horse is a good horse, the second day without food or water, and if not He, why then the devil, for he is very old.' In all countries the intelligent are aware that you cannot estimate a horse's goodness by his stature. The average stature of the Pampas horse is about 14½ hands — what we should call a pony in England. In his case, however, his length of loin, his lean neck, and relatively immense stride, show that it is no pony we have to deal with, but a horse, of low stature if you will, but one that wants a man to ride him.

Intelligent and fiery eyes, clean legs, round feet, and well-set sloping shoulders, long pasterns, and silky manes and tails, form the best points of the Pampas horse. His defects are generally slack loins and heavy head, not the 'coarse' head of the underbred horse of Europe, but one curiously developed that may or may not be, as Darwin says it is, the result of having to exert more mental effort than the horse of civilisation.

Of his colour, variable is he; brown, black, bay, chestnut, piebald, and gray, making a kaleidoscopic picture as on the dusky plains or through the green *monte* (wood) a herd of them flash past, with waving tails and manes, pursued by Gauchos as wild and fiery-eyed as they. As on the steppes of Russia, the plains of Queensland and Arabia, the trot is unknown. To cross a Pampa loaded with the necessaries of desert life, without a path to follow, it would be a useless pace. The slow gallop and the jogtrot, the Paso Castellano of the Spaniards, the Rhakran of the Turks, is the usual pace. The pacer of the North American, the ambler of the Middle Ages, is in little esteem upon the Pampas. You spur him, he does not bound; he is a bad swimmer. As the Gaucho says, 'He is useless for the lazo, though perhaps he may do for an Englishman to ride.' 'Manso como para un Ingles' (tame enough for an Englishman to ride) is a saying in the Argentine Republic.

Where did these horses come from, from whence their special powers of endurance? How did these special paces first characterise them, and how is it that so many of the superstitions connected with them are also to be found amongst the Arabs? My answer is unhesitatingly, From the Arabs. All the characteristics of the Arabs are to be observed in the Argentine horses; the bit used is that of Turkey and Morocco, the saddle is a modification of the Oriental one, and the horses, I think, are in like manner descended from those in Barbary.

It is pretty generally known that the conquest of America was rendered much easier to the Spaniards by the fact that they possessed horses, and the natives had never seen them.

Great, well-watered, grassy plains, a fine climate, and an almost entire absence of wild beasts — what wonder, therefore, that the progeny of the Spanish cavalry horses has extended itself (in the same way as did the horses turned loose at the siege of Azov in the sixteenth century on the steppes of Russia) all over the Pampas, from the semi-tropical plains of Tucuman and Rioja right down to the Straits of Magellan? Spanish writers tell us that Cordoba was the place from which the conquerors of America took most of their horses. To ride like a Cordobese was in the Middle Ages a saying in Spain, and such it has remained unto this day. Cervantes makes one of his characters say 'he could ride as well as the best Cordobese or Mexican,' proving the enormous increase of horses in the New World even in his time, not much more than a hundred years after the Conquest. In the plains of Cordoba, to this day, large quantities of horses are bred, but of a very different stamp from their descendants of the Pampas. Whence then did the original stock come from? Cordoba was the richest of the Moorish kingdoms of Spain in the thirteenth century. It was directly in communication with Damascus. Thus there is little doubt that the Cordobese horses were greatly improved by the introduction of the Arab blood. However, Damascus was a long way off, and the journey a difficult and a dangerous one. It therefore seems more probable to me that the most of the Cordobese horses came over from Barbary. A remarkable physical fact would seem to bear out my belief. Most horses, in fact almost all breeds of horses, have six lumbar vertebræ. A most careful observer, the late Edward Losson, a professor in the Agricultural College of Santa Catalina near Buenos Ayres, has noted the remarkable fact that the horses of the Pampas have only five. Following up his researches, he has found that the only other breed of horses in which a similar peculiarity is to be found is that of Barbary.

Taking into consideration the extreme nearness of the territories of Andalusia and Barbary, and the constant communication that in Mahommedan times must have existed between them, I am of opinion that the horses of the Pampas are evidently descended from those of Barbary.

It is not within my knowledge to state whether a similar configuration is to be observed in the Cordobese horses of to-day. But this is a point very easily cleared up.

The genet, too (the progeny of the ass and horse), has the same number of vertebrae. Is it impossible that in former times the union of an African mare and a genet may have produced the race of Berber horses which were taken by the Moors to Spain, and thence to the Pampas? The genet and the mule are not characterised by the same infecundity. During the last fifty years, in the south of France, many cases have been observed of the reproductiveness of the former animal.

The following story may serve to show that the idea of a mixed race of horses and asses that were not mules has been considered by the Arabs from the remotest ages as possible.

In the Western Soudan there are three celebrated breeds of horses, according to the Emir Abd-el-Kader — the Hâymour breed, the Boughareb, and the Meizque. Of these, the Hâymour breed is considered the best, and possesses many of the same qualities that are so striking in the horses of the Pampas — speed, bottom, and robustness. The Emir says that it is not uncommon for them to perform a journey of 130 kilometres in 24 hours. I myself have frequently ridden horses of the

Pampas 90 miles, and on one occasion 103 miles, in the same time.

The origin of the Hâymour breed is thus related. An Arab chief was obliged to leave a wounded mare in a small oasis, where there was grass and water, but near which no tribes ever passed. About a year afterwards, happening whilst hunting to pass the oasis, he saw his mare, well, and about to foal. Having taken her to the tents, her foal proved of singular excellence, and became the mother of a famous desert stock. The Arabs, knowing that no horses ever passed there (the wild horse is unknown in these deserts), believed that the foal was the progeny of a wild ass, Hamar-el-omâkheh, and to the foal they gave the name of Hâymour, the foal of the wild ass or onagar.

Be this as it may, whether Pegasus or an onagar was the progenitor of the horses of the Pampas, the fact remains that they are renowned for the rare qualities that made the horse of Barbary famous in the Middle Ages. Nothing more enjoyable on a frosty morning than to career over the plain, hunting ostriches on a good horse; nothing more fascinating (at twenty-two) than to rattle along behind a good tropilla of ten or twelve horses, following their mare with tinkling brass bell. Then indeed, with silver-mounted saddle and toes just touching the heavy silver stirrups (the Gaucho rides long and never puts his feet home into the stirrups, for fear of sudden fall), you bound along over the grassy seas, and cover perhaps 100 or 120 miles a day.

It is not only necessary in La Plata to ride well; a man must always fall well, that is, on his feet. Standing once watching the always interesting spectacle of a *domador** on horseback, with bare head and red silk handkerchief laid turbanwise round it, struggling with a violent colt, I rashly remarked that he rode well. 'Yes, he sits well,' was the answer; 'let us see how he falls.' Fall he did, after one or two more plunges, and his horse, a blue and white (*azulejo*) colt, on the top of him. The colt, after a struggle or two, regained its feet; the man never stirred again. His epitaph was, 'What a pity he did not know how to fall!' 'But, after all,' remarked a bystander, 'he must have died *de puro delicado*' (of very delicateness), so incredible did it seem that a man could have been fool enough to let a horse fall on him. The same superstitions exist amongst the Arabs and the Gauchos as to horses and their colours. Thus, the horse with a white fore and white hind foot is sure to be fast. The Gauchos say he is crossed, *cruzado*, and that accounts for it. In the same way the Arabs say he is sure

*Horse-breaker.

to be lucky. Both peoples unite in praising the dark chestnut. 'Alazan tostado, mas bien muerto que cansado,' says the proverb. The Arabs have a similar one. Both unite in distrusting a light chestnut with a white tail and mane. 'He is for Jews,' say the Arabs. The Gauchos also assign him to an unlucky caste. 'Caballo ruano para las putas.' A dun horse, unless he have a black tail and mane and red eyes, can never be good. Only a madman would ride a horse of any colour that had a white ring round its fetlock. It is unlucky. In peace it will stumble, in war fail you. Greys will not stand the sun. The roan is slow. One striking difference though. The Arab dislikes the piebald. 'He is own brother to the cow.' The Gaucho esteems him highly. The object in life of a rich Gaucho is to have a tropilla of piebalds. The author of 'El Fausto,' a well-known Gaucho poem, makes his hero ride a piebald.

Like the Arab, the Gaucho uses long reins open at the end, to hold a horse by if he is thrown. Like the Arab, he rides upright in the saddle. Like him, too, he stands at the horse's head to mount, looking towards its tail, and catching the saddle by the pommel, instead of the cantel, like Europeans and Australians, and throws himself at one motion into the saddle without pausing in the stirrup, his horse in the meantime going on, for no one has his horse held in the Pampas from one end of the 900 miles of territory from Buenos Ayres to the Andes. From the frontier of Bolivia to Patagonia you will never find a man with the heavy hands so common in Europe. This I attribute partly to the severe bit and partly to the fashion of never passing the reins through the fingers, but holding them in the hollow of the hand, which is carried rather high with the elbow turned down, and not at right angles to the body, as with us. The Arab habit of mounting on the off side has been dropped by the Gaucho, but it is practised both by the Indians of the Pampas and those of the prairies of North America. I had once to mount an Indian's horse. It proved unmanageable till the owner called out in bad Spanish, 'Christian frightening horse, he mount quiet on Indian side.' In the Pampas he who is not an Indian is a Christian.

Any details, even as incomplete and rambling as are these, about the Gauchos and their horses will soon be valuable. This race of tender-hearted, hospitable, nomad creatures is passing away. I shall regret them. I shall remember the Gaucho sailing over the Pampas, his eye fixed apparently on nothing, yet seeing everything. I shall remember him in his quaint costume at the great cattle brandings, see him catch the ostrich with the bolas, and never forget him in his most characteristic action, viz. when twenty-eight or thirty of them, proceeding to their respective horses, seem like drops of water to have incorporated themselves with the horses, without noise and without effort, and then, without the clatter that characterises all European equestrian performers, take wing as it were a flight of swallows. Often during the babble of the House of Commons, when in the hot summer nights we are hard at work substituting the word 'and' for the word 'but,' and leaving out all the words from 'whereinsoever' down to 'which in so after' in some senseless Bill, I shall think with regret of the seven wild horses and the stubborn mules which I have so frequently seen harnessed to a diligence.

The strange, wild customs, soon to be forgotten; the old-world life, so soon to fade away. Impressed as lines upon a picture in my memory remain the Gaucho wakes, in which the company, to light of tallow dips and the music of a cracked guitar, through the long summer nights danced round the body of some child to celebrate his entry into Paradise.

The races at the Pulperia, the fights with the long-bladed knives for honour and a quart of wine, the long-drawn melancholy songs of the Payadores, the Gaucho improvisatores, ending in a prolonged Ay — celebrating the deeds and prowess of some hero of the Independence wars — these things, these ways will disappear. Gaucho and horse, Indian with feathered lance, will go, and hideous civilisation will replace them both. In their place will rise the frightful wooden house, the drinking-house, the chapel, the manufactory. Those who are pleased with ugliness will be contented. Those who, like myself, see all too much of it already, may regret that light and colour, freedom and picturesqueness, are so rapidly being extirpated from every corner of the world.

At least we may be allowed to express the hope that in the heaven the Gaucho goes to, his horse may not be separated from him.

R.B.C.G.

IX. A Vanishing Race

A melancholy interest attaches to anything about to go for ever. Especially so to a people who with their customs, superstitions, and mode of life, are doomed. So with the Gauchos of the Pampa. Pampa, in the Quichua tongue, signifies the 'Space.' In truth the Pampa gives a good idea of space. Perhaps the loneliness, the immensity of it, has given the melancholy tinge to the Gauchos, which is their chief characteristic. Civilised enough to have (sometimes) a picture of a saint in his house, to cross himself if he hears a sudden noise at night, still savage enough to know by the footprint if the horse that passed an hour ago was mounted or running loose. A strange compound of Indian and Spaniard, of ferocity and childishness, a link between ourselves and the past. A Centaur never to be seen on foot, apt at a bargain, yet careless of money, an inveterate smoker, long-sighted, a poet withal, a singer and improviser of melancholy wild songs. Clearly for such a type civilisation reserves no place. He must go. Already, I am told, he is hardly to be met with, except on the frontiers, and in the upper provinces of Catamarca, Corrientes, and Santiago del Estero.

The Race Twenty Years Ago

I knew him but twenty years ago a force, a maker and unmaker of presidents, a stirrer up of revolutions, a very turbulent fellow. He and his horse — the untiring, angular, long-maned, fiery-eyed horse of the American desert — must be replaced by the heavy-footed Basque, the commonplace Canary Islander, and the Italian in his greasy velveteen suit. As the Gaucho replaced the Indian, the European colonist will replace him, one more type will have faded from the world, one more step will have been made to universal ugliness. It becomes important therefore to preserve, however imperfectly, any characteristics, any customs that to the next generation will seem strange and incomprehensible as those of the heroes of the Niebelungen Lied. In that generation the 'Gaucho

157

haragan,' the wandering Gaucho, with his lean horse and rusty spurs, never settled, always wandering, restless-eyed, will have disappeared, perhaps has done so already.

A Characteristic Incident

He would ride up to your house, ask for a glass of water, without dismounting pass a leg over his horse's neck, and sit talking; perhaps make a cigarette the while, chopping the tobacco from a lump with a knife a foot long, holding his cigarette paper between his bare toes till the tobacco was fine enough cut, cursing his horse if it moved, yet annoyed if it stood still, his glance fixed on nothing apparently, yet conveying to you somehow that it took in everything of value. 'Did he want work?' 'No, Señor.' 'Was he going anywhere? 'Nowhere in particular.' 'Where would he sleep?' 'Where the night caught him.' 'Had he no arms except that knife (*facon*)?' 'No, Señor, God is not a bad man.' I can see him ride off, carrying a piece of meat tied to his saddle, his horse cantering like a wolf. I can see his torn poncho fluttering in the air, hear the rattle of his iron spurs, catch the gleam of sun falling on the handle of his knife stuck through his sash, and sticking out on both sides like the lateen of a Levantine boat, and reflect that usually the morning after his visit a good horse had disappeared, or a fat cow would be found dead — killed for his supper.

Let him go with God, if go he must.

His long hide reins, his broken saddle (*recado*), covered with a dirty sheepskin, his ragged black hair, tied up in a red handkerchief, the two bags of maté and sugar tied to his belt, the tin kettle hanging from his horse's headstall, his brown bare legs shoved into top-boots (the skin of a horse's leg, the hock forming the heel), and his general look of contented villainy, will not fade easily from my memory. How he lived no one knew. Where he slept only the thickest woods and most desolate watercourses could tell you.

Present at every race; though a fine horseman, always riding a broken-down horse; at Bahia Blanca one month, and on the frontiers of Paraguay the next; feared by all, yet welcome for the news he brought, the Gaucho haragan was indeed a type of a past order of things.

The Tracker

The *rastreador*, the tracker who looked for strayed animals, found thieves, and performed feats that Europeans would look on as impossible, is, I suppose, also going or gone. Generally he was a little taciturn Arribeño from the upper provinces. He would arrive when horses had been stolen, dismount, seat himself by the fire, smoke a cigarette, get up, and walk out, peering at the ground, and say, without apparently looking, 'Your horses were driven off about three this morning. Two men took them, they went to the southward, one of them riding a lame horse.' 'A lame horse?' 'Yes, look at this sandy place, the horse did not put his off fore-foot down firmly.' You wondered, thinking it was chance, but saddled your horse, and followed your men, the *rastreador* every now and then pointing apparently to nothing, and saying, 'They changed horses here. Look where a saddle has been laid on the ground,' or something of the sort. Eventually he generally brought you to where the horses were, or the trail was lost in a town; for nothing but riding through a town ever threw the human bloodhound off the track. Sometimes even then he would take up the track on the outskirts, and start off afresh. Indeed, sometimes he has been known to lead the search for stolen goods to the house of the chief magistrate of some little town, point at it and say, 'Your things are there.' This generally ended the day's sport, as Justice was, of course, blind and deaf in such cases (as in most others).

Without Horses

'Why do you not work?' said Darwin to the Gaucho. 'I cannot, I am too poor,' was the answer. Astonishment of the great naturalist. However, the answer was most obvious to all who knew the Gaucho. The man had no horses. God had left him on foot. A Gaucho never worked except on horseback. On horseback, no matter if seventy years of age, he always appeared young. On foot he waddled like an alligator. Whether herding sheep or cattle, marching, hunting, drawing water from a well, the Gaucho always worked on horseback. He even drew a net on horseback; or churned butter by galloping about with a hide bag of milk tied to the end of a lazo. He lived on horseback, climbing when a child on to the back of an old horse, putting his little bare toes on the animal's knee and scrambling like a monkey to his seat. On the march he slept on horseback, never falling off. Coming from the Pulperia (camp stores), drunk, but quite the gentleman, he swayed backwards and forwards but kept his seat. In death, too, not seldom has a horse been found straying about with his rider, the hand that guided dead, but the sinewy legs maintaining the wild horseman seated in the saddle as in life.

The Great Misery

The beggars, what few of them existed, begged on horseback, extending a silent hand as you passed by them. In an alarm at night every one ran to his horse, and, mounting, was ready for what might betide. We thought a horse or Gaucho was but half complete separated from each other. To be on foot was his idea of the greatest misery. A paternal Government sentenced murderers, horse thieves, and other miscreants, not to death — why rob the Republic of a man? — but to serve so many years with infantry. Miserable enough that infantry sometimes was, and those who served in it comparable as to fortune with the Christian captives who, in the Middle Ages, rowed in Turkish galleys.

The poorest man usually had at least one tropilla of horses and a hundred mares.

Marking Horses

Every horse was branded with the mark of his owner — a hat, a spur, a letter, a device. The marks were the books of the Gauchos. On summer evenings they sat talking and 'painting marks' (*pintando marcas*) in the dust. 'Si Señor, I once saw this mark on a horse ten years ago in Entre Rios.' If you came upon a group of Gauchos talking, ten to one it was about horses' marks. The subject was ever new, as different marks were taken out nearly every day. When a horse was sold the owner put his mark on him twice. Thus, if the horse was marked B, the addition of another B rendered the horse unmarked — *orejano*, as it was called. The seller placed his mark on him, and he became his property. Good horses were frequently found with six or eight marks upon them. The lazo and the bolas were the tools the Gaucho worked with. With the lazo he caught horses or cattle, then threw them down and killed or branded them. With the bolas he caught wild or runaway horses, and ostriches or deer. To go upon the *boleada* — that is, to go out to catch ostriches with the bolas — was the great sport of rich and poor.

An Ostrich Hunt

The twilight ride to the hunting places (many a time have I ridden it in agony of fear on a half-wild horse) resembled a procession of shadows, the light going, unshod horses hardly brushing the dew from the grass, the greyhounds led carefully for fear of startling the game. Arrived at the places where ostriches had been seen the day before, the company spread out in the shape of fans, striving to encircle the birds. Then a rush forward at full speed was made, and the bolas commenced to whistle through the air. Sometimes an old ostrich or two would dash through the line, and be madly pursued by an eager horseman twisting the bolas round his hand, his horse rushing like a deer, himself sitting like a statue of bronze upon his horse. Sometimes a horseman, rushing downhill, turned a complete somersault with his horse, but never failed to come off on his feet, his great iron or silver spurs clashing on the ground like fetters. It wanted a good horse, a bold rider, and a strong arm to make a successful ostrich baller. But good horses, strong arms, and bold riders were plentiful on the Pampas in those days.

The Pampa Indians

All the Gaucho's life, though, was not ostrich-hunting. He had the grim reality of the Pampa Indians ever close to him. The wild Indians (*Indios bravos*) for three hundred years kept the frontiers in a turmoil. Compounded as the Gaucho was of Indian and Spaniard, still the hatred between him and his wilder cousin the Indian was keen, as if they had been both Christians of different but nearly approaching sects. To the Gaucho's heaven no Indian went. On the plains around the mythic city of Trapalanda no Gaucho rode.

Like the Arabs of to-day, the Indians chiefly came to steal the Gauchos' women and horses.

In the mysterious country known as *Tierra adentro* (the inside country) quite a colony of so-called Christians lived. These Christians, chiefly unattached to any especial form of Christianity, were as a general rule Gauchos who had committed crimes and fled to the Indians for protection. Sometimes, however, after the *pronunciamiento*, which followed usually upon an election for the presidentship, some leader of the opposition had to cross the mysterious shifting line known as the frontier and sojourn for a while amongst the Indians. If so, he generally became a sort of minor chief, a *caciquillo*, as the phrase was, and took to himself a wife or two, or even three, and amongst them generally a Christian captive. About forty years ago an officer called Saá, forced, from some cause or other, to make his habitation with the Indians, rose to such eminence as almost to imperil the republic.

Don José Hernandez, the Gaucho poet, relates the adventures of one Martin Fierro, who suffered many things with the Pampas and Ranqueles. In the long evenings, seated round the fire, passing the maté round, the adventures of Martin were sure to be discussed. The Gauchos seemed to take him as an embodiment of themselves and all their troubles (surely the greatest test a poet has of popularity), and talk of him as if at any moment he might lift the mares' hide which acted as a door and walk into the hut. Those of the company who could read (not the majority) were wont to read aloud to the unlettered from a well-worn greasy book, printed on flimsy paper in thin and broken type, after extracting the precious books from the recesses of their saddle-bags, or from their riding-boots. The others got it by heart and then repeated it as a sort of litany.

Almost all the founders of the Argentine Republic were of the Gaucho class. Rosas, the tyrant of Buenos Ayres, who died a quiet and respected country gentleman close to Southampton, had passed his youth on the great cattle farms (*estancias*). It is said he could take his saddle into the several pieces of which the *recado* (the saddle of the Pampas) is composed, and place it piece by piece upon the ground whilst galloping, and then replace it without dismounting from his horse. It is certain that in his youth he often performed the well-known Gaucho feat of jumping on a bare-backed, unbroken horse, and forcing it to obey him by sheer strength. This feat, which seems so impossible in Europe, I have often seen attempted, and sometimes executed. Urquiza, the great rival of Rosas, also was originally a country man, and so of Quiroga (the Tiger of the Llanos), Artigas, and many others. Take them for all in all, perhaps no other country ever has produced a similar class of men. The Tartars of the Steppes have been since the commencement of history banded in tribes; so of the Arabs, Cossacks, Berbers, and Indians both of the Pampas and the Prairies of the North. The Gaucho, on the contrary, has lived a solitary life since he first came into existence as a class. In a thatched hut upon a plain as boundless as the sea without a tree, without a land-mark, used to be his home. There, with his wife and children and his animals, he lived; his nearest neighbour perhaps a league away. He hardly ever had a gun, or, if he had one, seldom ammunition, his arms being the bolas, which he jocularly called 'Las tres Marias', a sword-blade, broken to convenient length and made a knife of, and the lazo. With this equipment he passed his life, living on meat and maté (Paraguayan tea), without a drop of milk in the midst of herds of cattle, without a vegetable, without a luxury except tobacco and an occasional glass of caña. So he became a kind of link between the Indian and the white man, a better rider than the latter, even more savagely careless of his own and others' life than the Indian of the Pampa. Not of a jealous temperament, leaving his wife and family for months, sometimes for years, and on returning not objecting to a new child or two about his hearth. Children of course are useful in the Pampas, where boys climb up the legs of a horse and ride at five years old.

A patriot too, hating all Europeans (Spaniards especially), and despising them for their poor riding, and, like most patriots, easily befooled by knaves and made to leave his home and scour the country to restore the liberties of the republic which had never been in danger. Though quarrelsome, seldom apparently excited, but when aroused ready to kill a man with as much indifference as a bullock. Azara relates that one of them, having a quarrel with another, got off his horse and said, 'I now intend to kill you,' and taking out his knife instantly did so, the other not resisting. So it is said a Gaucho, seeing his brother groaning with rheumatic fever, unsheathed his knife and took him by the beard and cut his throat to ease his misery. Patient of hardship and starvation the Gaucho was, beyond belief. As he would say himself, it is incredible what the male Christian (*Cristiano macho*) can undergo. The race seems to have begun in the first fifty years after the Conquest; by the middle of this century it had reached its apogee, in the time of Rosas; when I lived amongst them they were still the dominant class in all the immense prairies of the republics of Uruguay and the Argentine Confederation. Then you might see them on a Sunday at the *pulperia*, gorgeous with silver trappings on their horses, dressed in ponchos of vicuña wool, loose black merino trousers like a Turk's, and riding-boots of patent leather stitched in patterns with red or yellow thread. Now so great has been the change you scarce can see them, and, horror of horrors, I am told that when you do, they dress in flannel shirts and trousers stuffed into their boots like Texans. Shortly, I take it, the Gaucho will wear a morning suit and buttoned boots, and play at whist instead of *truco** and the taba†. When he gets off his horse, he will give it to a boy to hold, instead of sitting on the *cabresto‡*, with his knife stuck upright in the ground over his social game. It may be he and his 'china' will be married in a church, and that the intrusion of a little fair-haired 'Inglesito' in his family will be a thing not to be tolerated. Polo will take the place of barebacked races on the *caucha*, and when his horse at night falls into a hole the man will fall upon his head instead of on his feet. Before that time I hope in Buenos Ayres some sculptor of repute will do a statue of a Gaucho and his horse, for since the riders in the Parthenon no horseman has been at once so strong and picturesque upon his horse.

Bolas, lazo, Gaucho, Indian, all will soon have gone, if to Trapalanda I know not, but I hope so. Men will rob in counting-house and on exchange with pen and book, instead of on the highway with *trabuco* and *facon*. The country is getting settled, I have little doubt; cheap Spanish Bibles will soon be forced on those who cannot read them; the long-horned Spanish cattle will be replaced by Hereford or shorthorn; where the ostrich scudded, the goods train will snort and puff. Happy those who like the change, for they will have their way. Civilisation, which more surely plants its empty sardine tin as a mark on the earth's face than ever Providence placed its cross (on purpose to convert Constantine) in the sky, and the hideous pall of gloom and hypocrisy which generally accompanies it, will have descended on the Pampas. Instead of the quaint announcements of strayed horses, signed by the Alcalde, on the *pulperia* door, a smug telegraph clerk at the wooden wayside station will inform the delighted inhabitants of the continued firmness of grey shirtings. *Ay de mi!* Pampa!

R.B.C.G.

---

* *Truco* was a superior kind of whist, in which the partners made signs to one another, so that the call for trump was rendered unnecessary.
† The *taba* was a most exciting game played with a knuckle-bone.
‡ *Cabresto* is a halter.

X. Yuste

The muleteer, answering some unexpressed questioning of my eyes, says, 'Yes, that is Yuste.' For more than an hour the bridle-path has twisted and turned in serpentine convolutions, under the shadow of deep chestnut forests, and we have come out on to a vast country, rolling into hills and valleys until it is met by the great wooded mountains profiled against the vivid midday sky. In the midst of this immensity of mountain and forest and sky, high up on the mountain side, a speck amidst the billowy undulations of the forests in which it is almost buried, a white building glitters in the sun. It can only be some decaying and desolate monastery nestling amidst solitudes so austere and unpeopled — 'the grim and horrid' deserts of the monastic chroniclers of the seventeenth century, already alien to the spirit which took men to the wastes and mountains, already oblivious of the charm which these sweet and savage spots exercised on the simple and enthusiastic contemplative of a bygone generation.

Presently we begin to descend the heights which command this great unbroken landscape — these green distances, which convey an undefinable and vague expression of eternity, of a something that never ends. It is now too steep to ride — the path too rough, too narrow. The sun is burning, and the cistus, the heather, and the furze — the only and universal vegetation which covers the burnt and sandy soil — fill the air with strange and arid perfumes.

A river, agitated, bubbling, merry, rushes through the bottom of the valley, sending a thousand rhythmical cadences through the hot silence — a silence that is almost oppressive. We cross its mediæval bridge, too narrow except for mule and man. It is midday as the mules splash through the watercourses which form the streets of Cuacos — Cuacos, whence the little rascals of the sixteenth century stole the Emperor's favourite cherries; Cuacos, with its brown, unwhitewashed houses, which conserve all the dim mystery of their antiquity, their wooden balconies mouldering slowly to dust in the sun. On either side of the all-but-intransitable street the impenetrable shadow of arched doorways form dark spots, which cut trenchantly on the glaring sunlight. We are in full mediævalism. Time has stood still, and we are in a town of the time of Philip II.

Mediæval the wine-shop, open to the street, before which our mules stop instinctively. Mediæval the dark-green bottles, shaped like an alchymist's alembics, in which the swarthy, merry-faced *posadera* (innkeeper) hands us wine. Mediæval her costume, the bundle of gay-coloured petticoats which she sways with that undefinable movement of the hips peculiar to the Spaniard; her hair, braided in a fashion that one may still see in Velasquez' pictures, combed into great glossy wheels which curl in front of each ear, from which dangle rough earrings of massive silver; silver rings gleam on her supple, brown hands, a silver necklace round her throat. Presently the whole town surrounds us, but she is still the spokeswoman. Curious questioning, merry answering, sly jesting with my handsome young muleteer; but it is neither prudent nor safe to linger too long in a Spanish village, lost to the world in the depths of Estremadura, and, followed by the curious gaze of man, woman, and child, we take our way to Yuste.

We have ridden, perhaps, half an hour under a burning sun. We are ascending always — a slow, almost imperceptible, ascent up the side of the mountain, which a few hours ago, as we looked at it from the shadow of the chestnut-woods, seemed so far away. A grey wall, into which is built the sculptured arms of Austria, peers through the leaves of the oak-forest. A moment more, and we enter the great convent gates of Yuste, where, centuries ago, a prior, moved by intensest emotion, welcomed a wearied and disillusioned man, who was nevertheless the greatest monarch of Europe and of his age.

A courtyard, green, mouldering, sunlit, invaded by the gigantic shadow of the historic walnut-tree under which Charles loved to sit, and which even then was accounted a patriarch of the forest — a courtyard moss-grown, strewn with withered leaves, its corners full of damp and vague dimness; a fountain decaying slowly in the centre, from which the water trickles feebly into a great granite basin choked with leaves and rubbish. My muleteer stares somewhat vacantly around him. Is it for this, then — to see an old ruined building, full of sadness and decay — that a sane person braves the chilliness of dawn, the broiling heat of the midday sun, to take a long and comfortless journey, with its accompanying hunger and fatigue? The shadow of the walnut-tree has crept on and on through the centuries, until it has gained the granite mounting-block on the other side of the court. There for the last time the 'prince of light horsemen' mounted feebly his old blind pony. There, too, I insist on getting down.

In front of us stands the 'palace' — for so it has remained, and will remain for ever, in the mouths of these simple country people — a modest building two storeys high, the upper one opening on to a balcony supported by wooden pillars, exposed to the full blaze of the sun. It is reached by a vaulted causeway, the incline of which is almost imperceptible. In a moment we are standing on the very spot in the corridor whence on a bright placid day in early autumn Charles watched for the last time the afternoon sun shining over the great walnut-tree full into the gallery. It was here that he felt the premonitory pangs of his fatal illness, and gazed for the last time on the sunlit Vera. The key grates in the lock, and we are suddenly invaded by a sense of shadow and gloom. And yet these small, low-roofed rooms, which differ but little from monastic cells, still full of the strange atmosphere of the past, witnessed the closing scenes of a life and a career than which none has ever been more brilliant, and for which Europe itself was all too small a stage. Transverse beams of heavy chestnut-wood, cut in the neighbouring forests, cross each other overhead. Time has tinged them with a darker hue, and generations of spiders have spun their webs unchallenged in the deep recesses of their angles. Narrow casements pierced in the profound thickness of the massive walls admit the light, but a light already attenuated by the deep shadow of the roofed balcony without. The inner rooms are dimmer still. That one dimmest of all where, centuries ago, the gentle William van Male, watching the royal deathbed, whispered breathlessly to the Archbishop of Toledo, standing in the shadow of the doorway, *Domine, jam moritur* — 'My lord, he is now dying.' The mystery of that death — that last scene of agony and struggle — still envelops it.

The wooden shutters are thrown back, and the hot sun streams into what was once the Emperor's cabinet. Heaving a sigh of relief, we step out into the balcony and lean over the roughly-carved balustrade which overhangs the terraced garden. If any scene can dispel the melancholy conjured up by these faded reminiscences, it is that which lies stretched before us in the dreamy stillness of the afternoon. A tangled wilderness of beauty sleeps beneath us in the sun. The grey walls and wooden balconies, the glossy orange-trees, the roses which trail over the little path which skirts its brim, are reflected vaguely, dimly, in the motionless depths of the fish-pond embowered amidst the interlacing foliage of mulberry and orange trees. Here and there a thick curtain of green slime, which seems the slow and undisturbed deposit of centuries, blots out the images which lie in its slumbrous depths. The low walls which surround it, grey with the greyness of the ages, are crumbling gently to decay — but a decay how graceful, how sweet and gentle! Tufts of wild mint grow out of the interstices of the stonework, and kiss their own reflection in the placid water. And over all is the sun, and all is unchanged. Time has stood still for Yuste, and only the forms are wanting which have flitted through it and rotted to dust — the footfall of a royal solitary, the vague hum of life, the sound of voices.

'And here lived,' says my muleteer musingly, dimly comprehending, 'a king — he whom they say was Emperor' (Mikado would have conveyed as much to him); 'and this is El Palacio!'

The sunlight is once more blotted out, and we are standing in the raised choir of the church — silent, cold, and desolate — from which, not so many years ago, midnight orisons, sad monotonous *misereres*, still rolled so sadly into the vaulted nave beneath. It may be that those grey walls still retain, chained up in their stony impenetrability, the far-away reverberations of those forgotten prayers. Great choir-books lie rotting on carved stands. I open one. The dust and mildew fly out in a cloud. It shuts down with a clang which echoes through the empty church, and sends a sudden chill to the heart.

High above, in the dim recesses of the roof to the left of the high altar — that high altar which not half a century ago was ablaze with ornament and gilded sculpture; before which silver lamps swung before the Host, and monks passed up and down the tall steps before it, their habits scarcely brushing them as they passed; now stripped, desecrated, heartrending — hangs the chestnut coffin in which the monks of Yuste laid their royal benefactor and brother — yea! death makes us all brothers — to rest. Long did it lie beneath the high altar, so that the priest in the solemn act of consecration might stand over a dead man's prostrate face — long after the body which it contained had been borne away from those peaceful glades, to lie decaying in the Royal Pudridero of the Escorial, and to afford Philip IV the opportunity of saying his one recorded sentence. When the coffin was opened and the body of his great ancestor, who in life ruled from Wurtzburg to Acapulco, was exposed to view, he turned to D. Luis de Haro and remarked, 'Honrado cuerpo, Don Luis,' receiving the formal Castilian reply, 'Muy honrado, Señor.' Curious visitors, possessed of the vapid irreverence of our age, chipped bits of the strong chestnut-wood to bear with them to those stupid collections of bric-à-brac and bad museums which modern man calls his house. But it was not until a rich American offered to buy the relic and transport it bodily to Boston that Spanish pride caught fire, slung it up there in the shadow of the roof, where even the long lean arm of an American was powerless to reach it, and so saved it from the devastating hands and vulgar greed of the sightseer.

Little remains of that great monastery which hid its splendour amidst the shadowy chestnut glades and mountain fastnesses of that wild Estremeñan desert. Like that most gorgeous relic of the Geronomites, the Parral of Segovia, heaps of carved stone lying buried amongst the débris encumber the great cloisters. Here and there a wall stands intact, in which arched windows, framing the sunshine, are like the vacant orbits of a dead man's eye.

A little wind — a sough, a sigh almost imperceptible — sweeps through the oak-trees, and the dead leaves of the year that is gone rustle slowly and gently on the path, which, through alleys of box which have long since lost all shape and form and curious culture of man's hand, leads through the oak forest to the Hermitage of Belem. Most pathetic of all is the desolation of this little ruined sanctuary — a veritable sanctuary of the forest, enclosed within the monastery bounds — the goal of the Emperor's walks.

As we turn away from the great courtyard of Yuste, and as our mules clatter sharply over the stony path, we are invaded by an immense sadness. It is as if we had buried a friend — laid to rest some phase of life never to revive.

We sleep under the shadow of those same chestnut forests whence we had caught our first glimpse of Yuste in the morning — a spot well retired from the road, which I had then mentally chosen for our camping-ground that night. All night I lay in a sort of stupor. All sorts of travellers are passing on that silent road beneath! — but, no; it is only the sound of a mule browsing amongst the ferns and oak-scrub, or the twitch of the rope which hobbles his feet.

In the grey, vague, vaporous light of dawn the fire has burnt low, and the muleteer is bending over a heap of white ashes lighting his cigarette. It is time to saddle up. As we emerge on to the road again, as before, he turns — 'Señora,' he says, and there is an inflection in his voice which it had not the first time, 'that is Yuste.'

That is Yuste — those great mountains over which the mist is sweeping, and which throws a curtain of hazy uncertainty over wood and vale and dale, in which I can distinguish nothing but a dark spot, yet so faint and ill defined that it may be only fancy. But both the muleteer and I know where that lies which we vainly seek with our eyes, and we both say together, 'Adios, Yuste!' And my servant adds, 'Hasta siempre!' — 'Until for ever!'

G.C.G.

XI. The Batuecas

I have been in the strangest, wildest, most forgotten corner of Spain, molested by the feet of few wanderers from civilisation since the Middle Ages, and those eccentrics like myself, to whom the past lives more vividly than the present; a corner round which cluster legends half-terrible, half-comic, in their fantastic weirdness and strangeness. As I write in the long low whitewashed room of the rude *venta* or wayside inn — the *fondak* of the Arabs, the *meson* of Mexico; its floor on the same level, and paved with the same rough cobble-stones, as the street outside, and the zaguan, or great covered porch, into which it opens from the inside, around which last night muleteers, shepherds, charcoal-burners, laid their blankets, and slept in close proximity to their mules and donkeys — it seems that I have awakened from a dream. And yet nothing can be stranger, farther away from the regions of commerce and railways, than those roughly-hewn massive beams of chestnut-wood of the roof above my head, or the thick solid plank of chestnut-wood which serves for a door, with its leathern latch hooking on to a nail inside.

Nothing more curious and old world than the figures which gathered last night around the corkwood fire in the middle of the kitchen, seeking a night's shelter like myself for themselves and beasts, alternately lit up or thrown into sudden shadow by the fiery glow of its fitful blaze — rich labourers and farmers from the wild mountain districts of Salamanca and Estremadura, bound to the cattle fair at Plasencia — shepherds, goatherds, muleteers. Their coarse embroidered shirts made by the women at home; loose knee-breeches with silver buttons and gay silk tags, the last decree of fashion in Philip IV's time; short, bright-coloured velveteen coats and broad sashes conserved something of the antiquity of another age, kept alive in villages and rude farmhouses, which the restless changing world has passed over as beneath its notice. Mediæval, too, our hostess stooping over and tasting the contents of her pipkins and brown dishes, stirring up the savoury mess of dried codfish and red peppers for our supper.

And yet to me, who am still dreaming of the fantastic fairyland between which and me lie days of weary travel, how tame, how conventional, how trite seems this scene, so quaint and picturesque! I have come from a place and scenes so dreamlike that what would at other times have been so strange to me rouses in me the faintest, most languid interest.

My muleteers have said good-bye to me in the cold light of the dawning day. What the strange reluctance? — the dollars clinked and counted and stowed away in the coarse canvas bag between the folds of their sash; what this strange reluctance to say farewell which overpowers both me and them? — me, the inhabitant of another world, in whose ears still linger the bustle of cities and the rattle of the railway train, although at heart half a sylvan; and these wild mountaineers, who wish me God-speed in strange guttural accents — half-unintelligible accents — which conserve the trace of something noble and musical — of a race as free as the winds, as careless, as unrestrained.

The long days spent together amidst fragrant wastes, where the silence which reigned over the monotony of mountain tracks so interminable that it seemed they would never end was alone broken by the mules' hoofs, forge a bond which costs a pang to sunder. Hence this sudden irresolution, this mysterious emotion, spontaneous and instinctive, which overpowers us both.

A week ago we had never seen each other's faces. To-morrow I shall be absorbed into a world which exists only to them as a sort of fairy-like fantastic legend, and they will traverse and retraverse for many, many morrows those wild mountain paths and deserts of Estremadura, which will for me alone exist in fancy and in memory.

Within an hour I shall be rattled back again, in a ramshackle coach drawn by six mules, into the world. I shall bear away with me a recollection of long sunlit days spent in traversing flowery wastes; of mules creeping along goat-tracks winding zigzag along mountain-sides which never seemed to end, buried amidst giant heaths and cistus, with large white blossoms blotched at the heart with a single vivid stain of red, which caught at our clothes as we passed, and impregnated them with their strange, powerful, resinous fragrance; mountain and plain a tangled wilderness of flowery brushwood, penetrable only to its denizens, the wolf, the wild boar, the fox. Of essences of flowers crushed under the hoofs of the mules, and a thousand aromatic scents laden with life and healing, filling the hot balsamic atmosphere, which burned and scorched our faces and hands; of mysterious and unseen insect life, which buzzed and chirped, and filled the air with strange and drowsy murmurs. Then, the cistus left behind, of heights less clothed, more open, beneath which dashed rushing, brawling rivers, at which we dared not look for very giddiness; and the eye swept over the grand wide lines of horizons flowing one into another, until they seemed lost in eternity — depths of plain and mountain covered with an undulating growth of wild arbutus, which melted away at last in a faint haze that might have been the sea. I remember stopping for breakfast at a farmhouse, where scarlet peonies grew thick amongst a patch of green corn, which the mules snatched at as they passed, and the hum of bees round the sunlit porch, where we feasted on milk and goat's milk cheese. I remember passing through several towns and villages which plunged us straight into the Middle Ages (ourselves the only anachronism) — old, stained, lichen-covered, the streets, through the middle of which ran streamlets and watercourses, impassable on foot, where groups of men in their cleanest shirts and holiday velveteens and silver buttons (it was Sunday), congregated together in the market-place, stared at us curiously, as the smith shod one of our mules that had cast its shoe; and children crowded round us in wonder and amazement, but not impertinence; and an innkeeper — a veritable Sancho Panza — offered us wine in a Salamanca jug, and smacked his lips with glee when we told him it was good — and it was! Of villages where from year's end to year's end the entire population lives on bread and wine, and goat's milk is an expensive luxury.

Tired, hungry, footsore, shoeless, ragged, we forget it all as we limp past the rude slate cross which marks the enchanted boundaries of the Batuecas.

We have yet a league to go, but the road made by the monks is good. On this road hundreds of friars have passed, going to and from the monastery, many to their living grave in the Batuecas. I wonder if this savage grandeur, this brown and limpid river which flows beneath the beetling crags and towering peaks, clothed with woods untouched by the hand of man since the Creation, affected them as it does me, or if they passed on, their cowl lowered over sunken and lack-lustre eye, wrapped up in a Deity which they adored in the hidden recesses of their own mysterious imaginings?

Am I wandering — have I lost my head in reading those legends of a distant age? —or is this strange spot, whose existence the Middle Ages accounted a myth, under the spell of some enchantment? Those fantastic forests which arrest me with such a strange, such a weird impression of life petrified and arrested in the midst of motion, but not destroyed; where the blanched ghosts of half-decaying trees dead long years ago, from which the grey moss hangs in long ragged shreds, fling their ghastly skeletons against the fresh green foliage of early summer; those boughs which overhang the stream and bend down to kiss it; those trunks and branches which seem to fight and struggle with each other for space and light; that sense of life, expression, and feeling with which the very twigs seem to be instinct; — exercises a strange and undefinable fascination, and suggests strange secrets concealed within their depths.

A distant hermitage gleaming on a height amongst the cork-trees; a sudden widening out of the narrow glen; a clump of huge horse-chestnuts, brought by some brother from the 'Indies,' looking so strange here amidst a vegetation so different; tall cypresses of secular growth towering above the bell-tower of a gateway, forming depths of shadow impressed with I know not what obscure melancholy, to which the murmuring of the stream and the constant rush of its waters lend a monotonous undertone. It needs not the apocalyptic figure of a saint in the niche above to tell us that we have arrived at the famous — the most famous in Spain — Carmelite Desert of Batuecas.

Above the current of the waters, the bell rung by so many pilgrims, so many friars, so many wanderers and penitents in years which now seem so far away, clangs harshly on the silence, and once more the river takes up the burden of its song.

Wooden bars fall to the ground; a rough figure, clad in sheepskin, greets us as in surprise; we enter the gate-house, where the figures of kneeling saints in the niches in the corners contrast strangely with the donkey tethered there. A flagged causeway, bordered by an avenue of lofty cypress-trees, leads through a garden — out of which Time has not blotted the quaint shapes of the box-bushes, once so daintily trimmed, nor quite banished the tangled flowers, which fall about our feet — past a marble fountain in which the water still falls drearily, to the church. There is nothing of architectural curiosity in this plain brick church, in these rude and simple cells, each with its inclined plank which formed the Carmelite's bed, the invariable skull and cross rudely carved of cork: only a great pathetic sadness, an intense abandonment. It is strange to see their little altars which surround the cloisters almost intact, in each a figure of some strange solitary caged in a little grotto made of shells, in which here and there a skull or human bone preaches its stern sad lesson; strange to see the herbs still green and flowering in the herb-garden, although it is so many years since the hand of the Brother who doctored the sick and ailing gathered the last leaf, distilled the last healing essence. We wander through the cells disconsolately, touching the little odds and ends which the friars left behind them in their flight: a rude cross, left lying on a casement; the wine jars, untouched since then, which lie useless in the cellars; the buildings, once busy with the sound of adze and saw; the smithy, where they forged all the ironwork they wanted for church or monastery; the neglected vines and olive-trees, which still climb sparsely up the hill in the terraces of the monks; the corn-mill, which the water turns no more, ready for use to-morrow; the oil-mill, where the jars were filled for the use of the convent.

So lived this community, which built all and made all for itself; which turned a desert into a flowering garden, adequate to its own subsistence and simple wants; and when the last echoes of the sandalled feet of the expelled friars sank into silence — just retribution for the folly and pride of man — it became again a wilderness, useless, uncultivated, fit only to give pasture to a few herds of goats.

In the gathering twilight I climb up the hill to one of the sixteen hermitages which, like the Laura of the Cenobites of Egypt, perched on inaccessible crags, surround and overlook the monastery below. Lost amongst the thick forest of corkwood, up heights so steep that a false step would have hurled me down into the rapid river below, after half an hour's climb I reach the disroofed hermitage. The cypress still rears itself into the evening sky; the stream still runs before the door; the cupboard is there in which the hermit stored his meal of dried fruit; the altar, with its lovely sixteenth-century tiles, waits for the footfall of the sad and solemn solitary; the bell hangs in the bell-tower, only the touch of a hand is wanted!

As night came on, and the mists shrouded the Peña de Francia* from our vision, from the gateway of the monastery we watched the great herds of goats driven into the corral. All the evening we had heard their bells tinkling afar off in the rocky crags. The tinkling came nearer and nearer, and at last the barking of the wolf-dogs, the cracking of the whips of the brown savage who trudged along after them, dressed in sheepskin, winding his horn, heralded their approach.

An inexplicable sadness brooded over the dusky kitchen — the kitchen of the friars — where we sat far into the night round the red blaze of cork

*A high mountain which overhangs the valley.

logs, and goat-bells tinkled below or a wolf-dog bayed, and listened to the curious lore which Nature and legend teach to the half-inarticulate children who live closest to her bosom. Legends as fantastic as the blaze of the fire, which cast strange flickerings of light into the blackness of the patriarchal kitchen, become vivified, and receive substance and colour in the comments of these rustic mouths. They look upon me with almost mysterious awe, the same almost as that with which some great scholar might be looked upon by the simpler minds of the Middle Ages, as I produce my store of cheap-Jack learning got out of faded monkish chronicles and handbooks.

How the Batuecas, haunt of evil spirits and demons, shut away from all communication with the world outside, a malignant spot shunned by the shepherds, its very existence looked on as doubtful in the Middle Ages, until a lovely lady of the House of Alba, seeking shelter for her illicit love with a page, discovered these solitudes peopled with a wild sylvan race, speaking an unintelligible tongue which preserved a few words of Gothic; how by some they were supposed to be Goths, by others Arabs; how the appearance of a convent in a spot so wild and savage was looked upon with superstitious dread, as having sprung up in a single night by some dread miracle, and likely to disappear again in the same strange way; until we peopled the solitude with the creatures of our fancy, and heard the Carmelite habits brush through the garden alleys, and the simultaneous sound of the hermitage bells borne to us on the wind, and fancied as we looked out of the casement into the night that we saw lights flickering and shadowy figures passing to and fro against the glow in the ruined windows of the church.

On the rude bed strange visions and fantasies disturbed my sleep. By a physical reaction I was still counting the measured tread of my mules' hoofs, which rang rhythmically through my brain, when a figure stood before me, and, growing larger and gradually more distinct, a stern Carmelite brother of gigantic stature barred my progress ———, and I awoke to find the world soaked with rain.

We watched the goats milked below, and after a bowl of milk and a piece of bread — our only breakfast, our only food, indeed, throughout the whole long day — in the grey of the early morning, blotted out by the rain, the convent of the Batuecas disappeared from our sight.

G.C.G.

XII. La Vera De Plasencia

A district which it would almost seem that Nature herself has been at pains to isolate from the surrounding world; shut in by mountain barriers; little visited; innocent of roads; the communication between the towns and villages, difficult at all times, ceases entirely to exist in winter. An ocean of billowy prairie, which sweeps away until it melts into dazzling and radiant distances; shaggy chestnut forests untouched by the woodman's axe for centuries; wild streams which dash down roaring and impetuous from mountain gorges; red-roofed towns and villages hidden in undulations of the ground or clinging to mountain slopes; a brief compendium of aromatic waste and savage precipice, of forest glade and alpine solitude — this is the Vera; a brief compendium indeed, for the whole district can be ridden over with ease within a week. A district over which hangs a strange halo of romance; which is indelibly associated with perhaps the most curious and picturesque episode of Spanish history; for a white building, which glimmers midway up a mountain side, among undulating chestnut woods, is for ever haunted by the gigantic figure of a disillusioned man, who held the strings on which all Europe danced like puppets — is the Geronomite Monastery of Yuste.

Nor it alone, for it would seem that it hovers persistently over the immense solitude and tranquil loneliness of the entire Vera. He who has so long rotted to dust in the oblivion of the melancholy chamber of the Escorial, still lives in the memories of these rude villagers, whose unruly ancestors stole his cherries before they, too, faded from time and the memory of their kind. To hear them talk, it might have been yesterday that the great Emperor took up his abode among their midst; but yesterday that the funeral dirges rolled through the monastery church of Yuste. From Yuste it is only a summer afternoon's ride over a wide mountain pass to Jarandilla, where, in the feudal castle of the Counts of Oropesa, he lodged. Above Jarandilla, among the peaks of the snow-capped mountains, is the pass still known as the Emperor's, whence Charles for the first time saw rolled out before him in autumnal beauty the vast expanse of the Vera, and which he affirmed with truth would be his last. Strange that this wild nook of incomparable beauty, lost amid the burning deserts of Spain, should have haunted his memory on the hot battle-field of Germany; should have become for him, the active, fiery soldier, the consummate and crooked diplomatist, his desired haven of rest.

Night in the Old Towns

Nothing more picturesque than to reach one of the towns at nightfall after a long day on horseback. A light twinkling from an iron cresset points out the Posada, and the traveller is swallowed up in the shadow of its doorway. Round a corkwood fire, which blazes in the middle of the floor, the smoke going out through the rafters of the roof, sits a heterogeneous collection of travellers — muleteers, a wool merchant from Salamanca, a pedlar, a priest bound to a distant village. The hostess squats over the fire, preparing the supper in red pipkins, now and then taking part in the conversation, flinging back a sharp sarcasm in answer to the jokes of the assembly. We leave the Posada at break of day. In the plaza the smith is already at work, shoeing mules and donkeys, surrounded by a crowd of labourers. The women, their heads covered with their petticoats, for the air is sharp, chatter and scream and gesticulate around the fountain, above which tower the grey walls of the church. A lane, inundated at every step by cascades of water, winds down between banks and moss-grown walls, hung over with gnarled walnut trees and cherry blossom, to the ivied bridge we crossed last night. On a beetling crag which overhangs the seething stream is perched a little hermitage embowered in foliage. The entrances of all the villages in the Vera are thus guarded and sanctified.

All is silent except for the church bells, which still echo lugubriously on the stillness of the atmosphere, as if they centred all of life and motion in the ghostly town. Jarandilla, the most important of the towns of the Vera, once the residence of the Counts of Oropesa, a branch of the great house of Alba, in whose castle Charles was lodged pending his translation to Yuste, is abandoned to a few villagers, who cultivate the surrounding soil, and whose life, when all else around them has crumbled to dust, by a strange turn of fate remains virtually the same now as then. They are proud of the grim old castle, which gives such an imposing air of nobility to their conglomerations of picturesque huts. They ask as they point out the massive turrets and gates, which seem as if they would defy all time, and the musicians' gallery with its geometrical parapet of stone, which still faces the grass-grown courtyard, once the scene of many a tilting at the ring, and Moorish cane play and bull-fight, whether in 'those worlds over there,' pointing to a vague spot on the horizon, 'there can be such a monument as this.' 'Confess,' they say jealously, 'that you have never seen anything like it before.' I am fain to say I never have. The coloured tiles still cling to the mouldering walls. The rafters of the roof still cross each other overhead, whole and entire. In a garden of the neighbouring monastery, where, among the pleasant shade of orange and fig trees, the Emperor wiled away the sunniest hours of a December day, a fountain still bears his name.

The Vera Doomed

I have ridden through the Vera in early spring, when its villages are buried in white blossom; in the hot summer, when the air is full of scents of wild thyme and sage and rosemary; in October, when the first faint sigh whispers through the boughs of its great chestnut forests, and the leaves flutter down slowly on to the path beneath. I have slept under its clear starlight nights — the midday halts beside a pure stream or on the edge of a forest are still present before me. I see the great prairie rolling away to the sky — vague, undefined, suggesting infinite space, flecked with cattle or flocks of sheep, while some herdsman, a wild and imposing figure, breaks the monotony of the horizon. Its loveliness and loneliness affect me strangely. I may perhaps, however, be the last to see it as it exists to-day, with its patriarchal rural life, its antiquated and picturesque mode of agriculture, its strange atmosphere of mediævalism, for the last time I was at Yuste I heard an ominous whisper that it was to be purchased by a rich capitalist, who was about to make a carriage road and gradually open up the district. If so, the loveliest, the strangest, the wildest district of Spain is doomed to destruction. The discontent with existing conditions will make itself felt. The people will exchange the very solid and real happiness they now enjoy, together with their freedom, for an illusory phantom in the air. The sons will barter the lands of their fathers to flock into the neighbouring town to become the prey of the capitalist, while the latter, patting his stomach with self-conscious virtue, points out to a melancholy plain, intersected by enclosures, shorn of its forests and the aromatic growth which covered its interminable prairies, and which is all that remains of the lovely Vera as Charles V saw it, and as it may still be seen to-day. Nay, more, we may even hope that civilisation may make such rapid strides that a Bible pedlar shall yet be seen at the entrance of the Great Geronomite Monastery, speaking to the people in an unknown tongue, or a strange dialect purporting to be Spanish; while in the courtyard, where the Prince of Light Horsemen mounted for the last time his old white one-eyed pony, a red cigarette machine 'functions,' bearing the inspiriting inscription of 'pennies only.'

G.C.G

XIII. In A Garden

I fancy that at the beginning of this century soldiers were not much given to analysing motives. They fought, marched, counter-marched, killed, and were killed, without inquiring why or caring wherefore. I am aware that their behaviour was *du dernier bourgeois*, but I do not care in the least. Not that war — its pomps, military bands, forage caps, wounds, ulcers, hospitals, and national neglect of the survivors — delights me much, or at all. No; would that soldiers were only to be seen stuffed, or preserved in spirits in museums. Save only, of course, the Life Guards, who should survive if but on account of their helmets and their black horses. Still, a soldier who 'done his level best,' through snow, through heat, in hunger, and in thirst, despite the follies of the War Office, and who at last rests in a garden overlooking his last stricken field, appeals to me somehow, if only for the garden's sake. Such a garden too! — shaded by acacias, girt by grey walls grown over with valerian and with umbelliferæ, on a peninsula jutting out to sea. *In proelio occisus*, etc., the Latin has it. The English : 'To the memory of General Sir John Moore, killed at Elviña, near Coruña, while covering the embarkation of the British troops.' Somehow, I like 'In proelio occisus' better than 'killed in action'; it sounds more martial.

Coruña, the Groyne of the Elizabethans, a busy little place with trade in oxen and in onions, tobacco factory (La Palloza), like a scene in *Carmen*, its three fiords of El Ferrol, Betanzos, and la ria de Coruña; with its barelegged fisher-girls, its ox carts in the streets, its churches, houses with balconies enclosed with glass, and Plaza de Maria Pita, is known, I fancy, best in England by its association with him who lies in the Jardin de San Carlos, *In proelio occisus*. If not, it should be so. Let them cremate who will, bury in vaults, in churches, under alabaster, with due (unfaithful) epitaph, I still hold that in the sea or near the sea a man rests best. Not that I love the sea, with memories of stewards, smell of oil, and stuffy cabins. Far from it!

Yet the sound of waves should (nay does, I am sure) sound pleasant to ears that have heard much noise in life of cannon, rattling cabs, or prattling fools. Besides, the vegetation by the sea grows sparsely, as if it were not nourished by what lies under it, the only thing repulsive in your country churchyard, though even that is mitigated when one sees the parson's pony feeding among the tombstones. Therefore, when the question comes to local option I shall vote for cemeteries by the sea. Along the narrow streets is the Church of Santiago, Romanesque in style, with low round doors, the arch supported on bullocks' heads of stone, with the fattest lamb I ever saw in stone in the middle of the arch; above St. James himself, on a somewhat long-backed horse, trampling upon the Moorish dogs like a true Christian. Within, a fledgling priest essaying his first Latin sermon, with much of 'Autem mei filii; dixit Sanctus Ambrosius,' to a congregation chiefly composed of brother priests, apparently assembled like actors at a *matinée* to 'give a hand'.

Leaving the church, the assembled priests, the fishermen, the villagers, and the perspiring neophyte in the pulpit, across the Plaza de la Constitucion, passing the Audiencia, at last one reaches a curious, fort-like structure, circular in form, with the embrasures all glazed like windows, God knows why; and the usual Spanish gateway, built for all time, with the arms of Castile and Leon sculptured upon it, with two tall, shady elms on either side the entrance. Inside, a sort of half-Italian garden cut in squares by myrtle hedges, and with tall bushes of purple veronica and escalonia, Italian as to form, but Spanish, purely Spanish, in neglect. Gardens, I fancy, should be wild in spite of Verulam; even a weed or two (that is a Southern weed) lends grace to the formal garden plants. It is as if a gipsy (from the Bohemia of our dreams) had strayed into a ballroom. In the middle, the grave; like most graves, leaving something to be desired in taste, still not unpleasing, with its plain sarcophagus of granite, supported on a massive slab of stone. It had been better had not the Municipality, in its zeal and kindliness, painted the stone in buff and grey to the glory of God and England. About the square acacias stand sentinel, at the four corners clumps of pampas grass. It always seems to me that pampas grass looks sad in Europe, and hangs its head as if it missed wild horses bounding over it, and sickened for the calling of the Teru-tero.

It may be, too, that want of water in this case was the cause, for your Spanish gardener, I should fancy, watered but fitfully, except, perhaps, in winter. Be this as it may, if pampas grass does not mourn itself, it makes me sad, as when I see a branded horse from the pampas in a London cab. Surely to the horse at least remembrances must come in the fetid streets of his *querencia*, of the free life, fresh grass, the little foals he played with, and the wild gallops under some Gaucho wilder than himself; for have not 'learned clerkes' assured us that animals do think, though, if they do, I am glad they cannot write their impressions of mankind? So round the grave grow pampas grass, veronica, myrtle, escalonia, datura, golden rod, and fennel, and many another flower the General trod upon in life and may be never saw, being occupied with things as transitory and quite as unimportant.

Let him sleep on in the little garden by the sea, close to the barracks where the Spanish soldiers cry, 'Alerta centinela!' Perhaps the sound of arms and drums and barrack life would please him better, could he hear them, than the swishing of the sea.

They say that once a sailor brought a spotted shell from the Pacific to his sweetheart (some Bet Bouncer of those parts) and put it to her ear, asking her what she heard, and that she answered that it made a noise 'like people coming out of chapel of a Sunday.' Still, there are some ears which, listening in a shell, hear other sounds than that. Leaving the garden of San Carlos, a passing boy turned to his father and asked him who was buried there. The father, who could read and write (*sabia de pluma y de cuentas*), answered him, 'El General Francés.'

El General Francés! So pass fame, honour, and glory, even remembrance. All is vanity, vanity of vanities; all except your gardens by the sea; your gardens wild, neglected, or, at best, cared for by Spanish gardeners, with or without a hero buried in them. These will blossom, do blossom, when the rider and the horse have mouldered into dust, cannons have rusted or been turned to sickles and to horseshoes; and when gallant deeds have been forgotten. At least they blossom to those who, listening in a shell, hear something different to the noise of people leaving a music-hall.

R.B.C.G.

The Ipané

R. B. Cunninghame Graham

Introduction

Father Archangel of Scotland, and other essays, the collection of essays and sketches that Robert Cunninghame Graham published jointly with his wife, Gabriela, in 1896 marks Graham's entry into the world of published authorship. These essays, sketches and stories seem a random collection, drawn as they were from the pieces that Graham had been contributing to periodicals throughout the 1890s. He had already produced the short guidebook, *Notes on the District of Menteith* (1895), and was to follow up these two tentative starter books with the more ambitious full-length travel book, *Mogreb-el-Acsa: A Journey in Morocco* (1898). However, it was the influence and encouragement of the literary reader and publisher, Edward Garnett, through their friendship beginning in the year 1898, which brought about Graham's first solo collection of short stories and sketches, *The Ipané* (1899).

The selection of pieces presented to the reader seems to be utterly random. Graham goes so far in his Preface as to say, "None of the following sketches and stories have the least connection with one another, or with each other (*l'un et l'autre se disent*)". This slightly teasing opening to the Preface may be to some extent discounted, because it is in fact possible to see links and thematic connections in the contents. Graham does not specifically dedicate *The Ipané* to any individual, unlike all his later collections. Yet he casts a romantic and faraway tinge over the book with his epigraph, 'Norroway, Norroway, beyond the Sea.' In his mind, a lot of what he presents is already of the past, dealing with places and times that are changing, living mainly in his memory and beginning to partake of myth and the stuff of ballads. Yet this too is misleading. Some of the sketches in *The Ipané* are very contemporary to his time of writing.

The title story, "The Ipané", however, looks back to a time that Graham remembers from his early years in South America. The setting is Asunción, the capital of Paraguay, in the immediate aftermath of the disastrous Triple Alliance War of the 1860s, a war with its three neighbours — Brazil, Bolivia and Argentina — in which Paraguay lost a high proportion of its male population. Graham describes a town under the control of the Brazilian navy, in which women do most of the work but where life goes on in the traditional colourful easy-going manner. He vividly describes the Hotel Casa Horrocks and the foreign residents living in it, and by easy degrees comes to focus on the two main subjects of the story, the scholarly German exile, Hartogg, and the death-trap river steamer, Ipané, on which Hartogg sets sail towards the yerba plantation he has bought miles upriver. In the slight narrative, the main events are the farewell accorded to Hartogg and his family, the bursting of the Ipané's boiler with the deaths of several passengers, including Hartogg, from scalding, and the burial of the atheist Hartogg in the Protestant Cemetery. It is a brief yet striking sketch, setting the pattern for many of Graham's earlier stories: a setting in an exotic location, a detailed evocation of the place and its people, in which Graham can deploy his first-hand knowledge of Latin-American life and manners, and a narrowing of focus to recount an episode or tell an anecdote, ending on a vivid, even elegiac image.

The two stories that follow "The Ipané" exhibit the same approach. "Un Pelado" (a very poor man) is set in the town of Encinal in Texas and describes the circumstances leading up to the hanging of a poor Mexican, José María Mendiola, for the murder of an American storekeeper, Hodges. Graham bases his account on a newspaper cutting of the real event, which is still among his papers. He uses the words of the journalist, his own description of the place and its people, with some probably elaborated dialogue, to conclude on an ironic twist, in which the courage and fatalism of the Mexican facing death are dismissed by a Yankee settler as mere animal stupidity. Graham's sympathy for Mendiola is left for us to infer. "Un Angelito" (a little angel) is a story recounting a bizarre experience that Graham had in Argentina when he was engaged in a horse-droving venture. In the house of an acquaintance to which the narrator comes on horseback, a dance is in progress, well attended by the local ranchers, and many gauchos and 'china' girls (prostitutes). The occasion is the 'sending off' to heaven of a recently-died child, whose body is on display, dressed and sitting in a chair as if blessing the dance with his presence. He is the angelito playing his part in a long-established practice on the pampas. Graham meditates on this custom and its inevitable disappearance as part of the gradual process of change that is transforming the Latin-American and gaucho way of life into a mere imitation of modern civilisation.

Graham's fascination for the gaucho way of life, whose passing he regrets, is directly shown in the sketches, "The Lazo" and "The Bolas", where Graham goes into great detail about the nature, purposes and techniques related to the lazo, or lariat, for roping horses, and the bolas (three balls of stone joined by ropes) for bringing down or stunning wild animals. Graham is clearly fascinated by these necessary elements of the life and work of the gauchos, and distinguishes the varying types of lazo and bolas to be found in different parts of South America. He is clearly writing under the influence of his reading of Alfred Ébélot's vignettes of gaucho life, *La Pampa* (1890), brought to his attention by his close friend, W.H. Hudson.

Interestingly, despite his obsession with Latin America, these five opening sketches virtually conclude his treatment of Hispanic subjects in *The Ipané*. Graham's other big exotic setting for stories was North Africa, especially Morocco. It figures very prominently in most of the later collections, but Africa more generally is the setting for three pieces in this book. "Bristol Fashion", "Tanger La Blanca" and "At Torfaieh". It is difficult to know how to take the story, "Bristol Fashion". After a colourful description of the west coast of Africa from Mogador (now Essaouira) in Morocco in the north right down to Mossamedes (now Namibe) in Angola in the south-west, the story turns into a disturbing anecdote about a dubious trading sea-captain, 'Honest Tom Bilson', whose true racist and brutal nature is overlaid with a veneer of civilised sentimentality. He employs Krooboys, men of a specific West African community who have become sailors crewing the European coastal trading ships, and treats them harshly. When some of them steal a boat and desert his ship, he follows and recaptures them. He then exacts a terrible revenge on them, which he loves to recount in later years with great satisfaction. Graham's attitude towards him is certainly disapproving, and yet Bilson is brought to life as a character with such relish that the reader is drawn in to savour his words and deeds, almost at the expense of sympathy with the largely anonymous supporting cast of African characters. It is perhaps Graham's first triumph in the realm of fiction, presenting an undoubtedly detestable character with powerful, almost attractive, conviction. By contrast, "At Torfaieh" explores the dilemma of the Christian Syrian Arab, Najim, manager of a Scottish-run trading factory at Cape Juby on the Sahara Desert coast of Morocco. Najim feels a conflict within himself between his Christianity and the company's commercial ethos on the one hand and his sentimental attachment to the Moslem Arab nomadic way of life and ethos displayed by the local chiefs, between his responsibility for making profit for the Cape Juby Company and the lavish generosity expected of him by the visiting Arabs. It is not a dilemma that can be easily resolved. Finally, in "Tanger La Blanca" (Tangier the White), Graham confines himself to a descriptive and historical sketch of the Moroccan city of Tangier, a place he had come to love, and to which he often returned in later years.

Graham's relationship with his native country of Scotland was always an ambiguous one. As the descendant of a noble family, with roots firmly embedded in Scottish history and a particular region of Scotland, he felt strong emotional ties to the traditional rural elements of his native land. As his Socialist principles developed over the years, he undoubtedly felt a strong sympathy for the ordinary Scots people of city and country in their poverty and deprivation, and wished to see the conditions of their lives improved by political action. Yet there were aspects of Scottish life and manners that repelled him strongly, and which he felt obliged to write about in terms of disdain and disgust. The main targets for his scorn were narrow-minded religion, excessive drinking and a general boorish lack of civility and sophistication. Graham himself never professed any religious beliefs, although he was drawn to write sympathetically about the Catholic faith that was held so strongly by his wife, Gabriela, and that was a mainstay of the Spanish culture that he so admired. Similarly, for much of his life, he did not normally drink alcohol. As a much-travelled man, at home equally on the pampas of South America and the salons of London and Paris, Graham had observed the manners of the wider world beyond Scotland and could not fail to make unflattering judgements of the behaviour he encountered among his fellow-countrymen. In the stories and sketches in which Graham looks at and describes Scotland, there is usually a strong element of bitter criticism. The story, 'S.S. *Atlas*', encapsulates such criticism in an account of a trip on a Scottish ship from New York to Glasgow and back across the Atlantic to Montevideo, picking up emigrants at Bordeaux and Lisbon on the way. The Scottish Bible-wielding captain and the drunken crew epitomise these feature of Scottish character that Graham detests within the framework of the vividly-described uncomfortable voyage.

Three other sketches in *The Ipané* focus more specifically on Scotland. "A Survival", "Heather Jock" and "Salvagia" allow Graham to develop his thoughts about the subject in a mingling of description, narrative and explicit personal opinion. "A Survival" shows Graham addressing 'you' English readers from the standpoint of 'us' Scots. His tone is ironical as he surveys a Scotland enfeebled and demeaned from what it once was into an unworthy caricature Kailyard dominated by narrow religion, sentimentality, penny-pinching commercialism and linguistic parochialism. The climax of the sketch is a cynical anecdote (not obviously related to what has gone before) where Graham implies that human nature is fixed, unable to be changed by a different environment, exemplified by the self-made man of trade who becomes a landowner or the Celtic Highlander transplanted on to a Lowland farm. It must be said that Graham ultimately does not come across very sympathetically in this story, as several aristocratic prejudices are being arrogantly aired. The story, "Heather Jock", is more sympathetic to its subject, a West of Scotland eccentric 'character' who wanders round the countryside making a poor living as a pedlar, singer and clown. Graham knew him from his own young days beside the Clyde and is reminded of him years later in South America when he receives letters from home, including a newspaper cutting of Heather Jock's death notice. The power of the story lies in the contrast that Graham makes between Jock's distant life in Scotland and Graham's pressing and deadly concerns on his ranch in Argentina. "Salvagia" sees Graham returning to his tone of bitter irony about Scottish life and manners. His specific target here is the dehumanising influence of Calvinism, with its pernicious doctrine of predestination. Salvagia (the land of savages) is Scotland under the name given to it by medieval Italian map-makers. Graham focuses on a particular village, undoubtedly a real place near his house of Gartmore, where the dead hand of religion lies over everybody, dulling sensibilities, coarsening manners and demeaning human relationships. Graham is at his most pessimistic in this satire on Scotland, yet it is a story that stands greatly to his credit, because he betrays no class prejudices but rather the sensibilities of a humane and compassionate person.

In these stories about Scotland, Graham has shown that he has the literary power to startle his readers with strongly-worded and unconventional, even unpopular, ideas. In *The Ipané*, he achieves this most effectively in the sketch with the arresting and even alarming title, "Niggers". The modern reader's immediate reaction is one of repulsion, perhaps horror. How can Graham so flagrantly flout our politically correct beliefs with such a blatantly racist title? Our immediate reading of the word suggests to us that the story will be an intensely biased and unacceptable treatment of black people. The inference drawn by Graham's readers in 1899 would have been a similar, if less offended, one.

Graham's purpose, however, is infinitely more subtle and satirical. After an eloquently and sympathetically written survey of the infinitely varied wonders of God's creation on Earth, his true subjects are revealed to be none other than Englishmen. It is they who in their blinkered Imperial delusions categorise all other human beings, of whatever nationality, as "Niggers". It is the racism of imperialism that Graham condemns, the pernicious belief that all other people exist for England to exploit for its selfish purposes. "Niggers" is a rare venture by Graham into the fully satiric mode, but he shows in the story, with his controlled anger and eloquent contempt, that he could manage it very skilfully.

Two stories in *The Ipané* remain for brief consideration. "Snaekoll's Saga" is set in Iceland, a far cry from Graham's normal story locations. In the summer of 1874, Graham had sailed north with his brother Charles on a brief visit to Iceland, and more than twenty years later this story captures the atmosphere of the sagas and the hard northern landscape. It is a strange story about a successful farmer, Thorgrimur, who is obsessed by the sagas and develops an overwhelming ambition to perform a feat worthy of these stories. With his strange horse Snaekoll, he sets out on an epic journey, which comes to a disturbing and horrifying conclusion. Graham is here writing out of his normal comfort zone, but shows that he is fully in command. There is an Icelandic connection with the final story to be considered. "With the North-West Wind" deals with the funeral in 1896 of one of Graham's many artist friends, the much-loved and multitalented William Morris. Morris, of course, was a passionate lover of the sagas and of all aspects of medievalism, which came to the fore in his writings, and in his commitment to the restoration of traditional arts and crafts. In this tribute to Morris's achievement, Graham is caustic about the Establishment's neglect of Morris in death as in his later life. Graham admired Morris for his Socialist principles and for his attempts to restore a simpler society freed from some of the blight of industrial progress. This is the first of several such tributes that Graham wrote in short story form about people he admired in the worlds of politics, literature and art.

The Ipané can be viewed as Graham's most successful literary work before the new century. It initiates Graham's eclectic approach to his story collections. He establishes within the frame of these fifteen stories and sketches a characteristic mix of locations and styles and narrative conventions. The result may appear to be random and heterogeneous, but it is possible to see that Graham is evolving a highly personal and original approach to his literary output. He was able to capitalise on a wide experience of life in many parts of the world, a seemingly unlimited range of friends and acquaintances, a great store of reading, a tenacious memory and a writing style that continued through his middle years to gain in sharpness and vigour. Cunninghame Graham is certainly one of the most individual and distinctive of Scottish writers, and *The Ipané* is a worthy introduction to his best work.

Alan MacGillivray

Contents

Preface 197

The Ipané 199

Un Pelado 209

Un Angelito 215

The Lazo 221

The Bolas 227

S.S *Atlas* 233

Bristol Fashion 243

Tanger La Blanca 251

A Survival 257

Heather Jock 265

Salvagia 271

Snaekoll's Saga 277

With The North-West Wind 285

Niggers 291

At Torfaieh 299

Norroway, Norroway, beyond the Sea

Preface

None of the following sketches and stories have the least connection with one another, or with each other (*l'un et l'autre se disent*).

But it may chance that thus collected some one may see in them a nexus undiscerned by me: mystic, I hope, for it is in the fashion, and no one, even in literature, who cares to lag behind.

Now, to my thinking, misapprehension still is rife as to the motives which cause men to write. Books have been written for many purposes, moral, religious, lewd, improving, ethical, and to make people stare; but many think, even to-day, when education, which, as we all know, intensifies artistic comprehension, spreading it even amongst the educated, is so diffused, that men write books to please a mysterious entity known as the public; that they regard this Mumbo-Jumbo as politicians do, or as the county councillor who is uncertain even if he be a cuckold till he has duly put the matter to the democratic vote.

Nothing more false. For the most part all books are written from vanity, for hope of gain, either pecuniary or of some other nature, and now and then to please the writer, for it is known that some have gone to sea for pleasure, and sailors say that those who do so would go to hell for fun.

And so of books. Few men know why they write, and most men are ashamed of all they do when once it stares them in the face in moulded type.

Thank Heaven I wrote that which is here collected to please no single being, and if my own feelings may be taken as the measure of the discerning public's generous judgment, I have succeeded well.

R. B. Cunningham Graham
January, 1899

The Ipané

The "Casa Horrocks" stood at the junction of one of the sandy staircased watercourses which did duty for side streets in Asuncion de Paraguay, and a deserted plaza overgrown with castor-oil plants and with wild indigo, bounded by ruined houses on one side and on the other by a few mameys, and by a hedge of orange-trees, in which at night the fireflies glistened, flashing to and fro as they were humming-birds all dipped in phosphorus. By day the horses of the neighbours played about and fought with one another; or, tied with a "maneador" to a stout peg, stood drowsily stamping at flies and hanging down their heads in the fierce sunlight. Sometimes a company of prisoners armed with machetes made pretence to cut down grass, their guards meanwhile unarmed and smoking in the shade. In South America at the time I write of (for now I fear that competition has brought about an economic change), prisoners seemed to think themselves an honoured class; few took the trouble to escape, but if their guards got drunk or misbehaved themselves, the prisoners not infrequently escorted them back to the gaol. Yet so strong is habit that these selfsame men, who most of them could have escaped at any moment, and many of whom came, went, and worked about the country towns, spoke of themselves with tears in their eyes as "los cautivos" and seemed to think their not uncomfortable lot, most undeserved.

The Casa Horrocks had scant architectural pretentions, and yet was not less pleasing than an "aesthetic" house "faked" up with terra-cotta work looking like ill-burnt piecrust, and with the woodwork gaping after an English winter's rain. Built round a courtyard with an "algibe" in the centre to catch the rain, the walls "adobe," solid and well cemented over; the open ceilings showed great beams of "jacaranda" or of "canela"; flat the roof as roofs of houses in the East; eaves deep, and from them slender tubes of hardwood sticking out a foot or two to carry off the rain, which in the rainy season spouted like waterfalls upon the passers-by; the rooms all opening into the court and into one another; the door of solid "urunday," studded with wrought-iron nails, and from it a dark passage called the "zaguan," which led to a second floor furnished with spy-hole, and with two small embrasures to fire from, should the "infidel" in times gone by have ventured an attack. Inside, scant furniture, no beds, but hammocks made of ornamental cotton with long lace fringes swinging in every room or to the pillars of the court; the chairs apparently contrived for giants, with seats of Spanish leather kept in their place by large brass nails; the tables solid and on each of them a porous jug of water, on the outside of which by day and night thick drops of moisture hung. No pictures and no clocks and all the walls inside dazzling with whitewash, whilst the house itself — which may, for all I know, have been contrived by a "conquistador" — shone like a ripe banana, with a coat of saffron-coloured paint. From "Azotea" or from "Mirador," across the river, you saw the "Chaco," which, with its palms, its billows of waving Pampa grass, and with its air of prediluvian impregnability, gave the lie direct to the sporadic civilisation of the capital of Paraguay.

The tramway running from the harbour to the railway station, the "Tolderia" of the Payaguas, who stalked about in all the glory of their feathers and polygamy; the "Correntinos" riding half-wild horses through the streets; and yet again the bank, the post-office, telegraph station and the steamers in the port, set forth that barbarism and progress had met and kissed (but out of mere politeness), and after kissing had drawn apart again, determined never to be friends. Cave of Adullam, Club, general meeting-place, give it what name you will, the Casa Horrocks served as rendezvous for all those waifs and strays who in the islands of the Pacific must have been "Beach Combers," but who in Paraguay, perhaps restrained by a life on horseback, never attained to the full meanness of a Pacific Beach Comber's estate. The Spanish proverb says, "There is no sane man on a horse's back" — "No hay hombre cuerdo à caballo" — and it may well be said no horseman, with the exception of the jockey now and then, is quite a cur. Riding, Cervantes says, "makes one man look a gentleman and yet another show like a groom"; but still the groom himself, by virtue of the company he keeps, remains more self-respecting than do the other members of the class who live upon the follies of mankind. So in the Casa Horrocks was assembled a heterogeneous crew. Firstly, the master of the house, together with his Paraguayan wife, he having left a legally qualified helpmate in Buenos Ayres, to mourn his loss. Rarest of types, a clever fat man; like Falstaff loving meat, drink, women, comfort, and horses; a good musician, a "plum centre shot," capable engineer; ingenious linguist, having travelled the whole world over, and eking out Guarani with Turkish, Spanish, and with Portuguese, and still in such a manner as to seem rather eclectic than ridiculous.

Lieutenant Hansel, late of the British navy, a choleric Celto-Briton, á lo Correntino — that is, in black merino Turkish trousers, high riding-boots, vicuña poncho, red silk handkerchief tied round the neck with the two points neatly spread out behind upon his shoulders in the same style the artist's "contadina" was assumed to wear her headdress in the 'fifties. Like a fire of Vesta was his short clay pipe, cigar, or cigarette; impervious he was to all known fermented drink, nervous by temperament, and yet with nerves of iron, manacled day and night in huge iron spurs, which report said he wore to prove he had never been a sailor; hating "Old Gladstone" as the first Article of his creed; Liberal in theory but of the "roaring forty" breed of Liberals, who in reality are more Tory than the Tories; a gentleman withal and a bold horseman, mixed in his metaphors at times, as when he spoke of "carrying weather helm" to characterise a "borer" or described a "bucker" as having got him in a jabble of a sea.

Crosskey, a youth caught fresh from College, and sent to the River Plate in order to acquire colonial experience, which he appeared to do by most assiduously frequenting "bailes," "fandangos," "novenas," or any function where the Paraguayan female population used to congregate. A female population in the ratio of thirteen to one man, the men having been all killed in the long, lately terminated, struggle with Brazil. A war which left the country all but depopulated, the President himself having been killed when riding the last horse (a little roan), upon the plains of the Aquidabán.

Women did everything; gathered the crops, tended the flocks, shot, fished, and hunted, and in some villages the very Alcalde was an old Indian woman, who, with a European footman's hat, long cane with silver top, and air of office, administered such justice as the times required, to the full as well as had she been properly qualified with beard and University degree. The national female dress even in ordinary times was most exiguous: a loose, coarse cotton-shift, called a tupoi, doing duty for all the pomps and circumstance which the female form divine seems to require in richer lands. Being *en famille*, so to speak, or at the least *en sexe*, even the tupoi in country places was not infrequently held all too cumbersome, and when a traveller came to a rancho a general stampede ensued till some one found the single garment in the place, clothed herself in it, and came forth, full of most courteous salutations, half Spanish and half Guarani, and a request the stranger would take possession of "his" house. A Portuguese from Goa known by the natives as the "English Indian," a Greek who greased the boots, and an Australian bookkeeper who never kept a book, with numerous Paraguayan women who seemed to come and go in a kaleidoscopic fashion and who smoked cigars as thick as candles all day long, made up the tail of the establishment. Order and regularity were things unknown; meals were served up when men were hungry, and consisted chiefly of jerked beef, stewed up with rice and pepper, sprinkled with mandioca flour, or of a vile concoction known as "Angou," in which eggs, mandioca, fish, and general "menavellings" were the ingredients. Bottles of square-faced gin (Albert Van Hoytema, the Palm Tree brand) were used as candlesticks. The heat was like a furnace, and clouds of insects, all most interesting to entomologists, rendered life one perpetual battle, and proved the aptness of the Spanish proverb that "eating and scratching is but to begin." During the day the horses fed about the streets and in the plaza, and at evening women led them down to the river to drink and bathe. The world went on, no doubt, in Paris and in London as of old, posters appearing in the streets with statements calculated to deceive the general public writ large upon them. Empires were struggling for their life. Sedan and Gravelotte, the Siege of Paris, the Commune, and the rest of the events of 1870 were going on; but we recked nothing of them, taking our recreation quite contentedly, watching the negro regiment of Brazilians, cantoned outside the town, perform what it considered drill, looking with admiration on the squadron of Rio Grandense cavalry manoeuvre, or on occasion strolling to the station to see the train come in driven by a sort of Belgian engineer assisted by two female stokers, naked but for tupois. Right underneath the Casa Horrocks lay the Brazilian fleet, the flagship, the *Aquidaban, Jequitinhonha Paraiba, Terror do Mondo*, and the rest, in the positions where they had anchored eighteen months ago, at the surrender of the town. Italian schooners like that which Garibaldi once commanded, plied up and down, making the passage to Buenos Ayres, "aguas abajo" — that is, with the stream — in twenty days, but taking fifty, sixty, a hundred, or as many as God willed, "aguas arriba," or against the stream. Canoes with Indians came and went, bringing great piles of oranges, bundles of mandioca, maize, and "pindo" for the horses, and blending with the landscape almost as perfectly as the great rafts of "camalote" which floated with the stream, gathering in magnitude as they advanced and carrying with them now and then monkeys and snakes, and once a tiger, which tradition said landed at Santa Fé and, walking through the streets, devoured a Christian. More or less ill-appointed steamers sailed for Corrientes or for Corumbá, taking the futile merchandise which Europe "dumps" on countries such as Paraguay; and in the cabins a Brazilian Governor journeying to "Cuyabá," some generals, colonels, a priest or two, a demi-mondaine changing her garrison, an orchid-hunter much bemused in gin, and all the waifs and strays of cosmopolitan humanity who, "outside our flag," pursue their useless lives, under the sixfold international code of law so neatly codified by Colonel Colt.

A nondescript society which set me thinking whether if after all Pizarro had not better have herded swine in the "dehesas" between Truxillo and Medellin until his death, Almagro kept his shop in Panama, Cortes continued to make love and fight in Cuba, and Alvar Nuñez have remained in Florida amongst the Seminoles. But had they done so, perchance America had been reserved for us and over it our flag had floated with "Empire," "Pauperism," "Sunday," and a contingent of the "native" troops from every State to tramp our streets at the recurrent ten years' Jubilee.

Pleasant as the spectacle would be of a whole world taking its speech from Whitechapel, still, *à la longue*, it might become monotonous, and had it been so, such an assembly as used to meet at Casa Horrocks could never have been seen. Somehow or other none of us liked Hartogg; perhaps it was his learning, his nationality, his way of stating what he knew was false, in such convincing fashion that it seemed more feasible than truth; it may have been his Paraguayan wife, to whom, being an atheist and violent Bible-smasher, he had been married in a church, thus losing caste according to our notions, for, with us, concubinage with "native" women was an honourable state, but marriage carried with it something of degradation. In the same fashion I believe in British India that the Briton thinks no shame to pass an hour or two in amicable converse with a "native" woman, but thinks himself disgraced if he promotes the selfsame woman to the state of mistress. These points of morals are so nice, so intricate, and so fallacious that it is well to set them down whilst they exist, in order that in future generations men may have subjects to enlarge upon, after the question of the due relation of the sexes has been pronounced upon and settled by some County Council, or other body duly elected on a democratic suffrage, and therefore competent to deal with matters such as this in such a way as to be pleasing to the greatest number of the greatest fools. The Paraguayan wife was harmless, servile, serviceable, and would have been pretty had she enjoyed the boon of European birth; the children well brought up, labouring by education to supply deficiency of blood. Strangely enough, and unlike all philosophers one reads of, Hartogg feared death. Why, he did not say, perhaps it was from seeing men so frequently take leave of life upon short notice. We reasoned with him, striving to show that death by violence was natural in Paraguay; that it was over soon, could not hurt much, and when got through with, it was ten to one it was as pleasant as the most orthodox departure from a bed. In fact, we used the arguments used by the friend who walks beside one to the dentist's door, and, conscious of the soundness of his teeth, pours all his wit, all his philosophy upon one, and at last departs, leaving one on the doorstep half irresolute to enter and still resolved, at any rate, to place a barrier between oneself and the unseasonable philosopher.

So seated, capping verses, smoking, listening to Paraguayan "tristes" on the guitar, watching the fireflies, waiting for the revolution and the rising of the stream, drinking innumerable matés, and "making time" in the best way we could, it came upon us as a relief that Hartogg had invested in a "Yerbal" some fifty leagues "aguas arriba," and with his wife and children, books and favourite mule, was soon to start to take possession of his place upon the steamer *Ipané*. I think it struck us all that the reproach was going to be removed. Why should a man in Paraguay read books on botany, study the flora and fauna, write to societies in Gotha, make plans of things, search for antiquities, collect old manuscripts, ride like a Neapolitan, lose himself whenever he went out, and spend his life in useless studies when gin, caña, horses, cards, politics, business, and other things were much more obvious?

Of all the miserable and patched-up craft that, to the imminent danger of their engineers, plied in asthmatic fashion on the Paraguay, the *Ipané* was worst. Condemned in Buenos Ayres, bought for a song by an Italian for the Paraguayan trade, broken down a hundred times, engines a mass of rust, pipes served with rope-yarn, cylinders doubtful, paddles with half the floats long broken from running upon sand-banks, smoke-stack stayed on the one side with a rusty chain and on the other with a raw-hide rope, paint cracked, the glass of half the scuttles gone, the seams of decks gaping like cat-fish in a drought, her single wretched quarter-boat used as a hencoop, the *Ipané* was known from Santa Fé to Cuyabá as the most perfect death-trap in the trade. Sensible engineers — these chiefly Scotchmen who had drifted borne by the northeast trade of whiskey which sets out of Greenock and takes a Scotchman round the world, leaving him sometimes weather- (or whiskey-) bound in Paraguay — had long forsaken her, the last remarking with an oath that, blast him! he would never undertake again to navigate "a blamed revolving scrap-heap." Basques and Italians, Swedes and Norwegians, one and all, had left declaring that the partition betwixt the *Ipané* and hell was far too thin for them. But as a fool or wise man (for the result places him in his proper category) always turns up for such a job, a stranded stagecoach driver who once had worked a donkey-engine in Bahia Blanca stepped into the breach, and with a crew of negroes, Neapolitans, Indians, and an Irish fireman, used to force the *Ipané* from Asuncion to Corumbá, running the pressure up to a hundred pounds an inch instead of the forty which her clattering engines tested to sixty might have borne with tolerable ease. So to this Argo, made as clean as holystone and paint laid on the night before could make her, we all turned out to escort the German Argonauts about to sail.

A curious appearance we must have made with Horrocks on an enormous horse riding like a Silenus at the head, dressed all in white, decked in a "jipi japa" hat and patent leather riding-boots, on the legs of which the Paraguayan eagle flapped his wings, embroidered in red silk. The rest dressed chiefly in the Correntino style except the Consuls, of which Asuncion boasted a mighty store, and the apothecary, also a German, together with a German captain in the Brazilian fleet; these last in European clothes, to which the Germans added spectacles, as being the hallmark of their nationality. Hartogg, his wife and children, came in a bullock-cart drawn by two apocalyptic oxen, conducted by a Paraguayan who, clad in white and with a red "bayeta" cloak over one arm, sat on the yoke and beat the oxen on the horns with a stout wooden mallet, or, jumping off, prodded them lustily with a long cane, pouring a torrent of continuous blasphemy in Guarani upon the unoffending beasts. Lastly a negro led a mule, the only animal tradition said that Hartogg dared to ride, for as he said "the mule is by so much the most damnable of all the beasts that I prefer him, for when he throws you off he also kicks the men that catch him, in the stomach, with his feet." Cocktails discussed, the passengers aboard, the mule secured close to the windlass, the wretched steamer, after the boiler duly "primed" upon the lookers-on, got under way, and heaving, rattling, with a noise below as of a thousand rusty chains, staggered into mid-stream, fired off her green brass gun, and dipped her flag as she passed underneath the stern of the

Brazilian flagship, sweltering at anchor in the blazing sun. Hartogg, after a hurried leavetaking, leaned upon the rail, and the last sight of him alive was his square German face, red nose and bushy beard, bent shoulders, and greasy alpaca coat, as, holding a child in one fat hand, he waved his black straw hat and shouted out, "Atios hasda odra vez."

The cavalcade returned to town racing along the sandy half-deserted streets, rushing through clumps of castor-oil bushes, "pechando" — that is, riding their horses "breast on" upon their neighbours, trying to unhorse each other by putting a foot under the nearest rider's foot, stooping and picking up handfuls of the red sand to throw in one another's eyes, and, galloping to the Casa Horrocks, drew up with a jerk, and each man after hobbling his horse got off to mix a cocktail and to drink success to Hartogg and his "Yerbal," whilst the opinion seemed to be that for a German and a fool, Hartogg was not so bad a fellow as he looked. Over a cocktail in Asuncion time soon slips by, and whilst the horses hung their heads outside, hobbled and hitched to posts, day faded tropically into night no twilight intervening, and as the company sat talking in broken Spanish so that all might understand a little of what was said, a sound of lamentation rose from the port and spread through every street of the half-peopled town. Rockets shot up, lights flashed in the Brazilian squadron, steam-launches came and went, and from the Camp, Rio Grandense orderlies rushed past towards the port, their horses flying through the black Paraguayan night as they were horses of the Walkyrie. Down at the port the loafer, without whose presence no port in any land is quite complete, imparts the news. About ten miles above the town a rapid known as "the Pass" ran strongly, the current sweeping through it at the rate of seven knots. In trying to surmount the difficulty the old machinery had failed, the boiler burst, and Hartogg and some dozen passengers been killed. The loafer seemed to see the hand of God in the calamity, for, with some quite unnecessary oaths, he told us that the mule when blown into the water had emerged upon an island, in which he saw that God had not been willing that such a good "sobre paso" beast should die. On the gun deck of the Brazilian flagship the survivors were laid out, wrapped all in cotton-wool, livid and horrible, and looking like so many scalded pigs, and gasping their lives out tortured by mosquitoes and by heat.

Amongst them Hartogg, just at point of death, conscious and cynical, scalded so horribly as to be all one wound. Beside him stood his wife and children quite unharmed; Brazilian sailors gathered in groups, all weeping, for a negro soon is moved to tears; doctors went to and fro with ice and bandages, ostensibly to aid, but really studying the cases, and as pleased as vivisectors when they hit upon some curious way of giving useless pain. A priest prepared his tackling, and stood by ready to hear confession, soothe the mind, and give the soul its passport into bliss.

Then Hartogg beckoned feebly to his wife, and said in Spanish, "Your good God is careless; let the priest bless me, it will do you good; I am glad the mule is safe — it must have been a true believer all the time. Adios, God is great, but inconsiderate." Then stretching out his miserable hand towards the frightened children he expired, and the scared priest advancing signed the atheist's body with the cross.

Out towards Lambaré, along a narrow, deep-cut road, planted with orange and "paraiso" trees, ruinous but yet walled in with mouldering Tapia walls, is situate the "Cementerio Protestante," where Germans, Englishmen, atheists, and those who die outside the Christian faith in Paraguay are suffered to remain, until the armadillos dig them up.

There all the sojourners at Casa Horrocks brought Hartogg's body in a bullock-cart, stretched on an open bier, and with his snub red nose, looking more like a radish than in life, emerging from the flowers which served to hide the horrid marks upon his face. Some sort of "dust to dust" and pistol-firing, snorting of horses; and, whilst they lowered the body with lazos into the sandy grave, a glass fell from the clothes, and as his youngest daughter picked it up she smiled, remarking that she thought it must be one of the glasses of "el microsposio de papa."

Un Pelado

Not far from where the Old Comanche Trail crosses the Nueces lies the little town of Encinal in Western Texas, county of La Salle, upon the International and Great Northern Railway track. A little one-horse place, just where the "post oak" country touches the great open but mesquité-covered prairies of the south. Oak forests to the north, oak and more oak, as "post oak," "black jack," "live oak," with hickory, pecan, red bud and hackleberry; bottoms rich and alluvial in which grow cotton; "bayous" alive with alligators; woods, woods, and still more woods, right up to Texarcana, on by Nacodoches, and from thence to Little Rock and the Hot Springs upon the Arkansas. To the south the prairies stretching to the Rio Grande, once open grassy seas, when the Comanches and Lipanes burnt them every spring, as sheep farmers in Scotland fire the heather, but now all overgrown with chaparral*, composed of dwarf mesquité and sweet flowering guisaché, low-growing ahuehuete intermixed with cactus, till nearing the great river, the very Nile of North America, all vegetation ceases, and salt plains replace the scrub-grown prairie, and at last even the salt grass vanishes and a stone-covered sandy waste serves as a barrier between the rival States.

The town itself a Helot amongst cities, and contrived, apparently, to fill the double object of showing what a town should never be and of example to the world at large of how much uglier a modern mushroom town can be than an encampment of the Diggers or the Utes. Frame-houses made in the North, then numbered in pieces and railed South, and put together like a Chinese puzzle, shingles for roofing, and each dwelling raised on blocks after the fashion of a haystack. No shade, no trees, except a straggling China tree or two in the sand waste known as the Plaza. A tramway running down the thoroughfare called Constitution Street. A coloured Baptist church, a second Presbyterian ditto, and the

---

*Chaparral, from chaparro, a dwarf oak, has come to mean in Mexico and Texas any underwood or scrub.

cathedral, half of adobe* and half of "rock," conveyed at great expense from Goliad by the members of the Pioneer faith, as Roman Catholics are styled in Texas. Three bar-rooms known as "saloons," a bank, some stores, in which all kinds of notions, from "ladies' fixings" down to waggon grease and coal oil, were on sale, and where hung "quirts," Mexican bits and horse-hair reins, with "cinches," Winchesters and white-handled pistols for cowboys on the spree. Before each house a horse tied by a lariat and saddled with a high-peaked saddle, with a rifle hanging to the horn, stood sleepily.

Horses in every street, in every yard, in waggons, buggies, hacks; mares hitched to Milburn waggons, with foals running at their feet. Horses asleep right in the middle of the Plaza; horses that strayed about like dogs in an Oriental town and seemed to have no owner; some tied to posts, apparently asleep, till an incautious stranger passed too near, when, with a squeal, they bounded from the ground and stretched their lariats quite taut, till the strain slackening they plunged against the post, like boats left at a stair and bumping on the steps as the waves rise and fall.

Nothing æsthetic in the whole town, and still the people not without the attraction that energy imparts. "Cleargritted" to a man, shooting "plum centre," riding a "pitching" horse as they were Indians, free-swearers, proof against all kinds of drink, not civilised and yet not savages, voting the Democratic ticket straight, and determined to uphold what they thought justice, especially when "niggers," Mexicans, or Indians transgressed their code.

Across the creek straggled the quarter of the Mexicans known as Chihuahua. Entering its purlieus, one came upon another world. The houses either made of adobes, or else mere huts, a cross between an Indian "wickey-up" and a Mexican "jacal," were made, as nests of prairie dogs are made, of everything that came to hand. Kerosene-tins and hides, sides of stage-coaches, ends of railway cars, with all the wreckage of a prairie town, were used in their make up. Still they seemed adequate for men in blankets to lounge against and plan what they could steal. Wrapped in "serapes," overshadowed by "Poblano" hats, their feet encased in high-heeled riding-boots, and in their eyes a look of half good-natured villainy, the population stood confessed a rogue. Few worked, all owned a horse, a game-cock, and every self-respecting man

---

*Sun-dried brick.

on feast-days went to play monte in a building lettered "Restoran and Koffe". So Encinal sat facing its suburb, the two destined, like man and wife, never to understand each other's motives though living side by side. In Encinal the people, go-ahead commercial men, but yet idealists like all the members of the Celto-Saxon race, determined to deceive and be deceived on all those points which the uneducated and slothful Mexicans in the suburb of Chihuahua perceived quite clearly and acted on like true materialists. In Encinal, Sunday, with all its horrors of closed shops, the "bell punch" in the bar-rooms, and an air of gloom congealed the town like a black frost at each week's end. Across the creek it was a holiday, with cock-fights, races, and an air of merriment which in itself went far towards atoning for the past week's villainy. On one side, moral citizens, under cover of the night, slipped when they could up to the "Mansions," mysterious, strongly fenced in, and solitary houses on the bluff which all the day looked dreary and deserted, and by night were all lit up, and flared with the electric light, which of course found its way to Encinal whilst Paris, London, and Berlin still clung to gas. But still these stealers to the "Mansions" in the dark were moral men, because on Sunday they all sat in church ejaculating Hallelujah or joining in the responses audibly, according to their creed.

No one was moral in Chihuahua, or made the least pretence to be. If men disliked their wives, they took another to help them bear their cross; and if a wife found that her husband treated her unkindly, she too looked round and cast her eyes upon some able-bodied unconnected man to help her bear her woes. Still, in Chihuahua the women understood woman's first duty — that is, to be a woman — more clearly than the elliptic print-clothed "females" or elaborately arrayed "white ladies" in the town of Encinal.

But as mankind is ever wont to typify, making the virtues feminine, the vices (if I mistake not) male, calling the Spaniard proud, the Italian treacherous, the Frenchman fickle, and so on, and understanding best what a town, country, race, or what not, is like by summing up his, their, or its characteristics in some man, I do the same.

Therefore, I take José Maria Mendiola and G. M. Hodges as prototypes, both of Chihuahua and of Encinal. The one a Mexican, working at what is called "freight hauling" in the United States, that is what we should style a waggoner. The other "Station Agent," and a keeper of a local store. Both rogues, but different in degree, and each unable to discover any taint of virtue in the other's life.

José Maria, long, brown and thin, his lank black hair showing his Indian blood, his furtive eye and nervous hands all proving him to be what the Americans, for reasons not explained, refer to as a "Greaser."

Hodges, a "real white man," fresh-coloured with the sandy hair and clear blue eyes which mark the man destined by Providence to keep a shop.

Just how the thing "kim round," as Texans say, no one was ever sure.

Some say that Hodges cheated Mendiola about a pistol, and others that José had swindled Hodges about some bill. That which is certain is, that in full day José Maria "filled Hodges up" with bullets from a Winchester that he had borrowed from the man he shot. Sheriff McKinney of Cotulla took the murderer, and twelve citizens, all in due course, brought in the verdict "murder in the first degree."

What follows, the reporter of the San Antonio *Evening Light* shall tell.

"Justice in Encinal: conviction against José Maria Mendiola, one of the Mendiolas of La Salle, a low-down crowd of 'Greasers,' located between Cotulla and Encinal.

"The victim's brother travels from Jacksonville to see José turned off, says that he guesses he would have come ten thousand miles to see the man who shot poor Gus buck in a horsehair rope. He complains of the accommodation in the 'sleepers' on the third section of the 'doodlebug,' and remarks he guessed he almost lost the 'round up' after all, as 'road agents' held up the car in which he travelled, at the long switch in the 'perara' outside Vermillionville. After a drink I started out to interview 'our Mary,' as you might call José Maria. Found him quite chipper, mighty peart, and sassy as an Indian pony on the young grass, smoking a loud cigar. Maria allows that he was raised at Las Moras, Kinney County, Texas. Has no record of his birth, but guesses he is twenty-five. Was reared in Western Texas and says: 'I have always lived there, never lived nowhere else. I have never wanted to live anywhere else. No wife (sabe), therefore no children to mourn for me. Old man and mother still both living near Encinal; sisters, brothers, two or three will see me die. I reckon they will also see I am not afraid to die.'

"As he said this, he drew his blanket (called it a serape) round his shoulders and shivered, for it was a mighty piercing norther, and he was dressed like most 'Pelados'* in cotton fixings, all except his blanket.

" 'Yes, señor; I have no trade, but little education, speaky no English.

---

*A Pelado is a poor Mexican, literally "stripped".

Understand him? Yes. All my life I have been a hauler, with a mule-wagon.'

" 'Home influences?'

" 'No, señor; very poor Mexican. Have drunk some mescal — not very much — too much. Yes, I killed Hodges; he took my ivory-handled* pistol. He swindled me, and I shot him.

" 'What do I think of my sentence?

" 'There is no justice in it. If there was any justice anywhere they would not take my life on the thing they are building out there. All the proceedings were in English. I did not understand a word. They told me I was to be hung. I said "Bueno." Curse your Corregidors; curse your Courts! No, I am not religious; born a Roman Catholic, but am a Universalist; think all religions should get a fair show. That saw and hammer go all day, only at night I get some rest. Sabe, eh? They finished the scaffold and pulled it down again because it was not quite level. Oh, these Americans; what does it matter if it was level or not? Even the earth is not quite level, for a poor man, very poor Mexican.'

"This let me out [remarks the talented reporter] and I lit for the Maverick House, and after some 'Rock and Rye,' sat down to think about what I had heard. I allow that Mendiola was, like most picayune 'Greasers,' really a fatalist, reckoned he had a Kismet or a something which predestined him to do the deed. Anyhow, he is not the first citizen of La Salle who has gone up the golden stair with the assistance of a half-inch rope.

"Back at the Maverick House — all over now. José Maria just turned off. He looked pale, but showed grit, and in a neat-fitting black suit (Dollar Store cut) made an elegant appearance. One of the most singular features of the whole show was that there was little swearing or ribaldry amongst the crowd; even the Aztecs, who had turned out in force, some coming from Carrizo Springs, the night before, and camping in the Plaza, seeming not much excited. Father Kosbiel, a Polander, had 'corpse' in charge. José stood mighty quiet, and as the City Marshal finished reading the warrant, slightly shrugged his shoulders and said 'Muy bien.' The reverend father then performed the offices for the deceased, and turning to the people said: 'Citizens of Encinal and of

---

*It is the ambition of every Texan and most Mexicans to own either an ivory-handled or a mother-of-pearl handled pistol. It gratifies them just as much as a baronetcy does a successful sweater, and is more readily compassed by the poor in spirit.

Cotulla, this poor Mexican, who stands beside me, will shortly stand before his God. He asks your pardon, and regrets that he can speak no English so as to express to you that he is penitent, but he humbly asks for the sympathy of all men as one about to die.' The reverend father seemed much overcome, but Mendiola remained unmoved, and merely saying, 'Adios, Padre,' stepped on the scaffold, and in an instant was jerked into eternity. 'Dead,' said the physician, 'in four minutes.' The people gossiped awhile, unhitched their horses, and then dispersed. I guess Maria Mendiola was a stupid animal, but he showed 'clear grit' right to the end. Father Kosbiel says he died a Catholic, and that the manner of his going showed his trust in God. Dunno, guess he said he was a Universalist, but any way he seemed the least concerned of the whole outfit, and looked as if he would be thankful when the affair was done."

Thus far the reporter, but an aged settler, as the shavings flew from his pocket-knife and whittling stick pronounced the epitaph:—

"No sense at all," said he, turning towards the nearest saloon; "just didn't have no sense at all. Like killing a goat, didn't have sense enough to be afraid."

Un Angelito

All day we had been riding over the south "campo" of the prairie of Buenos Ayres, between the mountains of Tandil and where the trail which led to Bahia Blanca crosses the Tres Arroyos.

It seemed that never had our "tropilla" given so much trouble to drive; still it was well selected, both as to colour and general undesirability to ride. The mare was brown and white, the foal which followed her, lemon and white with four black feet, the horses black and white, all with their manes well hogged after the Gaucho fashion, leaving a lock upon the withers by which to mount; and all in such condition that one could have counted money on their backs — two of them were neither tame nor wild; two neither wild nor tame; two but half broken (*medio bagualon*), one difficult to mount, another almost impossible to catch, and when caught, worth nothing but to fasten to a stake at night to drive the others up on, in the morning; and one but fitted, as the Gauchos say, to make a perch for a wild bird.

The suffocating north wind blew hot and fatiguing as the Hamsin. On every side a sea of grass, grass and more grass; "paja y cielo "(grass and sky), as the natives of the country style their favourite landscape.

Nothing to break the brown eternity of the Pampa but here and there a green ombú, shaped like an umbrella, or an occasional straggling line of Pampa grass, which marked the edges of some watercourse, and by comparison seemed as tall as does a poplar in the plains of Lombardy.

An ostrich now and then scudded across our path, with wings spread out to catch the wind, like a ship running down the North-East Trades.

Sometimes a Patagonian hare sprang from the grass and lurched, apparently quite slowly, out of sight.

In the district we were crossing, all the rivers salt, and, though as clear as crystal, bitter as gall. The rare travellers, seen from afar, almost hull down like ships upon the sea, grew by degrees larger as they approached, and hat, and poncho, and then saddle and horse came into sight.

When they drew near, they drove their horses all together, and coming forward, riding from side to side, holding their pistol or "facon,"* advanced, halted a stone-throw off, shouting their salutations. If all seemed right, they then advanced and asked for news about the Indians; for all the country had been laid waste, the houses burnt, men killed, and women and cattle carried off, about a week before.

It usually appeared that the next house — that is, the one the traveller had left three leagues behind — was smouldering, the body of the owner lying before the door, swollen to the dimensions of an ox, and festering in the sun.

We in our turn related how at the "puesto" five leagues away, close to the pass of the Quequen Salado, we had seen a woman's body hanging naked to a post, and decorated with leaves torn from a Bible skewered artistically about it where decency required.

With mutual recommendations to have prudence, to beware of smokes†, to ride with care, to get off at the little hills which break the Pampa into inequalities, and crawling up to scan the horizon well before descending, we separated with a fallacious "Go with God," knowing full well our only trust was in our spurs.

Not quite the sort of time that any one would choose to sleep out on the open "camp."

Towards evening we reached what in those countries is called by courtesy, a fort — that is, it had been once a fort, and therefore had a shallow ditch all round it, and a flat roof, on which reposed a rusty cannon, choking the embrasure.

Around the fort a grove of peaches, known as the "Monte," straggled and furnished a fruit, hard as a turnip, but esteemed a delicacy upon the plains.

A strong corral of posts of ñandubay, all bound together with strips of hide, and a "palenque" — that is, a post to fasten horses to — formed the outworks to the place.

The "palenque" marks the boundary to which the wayfaring man, if not a fool, may safely venture on his horse.

To pass beyond it uninvited, especially at night, exposes one to the chance of a casual shot, or at the least to the assaults of a pack of dogs

---

*A "facon" is a long knife which serves either to eat with or to cut a man's throat (in the slang of the Pampas, "hacer la obra santa").

†The Indians signal to one another by the smoke of fires.

which seize your horse's tail.

Your caballero leaves his horses some way off, and rides up slowly, and still sitting on his horse, calls "Ave Maria!" in a loud voice, to which the owner answers, "Sin pecado concebida," and invites him to get off.

Religion and politeness being thus satisfied, the traveller dismounts, ties up his horse, enters the kitchen, and sits down on a horse's head beside the fire.

The quantity of saddled horses standing outside the house portended something of an unusual kind.

To the "palenque," to the wheels of bullock-carts, to posts in corral, to tufts of grass, to bones half-buried in the ground, stood horses tied.

Every variety of the piebald race was there — "overo negro," "alazan overo," "entrepelado," "overo porcelano," "azulejo," with "tuviano" and "yaguané" — they all were there, looking as bright and variegated as is a bed of tulips in the setting sun.

Some of them merely hobbled by the forefeet, and weighted down with silver bridles, with heavy "cups" on either side of the mouth, with silver reins seven feet in length tied back upon the saddles, making them arch their necks like rocking-horses; the saddles silver-mounted, silver their "fiadores" and "pretales," silvered so to speak, like clippers, to the bends; the very rings which formed the buckles of their broad hide girths being of heavy plate. Others, again, were saddled with an old "recado," not worth a dollar (even of Bolivia); a sheepskin on the top, the stirrups merely knots of hide made to be caught between the naked toes. These last sat back on their "Cabrestos" and snorted as you passed them, causing their owners to rush hurriedly from out of the house to see if there was danger of their saddles disappearing, and then to mutter, when the horse was quieted, that he was "*medio redomon*" (that is, but mounted a few times), "for the accursed infidel had taken all the tame horses and left the 'pago' upon foot." It puzzled me to think why after an invasion of the Indians so many people had come to visit my acquaintance, Eustaquio Medina, known also as Eustaquio el Tejon.

Soon he came out and welcomed me, asking me to dismount, hobble my mare, and carefully tie up a horse, remarking that in the times we lived Christians should take precautions and always live prepared.

The flesh, the devil, and the world were not the things against which Eustaquio thought a true believer should prepare — at least I think so — for, if he ever thought about such matters, he judged most likely it was the business of his priest to shield him from the devil; the world in the Pampas is not too distracting to the mind, and for the flesh he made no struggle, thinking that that which God had made, must of necessity be good for man.

After most minute inquiries after the health of all my family, of whom he knew no member, he said —

"We have 'un angelito' in our poor house — that is, his body; for his soul is with the blest."

The conscious pride of being, as it were, in direct touch with heaven itself had caused him to forget his grief for his son's death. No people upon earth can be more absolutely material than the Gauchos of the Pampa, yet one is just as safe amongst them, even in a bargain, as amongst those who analyse their motives and find a spiritual explanation for the basest of their deeds.

Amusements, except ostrich-hunting, cattle-marking, with racing, and others of a nature in which it is not easy for women to participate, are scarce. When a child dies it is the signal for a dance to celebrate its entrance into bliss.

If the Christian faith was really held by anybody in its entirety, this custom would not be solely to be observed amongst the Gauchos. As it is, humanity in almost every other country rises superior even to faith, that first infirmity of uninstructed minds.

So in a long, low room lit by a score of candles, made in tin-moulds, and smoking blackly, were assembled some fifty people, Gauchos, estancieros, a Basque or two, and the ubiquitous Italian with his organ, who in those days used to pervade the Pampa from the Arroyo del Pabon to Tapalquén.

The women, known as "Chinas" (Chinese), though none knows why or wherefore, did not err much upon the score of great expenditure in dress — a cotton gown, apparently in many cases their only garment, except their shift — sat, when not dancing, in rows on chairs along the wall, like swallows on a telegraph-wire, waiting as patiently for any man to hire them as the eleventh-hour labourers in Holy Writ.

The "Angelito," dressed in his best clothes, sat in a chair upon a table, greenish in colour, and with his hands and feet hanging down limply — horrible, but at the same time fascinating. Over his head a cheap Italian lithograph of the Madonna hung by a strip of hide from a deer's horn stuck into the wall. On either side a pious and frightful German print, one of the Prodigal amongst his swine, another flanking it setting him forth in better circumstances, seated in pomp between two German ladies, monstrously fair and fat.

Just underneath the "Angelito" sat an old "Gaucho" playing the guitar with the fatuous air with which musicians in countries such as South America invest their trade. Two or three men of the richer classes, as their silver-handled knives and spurs made plain, smoked in a knot apart; whilst in a corner sat some old men talking of horses' marks, and illustrating any difficulty by "painting" the mark in question on the table with their finger dipped in gin.

The younger people danced "habaneras," "el cielito," the "gato," "manguri," or one of those slow valses with much balancing of hips affected by the South Americans. Evidently they had been drinking to the fair passage of the new angel into the realms of bliss. Above the rasping music the rattle of the dancers' spurs was heard, and now and then the man at the guitar broke into a shrill falsetto song, in which the company took part. Stretched on a catre lay a man wrapped in his poncho, with a deep lance-wound in the groin, given by an Indian a few days before. To keep his blood in order and heal his wound he ate great pieces of beef cooked in the hide, and smoked incessantly.

On passing opposite the body the girls occasionally snatched loose their hands from the clutches of their partners and crossed themselves, and then, as if ashamed of thus indulging in a religious exercise in public, broke into laughter.

Why the presence of a child's body, even if its soul is with the blessed, should set on folk to dance passes my comprehension. Yet so it is, and a commercial element has crept into the scheme.

At the country stores, called "pulperias" in Buenos Ayres, sometimes the owner will beg or buy the body of a child just dead to use it as an "Angelito" to attract the country people to a revel at his store.

The pulperia is the Pampa Club, news, calumny and scandal take their rise in it, and there resort all the elite of frontier ruffianism.

One says as naturally, "What do they say at the pulperia?" as in England, "What is the news at such and such a club, or on the Stock Exchange?" An "Angelito" stored in a cool, dark room to keep him from the flies, and then brought out at night to grace a sort of Agapemone, shows past and present linked together in a way which argues wonders, when they both make way for that unfathomable future, the fitting paradise for unimaginative men. From where the custom came, whether from Europe or from the Indians, or if in some form or another it is to be observed in every nation, that I cannot tell: one thing I know, that in the Pampa of Buenos Ayres it and all other customs of a like kind are doomed to disappear.

A cultivated prairie cut into squares by barbed wire fences, riddled with railings and with the very sky shaped into patterns by the crossing lines of telegraphs, may be an evidence, for all I know, of progress; but of all that which makes a Pampa what the Indians imagined it when they gave the plains the name — for Pampa in the Indian tongue signifies the "space" — no traces will be left.

The semi-nomad horsemen will have vanished; the Indians have gone within my memory, leaving, though savages, by their disappearance a blank in the world more difficult to fill than if the works of all the Greeks had vanished into air.

The Gaucho will go next, the ostriches and the huanacos; little by little the plants of Europe, those parasitic prostitutes the nettle and the thistle, which follow us to every climate, will usurp the place of native and more congenial kinds.

His will will be accomplished who, having made the earth a paradise, gave it to us to turn into a purgatory for ourselves and all the dwellers in it.

In this monotony of mud and stucco, through the noise of cabs, of railways and the multitudinous sounds which rob the dweller in a city of any power of hearing, such as wild people have, I sometimes see my "Angelito" seated in his chair, and wonder in what kind of heaven he is. Often I have assisted at a "velorio," and done my best to honour the return of some small angel to his native land. Yet this first occasion on the Tres Arroyos still remains most firmly printed in my mind. Eustaquio Medina, the wounded man lying smoking on his catre, the decomposing "Angelito" in his chair, his mother looking at nothing with her eyes wide open, and the wild music of the cracked guitar seem to revisit me.

Lastly, the Pampa stretching away like a great inland sea, silent and bluish under the southern stars; and rising from it, the mysterious noises of the desert which, heard and comprehended, appeal to us in the same fashion as the instinct calling them north or south, stirs migratory birds.

The Lazo

The lazo is of great antiquity. It is said to be depicted in the ruins of Nineveh. An early Persian manuscript, preserved in the Escorial, shows a sportsman (whom I suppose royal by his Olympian expression and careless seat) in the act of catching a wild ass with a nicely plaited rope. The monarch bestrides a rather stocky-looking, dark-coloured horse, with four white feet and a white face. A bow, quiver and a sabre are hung from his saddle, and a sort of housing half covers the horse. How the wild ass is to be restrained, even by the hand of a monarch, is not at first sight evident, for the lazo is neither fixed to the saddle after the fashion of the Gauchos, nor is a half-turn taken round the pommel, in the style adopted by Vaqueros in Mexico and Texas. Apart from this detail, all is as realistically set forth as it would be to-day in a photograph. The horse bears away from the beast lazoed, and the king sits a little to one side, exactly as a Texan Cowboy or an Argentine Gaucho sits under similar circumstances. Irises and narcissi spring up under the horse's feet, and an applauding group of angels peep out of a cloud, whilst in the middle distance another Persian Gaucho shoots an antelope with an arrow whilst galloping at full speed.

One could have wished that the lazo had been depicted nearer to the ass's head, for hanging as it does, just on the withers, the line of most resistance (so dear to monarchs) has evidently been adopted.

The Laplanders are said to lazo their reindeer, and the Tartars and modern Australians use a rudimentary lazo fixed to a long pole in order to catch wild or refractory horses. The Poles, Croatians, and Wallachians, with the Hungarians, seem to have used the lazo till about the beginning of the present century. A picture by the German artist, Richter, shows Polish remounts for the German cavalry being lazoed in the Zwinger at Dresden. The horses look as wild as a Texan "bronco"* or an Argentine

---

*Bronco = rough or untamed.

"bagual,"* and the attitude of men and animals, and the way the ropes are coiled and thrown, are identical with those adopted in Spanish America to-day. The lazo appears to run through a ring in the pommel of the saddle.

It is, however, in Spanish America where the art has been most developed. This is on account of the open country and the vast numbers of wild and semi-wild horses which, up to the middle of the present century overspread its plains. The lazo may be said to have two great schools: one the style adopted in the Argentine Republic, and the other what may be called the school of Mexico. The Argentine Gaucho and the Brazilian of the province of Rio Grande use a raw-hide lazo, plaited generally in four till within about eight or ten feet of the end, where the plaiting is usually of six, eight, or ten strands, as fancy leads. The lazo terminates in a strong iron ring, which is spliced into the hide so as to remain stiff, and stick out in a straight line from the rope. At the end kept in the hand or attached to the saddle a Turk's head and plaited loop form the finishing. The thickness of the lazo is about that of the little finger, and the hide is kept soft and pliable by frequent applications of grease, for which purpose a piece of raw mutton fat is found to answer best. The Indians use mare's grease, but bacon, oil, or any salted grease is said to burn the hide. To make a lazo the hide of a cow is procured, denuded of hair, and the various strands are softened, either by beating with a mallet or being run through an iron ring, or worked between a piece of split wood (called a "Mordaza"). When properly softened, the inside of the hide is as white as flour, and, if well cared for, will last soft for many years. The ordinary length of an Argentine lazo is about sixty-six feet, though exceptionally tall and powerful men sometimes use lazos of eighty and even ninety feet in length.

A skilful man on foot will catch a horse in a corral at the distance of ten or twelve yards, throwing at the neck. At ten yards he will secure the two fore feet, or a fore and a hind foot, both hind feet, or, catching the animal round the neck, will, by imparting a vibratory motion to the rope, place a half-hitch round the nose, thus forming what is called a "medio bozal," or half-halter. To catch the feet is called "pialar" from *pie*, a foot. The effect of catching by the feet is to throw the animal

---

*Bagual in the Argentine Provinces is sometimes used for a wild and sometimes for a half-tamed horse. The word is of Quichua origin, and is said to have been originally "Cahual," and to have been a corruption of the word "Caballo".

violently to the ground. Catching round the neck chokes the animal to the ground, if enough force is used. In either case, the moment the lazo tightens, the lazoer throws himself back on the rope, like a seaman hauling on a sheet, and, digging his heels into the ground, bears heavily on the rope with his left hand, which he puts as far behind his back as possible. The strain is most severe, cutting the unaccustomed hand and destroying the clothes, so that in many cases a leather apron is worn to keep off the chafe. A strong colt of five years old will drag three or four men round a corral, if they try to stop him by sheer strength, and the lazo be not tightened high on the neck near the ears; but a boy of sixteen, used to the work, by watching his opportunity, will easily stop the same animal.

To throw a long lazo, height is of great advantage, as, other things being equal, a tall man can throw a longer lazo than a man of low stature. The lazo is prepared for throwing by making a noose from two and half to four yards in circumference at the ring end of the rope. The ring should be slipped down to about a third of the circumference of the noose. The remainder of the rope is coiled, and two or three coils taken into the right hand together with the noose; the rest of the coils are held in the left hand. Care must be observed not to leave too much slack rope between the coils in the right and left hands, as it is apt to get entangled when the lazo leaves the hand, especially on horseback. Swinging the noose as many times round the head as is required to give the sufficient momentum, and taking care that the noose flies open and with a slight upward inclination, it is then let go, rather than thrown, when the hand is just above the head on the right side, and slides through the air, uncoiling as it flies.

Like throwing a fly, putting screw on a ball at billiards, and taking a close counter of carte, it is an art not easily described, and best learnt by demonstration and by practice.

To become a perfect lazoer (the Spanish word is *enlazador*), the lazo must have been familiar to the thrower from his youth. To be able to catch a horse in a corral round the neck, with some certainty, can be learnt in about six months by a young and active man accustomed to athletic exercises.

The lazo on horseback is a very different and far more dangerous affair. Accidents are frequent and often fatal, and the business should not be attempted by any one who has not learnt the art in youth. In all cattle districts, in both North and South America, men maimed with the lazo

— having lost either fingers, or a hand, or foot — are as common as "mainsheet men" used to be in seaport towns in the days of "windjammers."

The lazo on horseback can be used with far greater effect than on foot. From sixteen to eighteen yards is a fair distance at which to catch an animal when going at full speed. The faster the horse is going, the more easily is the rope thrown; and of course the danger increases in the same ratio. The method of casting on horseback is precisely similar to that used on foot. A larger loop or noose (called *armada* in Spanish) can be used, and care must be taken not to entangle the coils of the "slack" with the reins, or to catch the horse's hind legs, or head, or his fore feet, or to touch him anywhere with the rope, unless he is extremely tame and tractable. For this reason a less elevation must be given to the point of the noose, as it gyrates round the head, on horseback than on foot; that is to say, it should be swung almost level round the head before casting. The end of the lazo retained by the thrower is buttoned into a strong iron ring fixed behind the rider's right thigh to a piece of hide about three inches in length, which piece of hide is firmly sewn into the ring of the upper part of the strong hide surcingle which forms the girth of the Argentine saddle.

This saddle is called *el recado*; it is a modification of the old "Bur" saddle of the time of Charles V, and is known as *albarda* to the Spaniards and *barda* to the Moors. It is composed of several pieces, and surmounted by a rug or sheepskin; the stirrups are hung long, from the middle of the saddle, and are so small as only to admit the toes. The Spaniards anciently called riding in this saddle riding "*à la brida*" as opposed to the short stirrups and high pommel and cantle of the Moorish saddle, which style of riding was called "*à la gineta*". The Mexican saddle has grown out of this latter style, the stirrups having been lengthened in order to facilitate mounting, and sticking to a wild horse.

When the lazo has been thrown on horseback, and the animal caught round the neck or horns, the difficulty and danger begin. Should the quarry be a wild horse or mare, care has to be taken not to let it cross either in front or behind of the mounted horse. If it does so, there is great danger of a half-turn being taken in the rider's arm or leg, or even a whole turn round his body. The least that can happen is that the mounted horse gets entangled in the rope, becomes frightened, and an accident is almost certain.

Should the animal captured be a bull or cow, the rider must manage to avoid having his horse charged, and for this purpose immediately the noose settles round the beast's horns, the horseman should turn to the near side, *i.e.* away from the animal lazoed, and endeavour to keep the rope always taut. If he succeeds in doing this, there is little danger of the strongest bull pulling over even a light horse; for it is to be remembered that the weight of the saddle and the rider is an assistance to the horse, as making his weight more nearly equal to that of the bull.

It must not be forgotten that in lazoing on horseback it is the horse that works and holds the animal caught; the rider merely throws the lazo, as no strength of his could hold an animal galloping at full speed. Some horses become so dexterous that the rider can slip off, leaving them to keep the lazo taut, and, approaching the bull, hamstring it, or kill it by plunging a long knife into its neck.

A high-spirited horse that starts, stops, and turns easily, and does not get too much excited, is the best mount for the lazoer. A low-spirited animal exposes its rider to danger from a charging bull, and an excitable horse is apt to get twisted in the coils of the lazo, or by throwing up its head, or swerving as the lazo is delivered, to make the aim defective. In almost every case the lazo is thrown on the off side of the horse (known from that circumstance in South America as the "lazo side"), but now and then a skilful lazoer will throw to the near side, and catching an animal, pass the rope over his own and his horse's head, or over the quarters of the horse. This process is always attended with danger, and, as the Gauchos say, should not be attempted by married men.

In South America the inhabitants of the Brazilian province of Rio Grande do Sul hold first place for skill with the lazo. After them come the inhabitants of the Republic of Uruguay and the Gauchos of the province of Buenos Ayres.

The Chilians use a slightly different lazo, without a ring, and with a loop and button at both ends. It is twisted in three strands, and known as a "torzal." They are skilful, but, their country being more broken, are inferior to the men on the east side of the Andes.

The second school of lazoers is that of Mexico. There the lazo is never made of hide, but of horsehair or *istlé*, or of the fibre of the aloe. No iron ring is ever used, and the lazo is all one piece, not having an addition* spliced on at the end, as in South America.

Being of lighter material, the Mexican lazo cannot be thrown so far as

---

*This addition is called La Llapa by the Gauchos, and is also used by them for a luck-penny in a bargain. The word is said to be of Quichua origin.

that of the Pampas. It is more easily carried, however, requires no grease, closes more readily on the neck of the animal lazoed, and neither cuts a horse's legs nor a man's hands so severely as a raw-hide rope.

It is on horseback that the difference between the two schools is most manifest. The Mexican lazo is made fast to the saddle in front of the rider, and hence the difficulty of throwing to the off side is largely obviated; as it is easy to pass the lazo over the horse's head and keep the strain on the rope, and hence far fewer accidents occur in Mexico and Texas than in the Pampas. The Mexican system is, however, less effectual against the efforts of a heavy animal, as, the lazo being fastened to the horn of the saddle when an animal is caught, the rope grazes the body of the rider during the process of the struggle, and it appears improbable that the horse can throw as much weight on to the rope as he can under the Argentine system of fastening. It is usual in Mexico not to tie or make fast the end of the lazo to the saddle, but to take a half-hitch round the horn, and hold the end in the left hand. It is considered very dangerous to tie the lazo to the bow of the saddle, and a man who does so is said to *amarrar a muerte* — that is, to tie a death-knot. Mexicans are very dexterous with the lazo on foot, as, owing to the lightness of their rope, it is very easily thrown. Texans, Kansans, and men of the North-West often use a common hemp rope without a ring or button, but merely tie a bowline, and pass the coil of the rope through a bight to form a noose. Texan cowboys are often extremely skilful, performing as many feats with the lazo as the Mexicans or Gauchos, but seldom equalling the Brazilians of Rio Grande, who are the smartest men with lazo or bolas, or on a wild horse, that I have seen.

The lazo, with the bolas, the boomerang, the spear, and bow, in a few years will be but memories. Rifle and gun will have replaced or rendered them unnecessary, and the descendants of the wild riders who mounted "bagual" and "bronco," holding them by the ear, and getting to their seats as a bird lights upon a bough, will wait to catch the tramcar at the corner of the street. Therefore this short description may have its interest, being a sort of record of a dream, dreamed upon pampas and on prairies, sleeping upon a saddle under the southern stars, or galloping across the plains in the hot sun, photographed in youth upon the writer's brain, and, when recalled, more vivid than affairs of State which happened yesterday.

The Bolas

"They have certain balls of stone" (says Hulderico Schmidel in his "Historia y Descubrimiento del Rio de la Plata y Paraguay") "tied to a long string like to our chain shot; they throw them at the legs of the horses (or of the deer when they hunt), which brings them to the ground, and with these bolas they killed our Captain and the above referred to gentlemen."

This happened in the year 1585, when the Flemish soldier Hulderico Schmidel fought with the troops of Pedro de Mendoza against the Indians called Querandis, on what is now the site of Buenos Ayres. The captain slain was Diego de Mendoza, brother to the general of the expedition; the "above referred to gentlemen" figure but as "los seis Hidalgos." And thus is chronicled the first description of the "bolas," destined since then to bring down to the ground many a good horse and stag, and even crush the skulls of captains and hidalgos not a few.

Confined entirely to the south of South America, the bolas, like the boomerang, seems to have been unknown to any tribe of savages apart from its inventors. It grew, like other national weapons, from the conditions of the life and country whence it sprang.

The Indians of South America before the Conquest had no horses, so, living on great plains, game must have been most difficult to approach, and when approached consisted chiefly of deer, guanacos, and of ostriches — all animals certain to escape (upon a plain) if slightly wounded by an arrow. Thus an invention like the bolas, which if it touched the legs was certain to entangle, was valuable, as, thrown by a strong arm, it could be used almost as far off as an arrow, was much more easily recovered after a miss, and ten times easier to make. Schmidel describes the weapon accurately when he refers to it as "three balls of stone fastened together by a cord after the fashion of our chain shot." Therefore, it will be seen that the bolas known (for euphony and other reasons) as "las boleadores" [= *boleadoras*] in the River Plate stands in the same relation to the lazo as the rifle stands to the ordinary gun.

Such as it is, no Indian, Gaucho, or any self-respecting countryman from Sandy Point to Paraguay, or from the Banda Oriental to Coronel, ever stirs out without at least one pair, either wound round his waist or placed under the "cojinillo"* of his saddle, ready to throw at ostriches, at deer, guanacos, or at the horse of some newcomer to the country which has escaped and scours the plain, the stirrups dangling to the accompaniment of shouts of "Yá se vá el caballo del Inglés." Sometimes it serves to fight with at a "pulperia,"† when the inevitable gin-born discussion as to the merits of the "Blancos"‡ and the "Colorados" waxes hot.

Bolas for general use are made of two stones about the size and weight of billiard balls, and of another about half the size and egg-shaped. All three are shrunk into bags of hide known to the Gaucho as "retobas." Each ball is fastened to a string of twisted hide about the thickness of a pencil, and three feet in length. The three are fastened in the middle like a Manxman's legs, so that the length from the hand ball to the two large balls does not exceed six feet, and the whole weight is not above a pound. For horses, wooden balls are used, and to catch ostriches, little balls of lead not larger than a pigeon's egg, fastened to strings of rather greater length than those I have described.

The Indians in the south of Patagonia sometimes use a bola made of a single string and with a ball attached, with which they strike and kill wild animals, as pumas, jaguars, and guanacos. The instrument is called "bola perdida," and, of course, cannot be used to take an animal alive, as it does not entangle but merely stuns the animal it strikes. At other times they use a single string with but a single bola and a hand ball, as being easier to throw, lighter to carry, and much easier to make, but it does not wind round the legs so firmly as do the bolas of the common

---

*"Cojinillo," literally cushion, is the sheepskin or mat of twisted goat's hair, which is placed over the framework of the "recado" (South American saddle); over the cojinillo is placed a piece of leather called a "sobre puesto," and the whole is kept in place by a strong hide sircingle, known as the "sobre-cincha."
†Pulperia is a country store where everything is sold, and where sardines, figs, bread, raisins, and "vino seco" or "Carlon," with square-faced gin, comprise the menu. The bar is defended by a strong grating, and the "pulpero" stands behind with his revolver and a pile of empty bottles ready for what may happen.
‡"Blancos" and "Colorados" are the Ins and Outs, and they are as hard to distinguish as are two black stones, or as the obsolescent political protoplasms known as Whigs and Tories.

shape. To throw the bolas, they are whirled round the head and circle through the air with the two heavier balls close beside one another, and when launched turn round and round on their own axis in their flight, and break in like a "twister" from the leg side, and if the strings strike on the legs of any animal, the motion of the bolas being stopped, the balls wind round and round and tie the animal as firmly as would a pair of hobbles. The heavier kind may (on a good horse) be thrown from fifty to seventy yards, the balls for ostriches nearly one hundred, and the single "bola perdida" a hundred and twenty yards and even more, according to the strength of the man throwing and the speed at which the cast is made. On foot, as with the lazo, much of the power is lost, though as a general rule the cast is made more accurately. When thrown the bolas are extremely hard to get away from, and the best plan is to run towards the thrower and lie down flat upon the ground. If the man thrown at tries to run away his chance is small, and even if armed with a revolver the odds are much in favour of the "boleador," especially if he has several pairs of bolas, as, at the distance of fifty to sixty yards, the pistol rarely does damage if the object at which the shooter aims is moving rapidly about; the fact of motion is of no consequence to the man who throws the "balls," their length giving such a wide margin upon which to work. The bolas are easier by far to learn than is the lazo, and the danger far less great; for as the bolas leave the hand when thrown, the only danger lies in the possibility of catching your own horse's legs, in which case it is probable he will start bucking "fit to knock down a town," and the unlucky thrower get a violent fall and rise to find his horse either with a leg broken or else scouring the plain with his new saddle, and himself afoot.

An average horseman and a cricket-player should learn the bolas in three months' practice, though to excel (as with the lazo) the "boleador" must have begun as a mere child, and have "balled" and "lazoed" chicken, cats, and dogs in order to acquire the skill of hand the natives of the Pampas enjoy with both. Such is the weapon (well greased with mutton fat) with which the Gaucho and the Indian fight, catch wild horses, deer, and ostriches, and with which their forefathers caught the horses of the soldiers of Don Pedro de Mendoza, and their grandfathers the artillerymen of the unlucky expedition under General Whitelock, the flags of which still hang in Buenos Ayres in the Cathedral aisle.

In the vast territory of the Southern Pampa, which stretches from Bahia Blanca to Sandy Point, and from Puan to Nahuelhuapi; in the green prairies that reach from Buenos Ayres to the Sierra de Vulcan, upon the park-like prairies of Entre Rios, and the vast rolling steppes of Rio Grande, and again amongst the apple forests of the Andes, the bolas are the chief pleasure, weapon, and plaything of the Gaucho of the plains. His habits, speech, and mode of life Azara first made known to the futile world which reads and writes, and thinks because it reads it knows, and to whose eyes the Pampa with its signs, its lore, its disappearing customs, its low horizons, flat-topped ombús, rivers and wastes, Guadal* and Biscacheras,† its flocks of ostriches, its cattle without number, herds of wild horses, whirling tero-teros, and its lone ranches, is a closed book. Nothing so pleasant in this machine-rid world as to bestride a half-tamed horse upon the Southern Pampas, and, well armed with several pairs of ostrich bolas, accompanied by two good greyhounds, to go upon the "boleada" — that is, to start out ostrich hunting with several well-tried friends, and with a "caballada" from which to take a fresh mount when the horse ridden tires. The Patagonian ostrich (*Rhea Americana*) frequents the stony uplands which so fascinated Darwin, and of which he said that all the wealth of vegetation of the tropics had not made so deep a mark upon his mind as the wild plains, the solitary huts, the lonely camp-fires where the dogs kept watch, the horses eating, tied with their green-hide ropes, and he lay smoking, wrapped in his poncho, looking at the stars. Whether in Patagonia, or on the rolling plains of brown and waving grass which stretched from the Romero Grande to Tandil, the ostrich goes in flocks ranging from ten or twelve up to a hundred or even more. Scudding across the plains before the wind, their wings spread out to catch the breeze, it takes a well-tried horse, with his utmost efforts, after a gallop of several miles, to bring a man within a bola's cast. The hunters range themselves in a formation like a fan, and try to join the outside edges of their ranks and get the ostriches into a circle, or else to force them into marshy ground on which they cannot run, or up against the margin of a stream, edge of a wood, or border of a precipice. Sometimes the birds scatter and break up into groups, and then the horsemen, whirling their bolas round their heads, bound over stones, rush through the mia-mia, thread through the scrub, and, with

---

*"Guadal" is a marshy tract of ground; the word comes from the Arabic "guahal," mud.
†Biscachera; the biscacha is an animal somewhat resembling the prairie dog of North America. The best description of the biscacha is perhaps that of W. H. Hudson in his "Naturalist in La Plata."

wild cries, incite their horses and their greyhounds to full speed. Ponchos stream in the wind, hair flutters, silver spurs rattle upon the raw hide girths, and now and then a horse, stepping into a "cangrejal,"* rolls like a rabbit, its rider seldom failing to alight "parado" — that is, on his feet — and, holding the long reins or halter in his hand, to rise before his horse, and mounting, when it regains its legs, straight to resume the chase.

To go upon the "boleada" is the chief ambition of every Gaucho of the south, and so that he can make enough to keep him in cigars and gin, to buy a new silk handkerchief or poncho now and then, no chance that he will hire himself for any settled work. Yet many of the "boleadores" die at their trade, either at the hands of Indians, by hunger or by thirst, or, failing to alight "parado" after a heavy fall, are left on foot with a limb broken, to die alone amidst the ocean of brown grass, from which no man left wounded, without a horse, escapes alive. Most of the frontier soldiers who, in the last two generations, themselves half Indians, have forced the Indians back into the wild valleys of the Cordillera of the Andes, have been "boleadores."

The couriers, who used to ride from Bahia Blancas to Patagonia, passing the Rio Colorado, and getting across the "travesia"† as best they might, all learned their desert lore in the pursuit of ostriches. Perhaps Bahia Blanca was the centre of the "bolas." Game was abundant, cattle mostly wild, Indians swept often in their "malones"*‡ over the settled lands, and the wild people known as "Badilleros" had a deep-rooted and most logical objection to all continued work. Even the lazo was too troublesome, and so they lived even less comfortably than did the Indians, raising no crops, shivering in wretched mud and straw-thatched huts, with a horse-hide for the door, eating no bread, and with a saddled horse tied night and day outside the house. Their conversation was all of horses, brands, fights with the Indians, feats with the "bolas"; of such a one who, on his journey to some place, was set on by the "infidel," and crossed the Rio Colorado with a pair of bolas on his horse's legs; of such another who, carrying the mails, lost the road, and was discovered lying dead on his exhausted horse, his last act having been to hang the mail-bag on a tree.

---

*"Cangrejal" is a piece of ground undermined by land crabs (cangrejos).
†Travesia = a crossing; it is generally used in the River Plate for a tract of desert country between two fertile districts.
‡"Malon" was the word used by the Gauchos for an Indian raid.

Such as they were, a hardy race — now passed, or passing fast, into oblivion — more savage than the Arabs, only a step advanced beyond the Indians; tall, lean, long-haired, hospitable, and thievish, abstemious as Icelanders, and yet as very gluttons as an Apache at a dog feast; born almost on their horses, sitting them like centaurs, living amongst them, talking and thinking but of them, and shying when they shied, as they had been one flesh. I see them, as I saw them years ago, out on the "boleada," riding towards some "pingo"* paradise, twisting "las tres Marias"† round their heads, bent just a little sideways in the saddle, as, at full speed, they plunged through the pajonales,‡ flitted across the stony wastes, sped through the oceans of brown grass, and disappeared out on the Pampa as a ship slowly sinks into the shadow of the world upon the sea.

---

*"Pingo" is the Gaucho word of praise and endearment applied to a fine horse.
†"Las tres Marias", i.e. the "Three Marys," a euphuism for the "Bolas." It is also used for the three bright stars in Orion.
‡Pajonales, *i.e.*, canebrakes or thickets of Pampa grass.

S.S *Atlas*

It was a filthy autumn day in New York, with Fifth Avenue looking more than usually vulgar under the leaden sky, and the streets carpeted with rotting plane-leaves, as I drove, jolting over the rough cobblestone, to a wharf near Dubrosses Ferry to go on board the *Atlas*. The S. S. *Atlas* was a type of ship well known in the Seventies, but now obsolete. In those days the "tramp" had scarcely made its appearance, and the liner was less frequent and less gorgeous than at present.

Vessels long, iron-built, flat-sided, and coffin-like, of the *Atlas* type held an intermediate position. They looked for cargo where it might be reasonably expected, and took passengers to whom a long passage, rough food and poor accommodation were rendered indifferent through lack of means. The American agent had informed me that the fare from New York to Glasgow was £10, and that the vessel was a Scotch boat, in which I should find Bible and whiskey, and might expect to be in Glasgow in twelve days, if (so the agent said) the Lord was willing and the Scotchmen did not overdrink themselves. I had no deck-chair, the decks were an inch deep in coal-dust, and the vessel went to sea at once. Leaving Sandy Hook we encountered the full force of a north-easterly gale, and I (the only passenger) retired at once to my athwartship bunk, to be miserable and endeavour to read the "Faerie Queene," my only book, and the only book on board except a Bible and a bound-up volume of the "Reaper" and some professional works. For weeks, as it appeared to me, it was "Burley Banes," rattle of ropes, racing of screw, banging of my portmanteau as it washed to and fro in a foot of water in the cabin, groaning of timbers, roaring of the wind, bellowing of the Blatant Beast (in the "Faerie Queene"), shouting of the boatswain, pattering of naked feet upon the deck; then a fitful dozing, broken but by the rare visits of the steward with a "cup of arrowroot and whiskey, sir," to tell me everything was battened down, and that the skipper had been sixteen hours on the bridge and looked like Lot's wife when she enjoyed her last wistful glance at Sodom. Air stifling, lamp smoking, drops of moisture on every plank, a continuous dropping of water on to

233

my pillow, rats running across the floor, a dense, steamy feeling which made one sleepy, crumbs of biscuit in the bed-clothes, a futile tin basin floating in the cabin, a brandy-bottle propped between a Bible and a sponge in the fixed washing-stand, guttering candles swung in gimbles, decks which seemed to rise and hit one in the face when staggering out in the rare intervals of the storm, to see yards of bulwarks swept away, feeling one's way between the seas, clutching a life-line to the engine-room to listen to the yarns of the chief engineer, a Greenock Ananias of the first water, and bushy bearded as befitted one who had "gone out in '47, second engineer aboard the craft what took out Rajah Brook." Then back to bed, wet through, and back into a trance between sleep and waking, more brandy, arrowroot, more "Faerie Queene," more stifling, and the vessel labouring so heavily that when the copper cargo shipped at Copiapo shifted on the fifth day out, it seemed she lay almost upon her broadside in the sea. And still I liked the voyage, and even took a pride in knowing we had sighted Rockall, hoped in my heart of hearts we should sight Iceland, and yet was miserably seasick all day long, and all night long lay half awake, meditating on the adventures of Sir Satyrane, of Britomart, Parlante, and the Faire Florimell, and all the other characters of Spenser's masterpiece, who in some curious way seemed to become connected with the ship.

After the seventh day no cooking, galley fire put out and steward staggering in drunk, with a Bible in his hand, white-faced and frightened, "rubber" sea-boots on, and plate of cold salt horse and biscuit, and, of course, more whiskey; fitfully came the strains of "Renzo" as the crew set the fore topmast staysail, and in my berth I learned how "Reuben Renzo" shipped aboard a whaler, "Renzo, boys, Renzo," heard his adventures, cruel treatment by the mate, and was most interested to find that for a change his virtue had its reward at last, and at the present time "he was the skipper of a sugar droger." Weeks seemed to pass, and on a day the Captain, clad in dripping oilskins, looking in for a moment with a speaking-trumpet in his hand, deigned to impart the information that we had a slant of wind, and though the smoke-stack had fetched loose, he reckoned to make Cape Clear, "damn his eyes, forgive him, God, for swearing," in a few hours.

Now floated down to me the cheering melody of "New Orleans," with its inspiriting chorus of, "Yah yer, ho, roll and go," and somewhat inconsequent but Demosthenic envoy of "Hell to yer soul, is it tay that ye want?" as the crew "set sail to steady her," as my familiar the steward, having discarded whiskey, fear and Bible, for the nonce, and bearing hot sea-pie came in to say.

At last on deck, with Rathlin Island on the starboard beam, steaming towards the Mull; a great sea change, no boats, bulwarks all washed away upon the weather side, doors torn off the hinges, the "fetched loose" smoke-stack, coated white with salt, and stayed up in a clumsy fashion with some chains; rigging a mass of tatters, halyards flying loose, the jack-staff gone, the Captain haggard and red-eyed, the officers all cheerfully profane, the crew going about like men after a long debauch, but cheerily, as hauling in the main sheet they bent their backs, taking the time from a Long Island fisherman who did not pull the value of a cent, and hauled together, keeping time to the innumerable verses of that old-world lyric of the seas, "Tom's gone to Hello." The Mull and Pladda, Lamlash Island, Cloch Lighthouse, and the winding river with its fairway marks, Dumbarton Castle, and Dumbuck, Elderslie House, and at the last the Broomielaw; black decks again, and then I step ashore in "Glesca" to find it "Sawboth," and be asked by the pious whiskey-seller, where I essayed to change a sovereign to pay my cab, if I was sure I was a "bona feede traveller."

Ten days flew past at home with theatres, dress-clothes, good dinners, and the unaccustomed feel of comfort, so strange to those who but a week ago have been the inmates of a tramp. Ten days amongst the faces, once so familiar, but which to-day may look quite strange if we should meet in limbo, purgatory, or wheresoever it is the souls of travellers pass their appointed time. Ten days and back again upon the Broomielaw, rain, fog, and coal-dust, and the lights of whiskey shops glaring like ogres' eyes upon the crowd, decks filthy, crew either half drunk or else disabled by disease; the skipper sulky, mates thinking about home and surly, the boatswain almost inaudible through a bad cold, and the poor draggled drabs upon the shore looking like animated rag-shops in the December gloom. Scuffling and cursing, creaking of blocks, throbbing of the screw, and then the vessel slides out into the foul-smelling, muddy drain they call the Clyde, slips past the shipyards, passes Blythswood, leaves the Cloch astern, runs past the Cumbraes, where the minister once used to pray for the adjoining islands, England and Ireland; leaves Pladda on the weather side, begins to dip and roll and sends me to my bunk to lie half stupid, torpid, a prey to nausea and foul smells, till the throbbing ceases, the heaving and the pitching stop, and going upon deck I see the sun and find that we are anchored in the Garonne under a vineyard, and about a mile outside Pauillac. Here we intended to take in emigrants for the River Plate, the vessel, during her ten days' rest in Glasgow, having been whitewashed down below and fitted up with tiers of bunks after the fashion of those vans in which sheep make their railway journeys, and just as comfortable. Visions of tugs coming sweeping down the yellow stream, crammed thick with people, all with Basque caps and carrying bags, bundles, and the inevitable bird-cage, without which no emigrant embarks. Glimpses of garboard strakes, as the tide sets the steam launches round, and the emigrants rush to one side chattering in Basque; clattering of donkey-engines worked by a grimy "greaser," and recollections of an interminable song about "Oh mariniers, bons mariniers, à combien vendez-vous votre blé?" sung by black-haired and red-sashed men, working the cargo under the direction of a much-bejewelled stevedore. Then all the emigrants crowd down below, kissing takes place, men hug their sweethearts, to wed whom they are going foreign, and hope in ten years' time when they return with dollars to find constant, unimpaired in virtue and in face, with the same figure which the dim but treasured photograph sets forth. A bell rings and the quartermasters clear the ship, the friends who go ashore holding their handkerchiefs, dirty with tears, to their red eyes; the friends on board waving their greasy hats, and neither trying in the least to keep their feelings in, but weeping lustily after the primitive and natural fashion which relieves a man and makes him feel that tears wash out his grief, rendering him happier than those whom education, custom, prejudice, or what you will, have forced to face their misery with dry eyes.

So past the Tour de Cordouan, and, after, Lisbon, where again the ship took in another freight of human cattle, this time chiefly peasants from the Galician hills, who emigrate *en masse*, leaving their villages deserted and the houses closed, for wolves to scamper through the deserted streets on winter nights, Then out into the "roaring forties," followed by a rising gale. Hell down below amongst the emigrants, and no one on board who could speak French or Spanish, still less Portuguese, except the wretched reader of the "Faerie Queene." So through those alleyways I weltered sick to death, when difficulties rose, and jabbered with the unlucky peasants, who bore their sufferings manfully, sitting on the deck all jammed together like sardines, from the grandmother to the new-born infant, and almost every family hampered with a great wicker birdcage, though they were going to a land of parrots, macaws, toucans, hummingbirds, cardinals and flying spots of jewelled rainbow, compared to which the birds of

Europe all seem made of sackcloth or of mackintosh; but were not Abana and Pharpar superior to all the waters of Judea? But it seems natural to man upon a journey to impede himself with all the living things he can, and to trail draggled birds, bound in their wicker servitude, beyond the seas. As he could not free man, body or soul, by all the strength of prayer and of example, St. Francis perhaps did well to open bird-cages and set their inmates free whenever he got the chance; at his beatification, had I been there I should have urged against the arguments of the Devil's Advocate, this fact, and pled that every rookery about the place, all larks, quails, pigeons, thrushes, blackbirds, linnets, and starlings should have had a chance to register their vote. And then the gale subsided, and the old semi-tramp lurched at nine knots before the following seas, till in a day or two we struck the north-east trades, carried them fair and light, and woke one morning in the dream world of sapphire sea, clear sky, and flying fish darting before the ship, Portuguese men-of-war on every side of us; warm air, a feeling of content, a heavy roll, sails flapping against the rigging, now and then filling with a jerk as if they would tear out of the bolt ropes, in fact, the magic of a fine day in a low latitude not to be represented to the mind by a curved line and straggling lettering, Tropic of Capricorn, as in a map. Like a white cloud we sighted Teneriffe, fully thirty leagues away, passed close to Santa Cruz, left Lanzarote on our lee, coaled at St. Vincent, passed under San Antonio rising a piece of Africa lost in the sea, and then headed across the ocean towards Brazil. Christmas Day caught us somewhere: no doubt the longitude and latitude is still recorded in some forgotten log-book with the due "observations" and "remarks": but we were Scotchmen and recked but little of such Erastian festivals, although the emigrants performed a sort of mutilated mass upon the deck, a Biscayan schoolmaster mumbling his mystery from a prayer-book and the faithful gathered in a crowd a little aft of the fore bitts, whilst the West of Scotland crew pushed through them now and then to trim the sails or make their way into the forecastle. At times a perspiring fireman emerged out of the stokehole, a "sweat rag" round his neck and lump of waste in his black hands, to breathe and see the show, sat looking for a minute as if the worshippers had been a tribe of savages, and then climbed down his ladder backwards, just pausing for a moment as his head sunk below the coaming of the hatch to mutter something of an uncomplimentary nature on the Whore of Babylon.

Days followed starry nights and we began to know each other, and the officers and men having emerged out of their oilskins, and the watch and watch duty which made them north of 40°, so to speak, fenced off from the mere landsmen and oppressed with work, they now began to take a patronising interest in the passengers and to chat freely with the emigrants, their deep-sea dignity laid on one side, perhaps because they could unbend more safely as no other sailors were about. The captain, who since then has risen to command big ships, to be commodore (I think) of a great line of steamers, and to retire upon his well-earned pension and laurels to Blackheath, to bore himself consumedly on shore, and to regret the days, no doubt, when he commanded the S.S. *Atlas*, was a pious, blaspheming Scotchman, built as it seemed to last for ever, hardy and wise, beard like a scrubbing-brush, quick-tempered and good-hearted, a perfect seaman of what I may term the transition school, having served all his early life in "wind-jammers," but "sceenteefic" in his way, and able, above all, to deal with a scratch, rough, skulking crew such as we had on board. The mates indefinite, all Glasgow men, well educated, reading "improving" books; one of them with a master's certificate, and all so boorish in demeanour that till you knew them it appeared that they were mad. Much is forgiven to North Britons, for they have drunk much, but why they should think that rudeness shows independence is not so clear, for above all men in the world they are the first to see a slight intended to themselves. The boatswain and quartermasters were all Englishmen, two of them old men-of-war's men, careful and tidy as old housemaids, and often in their watch off, on a fine night, I saw them washing their clothes amid the jeers of the Scotch crew, "who did not hold with it," and thought that water had only one use, to mix with whiskey, and that that use was only made of it by fools, by weaklings, and by Englishmen. At night I sat and yarned with them, tried unsuccessfully to learn to splice, thinking the art might turn out useful in mending lazos, listened to their jokes and forgot most of them, but still remember something about the "*Mary Dunn*, of Dover, a brig (I think) wot went to sea with three great bloomin' decks and 'ad no bottom." The crew appeared to be composed mainly of costermongers with a stray seaman here and there, longshoremen, and an occasional West Highland fisherman. The doctor (brother of a well-known portrait painter), who perchance may smile when he reads this, informed me that their habit was to come on board blind drunk, without a kit except a new jack-knife and new sea-boots, to pitch the latter down the fore peak and fall themselves upon the top of them, lie prostrate for a day or two, and then get up and ask him for "blackwash," of which he kept a mighty store, knowing the medicines by experience which were most likely to be useful in their case. The fishermen were quieter and had sea-chests, good stocks of clothes, and were sailors in a fashion, all having made a trip or two at sea. When sails were hoisted they always got close to the block, "lifted the shanty," yo, heave, ho! and made as if they were about to pull like oxen, but stopped there, and if some three or four of them had clapped on to the same rope the sail would never have been set in the whole watch they pulled so "cartiously."

The Spanish and French emigrants were mostly Basque, all wearing "boinas" and "alpargatas," speaking dialects of the Basque tongue quite comprehensible to one another, and yet hating each other to the full as much as Irish and English, merely because an arbitrary line ran through the mountains where they all were born. A long thin Bordelais called Pierre, but known as "Monsieur Pedro," because he spoke a little Spanish, ruled them like slaves, and when they fought knocked them about till they were quiet, at times coming aft to ask for medicines from the doctor with a grave face, often explaining with some detail that a woman was apparently ill with fever, but that he (Monsieur Pedro) thought that was untrue, and "the dam woman really make too much love." But this love or fever to the doctor were all one (perhaps they are to every one) and Pierre used to go off contented with a seidlitz powder and two pills. At night the emigrants danced to the strains of an accordion, sang "me gastan todas" to the guitar, or joined in chorus to the eighty verses of an old southern French song, known as "La Blonde," a damsel who was beloved by all "Les Chasseurs," but who incontinently flung herself away upon a "braconnier," perhaps because as the chorus used to set forth "Les braconniers sont dangereux et nombreux," — but why spy into the motives of a poacher and his wife?

The great Scotch festival found us off Fernando Noronha, the little island off the coast where the Brazilians had a penal settlement. The day broke hot, and as we passed the island it loomed low, the palm-trees standing in a sort of mirage so that they seemed to have no roots and float above the land like parasols, between the sand and sky.

How the crew got the liquor no one ever knew, but before twelve o'clock the ship was like a pandemonium or the east end of Glasgow on a fast-day night. From the stoke-hole came the sounds of "Auld Lang Syne," the watch on deck were stupid, and the emigrants scattered before them like chickens before the gambols of a large Newfoundland pup. Just when the skipper came on deck, his sextant in his hand, ready to shoot the sun, a man walked up to him and said, "Hoo are ye, Captin? Ye ken although my feyther aye sat under Dr. Candlish I'm a deevil wi' the lasses, and so are ye yirsel." The captain who, since early morn had been boiling with fury, growled like a bear, told the man roughly to go forward and lie down, received an insolent reply, then knocked him down, and had him put in irons, then carried to a spare cabin and locked in, where he continued to howl "Auld Lang Syne" until he fell asleep. But by this time the decks were filthy, men falling down and sick all over them, the mates and engineers working like slaves, punching and kicking, driving the drunken crew below, until at last they were all got into the forecastle, and a man planted at the door armed with a hand-spike to keep them in.

The day passed rather awkwardly, for though a special dinner had been prepared, a list of toasts drawn out, haggis and cock-a-leekie duly prepared, no one could eat it, for, till night fell, the mates, the passengers, doctor, purser, and such of the emigrants as were able were forced to work the ship; the doctor and myself steering occasionally and putting the helm invariably hard up, when it should have been put hard down, keeping the vessel yawing about as if we wished to write our names upon the sea. Next morning decks were washed, black eyes and broken heads attended to, the prisoner let out on promise of amendment, and a search made to find how the men had got the drink. Nothing, of course, came out, and we pursued our voyage, touching at Rio, and halfway to the Plate ran into a Pampero, which kept us out a day, till one fine morning we sighted Lobos, slipped past Maldonado, left the English bank upon our lee, passed close to Flores Island, and anchored finally just underneath the "Mount." The Neapolitan who rowed me to the shore said that the *Atlas* looked to him like a coffin, but having spent so long aboard of her I cursed him for a fool, told him the blood of St. Januarius would never liquefy if he went on like that, and turning saw the skipper leaning on the rail waving his hat and calling out "So long; don't forget New Year's Day." I said I would not, and the *Atlas* passed out of my life, and what became of her only the underwriters could possibly have told. Perhaps she was broken up for scrap iron, lost on a well-known shoal, sold for a tramp, and maybe dodges about between the Islands of the Chinese Seas, if she has not long ago foundered in the night after the fashion of so many of her class.

But anyhow my copy of the "Faerie Queene" still smells of cockroaches, is spotted on the cover with salt water, some of the leaves are foxed, the title-page is lost, and when I open it even the music of "Epithalamion" is dumb, and in its stead I hear the swishing of the sea, feel the screw racing and the long-drawn-out notes of a "forebitter" seem to quiver in the air, until I shut the book.

Bristol Fashion

From Mogador to Mossamedes runs a line of coast which from the time of Hanno to the present day has been the wonder and the despair of men. There barbarism has had its last entrenchments; even to-day some of them still remain unstormed.

Cannibalism, missionaries, "feitiço," "gri-gri," the gorilla, gold dust and ivory, the negro race, great swamps, primeval forests, stretches of barren sand, leagues of red earth as at King Tom, bar harbours, "factories," beads, amulets, slave trade, Liberia; the curious names of places, as Bojador, Bisagros, Portendik, with Jella Coffee, Fernando Po and Annobon, St. Paul's, Loanda, Half-Jack, and Ambrizette, form a strange hell-broth of geography, ethnology, fauna and flora, superstition and religion up to date, remnant of the pre-wages era, republic of the type of Gerolstein, an animistic fugue of barbarous music, in which "Marimba," war-whistle, and tom-tom all bear their part.

First, Mogador, called Sueira (the picture) by the Moors, almost an island, dazzlingly white, confined to Africa but by a rope of sand, kissed by the North-east Trade, and looking ever out on Lanzarote, towards which it seems to sail. Then Agadir, once Santa Cruz, and held by Spain, and now deserted but by some families of Jews and a few wandering Arabs, and then the country of the Troglodytes, whose caves remain, but from whose hills the warlike dwarfs described by Hanno have long disappeared: next the Wad Nun, the Draa where Arabs, mounted on their "wind-drinkers," chase ostriches and speak the dialect of the Koreish; then Cape Juby, and from thence to Bojador, the Cape known as the world's end till Gilianez, with Zarco and Tristan Vaz, passed to the Bay of Garnets, and claimed the land for Spain.

Edrisi, Ibn Batuta, with Leo Africanus and Ibn-el-Wardi, and before them Herodotus, Polybius, Procopius, and historians Roman, Arab, and Greek, have left accounts of some sort or another, down to the Senegal; but that they knew the land south of Cape Palmas is not made out. They tell us of vast deserts, burning sands between Cape Barbas and the Senegal; all this we know, and little more to-day, for, from the sea, the eye surveys the sand unbroken but by a palm-tree here and there, an Arab Duar, and now and then a rider on a camel, or a troop of ostriches.

Now by degrees the country changes, and great woods appear joining the mangrove swamps which fringe the coast and run from Bathurst, Sierra Leone, past the Grand Sesters, Piccaninny Sess, Cape Palmas, Accra, Acasa, through the Gold Coast, where a white vapour hangs over everything and obscures the sun as it were covered with fine gauze. Passing Fernando Po, which rises from the sea, an offshoot from the mountains of the Cameroons, past Annobon, the Congo, St. Paul's, Loanda, and Benguela, the dense bush continues till by degrees the vegetation grows more sparse, and below Mossamedes, after having passed more than two thousand miles from Mogador, again the land gets sandy, arid, and subtropical.

During the Sixties, along the coast laden with rum and gin, with gas-pipes muskets long as a spear and painted red, brass dishes, musical-boxes, trade powder, cheap German clocks and French indecent prints (as presents for the chiefs), beads, bells, and looking-glasses, well "sized" cottons, and all the other glories of our time and state with which we push the gospel truths, extend our trade, and bring the "balance" of the world under the shadow of our glorious flag, ran barques, all owned in Bristol, usually about five hundred tons, all painted chequer-sided, sailing short-handed out of Bristol, and at Cape Palmas shipping a gang of Krooboys for the cruise.

Between Cape Mesurado and Cape Palmas the Krooboys have their towns, the Little Kru, the Settra Kru, King Will's Town, and the rest. A race apart, the Lascar of the coast, the Krooboy for the last two hundred years has been in intercourse with men from Europe, and still remains a worshipper of gods which, in the latitudes of Aberdeen, of Sunderland, the Hartlepools, and other regions where the true faith reigns, are not accepted. A healthy pagan, tall, active, with muscles like a Hercules, head like a comic masque, speaking a sort of "petit negre," or "Blackman English," a jargon, call it what you like, the groundwork of it oaths; his face tattooed on either temple with a triangle, from which a line of blue, which starts below his hair, runs down his nose, giving him when he laughs a look of having two distinct faces. The Krooboy ships for a cruise, and then, on his return to the five towns, reverts to paganism; a merry misbeliever, over whose life no shadow of the Galilean tragedy has passed, and who, therefore, ships aboard an English ship in the firm expectation of returning home after a two years' cruise to invest his wages in the purchase of more wives, two hundred years of missionary labour having as yet proved ineffectual to eradicate the natural polygamistic tendencies which Providence (who one supposes acted after due consideration) seems to have planted in the fibre of all mankind, except, of course, ourselves. Strong, tall, a coward, animistic to the core, and called indifferently "Jack Beef," "Sam Coffee," or "Small Fish," the Krooboy is a man apart, and for the test of moral worth our Christian navigators put a bale weighing two hundredweight upon his head, and if he carries it safe through the surf, he is engaged.

Of all the barques none was considered smarter than the *Wilberforce* owned by the Messrs. Fletcher, commanded by one Captain Bilson (Honest Tom Bilson), a man who knew the coast by day and night, each harbour, inlet, mangrove swamp, and knot of palms, as the Lone Palm, Three Palms, the "Carpenter," and the rest from Sherboro Island to Kabenda Point.

"Honest Tom Bilson" all the traders called him with a laugh, and by the various chiefs he was best known as "Blistol Fassen" from his constant using of the phrase. "Ship-shape and Bristol Fashion" was his word, and after pouring out a stream of blasphemy at some unlucky Krooboy stowing a sail, he used to raise his eyes to heaven and exclaim, "Oh, Lord, Thou knows my 'eart, but these 'ere Krooboys make me peril my immortal soul ten times a day!" for Bilson was a member of a congregation in the rare intervals he passed at home, and even when at sea, on Sundays, read his chapter to his crew, not greatly understanding what he read, but reading, as he heaved the lead, took in top-gallant sails at night, or purged his crew on entering low latitudes, from sheer routine. Of course he had a wife at home legally married, or, as he said, "wedlocked" to him in a chapel; but matrimony, I take it, does not bind much below the "roaring forties," so in his cruises up and down the coast, when he had shipped his Krooboys, having no gift of tongues, he also shipped a negro girl to act as an interpreter and keep things "ship-shape" in his cabin, sew on his buttons, play on the "marimba," and act as intermediary in his dealings with the chiefs. This was the "fassen" of the coast, and in Accra a sort of seminary existed to train, instruct in English, and turn out young negro girls for "the profession," which was held an honourable and lucrative estate. These damsels, known as "consorts," used to affect great state and dignity, wearing their clothes so stiffly starched with arrowroot that, had you cut their legs off, still their skirts would have maintained their balance by sheer force of starch.

Aboard these trading barques the life was easy, running down the coast from town to town, for then the skippers seeking a cargo did the work which now is done by hulks, and got their cargo here and there, picking up palm-oil, camwood, ivory, gum copal, kola nuts, beeswax, gold dust, and ostrich feathers on the barter system, in direct dealing with the headmen of the towns. To-day upon the coast the days of "seeking" are long ended, for hulks in every river collect the country produce, and the captains of the "tramps" who take it off see little more of native life than what is seen by sailors all the world over, that is, the "tingel-tangel," gin-shop, and haunt of low debauchery, but in those halcyon days a captain of a barque shared with the missionary and the head trader of the "factory" the chief position of the unofficial white man from Cape Palmas to the Bights.

Pleasant it was to drop into some river where no trader lived, signal for a pilot to the chief, and either in his hut or in the cabin of the ship "set up a trade," after a long palaver where cases of gin from Rotterdam formed the chief arguments. Although the barques carried no guns, still they had arms aboard — muskets and cutlasses, which the skipper used to keep in his own cabin under key. At times the captain used to land, and with a guard of men and squad of Krooboys carrying merchandise (that is, of course, gin, rum, and powder, with trade guns), proceed to interview some chief in his own house. Then palm-wine flowed, tom-toms were beat, the negro women danced after a fashion which even at the Moulin Rouge would not be tolerated, presents were exchanged, and a great banquet was provided and discussed in the chief's own room, generally furnished with three or four iron beds, a cuckoo clock, two or three musical-boxes, and on the walls either religious pictures setting forth the Prodigal's Return, Rebecca at the Well, the Ark, or else French prints, all of the most superlative degree of "pornographickness." At least such was the furniture in Jella Coffee, *regnante* King Jo Tay, who with his consort Margo used to provide the skippers of the passing ships with yams and sweet potatoes, palm-wine and bananas, and send off canoes crammed to the gunwale with that special feature of his land, the "Jella Coffee runner." On shore at "factory" and port the straggling European population struggled with fever, fought with gin, lolled half the day in hammocks, imported horses from the Gambia, only to see them die within the year, talked of the old country, occasionally got up a prize-fight borrowing the missionary's steam launch when necessary to run the fighters into native territory. Flies and mosquitoes made life miserable, men took the fever overnight, were dead by morning, buried at gunfire, and none seemed happy but the "snuff and butter" coloured children, who swarmed in evidence of the philoprogenitiveness of the members of what Mr. Kipling calls "the breed." No nonsense about Bilson, "shipshape and Bristol fash," and "treat a bloody nigger well if he works well; and if he kicks, why then speak English to him," was the burden of his speech. Philanthropists, with missionaries and those who talked of equal rights for all mankind, he held as fools, calling them "bloomin' sentimentalists," which term he thought the most contemptuous a man could bear, and fit for landsmen, swabs, and those who sailed out of the northern ports in brigs and schooners, and all those mariners who had not attained to the full glory of a Bristol barque.

"I like a naked nigger" (he would say) "dressed in his breech clout", but the self-same "nig" rigged in a cheap slop suit he thought unnatural, and asked with many oaths, and tags of Scripture referring to the Amalekite dwellers in Canaan and the Cities of the Plain, if you would like to give your daughter to a negro man. This not infrequently produced unpleasantness, for no missionary, philanthropist, or any other man, no matter what he thought, had ever answered with a downright "Yes."

Then Bilson used to triumph and call for drinks, sweetening his gin with orange marmalade, and calling to his "Accra girl," tell her to dance, just in the way that Vashti should have danced had she not shown the proper spirit that has caused her to be handed down as an example to all self-respecting wives, in the immoral legend where the loves of Esther and Ahasuerus are set forth. After much rum, his "consort" bit by bit took off her stiff-starched clothes and stood half-naked ready to dance after the manner known as "Bonny Fash," a "Fash" which has its merits even compared to the gyrations of the half-naked, perspiring spinster at a London Ball. And whilst the negress danced to the accompaniment of a tom-tom and a flute, bending about her body like a snake, imparting that strange rotatory motion to the pelvis which so charms the Eastern and repels the moral Western man (accustomed as he is to London streets at night), waving her arms about in phallic gestures, turning her eyes back till the pupils become almost invisible, brushing against the knees of the spectators as a cat arches his back against a table-leg, Bilson would talk with tears in his eyes of home, about his wife, his children, and his wish they should attend good schools, his daughter learn the piano, French, dancing, and the mysterious things which make a girl a lady "all the way up" (as Bilson used to say), and that his son through the gradations of a mortarboard, college degree, and, what was necessary, become at last what his proud father styled a "blarsted gentleman."

Men's minds are built in reason-tight compartments, and what they do but little influences them, for the real life we live is one of thought, and it is not impossible even that in a brothel the mind may still be pure.

Honest Tom Bilson cared not for speculations, but acted in the manner he called practical, that is, he tried to square his conscience with his life, except when personal interest, hate, love, or any other human passion intervened. After the fashion of most common natures, he hated to be over-reached, and if a "nigger" was the over-reacher his fury knew no bounds. Seated in the caboose over his "okross" stew, which, as he said, reminded him of a fat eel well-stewed in glycerine, sipping his gin and talking to his mate (the Accra girl listening as solid as a joss), the chart spread on the table marked with rings where cups of cocoa had been set upon the paper, the picture of his wife dressed in her best silk gown with brooch large as a cheeseplate pinned on what he styled her "boosum," glancing down at him from the wall, his Bible and revolver handy, his naked feet in carpet slippers, shirtsleeves rolled up, the scuttles open, and the ship anchored outside the bar of a small river, his boatswain came below and told him in a report garnished with oaths that several of the Krooboys had stolen a boat, and having crossed the bar, had paddled up the river and disappeared. Now Bilson knew that to recover boat and "niggers" was beyond his power, for in the little native town no white man lived, and native chiefs never give up a man who seeks protection, but plunder him themselves, and make excuses saying, "Nigger, he no lib', gone into bush all the same turkey, we no catchey he." To quote the boatswain, "You could have shovelled out the blasphemy with a tin sugar-scoop, and the whole 'droger' seemed alight from stem to starn." To lose a boat upon the coast meant money, much inconvenience and the impossibility to get another till he arrived at Cape Coast Castle, Accra, Sierra Leone, or some considerable port. This did not move him near so much as the bewildering thought that he, the smartest skipper on the coast, had been outdone by his own Krooboys, "niggers," savages, heathens, and yet sharp enough to leave him in the lurch. The "palaver" which he held lasted till early morning; almost a case of "Palm-tree Brand" was finished, and when the sun at last broke through the heavy mist which in the tropics heralds day, and when the tree-frogs chirping like cymbals woke the echoes of the heavy-flowing tidal stream, mate, negress, and the boatswain lay asleep upon the cabin floor, and only

Bilson sat erect, his head quite clear, his resolution fixed, and taking down his Bible, assured himself that eye for eye and tooth for tooth was God's own law, then went on deck.

Having got "Scripture for it," Bilson would stick at nothing, and he knew that Kroomen stranded ashore far from Cape Palmas had but one course of action if they wished ever to see their native land again; that was, to sell the stolen boat and ship aboard the first returning vessel they could find: and this returning vessel Bilson resolved with many oaths should be his own.

The dog watch saw him almost hull down, and when in five days' time about six bells, the vessel entered the river from the eastward, she had suffered a great change. The chequer sides were gone and a red stripe replacing them caused her to look much higher, the cherished figurehead setting forth Wilberforce in the act of benediction, the joy of Bilson's heart, was out of sight, cased up in canvas and painted black, so as to scarcely show apart from the body of the ship, and a few heavy weights moved further aft gave her a different set. The square yards on the mainmast all had disappeared, and she presented (to a Krooboy's eye) the appearance of a Yankee barquantine sailing from Portland, Maine, and to make all things right the Stars and Stripes flew from her peak, and, as she anchored Bilson came on deck, dressed in white drill, a broad Bahama hat, his hair dyed black, moustache cut off, and beard and whiskers trimmed to the goatee shape which, in those days, bespoke the Yankee, in the same way as the full-shaped beard was held to be the trademark of the "limejuice" Englishman.

As Bilson had expected, a canoe put off, and, as it neared the ship, one of the missing Krooboys, known as Tom Coffee, hailed and asked, " 'Spose Massa Captain want Krooboy, Tom Coffee, Little Fish, Joe Brass lib' for ship one time." And Bilson answering in an exaggerated New England accent that he was short-handed and was going north, the unsuspecting Krooboys ran their canoe under the vessel's counter and came on board. As each man stepped on deck a heavy blow stretched him half-senseless, and he recovered to find himself in irons and listen to Bilson pouring out his rage in all the choicest phrases of the dialect of Sierra Leone, "You damn niggers, you tief ship boat, eh, you think you better man past Captain Bilson, eh, I tell you wash 'um belly, no see Cape Palmas dis one time," and calling to his boatswain he had the three poor wretches thrown into the hold upon the cargo, the dunnage of it being logs of camwood, every hole of which harboured a scorpion, a centipede, or mangrove crab, which, if you crushed it, sent forth a scent worse than a Chinese stinkpot, a tanyard, slaughter-house, or fashionable lady smothered in the newest perfume made from the dross of tar.

His "niggers" well secured, Bilson weighed anchor, and, sailing down the coast, ran into a small river that he knew, from whence Brazilian slavers shipped their "rolls of tobacco," and, backing his foreyard, lay to, going himself well armed in his own whale-boat to call upon the chief. Late in the evening he returned, and with him came a war-canoe manned by some sixteen savages all with their teeth filed to a point, with collars of leopard's claws, armlets of ivory, and armed with spears.

The wretched Krooboys, gagged and tied hand and foot, were dumped like logs into the war-canoe, and Bilson, after hauling in his boat, braced round his yards, and slipped into the night.

Years afterwards, when seated in his villa outside Bristol, after attending chapel, the Sunday dinner done, grog on the table, churchwardens alight, and feet in slippers, the sermon well discussed, the chances of the next election of the town council all talked over, his "wedlocked" wife and daughter having retired, Bilson was wont to tell how that in all his life he had been done but once and that time by some "bloody niggers;" but he would say, "They stole my boat, they did; their names was Little Fish, Tom Coffee, and Joe Brass, stole my boat, eh, but by Gawd's help I ketched 'em and sold 'em to a chief of one of them cannibal set-outs of niggers down Congo way; fixed 'em, I did, you bet, in Bristol fashion."

Tanger La Blanca

Gibraltar melts away, taking the outline of a sleeping lion, the peaks above Gaucin stand out as clearly as if cut out of cardboard, and on the other coast, Ape's Hill in Barbary rises up like a gigantic sugar-loaf.

Pillars of Hercules, Gibel Tarik, and Gibel Musa, Gate of the Road, the "Puerta del Camino" of the mediæval Spanish chroniclers, they still remain guarding the entrance to the great salt lake around whose shores all that was interesting in art and science of the ancient world, arose and fell.

From Gibel Musa, Tarik embarked on his adventure, one of the three or four in which whole peoples have engaged, and, landing on the other outpost of the then known world, overran Europe, and had his progress not been stayed but by an accident, we might to-day have heard the call to prayers arise in Aberdeen. From Gibel Tarik, after eight centuries of peace and one of bitter persecution, the Morisco remnant of the once conquering Yemeni hordes embarked, leaving the land which cast them out, priestbound and slothful and the poorer by their loss.

Next, Algeciras, the green island (El Jezirah el Hadara), from which it takes its name), lying athwart its harbour like an enormous whale. Coasting along La Tierra de Maria Santisima, with Africa on the port bow, one wonders which of the chosen lands, that of the Blessed Virgin or that of Sidna Mohammed, looks most inhospitable. On both sides mountains, all clothed with arbutus, dwarf rhododendron and the kermes oak, run to the water's edge. On either side the isolated farms are low, flat-topped, and white. The population both in Spain and Africa is pastoral, and flocks of goats and hairy sheep are tended, in Spain by a brown, wool-clad figure with a sling, and on the other coast by a white-robed statue armed with a sword-shaped club, bare-footed and bare-headed, and standing listlessly to watch the steamer pass, unmoved except perhaps to curse the strange "maguina" made by the Frank. From both the goatherds floats a song as wild and quavering as a heron's scream, taught to them both by their remote and common ancestor from Hadramut. Almost awash, the ramparts of Tarifa rise, then, bit

251

by bit, the crenelated wall, the Castle of Guzman el Blanco, identical, unchanged from that May morning when the Moorish Caid exposed the Christian captain's son upon the ramparts, promising his life, if but the father would consent to raise the siege, and upon his refusal hurling the headless body of the boy into his camp. Tarifa, the most African of all the towns of Spain, let Ronda, Cuenca, Granada, Niebla, Huelamo, and the white city, on the hill in Aragon called Arcos de Medina Celi, all contest her claim. Houses intact as when their Moorish owners left them; the gate of the town a horseshoe arch with due inscription, setting forth God's name in the linked characters of Cufa, which he loves. Outside the "noria" revolves, turned by a woman and an ass, palm-trees and canes, with Azofaifa, Ajonjoli, and Albahaca grow — all introduced, as Abu Zacaria tells us in his "Book of Husbandry" from farthest Nabothea. Lastly Las Tarifeñas, dressed in their curious straight mediæval petticoat, their black lace veil covering their faces all except one eye; which custom, had Mahommed ever foreseen, theirs would have been the greater punishment — that is, of course, when the Believers held the town; but what if Christians fall into the Tarifeñas' snare and, as the people say, drown in their eye, he takes no heed. Tarifa sinks into the sea, and the sandy plain through which the Guadalete runs, and where Don Roderick lost the land, God having given the victory to the Moors (the embraces of La Caba having detained him too long in the north), appears but for a moment and then sinks like Spanish glory with a long struggle, into the blue haze. Through the white tide-rip, which in old times must have been as a Syrtis to the banked galleys as they floundered through; under Cape Malabat, on which a Moorish Atalaya stands, guarding the coast with three old Spanish guns of brass prone on the ramparts, for the carriages have long ago been used as firewood, or have mouldered into dust. Under its semicircle of low hills, the houses on the Marshan standing well out against the sky, Tangier appears, the Alcazaba dominating the old white town. Palm-trees spring from the courtyards, no smoke curls up to spoil the atmosphere, and the mosque tower in the centre of the place reverberates the sun from its green tiles, the light flashing and turning iridescent on them as on the scales of some gigantic lizard's back. Row after row of flat, white houses, like an interminable terrace, constitute the town, all so distinctly seen in the clear air, that from the steamer's deck you fancy you could step from house to house, and from the last descend into the realms of the Arabian Nights. But thirteen miles from Europe, as the gull flies, millions of miles away in feeling and in life. Tanger la Blanca, Tangier the white. Whitewash and blinding sunlight on the walls; upon the beach, white sand; the people dressed in robes of dusky white, a shroud of white enfolds, a mist as of an older world hangs over it, coming between our mental vision and the due comprehension of the secret of the place. The town is old enough, God knows, older than London. Goth, Spaniard, Portuguese, Greek, Roman, Arab, and Carthaginian have fought for, conquered and possessed it (or it them), have left it, some have disappeared, their very countries knowing them no more, but still the city stands, enduring sun, dust, rain, wind, the lapse of time, neglect, and still but little changed from when Count Julian held it for the empire of the Greeks. Since Tarik sailed out of its port to conquer Spain is but a day in its existence. Ibn Batuta left it and wandered up and down the world for thirty years, visiting Persia, Irak, and Malabar, and penetrating to that strange land where, as he tells us in his "Travels," he found even amongst the dwarfish, yellow Djin-descended men, some friends of God. Then, tired of travelling, he returned to write and muse, and found the place, as he himself relates, unchanged; then died, and we may hope that Allah gave him rest at last, after his wanderings. But thirteen miles from Europe and yet less spoiled with European ways than is Crim-Tartary. Nothing has changed for centuries. In the narrow streets the porters stagger under burdens, swaying and shouting "Balak!" as they go; the water-seller, with his great skin bag, brass cup and bell, winds in and out amongst the crowd; women, all swathed in haiks, pass silently along, to meet their lovers, to the bath, to gossip with their friends, or sit in rows to tell their troubles to the reader in the mosque.

Othman, Ali, or Sidna Mohammed himself, appointed Friday to be the womens' day, and so it has continued, for time, rightly considered, but sanctifies that which itself is good and goes some way to make mankind endure even the most intolerable of ancient customs and of modern laws. As in the time of Jacob, women draw water from the well, the camels rest beside their burdens in the market-place, the grave-faced men sit selling trifles squatted in their little shops, whilst round the public writers covering their yellow slips of paper stand knots of people wondering at their skill, for writing of itself has something sacred which attaches to it, for all believers know the Cufic alphabet was sent direct from God. The rich man perched, all swaddled up in fleecy clothes, upon his pacing mule, his house secured and wives locked up, the key which guards their virtue stuck in his waistband, rides down a cobbled street, under an archway, along the beach, and then entering an aloe-planted lane comes to his garden, then dismounts and meditates or sleeps, perhaps reads the Koran, the verses of el Faredi, or perhaps does nothing, and returns home content. The poor man lounges all day about the streets, prays at the stated times, dozes and prays again, then sleeps face downwards in the courtyard of the mosque and is contented with all Allah sends, if bread be not too dear. The beggars sitting at the gate, flies settling on their sores, blind, maimed and scrofulous, ragged and filthy, yet are all content, for hath not Allah made all kinds of men — rich, poor and outcast, Caids, Governors and Sheikhs, sailors and camel-drivers — and all to praise his name? It may be that the entirely materialistic view of life conduces to content.

Again the mind of man perhaps can grasp the idea of a single God with greater ease than it can grapple with the Trinity. Still it is so: the sun, the sound of running waters and the hum of flies, the clear white light, the unchanging life — all seem to satisfy, and after all is not a palm-tree, with its leaves hanging quite listlessly against the trunk, perhaps more restful to the eye than is an oak, shattered and twisted, its branches swaying and tossing in the never-ceasing storm? Content and ignorance, delight in life, tears, joy and laughter unrepressed, the simple faith, few wants and no ambition — all conjoin to make the place as unlike Europe as it is possible to be. The Arabs tax us with our miserable looks, say we are all in terror of ourselves, afraid to be alone, and that we need no hell to punish us for lack of faith after the life we lead. It may be so, and that a group of horsemen flying on the beach, their horses' manes and tails streaming like seaweed in the wind, their clothes all fluttering out, firing their long, curved guns and calling on God's name, is just as pleasing as a group of grey-clad men, even though educated, who pass their lives in turning out sized cottons by the piece or an infinity of water-closet handles.

If in Tangier a man is owner of a horse, a wife or two, a camel or an ass, what does it matter if from the coast to Fez it takes a month to ride? When he gets there at last, he sells his bale of calico, packet of leather, or his box of spice, and after selling sleeps as peacefully as if a train had whirled him there in sixteen hours, packed like a sardine in a third-class carriage and obliged to plan to cheat his fellows against time. What matter if, to go a little lower in the social scale, a man has but a donkey and one wife, a little plot of land, or water-melon patch, and goes to market pushing, so to speak, his ass in front of him with all his merchandise perched on its back, singing the while in a falsetto key, if he is free from care?

So thinking of such things, my mind sometimes goes back to the white Arab town sleeping as peacefully as it has slept for ages, and looking out on Europe with an air of wonder tempered with contempt. And I am glad that the chief industry is intermittent, leaving full time for meditation and for faith; for all you have to do, is heap your orange-peel, dead cats, and any offal you can find, in an esparto basket and sling it on an ass, then drive him gently to the beach, unload, and after a due interval has passed, replace your basket, shout "Arranemook!" and then begin again.

A Survival

To be a Scotchman nowadays is to fill a position of some difficulty and trust.

It is expected that when he takes pen in hand that he must write, no matter what his predilections, antecedents, or education may have been, a language which no Englishman can understand. It is in vain to plead that all our greatest writers in the past have written in what they hoped was English.

Hume, Smollett, Thomson, and Sir Walter Scott, with Dugald Stuart and Adam Smith, endeavour to make themselves intelligible, even to Englishmen.

Dunbar, the greatest poet that Scotland has produced, wrote in a language but little differing from that of Chaucer, who, by the way, he styled his master, acknowledging him to be of "Makkaris Flowir."

Bishop Douglas did not translate Virgil into the rough jargon of the peasants of his day.

Master Robert Henryson, the author of "Robin and Makyne," one of the few pastorals tolerable to those who do not live in towns, is almost as easy of comprehension as is Spenser.

Drummond, of Hawthornden, rarely uses a Scottish word. Carlyle, it is true, made himself a language after his own image in which to express his philosophy, but neither language nor philosophy seem likely to endure, and future generations may yet remember him but as a humorist.

Burns occasionally "attempted the English," but his success in that language was not striking, and a man of genius is neither subject to rules, nor can he usually found a school to carry on his work.

Be all that as it may, the fact remains that the modern Scottish writer to be popular in England must write a dialect which his reader cannot understand. If novelists north of the Tweed must live (and write), they must perforce adopt the ruling fashion, if possible be clergymen and treat entirely of weavers, idiots, elders of churches, and of all those without whose aid, as Jesus, son of Sirach says, no state can stand.

Now, though I have but little skill of the jargon which these Levites have invented, let no Southron think that I depreciate the worthy folk of whom they write. They are all honourable men (I mean the Levites), and if it pleases them to represent that half the population of their native land is imbecile, the fault is theirs. But for the idiots, the precentors, elders of churches, the "select men," and those landward folk who have been dragged of late into publicity, I compassionate them, knowing their language has been so distorted, and they themselves been rendered such abject snivellers, that not a henwife, shepherd, ploughman, or any one who thinks in "guid braid Scots," would recognise himself dressed in the motley which it has been the pride of kailyard writers to bestow. Neither would I have Englishmen believe that the entire Scotch nation is composed of ministers, elders, and maudlin whiskified physicians, nor even of precentors who, as we know, are men employed in Scotland to put the congregation out by starting hymns on the wrong note, or in a key impossible for any but themselves to compass.

England today looks at a native of North Britain from a different standpoint from that of half a century ago. In the blithe times of clans and mosstroopers, when Jardines rode and Johnstones raised, when Grahams stole, McGregors plundered, and Campbells prayed themselves into fat sinecures, we were your enemies. In stricken fields you southern folks used to discomfit us by reason of your archers and your riders sheathed in steel. We on the borders had the vantage of you, as you had cattle for us to steal, houses to burn, money and valuables for us to carry off. We having none, you were not in a state to push retaliation in an effective way.

Later, we sent an impecunious king to govern you, and with him went a train of ragged courtiers all with authentic pedigrees but light of purse. From this time date the Sawneys and the Sandies, the calumnies about our cuticle, and those which stated that we were so tender-hearted that we scrupled to deprive of life the smallest insect which we had about our clothes. You found our cheekbones out, saw our red hair, and noted that we blew our noses without a pocket-handkerchief, to save undue expense. You marked the exiguity of our "Pund Scots," our love of sixpences (which we called saxpence), and you learned the word "bawbee." So far so good, but still you pushed discovery to whiskey, haggis, sneeshin, predestination, and all the other mysteries both of our cookery and faith. The bagpipes burst upon you (with a skirl), and even Shakespeare set down things about them which I refrain from quoting, only because I do not wish to frighten gentlewomen. Then came the road to England that we chiefly used, all others in our country being but fit for partridges, but that well worn and beaten down, just like the path to hell. King George came in, in pudding-time, and all was changed, and a new race of Scotsmen dawned on the English view. The '15 and the '45 sent out the Highlander, rough-footed and with deerskin thongs tied round their heads, dressed in short petticoats and claymores in their hands, they marched and conquered and made England reel, retreated, lost Culloden, and the mist received them back. But their brief passage altered your view again, and you perceived that Scotland was not all bailie, prayer-monger, merchant, and sanctimonious cheat. By slow degrees we rose from mosstrooper and thief to impecunious courtier, then became known as pious business men, ready to cheat and pray on all occasions, but still ridiculous, as those who have no money must of necessity appear to richer men. Our want of wit amazed you, for you did not know we wondered at your want of humour, and so both of us were pleased.

Then Scott arose and threw a glamour over Scotland which was nearly all his own. True we were poor, but then our poverty was so romantic, and we appeared fighting for home and haggis, for foolish native kings, for hills, for heather, freedom, and for all those things which Englishmen enjoy to read about, but which in actual life they take good care only themselves shall share. The pale-faced Master and the Highland chief, the ruined gentleman, the smuggler, swashbuckler, soldier, faithful servant, and the rest, he marked and made his own, but then he looked about to find his counterfoils, the low comedians, without whose presence every tragedy must halt.

Then came the Kailyarders, and said that Scott was Tory, Jacobite, unpatriotic, un-presbyterian, and that they alone could draw the Scottish type. England believed them, and their large sale and cheap editions clinched it, and to-day a Scotchman stands confessed a sentimental fool, a canting cheat, a grave, sententious man, dressed in a "stan o' black," oppressed with the tremendous difficulties of the jargon he is bound to speak, and above all weighed down with the responsibility of being Scotch. I know he prays to Gladstone and to Jehovah turn about, finds his amusement in comparing preachers, can read and write and cypher, buys newspapers, tells stories about ministers, drinks whiskey, fornicates gravely, but without conviction, and generally disports himself after a fashion which would land a more imaginative and less practically constituted man within the precincts of a lunatic asylum before a week was out.

All this I know, and I know virtue which has long left London and the South still lingers about Ecclefechan, hangs about Kirriemuir, is found at Bridge of Weir, and may yet save us when England is consumed with brimstone, as were the Cities of the Plain. But I object to the assumption that the douce, pawky, three per-centling of the kailyard has quite eclipsed the per-Culloden type. In remote places it still remains in spite of education, kodak, bicycle, cheap knowledge and excursion trains; it lingers furtively without a reason, but perhaps that of disproving Darwinism. The men who named the hills, the streams, the stones, who hunted, fished, and fought, who came out of the mist, who followed like dumb faithful dogs, the foolish Stuarts, and fought against the brutal Hanoverians to their own undoing, have now and then a type lingering pathetically and ghost-like from the dim regions of a pre-commercial age.

All that still lingers from another age is what we call a ghost — a ghost perhaps of happier, freer times, when men were less tormented about little things than we who live to-day. Even in Scotland there still exist some few remains of the pre-Knoxian and pre-bawbee days, though fallen into decay.

Not far from where I live there dwells a worthy man, Scotissimus Scotorum, a Scot of Scots, enriched by sweating of some sort, but still a kindly soul. Kindly, of course, in everything but trade, which is a thing apart and sacred, semi-divine, sent straight from God, and like divinity, the teinds, baptismal regeneration, and hell-fire, quite beyond argument. A Liberal, of course — that is, a Liberal wishing to drag down all men over him — a Tory of the Tories to all below him, but yet a kindly, worthy wealthy, and not intolerable man. A moralist, if such a thing there be, thinking all sins but fornication venial. A teetotaler — that is for others — but himself taking at times his glass of whiskey for the reasons which have been so cogently set forth by St. Paul the Apostle to the Caledonians. My friend lives in a house to which is joined a small estate called Inverquharity. Now, though a Radical, nothing rejoices him so much as to be designated territorially as Inverquharity, and to give out he is third cousin to the Earl of Bishopbriggs. These inconsistencies give zest to life and go some way towards redeeming even North Britain from the load of dreariness which Kailyarders depict. One of the themes the worthy ex-sweater, now turned bonnet-laird, delights to dwell on is, that race has little influence upon a man. For take (he says) a Highlander and place him in the same conditions as a Lowland Scot, and he at once alters his mode of life, becomes industrious, and soon assimilates himself to those with whom he dwells. Nothing so difficult as to discuss such questions with my worthy friend. What the true Scotsman wants is argument, and it angers him as much if you agree with him as if you argue and confute his argument. If you agree you are a hypocrite, and arguing shows your narrow-mindedness, so that the safest is to say nothing and be thought a fool. Talking one day, he broached the theory that the crofters of the Hebrides were really fond of work, and that their idleness arose from lack of opportunity. "See," he remarked, "in Manitoba how they improve in new surroundings, and without a landlord to rack-rent and oppress." All landlords, in my friend's opinion, are rank tyrants, and though he likes to meet them individually, even to dine with them if they have titles, in the bulk they are accurst. Of course there is no tyranny in trade, and if a strike takes place, why who so loud as he to call for extra police, to write for soldiers, and to complain that magistrates are weak, and that a whiff of melenite is needed just to clear the air? — for commerce, as all know, came down from heaven, took root in Glasgow, and never can do wrong.

Talking of earls and dukes, and of the shameless immorality of countesses, the iniquity of game laws (though he himself preserves), stakes in the country and the state of trade, the villainy of servants, the rate of illegitimate births and other things on which men placed as he is placed delight to dwell, he asked me if I knew a farm known as the Offerance. I knew the spot, a little croft with hideous little house, four windows and a door, with slated roof, and with two spruces ragged with the wind which sweeps across our favoured land on either side the "toun." A little garden, in which grew "berries," as we style gooseberries and currants, and those sub-acid apples and plums which flourish in the north. A barn, a byre, and a horse mill, with its mushroom-looking top and four wide openings, contrived on purpose to give the horses cold when resting from their work; and over all that air of desolation which the lack of flowers and neatness with the excess of wind and rain impart to Scottish farms. Withal not ill-appointed, the fields well-drained and top-dressed, the fences in repair, the gates well painted, and the whole place a thrifty, ugly, wire-fenced, and necessary blot upon the land. Though a small holding nothing was done by hand, crops were scientifically dropped from machines into the ground, and then the harvest ready, as artfully manoeuvred out, so that the acme of rural dullness and town desolation was attained.

The tenant of this paradise was just about to leave, and Inverquharity announced that he was going to put his theory of environment into immediate execution, to get a crofter family down from the Hebrides to occupy the place. It seemed to me that if he must have Islanders, he might as well have got them from Tahiti as the Hebrides, but still I held my peace.

Time passed, and Inverquharity and I drifted apart, and Offerance, crofters, and theories of rent escaped my mind. Riding one day to visit a hill farm, I passed the Offerance. It looked a little unfamiliar, and seemed to have passed into a different state. Outside the door a fire of peats was burning, on which a kettle, hung to three birchen poles, essayed to boil. Before the fire two ragged children sat, searching each other's heads as diligently as they had both been scriptures. A different air of desolation brooded on the place. The fences were all broken, ground untilled, and little zig-zag paths traversed the fields where short cuts had been made. The gates were off their hinges, lay on the ground or had been burnt, and in a gap a broken cart stood jammed into the hedge. The stock was not extensive, and reminded one of that one sees outside an Arab's tent, or Indian wigwam, mangy and full of ticks, and with the bones protruding through the hidebound skin. Two skinny ponies, with their feet hoppled with withy ropes, which left the flesh all raw, were feeding on the weeds. Some Highland cattle and a goat or two, some scabby sheep, a pack of sheep dogs, and a lean, miserable cow, comprised the lot, and left me wondering if the owner ever expected to pay rent, or looked upon the Offerance as a fee simple given to him by Providence on which to put out all his agricultural lore, and teach the natives the Ossianic mode of carrying on a croft. Close to the house a tall, athletic man, half drunk (but not so drunk as to have lost his wits), wrapped in a plaid and leaning on a stick, his fell of rough black hair descending to his small grey eyes, stood looking at a woman and a girl planting potatoes after the method known in the Highlands as the "lazy bed." That is, instead of ploughing, you dig lightly with a spade, turning the turf a little over on one side, then put in the potatoes and rearrange the turf. The plan is excellent, and saves much work, manure is not required, or sweat of brow, and the soil is exhausted almost as quickly as a crofter can desire.

To see and understand took me but little time, and mentally I said, "This is the crofter family which my worthy friend has brought." On my horse fidgeting the man looked up, came to the road unsteadily, and tried to seize my reins, then, taking off his hat, poured out a flood of compliments, all in the Gaelic tongue. I on my part caught a word here and there, learned he was glad to see me, and understood nothing particular, except the word "Tighearnas," which he repeated at the end of every phrase. It means a chief, and is used by Highlanders as gipsies use "captain" on a racecourse when they wish to flatter or delude. The rain poured down, and he stood there bareheaded, talking and talking till I thought I should go mad. In a mixed jargon of broken Gaelic, and that sort of idiot English that we use to make our meaning clear to foreigners, I asked him to put on his hat and not to be a fool. He answered, "Neffa," and though I found that he knew English pretty well, he beckoned to his wife to act as his interpreter.

"Donald," she said, "is out of Wester Ross, he does not like the digging, but Inverquharity is pleased with him, for he puts up such a bonny prayer." This with the sing-song accent which all Highlanders affect.

Knowing the species, I was sure digging and ploughing, and every form of man-ennobling work, was not his style, and asked why he stood bareheaded, and if he liked the place.

"Och, aye," he said, "Offerance of Inverquharity is a pretty place, and a vera pretty name it has itself whatever."

Strange as it may appear, the uncouth syllables sounded quite different when pronounced by him. His wife, continuing, informed me that Donald never put on his hat when talking to one he thought a "chentleman," and though he cared but little for hard work, he was a "pretty gamekeeper," and a first-rate man to beat.

The semi-sacrament of whiskey-money having duly passed, I rode away amongst a shower of what I took for blessings in the Ossianic tongue.

Turning I saw the Offerance through the rain, black but uncomely, ragged and wind-swept — a picture of the old-world Scotland, which has almost disappeared. Sloth was not altogether lovely, but prating progress worse.

I might have left the place quite discontented even with mankind had I not recollected that the world is to the young, and noted that the children's diligence had been rewarded, and that one was handing something to the other with quite an air of pride.

Heather Jock

To differ from the crowd, whether as a genius, an idiot, a politician, or simply to have a differently shaped beard from other men, will shortly be a crime. At present, out of pure philanthropy for ourselves, we seclude our madmen in prisons euphemistically called lunatic asylums. In the East the madman still walks the streets, as free as any other man, and gives his judgment on things he does not understand, like any other citizen. True, in the East there generally is sun, and every evil with the sun is less.

There is no sun in Scotland, but not so long ago our semi-madmen and our idiots philosophised about the world, taking the bitter and the sweet of life in public, just like the rest of us. The custom had its inconveniences; but, on the other hand, perhaps, was just as merciful as that which today shuts up all harmless, foolish creatures within four walls to save the sane the pain of seeing them.

What reasons influenced William Brodie, bred a weaver at the Bridge of Weir, in Renfrewshire, to first turn pedlar, or, as we say (Scoticé), "travelling merchant," and from that to transmigrate himself into a wandering singer and buffoon under the name of Heather Jock, are quite unknown. The status of a Scotch Autolycus has, no doubt, charms. We do not look on pedlars with the disdain with which in England the trading class is viewed. Rather, we honour them for the use we have of them, knowing the Lord created them for some wise purpose of his own not yet made plain. Hucksters and merchants both are prone to sin, and as a nail sticks fast between the joinings of the stones, so sin sticks close between selling and buying: at least so Jesus son of Sirach tells us, and though not quite canonical himself, his works are much esteemed in Scotland for their "pawkiness." But, being practical, we see as little honour in higgling for thousands as for halfpennies, and call men "merchants" whether they carry packs upon their backs or send out ships freighted with shoddy goods to sell to niggers.

So no one asked his reasons, but accepted him just as he was, with headdress like an Inca of Peru stuck all about with pheasants' and peacock's feathers, bits of looking-glass, adorned with heather, and fastened underneath his jaws with a black ribbon; with moleskin waistcoat; bee in his bonnet; humour in his brain; with short plaid trousers, duffel coat, and in his hand a rude Caduceus made of a hazel stick, and in the centre a flat tin heart, set round with jingling bells, and terminating in a tuft of ling. In figure not unlike a stunted oak of the kind depicted in the arms of Glasgow, or such as those which grow in Cadzow Forest, and under which the white wild cattle feed, as they had done since Malcolm Fleeming slew one with his spear and saved the king.

The minstrel's features of the Western Scottish type, hard as a flint, yet kindly, his eyes like dullish marbles made of glass, such as the children in Bridge of Weir call "bools," his hair like wire, his mouth worn open and his nose merely a trap for snuff. Hands out of all proportion large, and feet like planks, his knees inclining to be what the Scotch call "schauchlin," and imparting to his walk that skipping action which age sometimes bestows on those who in their youth have passed a sedentary life. A true *faux bossu*, and though without a hump, having acquired the carriage of a hunchback by diligence, or sloth. In fact, he seemed a sort of cross between a low-class Indian, such as one sees about a town in South Dakota, and an orang-outang which had somehow got itself baptised.

From Kilmalcolm [*sic*] to Mauchline, from Dalry to Ayr, at a Kilwinning Papingo, at races, meets, fairs, trysts, at country house or moorland farm, to each and all he wandered and was welcome.

His minstrelsy, if I remember right, was not extensive as to repertory, being comprised of but one dreary song about a certain "Annie Laurie," originally of a sentimental cast, but which he sang with humorsome effects of face, at breakneck speed, jangling his bells and jumping about from side to side just like a Texan cowboy in Sherman, Dallas, or some Pan Handle town during the process of a bar-room fight, to dodge the bullets. At the end he signified his wish to lay him down to die for the object of his song, and did so, elevating, after the fashion of expiring folk, his feet into the air and wagging to and fro his boots adorned with what the Scotch call "tackets."

Perhaps it was the dispiriting nature of the performance which drew sympathy from men whose lives were uninspired. They might have thought a livelier buffoon untrue to nature from his unlikeness to themselves. What he had seen during his wandering life he treasured up, relating it (on invitation), to his hearers in the same way an Arab or a

Spaniard quotes a proverb as if it was a personal experience of his own. Once in his youth "west by Dalry" he chanced to see a panorama of the chief incidents of Scottish history. What specially attracted his attention (so he said) was when the lecturer enlarged upon the fate of Rizzio: "Man, he just depicted it so graphically ye fancied ye could hear the head gae dunt, dunt, dunting, as they pulled the body doon the stairs."

Our northern wit runs ghastly and dwells on funerals; on men at drinking parties, dead but quite the gentleman still sitting at the board; sometimes on people drunk in churchyards; but always alternating, according to the fancy of the humorist, from one to the other of our staple subjects for jesting, whiskey, or death. But Heather Jock, like other memories of youth faded away, and the constant spectacle of much superior buffoonery in parliaments, in marts, at scientific lectures, literary clubs, and other walks of life, bore in upon me that all the world is but a pantomime, badly put on the stage by an incompetent stage manager, ourselves the mummers, and each man, according to the estimation he is held in by his fellows, a pantaloon or clown.

One day in Tucuman, amongst the orange gardens, mounting my horse, which for my personal safety I had to do with a bandage over his eyes and foot tied to the girth, and thinking that the business of my life, which then consisted chiefly in going out by break of day to round my cattle up (*parar rodeo*, as the Gauchos say), was not inferior after all to that passed in a European office — where men begin at twenty to enter nothings in a ledger, and old age creeps on them finding them bald-headed at the same task — I chanced to get some letters.

The messenger who brought them slowly got off his horse; his iron spurs, like fetters on his naked feet, clanked on the bricks of the verandah; he seemed perturbed — that is, as much perturbed as it is possible to be upon the frontiers — his hat was gone, around his head he wore a handkerchief which had been white when it left Manchester some years ago; his horse was blown and wounded, but still he stood impassively handing me the bag and asking after the condition of my health with some minuteness. Was he tired? "No, Señor, not over-tired." Would he take a drink? "Yes, to the health of all good Christians." Where was his brother who used to ride with him? "Dead, patroncito, and I hope in Glory, for he died like a Christian, killed at the crossing of the Guaviyú by the infidel who came on us as we were crossing, with the water to our saddle skirts." This with a smile to make the unpleasant news more palatable in the delivery. Christian, I may explain, upon those frontiers is rather a racial than a religious status. All white men are *ex officio* Christians, with the possible exception of the English, who, as they listen to their mass mumbled in English, not in Latin, are less authentic. However, said the Gaucho (always with my permission), he would saddle a fresh horse and with some friends go out to fetch the body.

Whilst he caught a horse — a lengthy operation when the horses have to be driven first to a corral and then caught with the lazo — I took the bag, with the feeling, firstly, that it had cost a man his life, and then with the instinctive dread which, when in distant lands always attends home news, that some one would be dead or married, or that at least the trusted family solicitor had made off with the money entrusted to him to invest.

Nothing of this was in the letters, only, as per usual in such cases, accounts of deaths and marriages of folk I did not know; of fortunes come to those I most disliked, and other matter of the regulation kind with which people at home are apt to stuff their letters to their distant friends.

One of the letters had a scrap of newspaper inside it, with the announcement of the death of Heather Jock. "At Bridge of Weir upon the 13th instant, William Brodie, at the age of eighty-two, known through the West of Scotland to all, as Heather Jock."

So Heather Jock would strive no more with life, with people just as foolish if more wicked than himself, struggle no more against the difficulties of English concert pitch, and be with "Annie Laurie" and the other puny dead who erstwhile plied his trade. Then I remembered where I saw him last: at an old house in Scotland perched on a rock above the Clyde and set about with trees, the avenue winding about through woods and crossing a little stream on bridges made the most of by landscape-gardeners' art. I saw the yew-trees under which John Knox is said to have preached and dealt with heresy and superstition, like the man he was, driving out all that kindly Paganism which is mingled with the Catholic faith, and planting in its stead the stern, hard, hyper-Caledonian faith which bows the knee before its God in a temple like a barn, and looks upon the miserable east end of Glasgow as a thing ordained by God. The tulip-tree, the yellow chestnut, and the laurels tall as houses all came back to me, the little garden with its curious stone vases and the tall hollyhocks. I saw the river with the steamers passing between the fairway marks, saw Dumbarton Castle on its rock and wondered how it could have been the seat of Arthur's Court, as wise men tell. Again I recollected that one day upon the sands I found the outside covering of a cocoanut and launched it on the Clyde just opposite to where the roofless house of Ardoch stood, and watched it vanish into nothing, after the fashion of an Irish peasant woman on the quay at Cork watching the vessel take her son away, and just as sure as she of the return.

Then it occurred to me that Heather Jock had been a different character from what he really was, and that there had been something noble and adventurous in his career. That he had, somehow, fought against convention, and preferred, after the fashion of Sir Thopas, to "liggen in his hood," and go about the world a living protest against the folly of mankind. But, God pardon me, for that way exegesis lies, with finding out of hidden, mysterious esoteric motives for common actions, after the fashion which would astonish many, who, if they came to life again, would find those worshipping who, in life, were their most bitter foes.

Nothing of moment was in the other letters, and when the neighbours mustered, armed with spears and rusty guns, lazo and bolas, but each man mounted on a first-rate horse and leading another to run away upon in case of danger, I mounted a "picazo,"* which I kept for such occasions, knowing he was a horse "fit for God's saddle," and taking my rifle with me unloaded, not from superior daring, but because I had no cartridges.

Just at the crossing of the Guaviyú, close to a clump of "Espinillo de Olor," we found the body, cut and hacked about so as to be almost unrecognisable, but holding in the hand a tuft of long black hair, coarse as a horse's tail, showing the dead man had behaved himself up to the last, like a true Christian.

At the fandango after the funeral, during the hot night, and whilst the fireflies flickered amongst the feathery tacuarás, and lit the metallic leaves of the orange-trees occasionally with their faint bluish light, above the scraping of the cracked guitar, above the voices of the dancers when they broke into the chorus of the "Gato," above the neighing of the horses shut in the corral for fear of Indians, I seemed to hear the jangling of the dead fool's bells, and listen to the minstrelsy, such as it was, of the hegemonist of Bridge of Weir.

---

*A picazo is a black horse with a white face.

Salvagia

Almost the most horrible doctrine ever enunciated by theologians is, in my opinion, the attribution of our misfortunes to Providence. An all-wise power, all-merciful and omnipresent, enthroned somewhere in omnipotence, having power over man and beast, over earth and sky, on sea and land, able (if usually unwilling) to suspend all natural laws, seated above the firmament of heaven, beholding both the evil and the good — discerning, we may suppose, the former without much difficulty, and the latter by the aid of some spectroscope at present not revealed to men of science — sees two trains approaching on one line, and yet does nothing to avert the catastrophe or save the victims. Withal, nothing consoles humanity for their misfortunes like the presence of this unseen power, which might do so much good, but which serenely contemplates so many evils.

I have often thought that, after all, there is but one idea at the bottom of all faiths, and that, no matter if the divinity be called Jehovah, Allah, Moloch, Dagon, or the Neo-Pauline Providence of the North Britons, the worshippers seem to esteem their deity in proportion as he disregards their welfare.

Some have maintained that the one common ground of all the sects was in the offertory; but more recent reflection has convinced me that the impassibility of Providence provides a spiritual, if unconscious, nexus which unites in one common bond Jews, Christians (whether Coptic, Abyssinian, Greek, or Roman), Mohammedans, Buddhists, the Church of England, with that of Scotland, and the multitudinous sects of Nonconformists, who, scattered over two hemispheres, yet hate one another with enough intensity to enable mankind to perceive that they have comprehended to the full the doctrines of the New Testament.

I know a little village in the country generally described in old Italian maps under the title of "Salvagia," where the providential scheme is held in its entirety. Nothing, at first sight, proclaims the fact why a great power should specially concern itself about the place. Still, is it not the case that, as a rule, blear-eyed, knock-kneed young men imagine that they touch the heart of every woman who pities their infirmities? Do not red-haired and freckled, cow-houghed maidens usually attend a fancy ball attired as Mary Queen of Scots, and think their fatal beauty deals destruction on the sons of men, unconscious that their lack of charms preserves them safe from those temptations by means of which alone virtue can manifest itself? That which holds good of individuals often applies to people in the bulk. So of my village in Salvagia. A straggling street looking upon a moor, bordered by slated living boxes, each with its "jaw-box" at the door and midden at the back, its ugly strip of garden without flowers, in which grew currants, gooseberries, with nettles, docks, potatoes, and the other fruits known to the tender North.

In every house a picture of Dr. Chalmers flanked by one of Bunyan, and a Bible ever ready on a table for advertisement, as when a minister or charitable lady calls, and the cry is heard of "Jeanie, rax the Bible doon, and pit the whiskey-bottle in the aumrie." Two churches and two public-houses, and a feud between the congregations of each church as bitter as that between the clients of the rival inns. No whiskey or no doctrine from the opposing tavern or conventicle could possibly be sound. No trees, no flowers, no industry, except the one of keeping idiots sent from Glasgow, and known to the people as the "silly bodies." Much faith and little charity, the tongue of every man wagging against his neighbour like a bell-buoy on a shoal. At the street corner groups of men stand spitting. Expectoration is a national sport throughout Salvagia. Women and children are afraid to pass them by. Not quite civilised, nor yet quite savages, a set of demi-brutes, exclaiming, if a woman in a decent gown goes past, "There goes a bitch."

A school, of course, wherein the necessary means of getting on in life is taught. O education, how a people may be rendered brutish in thy name! Behold Salvagia! In every town, in every hamlet, even in the crofting communities upon the coast, where women till the fields and men stand idle prating of natural rights, the poorest man can read and write, knows history and geography, arithmetic up to the Rule of Three — in fact, sufficiently to over-reach his neighbour in the affairs of life.

Still, in the social scale of human intercourse the bovine dweller in East Anglia is a prince compared to him. How the heart shrinks, in travelling from London, when, the Border passed, the Scottish porter with a howl sticks his head into the carriage and bellows "Tackets — are ye gaeing North?" No doubt the man is better educated than his southern colleague, but as you see him once, and have no time to learn his inward grace, his lack of outward polish jars upon you. After the porter comes the group of aged men at Lockerbie, all seated in the rain, precisely as their forebears sat when Carlyle lived at his lone farm upon the moor. Then come barefooted boys selling the *Daily Mail*, the *Herald*, and *Review*, till Glasgow in its horror and its gloom receives you, and you lose all hope.

Throughout Salvagia "Thank you" and "if you please" are terms unknown. In railway trains we spit upon the floor and wipe our boots upon the cushions, just to show our independence; in cars and omnibuses take the best seats, driving the weaker to the wall like cattle in a pen. In streets we push the women into the gutters, "It's only just a woman" being our excuse. Our hearts we wear so distant from our sleeves that the rough frieze of which our coats are made abrades the cuticle of every one it rubs.

Back to our village — "Gart-na-cloich," I think the name, meaning the enclosure of the stones. Stony indeed the country, stony the folks, the language, manners, and all else pertaining to it. Even the Parameras outside Avila, where every boulder is a tear that Jesus wept, is not more sterile. Not that Jesus had ever aught to do with Gart-na-cloich. The deity worshipped there is Dagon, or some superfetated Moloch born in Geneva.

In no Salvagian village is there any room for a gentle God. "Nane of your Peters; gie me Paul," is constantly in everybody's mouth, for every dweller in Salvagia studies theology. Faith is our touchstone, and good works are generally damned throughout the land as rank Erastianism. Only believe, that is sufficient. "Show me your moral man," exclaims the preacher, "and I will straight demolish him"; the congregation nod assent, being convinced "your moral man" is not a dweller in Salvagia, or, if he was, that the profession of a "cold morality" on earth must lead to everlasting fire, in the only other world they hear of in the kirk.

Our sexual immorality, and the high rate of illegitimacy, we explain thus. No thrifty man would buy a barren beast. Therefore, as we cannot buy our wives and sell them, if they prove unprofitable, 'tis well to try them in advance, and as our law follows the Pandects of Justinian, being more merciful to those who come into a hard world through no fault of their own than that of England, the matter is put right after a year or so, and all are pleased. That which a thing is worth, is what it brings, we teach our children from their earliest days; we inculcate it in our schools, at mart and fair, in church, at bed and board, and that accounts for the hidebound view we take of everything. Anger and love move us not much: we seldom come to blows after the fashion of the people in the mysterious region that we call "up about England." A stand-up fight with knock-down blows is not our way, not for the lack of courage but from excess of caution and the knowledge that we have intuitively that calumny kills further off than blows. How we get married is a mystery I have never solved, for no Salvagian ever seems heartily to wish for anything, or, if he does, is far too cautious to make his wishes known. Perhaps that is the reason why the Germans drive us out from business as easily as the Norwegian rat expels the original black rat, or the European extirpates the natives of Australia.

Withal, we have our qualities, but well concealed, and only to be found after a residence of fifty years within our gates. In spite of kailyard tales, we snivel little, and cant not much more than our neighbours do; and we have humour, though the kail-yarders record it not, for fear of troubling the Great Heart which only likes "a joke," and is impervious either to humour or to wit. Sometimes we have a touch of pathos in our composition which startles, coming as it does from an unlikely source.

In Gart-na-cloich there dwelt one Mistress Campbell, a widow and the mother of four sons, all what we call "weel-doing" lads — that is, not given to drink, good workers, attenders at the church, and not of those who pass their "Saw-bath" lounging about and spitting as they criticise mankind.

Going to church with us replaces charity — that is, it covers an infinity of things. A man may cheat and drink, be cruel to animals, avaricious, anything you please, so that he goes to church he still remains a Christian and enters heaven by his faith alone. Our faith we take from "Paul," our doctrine from Hippo, so that we need do nought but bow the knee to our own virtues, and be sure that we are saved.

No one could say that Mistress Campbell's cottage was neat or picturesque. No roses climbed the walls, nor did the honeysuckle twine round the eaves. For flowers a ragged mullein growing in a wall, a plant of rue, one of "old man," with camomile and gillyflowers, did duty. Apple and damson trees grew round the "toon," the fruit of which was bitter as a sloe. Beside the door the cheesestone with its iron ring, a "stoup" for water shaped like a little barrel, a "feal" spade, and a rusty sickle lying in the mud, gave promise of the interior graces of the house.

Inside the acrid smell of peat, with rancid butter, and the national smell of whiskey spilt and left to dry, assailed your nose.

All round the kitchen stood press beds in which the children slept. Before the fire grey woollen stockings dried whilst scones were baking, and underneath the table lay a collie dog or two snapping at flies.

The inner chamber had the peculiar musty smell of rarely opened rooms. Upon the walls a picture of Jerusalem set forth in a kind of uphill view, was balanced by a sampler which may have been the Ten Commandments, the Maze at Hampton Court, the Fountains at Versailles, or almost anything you chose, according to your view. Not tidy or convenient was the house, but still a home of the peculiar kind that race and climate has made acceptable.

The widow's faith was great, her household linen clean, and her chief pride, after her sons, was centred in her cows, called in Salvagia "kye." She liked to sit in church and fall asleep, as pious people do during the sermon. Seated between her sons, her Bible in a handkerchief scented with lavender, she had the faith not merely able to move mountains, but with her Bible for a lever, had she but got a fulcrum, to move the world itself. She knew her Church was right, the others wrong, and that sufficed her; and, for the rest, she did her duty to her sons and cows and to her neighbours.

Years passed by, the world wagged pretty much as usual in Gart-na-cloich; sometimes a neighbour died, and we enjoyed his funeral in the way we love, whilst listening in the house of woe to the set phrases of the minister which use has constituted a sort of liturgy.

Winter succeeded summer, and day night, without a thing to break the dreary life we think the best of lives because we know none else.

Years sat but lightly upon Mistress Campbell, for she had reached the time of life when countrywomen in Salvagia seem to mummify and time does nothing on them. Her sons grew up, her cows continued to give milk, the rent was paid in season. Nothing disturbed her life, and folk began almost to murmur against Providence for His neglect to visit her.

Then came a season with the short, fierce spell of heat which goes before the thunderstorm, and constitutes our summer. In every burn the children paddled, trout gasped, and cattle sought a refuge from the midges in the stream.

A little river, in which before the days of knowledge, kelpies were wont to live, flows past the town.

Its glory is a pool (we call it linn) known as the Linn-a-Hamish. Here the stream spreads out and babbling in its course wears the stones flat as proverbs in the current of men's speech get broadened out. The boys delight to throw these flat stones edgeways in the air, to hear the curious muffled sound they make when falling in the water, which they call a "dead man's bell."

Alders fringe the bank, and in the middle of the pool a little grassy promontory juts out, on which cows stand swinging their tails, and meditate, to at least as good a purpose as philosophers. The linn lies dark and sullen, and a line of bubbles rising to the top shows where the under-current runs below the stream. In a lagoon a pike has basked for the last thirty years. In our mythology, one Hamish met his death in the dark water, but why or wherefore no one seems to know. Tradition says the place is dangerous, and the country people count it a daring feat to swim across.

There the four sons of Mistress Campbell went to bathe, and all were drowned. Passing the village, I heard the Celtic Coronach, which lingers to show us how our savage ancestors wailed for their dead, and to remind us that the step which separates us from the other animals is short. I asked a woman for whom the cry was raised. She answered, "For the four sons of Lilias Campbell." In the dull way one asks a question in the face of any shock, I said, "What did she say or do when they were brought home dead?"

"Say?" said the woman; "nothing; n'er a word. She just gaed out and milked the kye."

Snaekoll's Saga

Thorgrimur Hjaltalin was known throughout all Rangarvallar, down to Krusavik, up to Akureyri, and in fact all over Iceland, for his wandering disposition, his knowledge of the Sagas, and for his horse called "Snaekoll." He lived in Upper Horgsdalr, near the Skaptar Jokull, and from his green "tun" were seen the peaks of Skaptar Jokull, Oroefar, and the white cordillera of the vast icy Vatna.

A Scandinavian of the Scandinavians, Thorgrimur was tall and angular, red-bearded, yellow-haired, grey-eyed, and as deliberate in all his movements as befits an Icelander, compared to whom the Spaniards, Turks, Chinese, or Cholos of the Sierras of Peru are active, quick in design and movement, and mercurial in mind.

His house was built of Norway pine with door jambs of hard wood, floated almost to his home from the New World. Unlike most Icelanders, he had not profited too much by education, leaving Greek, Latin, and the "humanities" in general for those who liked them; but of the Sagas he was passionately fond, reading and learning them by heart, copying them out of books in the long evenings whilst his family sat working round the lamp on winter nights after the fashion of their land.

People were wont to say he was descended from some Berserker, he was so silent and yet so subject to sudden fits of passion, which came on generally after a fit of laughter, ending in wrath or tears. Berserkers, not a few, had lived in Rangarvallar, and it may be that moral qualities become endemic in localities, in the same way that practices still cling to places, as in Rome and Oxford and some other towns where the air seems vitiated by the breath of generations long gone past.

Thus, in the future, when the taint of commerce has been purged away and the world cleansed from all the baseness commerce brings, it may be that for some generations those born in London, Liverpool, in Glasgow and New York, will for a time be more dishonest than their fellows born in cities where trade did not so greatly flourish, and so of other things.

Thorgrimur was married and had children, as he had sheep, cattle, poultry, dogs, and all the other requisites of country life. But wife and children occupied but little of his mind, though after the fashion of his countrymen he was kind and gentle to them, sought no other women, did not get drunk, gamble, or regulate his conduct upon the pattern of the husbands of more favoured lands. All his delight was to read Sagas, to dream of expeditions through the great deserts of his country, and his chief care was centred in his horses, and most especially in "Snaekoll," his favourite, known, like himself, for his peculiarities.

Whilst there are camels in the desert, llamas in Peru, reindeer in Lapland, dogs in Greenland, and caiques amongst the Esquimaux, Iceland will have its ponies, who on those "Pampas of the North" will still perform the services done by the mustangs of the plains of Mexico, the horses of the Tartars, Gauchos, and even more than is performed by any animal throughout the world. Without the ponies Iceland would be impossible to live in, and when the last expires the Icelanders have two alternatives — either to emigrate *en masse*, or to construct a system of highways for bicycles, an undertaking compared to which all undertaken by the Romans and the Incas of Peru in the same sphere would be as nothing.

No Icelander will walk a step if he can help it; when he dismounts he waddles like an alligator on land, a Texan cowboy, or a Gaucho left "afoot," or like the Medes whom Plutarch represents as tottering on their toes when they dismounted from their saddles and essayed to walk. Ponies are carts, are sledges, carriages, trains — in short, are locomotion and the only means of transport: bales of salt fish, packages of goods, timber projecting yards above their heads and trailing on the ground behind like Indian lodgepoles, they convey across the rocky lava tracks. The farmer and his wife, his children, servants, the priest, the doctor, "Syselman," all ride, cross rivers on the ponies' backs, plunge through the snow, slide on the icy "Jokull" paths, and when the lonely dweller of some upland dale expires, his pony bears his body in its coffin tied to its back, to the next consecrated ground.

So Thorgrimur loved "Snaekoll," and was proud of all his qualities, his size, for "Snaekoll" almost attained to fourteen hands, a giant stature amongst the ponies of his race. In colour he was iron-grey, with a white foot on either side, so that his rider had the satisfaction of riding on a cross, fierce-tempered, bad to mount, a kicker at the stirrup, biter, unrideable by strangers, but, as Thorgrimur said, an "ice-eater"; that is, able to live on nothing and dig for lichens on the rocks when snow lay deep, to feed upon salt cod or on dried whale beef, and for that reason not quite safe to leave alone with sheep when they had lambs. But for all that Thorgrimur did not care, and never grudged a lamb or two when he reflected that his horse could go his fifty miles a day for a whole week, and at the end be just as fresh as when he left the "tun."

Thick-necked, stiff-jawed, straight pasterns high in the withers, square in the croup, mane like a bottle-brush, tail long and thick, "Snaekoll" had certainly few points of beauty: still, as he stood nodding beneath his Danish saddle, hobbled with whale-hide hobbles, shod with shoes made by Thorgrimur himself, stuck full of large round-headed nails and made long at the heel and curving up near to the coronet to protect his feet in crossing lava-fields, he had a gleam in his red eyes like a bull terrier, which warned the stranger not to come too near. This was a source of pride to Thorgrimur, who used to say, with many quite superfluous "hellvites," that his horse was fit for "Grettir, Burnt Njal, or Viga Glum to ride;" then, mounting him, he used to dash full speed over a lava-field, sending a shower of sparks under his feet, cracking his whale-hide whip, and stopping "Snaekoll" with a jerk whilst sitting loosely with his legs stuck out after the fashion of all horsemen when they know they are observed.

To cross the Vatna Jokull, the great icy desert, which extends between the top of Rangarvallar and the east coast of Berufjördr, was Thorgrimur's day-dream. Others had journeyed over deserts, crossed Jokulls, as the icy upland wastes of Iceland are called, but in his time no one had yet been found to cross the Vatna. Now this idea was ever present in his brain during his lonely rides in summer from his home to Reykjavik, from thence to Krusavik, or as he jogged across the lava-fields or crossed the tracts on which grew birch and mountain ash a foot in height, which constitute an Icelandic forest; and in the winter, in the long, dark hours, he could not drive it from his head. Men came to laugh at him, as men will laugh at those who have ideas of any kind, and call him "Thorgrimur of Vatna Jokull, the Berserker of Rangarvallar," and the like, but none laughed openly, for Thorgrimur was hasty in his wrath, and apt to draw his whale knife, or at least spur his horse "Snaekoll" at the laugher's horse, as he had been a fighter in the ancient horse fights, and it was lucky if the horse that "Snaekoll" set upon escaped without some hurt.

In fact the man was a survival, or at the least an instance, of atavism strongly developed, or would have been so styled in England; but in

Iceland all such niceties were not observed, and his compatriots merely called him mad, being convinced of their own sanity, as men who make good wages, go to church, observe the weather and the stocks, read books for pastime, marry and have large families, pay such debts as the law forces them to pay, and never think on abstract matters, always are convinced in every land.

Think on the matter for a moment, and at once it is apparent they are right

The world is to the weak. The weak are the majority. The weak of brain, of body, the knock-kneed and flat-footed, muddle-minded, loose-jointed, ill-put-together, baboon-faced, the white-eye-lashed, slow of wit, the practical, the unimaginative, forgetful, selfish, dense, the stupid, fatuous, the "candle-moulded," give us our laws, impose their standard on us, their ethics, their philosophy, canon of art, literary style, their jingling music, vapid plays, their dock-tailed horses, coats with buttons in the middle of the back; their hideous fashions, aniline colours, their Leaders, Leightons, Logsdails; their false morality, their supplemented monogamic marriage, social injustice done to women; legal injustice that men endure, making them fearful of the law, even with a good case when the opponent is a woman; in sum, the monstrous ineptitude of modern life, with all its inequalities, its meannesses, its petty miseries, contagious diseases, its drink, its gambling, Grundy, Stock Exchange, and terror of itself, we owe to those, our pug-nosed brothers in the Lord, under whose rule we live.

Wise Providence, no doubt, has thus ordained it, so that each one of us can see the folly of mankind, and fancy that ourselves alone are strong, are wise, are prudent, faithful, handsome, artistic, to be loved, are poets (with the gift of rhyme left out), critics of music, literature, of eloquence, good business men and generally so constituted as to be fit to rule mankind had not some cursed spite, to man's great detriment, cozened us out of our just due. So Thorgrimur was mad, and pondered on the crossing of the Vatna, day by day; not that he thought of profit or of fame — your true explorer thinks of neither. But like a wild goose making north in spring, or as a swallow flying south without a chart to shape his voyage by; or as a Seychelle cocoanut adrift upon some oceanic current all unknown to it, your true explorer must explore, just as the painter paints, the poet sings, or as the sworn Salvationist must try to save a soul, and in the trying lose perhaps his only friend — a perilous business when one thinks that souls are many, friends are few.

And still the Vatna Jokull filled Thorgrimur's imagination. Surely, to be alone in those great deserts would be wonderful, the stars must needs look brighter so far away from houses, the grass in the lone valleys greener where no animal had cropped it, and then to sleep alone with "Snaekoll" securely hobbled, feeding near at hand; and, lastly — for Thorgrimur was not devoid of true Icelandic pride — the arrival one fine morning at the first houses above Berufjördr, calling for milk at the farm door, and saying airily, in answer to the inquiry from whence he came, from Rangarvallar, across the Vatna. That would indeed be worth a lifetime of mere living, after all.

Needless to say that no one in the time of Thorgrimur had ever passed over the Vatna from Rangarvallar, though the Heimskringla seemed to indicate that at the first settlement there had been such a road. Reindeer were known to haunt the wild recesses of the desert track, and some said, ponies long escaped had there run wild, and all were well aware that evil spirits haunted the valleys, for there the older gods had all retired when Christianity had triumphed in the land.

Two hundred miles in distance, but then the miles were mortal, without food, perhaps no water, without a guide, except the compass and the stars. Seven days' ride on "Snaekoll," if all went well, and if it did not, why then as well to sleep alone amongst the mountains, as in the fat churchyard, for there men when they see your headstone growing green forget you, but he who dies in the lone Vatna surely keeps his memory ever fresh.

All through the winter, Thorgrimur talked ceaselessly about the execution of his dream. In spring, when grass is green and horses fat, when forests of dwarf birch and willow look like fields of corn, ice disappears and valleys as by magic are all clothed with grass, he made all bound to set out on his long-projected ride. "Snaekoll is eight years old (he said) and in his prime, sound both in wind and limb, and I am thirty, and if we cannot now prove ourselves of the true Icelandic breed the time will never come, old age will catch us both still scheming, still a-planning, and men will say that had we lived among the Icelanders of old, Snaekoll had been of no use at the horse-fighting, and I, instead of going a sea-roaming with Viga Glum, with Harold Fair-hair, Askarpillir, with Asgrim, and the rest, would have remained at home and helped the women spin." His wife, after the practical way of womenkind, thought him a fool, but yet admired him, for she imagined that Thorgrimur in reading Sagas had come upon the whereabouts of some great treasure buried in times gone by, for she could not imagine that a man would risk his life without good reason, being all unaware that generally lives are risked and lost without a cause. Perhaps, too, she was willing enough for Thorgrimur to go, his musings, readings, wanderings, and uncanny ways rendering him an unpleasant inmate of the house.

But Thorgrimur cared nothing, or perhaps knew nothing of her speculations, but got his saddle freshly stuffed, made whale-hide reins strong, new, and six feet long; purveyed a long hair rope, new hobbles, and for himself new whale-hide shoes like Indians' mocassins, new wadmal clothes, and laid up a provision of salt fish and rye-flour bread all ready for the start.

News travels fast in Iceland, as it does in Arabia, the Steppes of Russia, in Patagonia and other countries where there are no newspapers and where wayfaring men, even though fools, pass news along with such rapidity that it appears there is no need of telegraphs or telephones, for what is done in one part of the land to-day is known to-morrow miles away, and just as much distorted as it had been disseminated through the medium of the Press. Thus Rangarvallar and all southern Iceland knew of Thorgrimur's intention, and people came from far and near to visit him, for time in Iceland is held valuable, or at the least folk think it so, and, therefore, spend what they prize most after the fashion that most pleases them, and that by talking ceaselessly, mostly of nothing, though they can work as patiently as beavers, when they choose. And thus it came about that at the little church in Upper Horgsdalr a crowd of neighbours had assembled to see the start of Thorgrimur into the unknown wastes.

To say the truth the church was of as mean a presence as was the author of the most part of the faith expounded in its walls. Built all of rubble, roof of Norway pine, the little shingled steeple shaped like a radish, nothing about the building, but the bell cast centuries ago in Denmark, could be called beautiful; but still it served its turn and as a mosque in a lone "duar" in Morocco, stood always open for the faithful to use by day for prayer, and as a sleeping-place at night. In the churchyard, curiously marked and patterned stones bore witness to the supposititious virtues of those long dead, and from the mound on which the church was built, the view extended far across lava-fields over the reddish mountains flecked here and there with green and crowned with snow, and in the distance rose the glaciers and the peaks of the unknown and icy Vatna. A landscape dreary in itself, unclothed by trees, wild, desolate, and only beautiful when the sun's rays transformed it, turning the peaks to castles, blotting the black and ragged lava out, and blending all into a vast prismatic play of colour, changing and shifting as the lights ran over limestone, rested on basalt, and lit the granite of the cliffs, making each smallest particle to shine like mica in a piece of quartz. The Icelanders do not hold Sunday as a day of gloom, devoted, as it used to be in England and still remains in the remoter parts of Scotland to which the beneficent breath of latter-day indifference has not yet penetrated, sacred to prayer and drink. So Sunday was the day on which Thorgrimur intended to set out; dressed in his best he sat at church, his wife and children seated by his side. The service done, he left the church, and pushing through the ponies all waiting for their owners outside the door, entered his house.

The priest, the "Syselman," the notables, and friends from far and near sat down to dine, and dinner over and the corn brandy duly circulating, Thorgrimur rose up to speak. "My friends, and you the priest and 'Syselman,' and you the notables, and neighbours who have known me from a boy, I drink your health. I go to try what I have dreamed of all my life; whether I shall succeed no man can tell, but still I shall succeed so far in that I have had the opportunity to follow out my dream. I hold that dreams are the reality of life and that which men call practical, that which down there in Reykjavik the folk call business, is but a dream. 'Snaekoll' and I depart to cross the Vatna, perhaps not to return, but still to try, and so I drink your health again and say farewell, 'Skoal,' to you all."

Then mounting "Snaekoll," who stood arching up his back, he kissed his wife, and saying to his children, "Stand aside, for 'Snaekoll' bites worse than a walrus," he took the road. His friends rode with him for a "thingmanslied" upon the way, and when the last few scattered farms were passed and the track ended in a rising lava-field stretching to the hills, bade him God-speed and watched him sitting erect on "Snaekoll" fade into nothing upon the lava-fields, his horse first sinking out of sight and then his body, bit by bit, till he was gone. The priest, spurring his horse upon a rocky hill, claimed to have seen him last, and said that Thorgrimur never once looked behind, but rode into the desert as he was riding to his home, and that he fancied as he saw him ride, he saw the last of the old Berserks disappear. And then the Vatna claimed him, and Thorgrimur of Rangarvallar went his way out of this story and the world's.

But in east Berufjördr, not far from Hargifoss, there dwelt one Hiörtr Helagson, a man of substance, owner of flocks and herds, and as he sat one morning at his "bær" door, drinking his coffee sweetened with lumps of sugar-candy in the Icelandic fashion, waiting until his horse was caught to ride to church, his herdsman entered to inform him that he thought "Hellvite," the devil had got amongst the horses, for he said, "they run about as if in fear, and the dark chestnut which you ride has a piece bitten out of his back as by a wolf." Then Hiörtr Helagson, although the "Syselman" of Berufjördr and elder of the Church, swore like a horseman when he knows his horse is sick or come by mischief, and, taking down his gun, went to the pasture where his horses fed. The horses all were running to and fro like sheep, and in the corner of the field an object lay, dark grey in colour, like a Greenland bear. But when the "Syselman" had raised his gun, it staggered to its feet, and he, on looking at it, said to his herdsman, "Ansgottes, this is the horse of Thorgrimur of Rangarvallar; he must be dead amongst the ice-fields, and his horse has wandered here." Time passed and "Snaekoll" once again grew round and sleek, although a pest to all the horses in the "tun," and Hiörtr, thinking to cut a figure at a cattle fair, saddled and mounted him. "Snaekoll" stood still, though looking backwards, and when the "Syselman" was seated on his back, arching his spine, the horse plunged violently, and coming down with legs as stiff as posts, gave Hiörtr Helagson a heavy fall, and — turning on him like a tiger — would have killed him had not help been nigh. So, from that day, no one essayed to ride the dead man's horse, who ranged about the fields, and, after years, slept with the horses of the Valkyrie. But Hiörtr Helagson had the best ponies in all Berufjördr, hardy, untirable, and "ice-eaters," fiery in spirit, hard to mount, kickers and biters, apt to rear and plunge, fit for the saddle only of such few commentators as can catch the stirrup at the moment they are up. And when the neighbours talked about their temper and their ways, Hiörtr would say, "Well, yes, they are descended from the horse of Thorgrimur of Rangarvallar; his name was 'Snaekoll,' and he came to me out of the desert, lean as a bear in spring. You know his master died trying to cross the Vatna, and 'Snaekoll' how he lived amongst the ice and found his way to Berufjördr, I cannot tell. Up in the Vatna there is naught but ice, and yet he must have eaten something; *what* it was, God knows!"

With The North-West Wind

As we never associated William Morris with fine weather, taking him rather to be a pilot poet lent by the Vikings to steer us from the Doldrums in which we now lie all becalmed in smoke to some Valhalla of his own creation beyond the world's end, it seemed appropriate that on his burial-day the rain descended and the wind blew half a gale from the north-west.

Amongst the many mysteries of enigmatic England few have more puzzled me than our attitude towards our rare great men. No one can say that in our streets they jostle other passengers, pushing the average man into the gutter, which is his own estate. Neither in Church or State, or in religion, the Press, the army, amongst the licensed victuallers, or at the Bar, do they abound so much as to take the profits of the various jobs I have referred to, from their weaker foes. It may be that we think them "blacklegs," working, so to speak, for too long hours at too high pressure; it may be that the Democratic sentiment, of which we hear so much and see so little, thinks them, as Gracchus Babeuf did, nothing but "aristos" sent by an unjust God (himself a *ci-devant*) to trample on us.

Genius in England is a thing accursed, and that it is unpleasing even to the creator of all Englishmen is manifest by the marked disapproval shown to it by the majority of the created. Therefore, I take it in the future, as the vote has, so to speak, been taken by the show of sneers, that we shall not be called upon to stand much more of it.

So the rain descended, and the north-west wind battled and strove amongst the trees and chimney-tops, swirling the leaves and hats into the mud, making one think upon the fisherfolk, the men aboard the ocean tramps, the shepherds in the glens of Inverness-shire, upon the ranchmen out on the open prairie riding round the cattle, and on the outcasts of the El Dorado, crouching the livelong night under some Christian bridge or philanthropic railway arches.

I have a standing quarrel with "*le grand capricieux*" called Providence, but at a funeral it generally appears he does his best so to dispose the weather that the principal shall not regret the climate he has left. Seen through the gloom at Paddington, within the station, moving about like fish in an aquarium, were gathered those few faithful ones whom England had sent forth to pay respect to the most striking figure of our times.

Artists and authors, archæologists, with men of letters, Academicians, the pulpit, stage, the Press, the statesmen, craftsmen, and artificers, whether of books, or of pictures, or ideas, all otherwise engaged.

Philanthropists agog about Armenia, Cuba, and Crete, spouting of Turks and infidels and foreign cruelties, whilst he who strove for years for Englishmen lay in a railway van.

The guilds were absent, with the Trades Unions and the craftsmen, the hammermen, the weavers, matchmakers, and those for whom he wrought.

Not that he was forgotten of those with whom he lived; for in a little group, forlorn, dishevelled, and their eyes grown dim with striving for the coming of the change, stood his own faithful house carles from Hammersmith, and they too followed their master to the end — standing upon the platform, as it were, on the brink of some new country over which they saw, but knew they could not reach.

When a great man dies in other countries all his last wishes are disregarded, even his family shrinks into second rank, and he becomes the property of those who in his life flung mud at or neglected him. Outbursts of cant, oceans of snivel, are let loose upon his memory, so that it may be that in this instance our Saxon stodginess preserved us from some folly and bad taste. Yet I would have liked to see a crowd of people in the streets, at least a crowd of workmen, if but to mark the absence of the dead man's friends. Thus moralising, the train slipped from the platform as a sledge slips through the snow, and in the carriage I found myself seated between some "revolutionaries."

Had they been cultured folk, it is ten to one the talk had run upon the colour of the dead man's shirt, his boots, his squashy hat, and other things as worthy of remark.

Bourgeois et gens de peu, seated upon the hard, straight seats provided by the thoughtful company to mark the difference betwixt the passengers it lives off and those it cringes to, we moralised, each in our fashion, upon the man himself.

Kindly but choleric the verdict was; apt to break into fury, easily appeased, large-hearted, open-handed, and the "sort of bloke you always could depend on," so said the "comrades," and it seemed to me their verdict was the one I should have liked upon myself.

So we reached Oxford, and found upon the platform no representatives of that old Trades Union there to greet us, and no undergraduates to throng the station, silently standing to watch the poet's funeral. True it was Long Vacation; but had the body of some Buluwayo Burglar happened to pass, they all had been there. The ancient seat of pedantry, where they manufacture prigs as fast as butchers in Chicago "handle hogs," was all unmoved.

Sleeping the sleep of the self-satisfied were dons and masters and the crew of those who, if they chance once in a century to have a man of genius amongst them, are all ashamed of him.

Sleeping but stertorous, the city lay girt in its throng of jerry buildings, quite out of touch with all mankind, keeping its sympathy for piffling commentators on Menander; a bottler-up of learning for the rich with foolish regulations, a Laodicea which men like Morris long ago cast from their mouths and mind.

So the storm went with us to Witney, which seems as little altered as when the saying was, "A badger and a Witney man you can tell them by their coat." Arrived at Lechlade, for the first time it appeared the ceremony was fitted for the man.

No red-faced men in shabby black to stagger with the coffin to the hearse, but in their place four countrymen in moleskin bore the body to an open haycart, all festooned with vines, with alder, and with bulrushes, and driven by a man who looked coeval with the Saxon Chronicle. And still the north-west wind bent trees and bushes, turned back the leaves of the bird maples upon their footstalks, making them look like poplars. The rain beat on the straggling briars, showering the leaves of guelder roses down like snow; the purple fruit of privet and ripe hips and haws hung on the bushes with the lurid look that berries only seem to have struggling through wreaths of bryony and Traveller's Joy and all the tangles of an unplashed hedge bordering a country lane in rural England. Along the road a line of slabs of stone extended, reminding one of Portugal; ragweed and loosestrife, with rank hemp agrimony, were standing dry and dead, like reeds beside a lake, and in the rain and wind the yokels stood at the cross-roads or at the openings of the bridle-paths. Somehow they seemed to feel that one was gone who thought of them, and our driver said, "We've lost a dear good friend in Master Morris; I've driven him myself 'underds of miles." No funeral carriages, but country flys driven by red-faced men in moleskins, carried the mourners, and in a pony cart a farmer, with a face as red as are the bottles in a chemist's window, brought up the rear, driving his shaggy pony with the air of one who drives a hearse.

Through Lechlade, with its Tudor church, its gabled houses roofed with Winsford slates all overgrown with houseleek and with lichens, and with the stalks of wallflower and valerian projecting from the chinks, we took our way.

There, unlike Oxford, the whole town was out, and from the diamond-paned and bevelled windows gazed children in their print dresses and sun-bonnets which Morris must have loved. Then Farmer Hobbs' van drew up before the little church which is now rendered famous by the description of the illustrious man who sleeps so close to it. The row of limes, flagged walks, the ample transept and square porch, the row of sun-dials down the wall, most with their gnomons lost, is known to all the world.

Time has dealt leniently with it, and the Puritans have stayed their fury at the little cross upon the tower.

Inside, the church was decorated for a harvest festival, the lamps all wreathed with ears of oats and barley, whilst round the font and in the porch lay pumpkins, carrots, and sheaves of corn — a harvest festival such as Morris perhaps had planned, not thinking he himself would be the chiefest firstfruit.

Standing amongst the wet grass of the graves, artists and Socialists, with friends, relations, and the casual spectators, a group of yokels faced us, gaping at nothing, after the fashion of themselves and of their animals. And then I fancied for a moment that the strong oak coffin, with its wrought-iron handles and pall of Anatolian velvet, was opened, and I saw the waxen face and features of the dead man circled by his beard, and in his shroud, his hands upon his breast, looking like some old Viking in his sleep beside the body of his favourite horse, at the opening of some mound beside the sea in Scandinavia.

So dust to dust fell idly on my ears, and in its stead a vision of the England which he dreamed of filled my mind. The little church grew brighter, looking as it were filled with the spirit of a fuller faith embodied in an ampler ritual.

John Ball stood by the grave, with him a band of archers all in Lincoln green; birds twittered in the trees, and in the air the scent of apple-blossom and white hawthorn hung. All was much fairer than I had ever seen the country look, fair with a fairness that was never seen in

England but by the poet, and yet a fairness with which he laboured to endue it. Once more the mist descended, and my sight grew dimmer; the England of the Fellowship was gone, John Ball had vanished, with him the archers, and in their place remained the knot of countrymen, plough-galled and bent with toil; the little church turned greyer, as if a reformation had passed over it. I looked again, the bluff, bold, kindly face had faded into the north-west wind.

Niggers

Jahve created all things, especially the world in which we live, and which is really the centre of the universe, in the same way as England is the centre of the planet, and as the Stock Exchange is the real centre of all England, despite the dreams of the astronomers and the economists. He set the heavens in their place, bridled the sea, disposed the tides, the phases of the moon, made summer, winter, and the seasons in their due rotation, showed us the constant resurrection of the day after the death of night, sent showers, hail, frost, snow, thunder and lightning, and the other outward manifestations of his power to serve, to scourge, or to affright us, according to his will.

Under the surface of our world he set the minerals, metals, the coal, and quicksilver, with platinum, gold, and copper, and let his diamonds and rubies, with sapphires, emeralds, and the rest, as topazes, jacinths, peridots, sardonyx, tourmalines, or chrysoberyls, take shape and colour, and slowly carbonise during the ages.

Upon the upper crust of the great planet he caused the plants to grow, the trees, bushes of every kind, from the hard, cruciform-leaved carmamoel*, to the pink-flowering Siberian willow. Palm-trees and oaks, ash, plane, and sycamore, with churchyard yew, and rowan, holly, jacaranda, greenheart and pines, larch, willow, and all kinds of trees that flourish, rot, and die unknown in tropic forests, unplagued by botanists, with their pestilent Pinus Smithii or Cupressus Higginbottomiana, rustled their leaves, swayed up and down their branches, and were content, fearing no axe. Canebrakes and mangrove swamps; the immeasurable extension of the Steppes, Pampas, and Prairies, and the frozen Tundras of the north; stretches of ling and heather, with bees buzzing from flower to flower, larks soaring into heaven above them; acres of red verbena in the Pampa; lilies and irises in Africa, and the green-bluish sage brush desert of the middle prairies of America; cactus

---

*Colletia Cruciata.

and tacuarás, with istle and maguey, flax, hemp, esparto, and the infinite variety of the compositæ, all praised his name.

Again, in the Sahara, in the Kalahari desert, in the Libyan sands, and Iceland, he denied almost all vegetation, and yet his work seemed good to those his creatures — Arabs, Bosjemen, reindeer, and Arctic foxes, with camels, ostriches, and eider ducks, who peopled his waste spaces. He breathed his breath into the nostrils of the animals, giving them understanding, feeling, power of love and hatred, speech after their fashion, love of offspring (if logic and anatomy hold good), souls and intelligence, whether he made their bodies biped or quadruped, after his phantasy. Giraffes and tigers, with jerboas, grey soft chinchillas, elephants, armadillos and sloths, ant-eaters, marmots, antelopes, and the fast-disappearing bison of America, gnus, springboks and hartbeest, ocelot and kangaroo, bears (grisly [*sic*=grizzly] and cinnamon), tapirs and wapiti, he made for man to shoot, to torture, to abuse, to profit by, and to demonstrate by his conduct how inferior in his conception of how to use his life he is to them.

All this he did and rested, being glad that he had done so much, and called a world into existence that seemed likely to be good. But even he, having begun to work, was seized with a sort of "cacoethes operandi," and casting about to make more perfect what, in fact, needed no finishing touch, he took his dust and, breathing on it, called up man. This done he needed rest again, and having set the sun and moon just in the right position to give light by day and night to England, he recollected that a week had passed. That is to say, he thought of time, and thinking, made and measured it, not knowing, or perhaps not caring, that it was greater than himself; for, had he chanced to think about the matter, perchance, he had never chosen to create it, and then our lives had been immeasurable, and our capacity for suffering even more infinite than at present, that is, if "infinite" admits comparison. However, time being once created and man imagined (but not yet perfected), and, therefore, life the heavy burden being opposed on him, the Lord, out of His great compassion, gave us death, the compensating boon which makes life tolerable.

But to return to man. How, when, why, wherefore, whether in derision of himself, through misconception, inadvertence, or sheer malignity, he created man, is still unknown. With the true instinct of a tyrant (or creator, for both are one), he gave us reason to a certain power, disclosed his acts up to a certain point, but left the motives wrapped in mystery.

Philosophers and theologians, theosophists, positivists, clairvoyants, necromancers, cabalists, with Rosicrucians and alchemists, and all the rabble rout of wise and reverend reasoners from Thales of Miletus down to Nietzsche, have reasoned, raved, equivocated, and contradicted one another, framed their cosmogonies, arcana, written their gospels and Korans, printed their Tarot packs, been martyred, martyred others (fire the greatest syllogist on earth), and we no wiser.

Still man exists, black, white, red, yellow, and the Pintos of the State of Vera Cruz. A rare invention, wise conception, and the quintessence of creative power rendered complete by practice, for we must see that even an all-wise, all-powerful God (like ours) matures as time goes on.

An animal erect upon its feet, its eyes well placed, its teeth constructed to masticate all kinds of food, its brain seemingly capable of some development, its hearing quick, endowed with soul, and with its gastric juices so contained as to digest fish, flesh, grain, fruit, and stand the inroads of all schools of cookery, was a creative masterpiece. So all was ready and the playground delivered over beautiful to man, for men to make it hideous and miserable.

Alps, Himalayas, Andes, La Plata, and Vistula, Amazon, with Mississippi, Yangtsekiang and Ganges, Volga, Rhine, Elbe and Don; Hecla and Stromboli, Pichincha, and Cotopaxi, with the Istacihuatl and Lantern of Maracaibo; seas, White and Yellow, with oceans, Pacific and Atlantic; great inland lakes as Titicaca, Ladoga, all the creeks, inlets, gulfs and bays, the plains, the deserts, geysers, hot springs on the Yellowstone, Pitch Lake of Trinidad, and, to be brief, the myriad wonders of the world, were all awaiting newly created man, waiting his coming forth from out the bridal chamber between the Tigris and Euphrates, like a mad bridegroom to run his frenzied course. Then came the (apparent) lapsus in the Creator's scheme. That the first man in the fair garden by the Euphrates was white, I think, we take for granted. True that we have no information on the subject, but in this matter of creation we have entered, so to speak, into a tacit compact with the creator, and it behoves us to concur with him and help him when a difficulty looms.

Briefly I leave the time when man contended with the mastodon, hunted the mammoth, or was hunted in his turn by plesiosaurus or by pterodactyl. Scanty indeed are the records which survive of the Stone Age, the Bronze, or of the dwellers in the wattled wigwams on the lakes. Suffice it that the strong preyed on the weak, as they still do to-day in happy England, and that early dwellers upon earth seem to have thought as much as we do how to invent appliances with which to kill their foes.

The Hebrew Scriptures, and the record of crimes of violence and bad faith committed by the Jews on other races need not detain us, as they resemble so entirely our own exploits amongst the "niggers" of today. I take it that Jahve was little taken up with any of his creatures, except the people who inhabited the countries from which the Aryans came. Assyrians, Babylonians, Egyptians, Persians, and the rest were no doubt useful and built pyramids, invented hanging gardens, erected towers, observed the stars, spoke the truth (if their historians lie not), drew a good bow, and rode like centaurs or like Gauchos. What did it matter when all is said and done? They were all "niggers," and whilst they fought and conquered, or were conquered, bit by bit the race which God had thought of from the first, slowly took shape.

A doubt creeps in. Was the creator omniscient in this case, or did our race compel him, force his hand, containing in itself those elements of empire which he may have overlooked? 'Twere hard to say, but sometimes philosophers have whispered that the Great Power, working, as he did, without the healthy stimulus of competition, was careless. I leave this speculation as more fit for thimbleriggers, for casuists, for statisticians, metaphysicians, or the idealistic merchant, than for serious men.

Somehow or other the Aryans spread through Europe, multiplied, prospered, and possessed the land. Europe was theirs, for Finns and Basques are not worth counting, being, as it were, a sort of European "niggers," destined to disappear. Little by little out of the mist of barbarism Greece emerged. Homer and Socrates, with Xenophon, Euripides, Pindar and Heraclitus, Bion, Anaximander, Praxiteles, with Plato, Pericles, and all the rest of the poets and thinkers, statesmen and philosophers, who in that little state carried the triumphs of the human intellect, at least as far as any who came after them, flourished, and died. Material and bourgeois Rome, wolf-suckled on its seven hills, waxed and became the greatest power, conquering the world by phrases as its paltry "Civis Romanus," and by its "Pax Romana," and with the spade, and by the sheer dead weight of commonplace, filling the office in the old world that now is occupied so worthily by God's own Englishmen. Then came the waning of the Imperial City, its decay illumined but by the genius of Apuleius and Petronius Arbiter. Whether the new religion which the pipe-clayed soldier Constantine adopted out of policy, first gave the blow, or whether, as said Pliny, that the Latifundia were the ruin of all Italy, or if the effeminacy which luxury brings with it made the Roman youths resemble the undersized, hermaphroditic beings who swarm in Paris and in London, no one knows.

Popes and Republics, Lombards, Franks and Burgundians, with Visigoths and Huns, and the phantasmagoria of hardly-to-be-comprehended beings who struggled in the darker ages like microbes in a piece of flesh, or like the Christian paupers in an English manufacturing town, all paved the way for the development of the race, perhaps, intended, from the beginning, to rule mankind. From when King Alfred toasted his cakes and made his candles marked in rings* (like those weird bottles full of sand from Alum Bay) to measure time, down to the period when our late Sovereign wrote her "Diary in the Highlands," is but a moment in the history of mankind. Still, in the interval, our race has had full leisure to mature. Saxon stolidity and Celtic guile, Teutonic dulness [*sic*], Norman pride, all tempered with east wind, baptized with mist, narrowed by insularity, swollen with good fortune, and rendered overbearing with much wealth, have worked together to produce the type. A bold, beef-eating, generous, narrow-minded type, kindly but arrogant; the men fine specimens of well-fed animals, red in the blood and face; the women cleanly, "upstanding" creatures, most divinely tall; both sexes slow of comprehension, but yet not wanting sense; great feeders, lovers of strong drinks, and given to brutal sports, as were their prototypes, the men of ancient Rome; dogged as bull-dogs, quick to compassion for the sufferers from the injustice of their neighbours; thinking that they themselves can do no wrong, athletic though luxurious; impatient of all hardships, yet enduring them when business shows a profit or when honour calls; moralists, if such exist, and still, like cats, not quite averse to fish when the turn serves; clear-headed in affairs, but idealists and, in the main, wrong-headed in their views of life; priding themselves most chiefly on their faults, and resolute to carry all those virtues which they lack at home, to other lands.

Thus, through the mist of time, the Celto-Saxon race emerged from heathendom and woad, and, in the fulness of the Creator's pleasure, became the tweed-clad Englishman. Much of the earth was his, and in the skies he had his mansion ready, well aired, with every appliance known to modern sanitary science waiting for him, and a large Bible on the chest of drawers in every room. Australia, New Zealand, Canada,

---

*Staple industry of the Isle of Wight.

India, and countless islands, useful as coaling stations and depôts where to stack his Bibles for diffusion amongst the heathen, all owned his sway. Races, as different from his own as is a rabbit from an elephant, were ruled by tweed-clad satraps expedited from the public schools, the universities, or were administered by the dried fruits culled from the Imperial Bar. But whilst God's favoured nation thus had run its course, the French, the Germans, Austrians, Spaniards, Dutch, Greeks, Italians, and all the futile remnant of mankind outside "our flag" had struggled to equal them. True that in most particulars they were inferior. Their beer was weak, their shoddy not so artfully diffused right through their cloth, their cottons less well "sized," the constitution of their realm less nebulous, or the Orders of their Churches better authenticated, than were our own. No individual of their various nationalities by a whole life of grace was ever half so moral as the worst of us is born.

And so I leave them weltering in their attempts to copy us, and turn to those of whom I had intended first to write, but whom the virtues, power, might, and dominion of our race, have caused me to forget.

I wished to show Jahve Sabbaoth made the earth, planted his men, his beasts, his trees upon it, and then as if half doubtful of himself left it to simmer slowly till his Englishmen stood forth. I felt he was our God, jealous and blood-thirsty, as in his writings he has let us see; our God, and we His people, faithful to bloodshed, not that we liked it, but because we knew we did His will. We are His people and it was natural that He should give mankind into our hand. But yet it seemed that we had grown so godlike in ourselves that perhaps Jahve was waiting for us to indicate the way. He made the world and stocked it, planting apparently without design the basest peoples in the most favoured lands; then we stood forth to help him, and by degrees carried out all he thought of from the first.

In Africa, Australia, and in America, in all the myriad islands of the southern seas inferior races dwell. They have their names, their paltry racial differences, some are jet black, some copper-coloured, flat-nosed, high-featured, tall, short, hideous or handsome — what is that to us? We lump them all as niggers, being convinced that their chief quality is their difference from ourselves.

Hindus, as Brahmins, Bengalis, and the dwellers in Bombay; the Cingalese, Sikhs and Pathans, Rajpoots, Parsis, Afghans, Kashmiris, Beluchis, Burmese, with all the peoples from the Caspian Sea to Timur Laut, are thus described. Arabs are "niggers".

So are Malays, the Malagasy, Japanese, Chinese, Red Indians, as Sioux, Comanches, Navajos, Apaches with Zapatecas, the Esquimaux, and in the south Ranqueles, Lenguas, Pampas, Pehuelches, Tobas, and Araucanos, all these are "niggers" though their hair is straight. Turks, Persians, Levantines, Egyptians, Moors, and generally all those of almost any race whose skins are darker than our own, and whose ideas of faith, of matrimony, banking, and therapeutics differ from those held by the dwellers of the meridian of Primrose Hill, cannot escape. Men of the Latin races, though not born free, can purchase freedom with a price, that is, if they conform to our ideas, are rich and wash, ride bicycles, and gamble on the Stock Exchange. If they are poor, then woe betide them, let them paint their faces white with all the ceruse which ever Venice furnished, to the black favour shall they come. A plague of pigments, blackness is in the heart, not in the face, and poverty, no matter how it washes, still is black.

Niggers are niggers, whether black or white, but the archetype is found in Africa.

Oh Africa, land created out of sheer spleen, as if to show that even Jahve himself suffered at times from long-continued work; in spleen, or else contrived out of his bounty to encourage us and serve as sweetener to his most favoured nation in its self-appointed task! A country rich in itself, in animals, in vegetation, and in those minerals in which we chiefly see the evidence of the Creator's power. Rich, and yet given up to such a kind of men that they are hardly to be held as men at all. Scripture itself has asked half doubtingly if they can change their skins, but we who know the Scriptures as we know Bradshaw, making them books of reference in which to search for precepts to support our acts, are ready to reply.

The Ethiopian cannot change his skin, and therefore we are ready to possess his land and to uproot him for the general welfare of mankind, smiting him hip and thigh, as the Jews did the Canaanites when first they opened up the promised land. Niggers who have no cannons have no rights. Their land is ours, their cattle and their fields, their houses ours; their arms, their poor utensils, and everything they have; their women, too, are ours to use as concubines, to beat, exchange, to barter off for gunpowder or gin, ours to infect with syphilis, leave with child, outrage, torment, and make by contact with the vilest of our vile, more vile than beasts.

Yet take us kindly, and at once the tender nature of our hearts is manifest to all. Cretans, Armenians, Cubans, Macedonians we commiserate, subscribe, and feel for, our feeling souls are wrung when Outlanders cannot get votes. Bishops and cardinals and statesmen, with philanthropists and pious ladies, all go wild about the Turks.

England's great heart is sound, it beats for all the sorrows of mankind; we must press on, we owe it to ourselves and to our God; ours to perform our duty, his to provide the field; the world is ours, let us press on to do our mutual will, and lose no time, in case inferior aping nations may forestall us, cut in between us and all those we burn to serve, and having done so, then shoot out their tongues and say: "These were but weaklings, and their God made in their image, merely an Anglo-Saxon and anthropomorphous fool."

At Torfaieh

A shade of dissatisfaction crept over the dark, handsome face of Najim, the Syrian, as he sat cleaning his pistol at the door of the factory at Cape Juby. In front the desert, flat, sandy, and grown over with low "sudra" bushes, as is the prairie overgrown with mezquite and with huisache in Western Texas. Behind, the sea, shipless and desolate, breaking upon the coast in long lines of surf, thundering and roaring ceaselessly. On the horizon a faint blue cloud just indicated the whereabouts of Lanzarote.

The factory itself, square-built and ugly, looking just like a piece of Manchester adrift in Africa, only redeemed from stark vulgarity by the cannon on the roof. Upon a little island, about three hundred yards to seaward, the fort looked frowningly, and showed the nozzles of its three guns through embrasures pointing towards the shore, as emblems of the milder faith the pious traders hoped to introduce.

Mecca and Galilee; the sword and fishing-net; on the one hand barbarity, upon the other progress; long guns, curved daggers, flying haiks, polygamy, the old-world life, opposed to cotton goods, arms of precision, store clothes, and the exterior graces which the interior virtues of our time and race induce. Outpost of progress, now, alas! submerged once more in the dark flood of Islam; portion of Scotland, reft from the mother country and erratically disposed in Africa in the same way that bits of Cromarty are found scattered sporadically about the map. Torfaieh was as Scotch, or even still more Scotch, than Peebles, Lesmahagow, or the Cowcaddens, for the setting went for nothing in comparison with the North British composition of the place. Decent and orderly the Scottish clerks, the tall, red-bearded manager; Scotch the pioneer, known to the Arabs down into the Sahara as "M'Kenzie," he who had found the place, surveyed it, planned to submerge the desert, and to sail to Timbuctoo, had got the company together, had sweated blood and water and regarded "Juby" as the apple of his eye. Order and due precision of accounts, great ledgers, beer upon tap, whiskey served out "medicinally," prayers upon Sunday, no trifling with the Arab women ever allowed, a moral tone, a strict attention to commercial principles, and yet no trade, for by a cursed fate the "doddering" English directors who controlled the cash had sent an order that no trading should be done, as they were waiting for the time when a paternal Government should equip them with a charter, and place them on a level with the Niger Company, and the philanthropists who smoked the "niggers" in the caves of the Matoppo Hills.

Therefore the order ran, "Let no one bringing trade approach the place," and natives having journeyed from the recesses of the desert with camels packed with wool, descried the factory low in the horizon, drank their last draught of water and hurried on their beasts, to find themselves greeted with rifle fire, and told to keep away. Then from the windows broke a fusillade of guns, and Najim, the Syrian interpreter, would mount upon his horse, and galloping towards the wondering, would-be traders, tell them on peril of their lives to keep away if they brought trade, but to come on and camp if they had none. This not unnaturally led to ill-feeling, for the wool had to be buried in the sand till, as the Arabs said, it pleased Allah to restore the Company to health.

And so they passed their lives like men upon a ship, not often daring to go far from their factory, occasionally venturing to hunt gazelles, but usually returning, hunted themselves by the exasperated Arabs, who fired on them when and where they got a chance. But not to lose their hold entirely upon the place, the Company paid all the more important chiefs allowances, which they thought tribute, and a feeling of contempt sprang up, tempered with kindliness and typified by the phrase "Our Christians;" these they protected and found necessary, but esteemed mad, as are, in fact, all Nazarenes and those who have no knowledge of the Faith. A pleasant, idle, not unhealthy, beery, and contemplative life; few stood it long, but sought relief in drink or else went mad, and all the time the Company were convinced the Arabs (whom they had never seen) were peaceably inclined, though they had had a manager murdered not half a mile outside the gate.

So all went well both up and down the coast, into the desert, and up to the Wad Nun, where Dahman-el-Beiruc reigned over the most fanatic of all the tribes. The legend grew about the mad Christians, who fired on traders, but yet paid good allowances to chiefs to encourage trade, and welcomed every one so that he came with empty hands. And then, as if on purpose to confirm the Arabs in their belief that Nazarenes are all stark mad, another rival band of Bedlamites appeared, all bursting to acquire the hypothetic trade and to supplant their brother madmen in the race.

Money was freely spent upon the chiefs, five thousand dollars falling to the share of one of them, who brought it loaded upon two camels to an employé of the Cape Juby Company to keep. Then these, too, faded into space, leaving some two or three of their adventurers captive amongst the desert tribes, and gloom settled upon Cape Juby, broken but by the three monthly visits of the chiefs for their allowance, and an occasional interchange of friendly shots at a long range with would-be traders from afar. But in the meantime Najim, the Syrian, rose from interpreter to manager, and all the while he did his duty, entering sacks of rice and bags of bullets, chests of tea, barrels of gunpowder, cases of gin, and bales of cloth in ledgers, or seeing it was duly done by the Scotch clerks, the desert life took hold of him as it has taken hold of many another of those sons of Adam whom a cynic deity has cursed with imagination, and rendered them unfit for ordinary work. The wild old life, the camels, the lean and worthless-looking but untiring desert horses, the blue clad, long-haired Arabs, with their close bargaining for trifles, and boundless generosity in larger things, the low horizon, and the pure language spoken by the people — always a pleasure to a man of Arab blood — took so firm a grip of him that all his sympathies were outside the fort, and his desire was to be like the natives in thought and dress.

When not on duty he wore the Arab clothes, talked with the tribesmen, learned their lore, rode in the powder play, heard of the "ould el naama" (son of the ostrich), the child, who, lost by his parents, had found a foster-parent in an ostrich, and in whose capture three good mares were tired, and by degrees insensibly grew to think the desert life the best which it has pleased Allah to show to man. All the chiefs knew him and looked on him as a sort of landmark set up between the Christians and Islam. Arab in blood, Arab in sympathy as regards the desert life, but yet a Christian, their wonder knew no bounds. "You speak like us, have our own skin, our eyes, read the Koran, and understand it; what then restrains you from saying you are one of us, joining the Faith, marrying amongst us, and leading amongst the tribesmen the life you say you love?" In fact, some thought he was a Moslem, but from policy pretended to be a Christian, until he, a Syrian of the Syrians, told them that for a thousand years his people had been Christians, and that, though not believing it, he yet would die a member of the Faith in which he had been born. This took their fancy, for Arabs are always taken with a bold answer, and they said: "Najim, you are a man, that is the way to speak, Christian or Moslem, you are still our friend." Then cunning, as only they themselves, they sought for his opinion upon the reality of the conversion of other Syrians who had left the Company and married in the tribe. But he, at least as subtle as they themselves, answered evasively that the heart of man is as the darkness of a starless night, and God alone can see into its depths.

The Arabs laughed and said, "By the Nabi he knows as much as we ourselves," they knowing nothing of any subject under heaven but camels' footprints in the sand, signs of the weather, the names of some few stars, together with the daily ceremonials of their faith, which constitute their life.

So, as he sat cleaning his nickelled Smith and Wesson pistol, bought in New York, that Mecca of all young Syrians, he saw far off upon the plain, dust rising, and was sure that it betokened the arrival of some chief, and as the allotted time for paying the allowances (or tribute) had not come, he knew, as trade by this time was well frightened off, that it portended the advent of some Arab come to beg. Nothing annoyed him more than these begging ventures of the chiefs. As manager he was tied down to a certain set allowance, and yet to send a man away after, perhaps, a three weeks' journey empty-handed, was impolitic, and besides hurt his feelings, for, like all generous-minded men, "No" stuck in his soul; and when pronounced, even with reason, rose up against him as a meanness, for, though quick-witted as most Syrians are, he was not of the race of men who, pending the due carrying out of Scripture, possess the earth.

Like ships almost hull down on the horizon, the caravan appeared, and first the riders, on the low scrubby plain, seemingly seated in the air, and then the camels heaving into sight, swaying and sliding through the sand, their long necks waving to and fro as every now and then they snatched a bite from the low, thorny scrub. Perched on them, their faces veiled, spears in their hands, their riders sat, and in the wake eight or ten semi-naked men on foot, driving the donkeys, without which, in the West Sahara no train of camels is complete. Lastly, a group of horsemen, all armed with guns and sitting on their high red saddles, swathed in their indigo robes, impassable and with the far-off look as if the eye saw through the middle distance and did not take it in, being fixed on the horizon, which is peculiar to all riders on frontiers, deserts, and to those whose safety rests on their power of seeing the approaching stranger first.

Arrived before the factory, the travellers halted, made their camels kneel, got off, and set about their preparations for a camp in the methodical but dawdling way that travellers on camels all affect. Then they sat talking fully an hour, for every movement in the desert is as much discussed as amongst Indians in America, or amongst county councillors deliberating what next to lay upon the ratepayer; and it by no means follows that men, having reached their journey's end, enter the city they have arrived at, or begin the business on which they have set out, for if the council so determines, it is just as likely that they may all return without a word. But in an hour or two, prayers duly said, dates and rice eaten, green tea discussed, a single figure, veiled to the eyes, wrapped in a blue burnoose, and holding in its hand a long flint gun, hooped round the barrel with brass, and with a Spanish dollar hanging from the twisted stock, stalked to the house and asked for Najim, Najim el Shami, and was admitted through the iron-plated door into the courtyard of the house. There Najim received him, and he began, "Ah, Najim, my heart has longed for you; in the desert below Sagiet-el-Hamara I said, 'I will arise and take my camels and will see my friend. Is he not chief of all our Christians?' So I unveiled my head, and in the sight of all men, openly, I took my way. All men know of me, my name is Bu Dabous; when men ask of me, Najim, say you know my name. Many have sought my friendship, letters arrive asking me to be true to them, some from the Sultan, five from Dahman-el-Beiruc. I tell you, Najim, five from Dahman-el-Beiruc. What did I do? I, Bu Dabous, give not my friendship lightly, so I said, 'The Sultan, well, he is far away, his messenger may wait, and Dahman-el-Beiruc, how can I answer so many letters all at once? I will seek Najim, and will tell him of my straits.' Ah, Najim, in my tents there is nothing; sugar, no sugar, tea, not a pound, no powder, and my children naked for want of cloth. So I took only five camels, and but ten of my best friends, and came to seek you Najim, knowing you are my friend, and that whilst you lived you would not let men say that Bu Dabous came to ask a favour and returned unblessed." Then Najim, sore perplexed, took up his parable. "Ah, Bu Dabous, right glad am I to see you, and the Company in all their letters write to me saying that they regard you as a friend. But, still, you know I am but manager, and it is far beyond my power to give you what you want. Each article I take is to be paid for, and you do not wish, I think, that I should be a loser by my friend. Yet, as a friend, I will exceed my power, and on my own account take from the store a bale of cloth, two chests of tea, a cask of sugar, and some gunpowder. These shall be yours, so that you may not say I am insensible to friendship, and disregard the trouble you have taken to come so far." Then Bu Dabous rose gravely from his seat and said, "Najim, I was deceived. I fear you are no friend, but a true Christian at the heart, one of these men who know no generosity, and whose sole God is pelf. Money, money, that is the Christians' God. That which you offer me is not enough for even one of my ten friends. Was it for this I sent the Sultan's messenger away and left five letters from Dahman-el-Beiruc without reply? But, Najim, not to shame you," and as he spoke he touched the Syrian lightly on the chest with his long, thin, brown hand, dyed blue with rubbing on his woad-stained clothes, "I will take credit from you, and all shall be arranged. The credit shall be large, not to disgrace me, and that the Company may say Najim does business with a wealthy man. Close to Shangiet, not fifteen days from here, I have five or six thousand dollars of fine wool. Now, therefore, give me forty chests of tea and twenty bales of cloth, a cask of gunpowder, ten guns, some lead, a hundred loaves of sugar, and add, just as a favour for myself, a pair of scissors and a little knife to trim my nails."

Poor Najim heard the demand with horror, and refused point-blank, and Bu Dabous, seating himself again, said, "Here will I sit, O Najim, till your heart speaks and I receive that which I want." His patience done, Najim called to his native police, and bidding them take from the store some tea and sugar and a bale of cloth, had Bu Dabous conducted to the gate. But from the middle of the men who pushed him roughly, a voice arose. "See how your soldiers use your friend. Give me, I pray, the scissors and the little knife." Then after a due interval had passed, slowly the "cafila" took the road towards the south, swaying and waving to and fro, passed out into the desert, raising a column of fine dust; the donkeys followed, and the horsemen bringing up the rear, turned in their saddles and fired a harmless volley at the fort.

Then, as he looked from off the roof, Najim beheld them slowly melt into the low horizon, the footfalls of their animals dulled in the sand, the riders perched high on their camels, or sitting upright on their horses, their guns carried erect like spears. Lastly they sank into the sand from whence they came, and Najim lighting a cigarette, descended from the roof, and going to his office turned to his ledger with a sigh.

Appendices

Beyond English: Graham's Use of Foreign Languages in

Father Archangel of Scotland, and Other Essays

A considerable part of the flavour of Graham's sketches and tales derives from the wide variety of physical settings and his understanding of their local cultures and languages. His range of foreign language references in this collection is extensive and occasionally challenging.

Latin units include : 'Odium Theologicum' ('hatred based on theological differences'); 'meum' ('my'); 'tuum' ('your'); 'partes infidelium' ('lands of the infidels'); 'bona fides' ('honest intention'); 'in extenso' ('at length'); 'De Potestate Pontificis Romani' ('Concerning the Power of the Bishop of Rome'); and in the climax of the title story 'Father Archangel of Scotland' 'Pretiosa in conspectu Domini est mors sanctorum ejus' ('Precious in the eyes of God is the death of His saints/martyrs'). The Latin title 'De Heretico Comburendo', initially unexplained, means 'Concerning the Burning of a Heretic'. A 'scandalum magnatum' is a defamatory speech or piece of writing directed against an important person. Some critics thought the Jesuit Missions in Paraguay an 'imperium in imperio' — an 'empire within the empire'. 'In pace requiescat' means 'May he rest in peace'. 'In proelio occisus' means 'Killed in battle'.

French items used include the oddly-spelt 'Xarentan' location near Paris, probably 'Charenton' near the Bois de Vincennes. Also logged are: 'plus haute gomme' ('the highest social classes'); 'esquin' ('dagger', from the Scottish 'sgian'?); 'fond de jupe'; and 'bourgeois'. He uses the French 'Soudan' rather than the English 'Sudan'.

The largest quantity of foreign language items derives from Spanish. Though his spoken Spanish was fluent, his printed Spanish was chaotic. He omits the Spanish stress mark in: después; Cristóbal; Ponce de León; lágrimas; pérfido; Río; María; Díaz; Julián; zaguán; Encarnación; Agustín; José; Solís; Joaquín; Rodríguez; chapetón; Fernández; Asunción; corazón; Inglés; Tucumán; Córdoba; sí; Martín; ría; Constitución; and Jardín. He uses old-style 'berengena' ('aubergine, egg-plant') and 'ginete' ('horseman') for 'berenjena' and 'jinete'. He stumbles when giving 'antiquarios' for 'anticuarios' and when he sets an unneeded stress mark on the 'e' of 'bayeta' ('a cleaning cloth').

Graham does usually insist on the Spanish tilde (ñ): Señor; Muñosancho; Nuñez (properly Núñez); año; compañero; España; vicuña; Coruña; and dueño, where his 'Soy de un dueño' ('I belong to an owner') remembered from old Iberian cannon barrels stamped with a king's coat-of-arms may be a very rare mis-recollection of 'Soy de mi dueño' ('I belong to my owner').

The cow-herders of the South American plains are capitalised as 'Gauchos'. Their beloved Paraguayan tea Graham presents as '(yerba) maté', where modern Spanish prefers '(yerba) mate'. The word for a horse's halter he gives as 'cabresto', where correct Spanish calls for 'cabestro': the gauchos in José Hernández's great protest poem *Martín Fierro* (1872; 1879) invariably speak of the 'cabresto', so Graham may be echoing their incorrect form.

He can be inconsistent: in the title sketch "Father Archangel of Scotland" the author surname initially given as Ajofrin (for Ajofrín) switches with Axofrin. The tribal group 'Guaycurús' conflicts with 'Guaycurus', and the southern hemisphere tree 'urunday' conflicts with 'Urunday'.

He seems to show care with units derived from American Indian languages: Guaraní (with one stumble on Guarani); Guayrá; Paraná; Yapeyú; Tobás; Guaycurús; Mocobíos; Tarumá; Payaguás; caraguatá; viraró; zamaú; Miní; Cuyabá; Humaitá; and Chiriguanás. Curiously, at two points in "In the Tarumensian Woods" he sets a stress mark over a final letter 'y': araguaý and Mondaý.

The single Portuguese item used is 'saudade', the piercing sense of longing for the homeland felt by the traveller, exile or expatriate.

In Italian the unit 'Cappucino' (Capuchin) is drawn from a book title and later in his own text becomes 'Cappuccino'. The unit 'l'arte de biondeggiar i capelli' is the art of turning the hair blonde. The unit 'Inglese Italianato diavolo Incarnato' means 'An Englishman turned Italian is the devil incarnate'. The Indians coaxed out of the forest into the Jesuit Mission have 'L'ultimo lasso! de *lor* giorni allegri' ('the last (stage?) of their happy times'): in quoting the first line of a Petrarch sonnet (*Canzonieri 328*) Graham changes the original 'miei' (my) to 'lor' (their), delicately signalling his change by setting 'lor' in italics. Is 'Raggionar' the verb 'to reason'?

His use of Scots terms is careful and accurate: 'to mak siccar'; '… to preach the Mass at her lug'; 'siller'; and 'oxgangis'. He initially offers both 'Aberden' and 'Aberdon'. He also cites the Celtic lamentation known as *coronach*.

His Arabic snippets seem to this inexpert eye quite authentic. They include locations such as Ras Doura; references to Mohammed, his wife Ayesha and the Koran; Ramazan (Ramadan, the Muslim month of fasting); the invocation Inshallah; holy places such as the Khutubieh at Marakish (the Koutoubia Mosque in Marrakesh) and the Muley Edris (Moulay Idriss) shrine at Fez; a tribe he calls the Zimouri; officials such as the Sultan, the Basha and the local township sherif; the feasts of Mulud (Birth of the Prophet) and Muley Busalham ('the patron of the riders'); the Marsa (port, natural harbour); the devil's trick known as Shaitanieh; imported English jockeys as 'ugly as Ginûn'; and items of clothing such as *haik* (a sheet-like outer garment) and *selhams* (hooded cloaks, burnouses). He mentions also the 'powder play' (Lab el Barod) where crowds of men on horseback ride frenetically back and forth firing off old-style muskets. His adjective 'Maroqui' may echo the English 'maroquin' (morocco leather) or the Spanish adjective 'marroquí' (Moroccan).

At the highest level, his apparent error in 'cabresto' may be a gaucho mispronunciation that Graham's ear utterly accepted, whilst his reformulation of the line from Petrarch is subtly and carefully done: he was an accomplished linguist and — all the evidence suggests — a superb speaker of Spanish. He shows very considerable skill in integrating these foreign language units into his sketches: they are usually deftly incorporated and smoothly explained or they can be grasped through the context. The educated reader is seldom bereft of understanding.

The occasionally wayward printed text of the first editions, however, would have benefited from more careful proof-reading.

John C. McIntyre

Aurora La Cuijiñi
A Realistic Sketch in Seville
With a Frontispiece

Si escribo veras nadie las entiende
Si burlas me prohibe que las haga
Si alabanzas nadie me las paga
Pues que tengo de hacer si todo ofende.

Licenciado Burguillos.

R.B. Cunninghame Graham

AURORA LA CUJIÑÍ

Aurora La Cujiñi
A Realistic Sketch In Seville

Isbilieh, as the Moors called Seville, had never looked more Moorish. The scent of Azahar hung in the air; from patio and from balcony floated the perfume of Albahaca and Almoradux, plants brought to Seville by the Moors from Nabothea. The city of the royal line of the Beni-Abbad was as if filled with a reminiscence of its past of sensuality and blood. The mountains of the Axarafe seemed to stand in a violet haze, a mile outside the town, instead of five leagues distant. The far-off sierras above Ronda looked jagged, and as if crenellated by the hand of man to serve as ramparts against the invasion of the African from his corresponding sierra in the country of the Angera across the straits. Over the Giralda came the faint pink tinge which evening imparts, in Seville, to all the still remaining Moorish work, making that finest specimen of the architecture of the Moors in Spain look delicate and new, as when the builder, he who in his life built at Rabat and at Marakesh, two other towers of similar design, completed it to the glory of the One God, and of Mohammed. Down the great river for which the Christians never found a better name than that left by the Moorish dogs, the yellow tide ran lazily, swaying alike the feluccas with their pointed tapering yards, the white Norwegian fruit schooners, and the sea coffins from the port of London, tramps out of Glasgow, and steam colliers from the Hartlepools or Newcastle-on-Tyne. The great cathedral in which lies Ferdinand Columbus, the most southern Gothic building in all Europe, built on the site of the great mosque said to have been as large as that of Cordoba, rose from the court of oranges silent as a vast tomb, and seemed protected from the town by its raised walk, fenced in with marble pillars taken from the ancient mosque. The Alcazar, Tower of Gold, the churches, especially St. John's beside the Palm, seemed to regret their builders, as I fancy do all the Saracenic buildings throughout Spain. Though ignorant of all the plastic arts, taking their architecture chiefly from the two forms of tent and palm-tree, their literature so constituted as to be almost incomprehensible to the people of the north, the tribes who came from the Hedjaz, the Yemen, and beyond Hadramut have left their imprint on whatever land they passed. They

313

comprehended that life is first, the chiefest business which man has to do, and so subordinated to it all the rest. Their eyes, their feet, their verse, and their materialistic view of everything have proved indelible wherever they have camped. They and their horses have stamped themselves for ever on the world. Even to-day their language, with English, Spanish, and Chinese, alone of all the speeches of mankind, gains ground.

Notable things have passed in Seville since Ojeda, before he sailed for the new-found Indies, ran along the beam fixed at a giddy height in the Giralda and threw a tennis-ball over the weather-vane, to show the Catholic Kings and the assembled crowd, the firmness of his head. Since San Fernando drove out the royal house of the Beni-Abbad, and Motamid, the poet king, took refuge in Mequinez, as Abd-el-Wahed chronicles in his veracious history of the times, much has occurred. In the Alcazar, Pedro el Justiciero had loved Maria Padilla; in it he had made the fishpond where the degenerate Charles the Second sat fishing whilst his empire slipped out of his hands. The Caloró from Hind, Multan, or from whatever Trans-Caucasian or Cis-Himalayan province they set out from, ages ago, had come, and spreading over Spain, fixed themselves firmly in the part of Seville called the Triana, after the Emperor Trajan, who was born there as some say, and where to-day they chatter Romany, deal in horses, tell fortunes, and behave as if the entire world was a great oyster to be opened by their wheedling tongues.

So on the evening of which I speak, a Sunday in the month of May, the bull-fight was just over, leaving behind it that mixed air of sensuousness and blood which seems to hover over Seville after each show of bulls, as it may once have hovered over Italica, the Roman city outside Seville, after a show of gladiators.

So the fight was over, and the British tourists, after condemning Spanish barbarism, had taken boxes to a man, and come away delighted with the picturesqueness of the show. In the arena the pæderastic-looking Chulos, dressed in their majo clothes, had capered nimbly before the bull, placing their banderillas deftly in his neck; waiting until the bull had lowered his head, they had placed one foot upon his forehead, and stepping across the horn had executed what is called 'el salto de trascuerno'; they had jumped with a pole over the bull, alighting on the other side like thistledown, dived behind the screen, caught and held the furious beast an instant by the tail, and after having played a thousand antics, running the gamut known to the 'intelligent' as 'volapie,' 'galleo,' 'tijerilla,' 'veronica,' and 'chatre,' escaped as usual with their worthless lives, for fortune, Providence, or the great motive but ill-regulated power which some think rules the world comes to the assistance of the strong, invariably. Perhaps Providence cares nothing, or perhaps, as bull-fighters, like other men, are all made in His image, is careful to protect what He has made, that men may see His image in themselves. Trumpets had sounded; and the horses, all of which had done more service to mankind than any fifty men, and each of which had as much right, by every law of logic and anatomy, to have a soul, if souls exist, as have the wisest of philosophers, had suffered martyrdom. Hungry and ragged, they had trodden on their entrails, received their wounds without a groan, without a tear, without a murmur, faithful to the end; had borne their riders out of danger, falling upon the bloody sand at last, with quivering tails, and, biting their poor parched and bleeding tongues, had died just as the martyrs died at Lyons or in Rome, as dumb and brave as they.

The 'espada' had come forward, mumbled his boniment in Andaluz, swung his montera over his shoulder upon the ground, and after sticking his sword in every quarter of the bull had butchered him at last amid the applause of the assembled populace. Blood on the sand; sun on the white plaza; upon the women's faces 'cascarilla'; scarlet and yellow fans, and white mantillas with 'fleco y alamares' in the antique style, and recognized by the discerning tourist as national because unseen except at bull-fights, and made in France or Germany; women selling water, calling out 'aguá!' in so guttural a voice it seemed like Arabic; Cordobese hats, short jackets, and from the plaza a scent of blood and sweat acting like a rank aphrodisiac upon the crowd, and making the women squeeze each other's sweating hands, and look ambiguously at one another, as they were men; and causing the youths, with swaying hips and with their hair cut low upon their foreheads, to smile with open lips and eyes that met your glance, as they had been half women.

Blood, harlotry, sun, gay colours, flowers and waving palm-trees, women with roses stuck behind their ears, mules covered up in harness of red worsted, cigar girls, gipsies, tourists, soldiers, and the little villainous-looking urchins, who, though born old, do duty as children in the South. The plaza vomits out the crowd, just as the Roman amphitheatre through its 'vomitorium' expelled its crowd of blood-delighting Roman citizens. "Civis Romanus sum," and all the rest of it.

The stiff dead horses were piled into a cart, their legs sticking out, pathetic and grotesque, between the bars. A cart of sand was emptied on the blood, then the 'espada,' some 'Culo Ancho,' or 'Lagartijillo,' got into his brougham, and all was done.

In the dark streets the women swarmed, in the Calle de la Pasion they stood against the open but barred windows, all freshly painted and expecting work.

In the dark lanes which lead in a sort of maze out of the 'Calle Sierpes' lovers stood talking from the streets to girls upon the balconies, whose mothers and the intervening distance of a storey guarded their virtue.

In the great palm-tree planted square, hard by the Casa Consistorial, the finest building of the Renaissance in Southern Spain, the salmon-coloured plaster seats were filled with men who seem to live there day and night, contributing their quota to the ceaseless national expenditure of talk. On this occasion they discussed, being all 'intelligent' (inteligentes), every incident of the recent fight, the old men deprecating modern innovation and sighing for the times and style of Cuchares, and of 'el Seño Romero,' he who first brought the art of bull-fighting from heaven, as his admirers say. If a woman, rich or poor, a Countess from Madrid, or maiden of the Caloró from the Triana, chanced to pass, they criticized her as a prospective buyer does a horse at Tattersall's. Her eyes, her feet, her air, everything about her, were freely commented on, and if found pleasing then came the approving "blessed be your mother!" with other compliments of a nature to make a singer at a Paris café concert blush. The recipients took it all as a matter of every-day occurrence, and, with a smile or word of thanks, according to their rank, pursued the uneven tenour of their way with heightened colour and perhaps a little more of what the Spaniards call 'meneo' of their hips.

In the Calle Sierpes, the main artery and chief bazaar, roofed with an awning from end to end, the people swarmed. The cafés were gorged with clients, all talking about the bull-fight, the Government, or disputing of the beauty and the nature of the women of their respective towns. The clubs, with windows of plate glass down to the ground, showed the 'haute gomme' lounging in luxury upon their plush upholstered chairs, stiff in their English clothes, and sweating blood and water in the attempt to look like Englishmen or like Frenchmen, and to keep up an unconcerned appearance under the public gaze. Girls selling lemonade, 'Horchata,' 'Agraz,' and the thick, sticky sweetmeats and white flaky pastry flavoured with fennel and angelica, left by the Moors in Spain, went up and down selling their wares and offering themselves to anyone who wished to venture half a dollar on the chance. The shops were full of all those unconsidered trifles which in Spain alone can find a market, cheap and abominably nasty, making one think that our manufactories must be kept running with a view to furnish idiots or blind men with things they do not want.

After the gospel, sermon, sherry after soup, so, in like manner, after a bull-fight the 'Burero' comes.

Theatres in Spain, in spite of Lope, Calderon, Echegaray, and the interminable plays of Moratin, of Ramon de la Cruz, and the immediate translation of every pornographic piece from Paris, never seem to thrive. Whether it is the badness of the scenery, or the casual manners of the actors, who stroll about and talk to one another without the slightest pretence of being letter-perfect, or from whatever cause it comes, I do not know.

Bull-fights and dancing-houses alone make money in a land where the inhabitants of Madrid hissed Sarah Bernhardt in "La Tosca," because they found the piece too quiet for their taste.

So on this evening the 'Burero' was packed with men. From the narrow doors, where old women sat selling flowers and obscenely-painted matchboxes, through the narrow passage, specially contrived as a death-trap in a case of fire, the people strove to push inside. An enormous music-hall, without a looking-glass, without a bar, without a velvet-cushioned seat, half lit by miserable oil-lamps, and bare enough of scenery to please a 'symboliste.' In the middle, rows of cane chairs opposite little bare wooden tables, at which sat drinking the flower of the rascality of Spain. In the gallery more cane chairs and wooden tables, three or four boxes in which, on this occasion, sat some foreign ladies come to see life, and over all the smoke of cigarettes filling the temple as with the fumes of incense. The audience almost mediæval as to type — Chulos and Chalanes, that is (*Arabicè*) loafers and horse-dealers, men with their hair drawn forward on the forehead, plastered to the head, close-shaved, dressed in the tightest of tight trousers, short jackets, stiff round felt hats, frilled shirts, and necktie like a shoe-string. Others, again, in tattered cloaks, and mixed with them some shepherds and herdsmen, and the not too anthropomorphic-looking scum which swarms in Seville and in every Southern Spanish town. Upon the stage eight or ten women, dressed in gay print dresses, Manilla shawls, boots with cloth tops, and highest of high heels, their hair dressed each one after her own idea, but generally high, sometimes hanging forward to hide the ears, and again in curls to almost cover up the eyes; flowers stuck about it, their faces painted in the Spanish fashion, without concealment of the paint, a comb surmounting all, sat chatting, smoking, pinching one another, and exchanging jokes with their acquaintances in the front.

On one side of the stage sat the musicians, two at the guitar, and two playing small instruments known as 'bandurrias,' a cross between a mandolin and a guitar. The women suddenly began to clap their hands in a strange rhythm, monotonous at first, but which at length, like the beating of a tom-tom, makes the blood boil, quiets the audience, stills the conversation, and focusses all eyes upon the stage. Then one breaks out into a harsh wild song, the interval so strange, the time so wavering, and so mixed up the rhythm, that at first it scarcely seems more pleasing than the howling of a wolf, but bit by bit goes to the soul, stirs up the middle marrow of the bones, and leaves all other music ever afterwards tame and unpalatable.

The singing terminates abruptly, as it seems, for no set reason, and dies away in a prolonged high shake, and then a girl stands up, encouraged by her fellows with shouts of "Venga Juana," "Vaya querida," and a cross fire of hats thrown on the stage, and interjections from the audience of "preciosita," "retrechera," and the inspiriting clap of hands, which never ceases till the dancer, exhausted, sinks into a chair. Amongst the audience, drinking their manzanilla in little tumblers about the thickness of a piece of sugar-cane, eating their 'boquerones,' ground nuts, and salted olives, the fire of criticism never stops, as everyone in Seville of the lower classes is a keen critic both of dancing-girls and bulls.

Of the elder men, a gipsy, though shouting out "salero" in a perfunctory manner, seemed discontented, and recalled the prowess of a gipsy long since dead, by name Aurora, surnamed La Cujiñi, and gave it as his faith that since her time no girl had ever mastered all the mysteries of the dance. The Caloró, who always muster strong at the 'Burero,' were on his side, and seemed inclined to enforce their arguments with their shears, which, as most of them maintain themselves by clipping mules, they always carry in their sash.

But just as the discussion seemed about to end in a free fight, a girl stepped out to dance. None had remarked her sitting quietly beside the rest; still, she was slightly different in appearance from them all. A gipsy at first sight, with the full lustrous eyes her people brought from Multan, dressed in a somewhat older fashion than the others, her hair brought low upon her forehead and straying on her shoulders in the style of 1840, her skirt much flounced, low shoes tied round the ankles, a Chinese shawl across her shoulders, and a look about her, as she walked into the middle of the stage, as of a mare about to kick. A whisper to the first guitar causes him with a smile to break into the Olé, his instrument well 'requintado' and his fingers flying across the cords as the old Moorish melody jarred and jingled out. She stands a moment motionless, her eyes distending slowly and focussing the attention of the audience on her, and then a sort of shiver seems to run over her, the feet begin to gently scrape along the floor, her naked arms move slowly, with her fingers curiously bent and meant perhaps to indicate by their position the symbols of the oldest of religions, and, as the gipsies say, she draws the hearts of every onlooker into her net. She twists her hips till they seem ready to disjoint, wriggles in a snake-like fashion, drags her skirt upon the stage, draws herself up to her full height, bends double, thrusts all her body forward, her hands move faster, and the short sleeves slip back exhibiting black tufts of hair under her arms, glued to her skin with sweat. Then she slides forwards, backwards, looks at the audience with defiance, takes a man's hat from off the stage, places it on her head, puts both her arms akimbo, sways to and fro, but still keeps writhing as if her veins were full of quicksilver. Little by little the frenzy dies away, her eyes grow dimmer, and the movements of the body slower, and with a final stamp, and a hoarse guttural cry, she stands a moment quiet, as it is called 'dormida,' that is, asleep, looking a very statue of impudicity. The audience remained a moment spellbound, with open mouths like Satyrs, and in the box where sat the foreign ladies, one has turned pale and rests her head upon the other's shoulder, who holds her round the waist. Then with a mighty shout the applause breaks forth, hats rain upon the stage, 'vivas' and 'vayas' rend the air, and the old gipsy bounds upon a table with a shout, "One God, one Cujiñi." But in the tumult La Cujiñi had disappeared, gone from the eyes of Caloró and of Busné, Gypsy and Gentile, and none saw her more.

Perhaps at witches' sabbaths she still dances, or perhaps in that strange Limbo where the souls of gipsies and their donkeys dree their weird, she writhes and dislocates herself in the Romalis.

Sometimes the curious may see her still dancing before a Venta, in the woolly outline of a Spanish lithograph, her head thrown back, her hair *au catagon*, with one foot pointing to a hat to show her power over, and her contempt for, all the sons of men, just as she did upon that evening when she took a brief and fleeting reincarnation to breathe once more the air of Seville, heavy with perfume of spring flowers mixed with the scent of blood.

R. B. Cunninghame Graham's "Aurora La Cujiñi": An Exploration

R. B. Cunninghame Graham published "Aurora La Cujiñi – A Realistic Sketch in Seville", a 17-page literary sketch in a limited edition of 500 numbered copies (Leonard Smithers, London, 1898). A copy, including the frontispiece, is available at Internet site "American Libraries Free Texts". Graham modified the original for publication in his collection *Charity* (Duckworth, London, 1912): this modified version can be read on the Internet at "Canadian Libraries Free Texts" > R. B. Cunninghame Graham > Charity > pages 146-162. This commentary deals with the 1898 limited edition version.

'Aurora' is one of the words for 'dawn' in Spanish and can be used as a girl's name. The unit 'La Cujiñi' looks strange: few words in Spanish end in '-iñi'. Where might this word come from?

The first clue comes from a French source. The writer and antiquarian Baron Charles de Davillier and the renowned illustrator Gustave Doré toured Spain together in the 1860s. Their reports were published in Hachette's major travel magazine *Le Tour du Monde* between 1862 and 1873. Hachette published the material in book form — including 309 wood-engravings by Doré — in Paris in 1874. The section on Cádiz and the introduction to Seville is available on the Internet: Le Tour du Monde (Paris 1860) > "1865/07 – (12) – 1865/12" > pages 353-432. This Internet presentation includes the drawings, set out in black on white, done by Doré.

The Davillier/Doré introduction to Seville at page 424 sets out a list of baptismal names preferred for southern Spanish gypsy girls: "Rocio…, - Soledad…, - Salud, - Candelaria…, - Aurora…, - Milagros…, - Gertrudis, etc., etc." Regarding the name Aurora Davillier writes: "Aurora (un nom illustré par une des plus célèbres danseuses gitanas de Séville: Aurora, surnommée la Cujini, mot qui, dans le langage des gitanos, signifie la Rose)". So Davillier and Doré either encountered or heard about a famous gypsy dancer in Seville known as 'Aurora La Cujini' [no tilde in Davillier], the unit 'La Cujini' being either a nickname or a stage name apparently meaning 'The Rose' in 'el caló', the Indo-European language spoken by Spanish gypsies.

The second clue comes from the frontispiece chosen by Graham — an image of an unnamed flamenco dancer: this ochre-coloured frontispiece image can be seen at page 312.

In April 2010 Grosvenor Prints (London) offered for sale a coloured lithograph entitled 'A Flamenco Dancer': a colour photograph in their catalogue illustrated the item. This catalogue photograph included at the top the information: "Costumbres Andaluzas" ("Andalusian Customs") and at the bottom "Aurora la Cujiñí. Chaman. Lith. G. Santigosa, Sevilla [no date, c. 1850]". The stage name is given with tilde and final written stress as 'La Cujiñí'. The lithograph was recently gifted to the present writer: a new colour image is available on the Internet.

The colour lithograph dated by the prints specialists at c. 1850 and Davillier's text from 1862 together suggest that Aurora La Cujiñí was a real person in the world of dance in Seville in the mid-nineteenth century. Graham may not have known her personally in the late 1860s or thereafter, but he was clearly familiar with the lithograph and the name. Aurora La Cujiñí was not invented by Graham.

The 3,230 words of "Aurora La Cujiñí" seem to contain five blocks of narrative. In the first section (up to "… wheedling tongues") Graham shows Seville's and the river's original Arabic names, Moorish-introduced plants, the Cathedral built on the site of a mosque and other Arab-style buildings recalling tent and palm tree. Graham identifies the Arabs' "materialistic view of everything". Long after the Christian capture, far-travelled gypsies settled on the Triana bank of the river.

The second section on the bullfight runs to "… all was done." On the opening page Graham had written: "The city … was as if filled with a reminiscence of its past of sensuality and blood." Here the bullfight leaves behind it "that mixed air of sensuousness and blood", the atmosphere becoming charged with a latent sensuality that threatens to disrupt conventions, with "… a scent of blood and sweat acting like a rank aphrodisiac upon the crowd …".

In the third section — as far as "… do not want." — the crowd makes its way back into town and Graham the costumbrist logs a range of typical behaviours, including men salaciously scrutinising the bodies of passing women and the young women selling soft drinks and their own bodies.

In the fourth section — up to "… in their sash." — the crowd packs into the "Burero" dancing-house where old women sell "flowers and obscenely-painted match-boxes…" and the flamenco troupe begins to create a strange tension. A solo dancer called Juana cannot, however, erase the memory of "the prowess of a gipsy long since dead, by name Aurora, surnamed La Cujiñi…"

In the fifth block, a young female dancer dances and is wildly applauded and acclaimed as the re-born Aurora from the 1840s. Her shuddering sensuality "draws the hearts of every onlooker into her net" until "she stands a moment quiet, as it is called, 'dormida,' that is, asleep, looking a very statue of impudicity". The sketch ends with further insistence on blood and sensuality.

The orderly progression from the opening bird's eye view of the city, through the collectively shared emotions of the bullfight, the crowd's return to town and the filling up of the dancing-houses into the concentrated focus on the young dancer in the last sequence is well planned and well handled.

The sketch is sub-titled "A Realistic Sketch in Seville", and Graham shows a sharp eye for realistic detail, as in: "The stiff dead horses were piled into a cart, their legs sticking out, pathetic and grotesque, between the bars. A cart of sand was emptied on the blood, then the 'espada,' some 'Culo Ancho' or 'Lagartijillo,' got into his brougham and all was done."

This last remark goes mischievously and mockingly beyond straightforward realism. Graham's use of the Spanish diminutive ending '-illo', which can be affectionate, here feels pejorative, suggesting that this bullfighter palely imitates an original. And 'Culo Ancho' means 'Broad Arse', the opposite of the slim hips yearned for by male flamenco dancers, classic bullfighters and their fans.

Graham's competence in standard realism shows again when he describes the upper classes in their clubs "… sweating blood and water in the attempt to look like Englishmen or like Frenchmen…" Graham suggests that as the dancer bewitches her audience, "the short sleeves slip back exhibiting black tufts of hair under her arms, glued to her skin with sweat." Graham is a clear-minded and clear-sighted realist.

Graham deploys extensive knowledge of Spain, regarding Seville's Moorish background, mediæval Spanish history, the migration of the gypsies — the Caloró — from India to Triana, bullfight routines and vocabulary, water-sellers crying out "in so guttural a voice it seemed like Arabic", and the dress, speech, eating and drinking habits and enthusiasms of the dance-hall crowd.

Graham, fascinated by foreign cultures, maintains a critical distance. The Arabs in Spain created wonderful buildings yet were "ignorant of all the plastic arts"; Spanish gypsies "behave as if the entire world was a great oyster to be opened by their wheedling tongues"; Southern children can be "little villainous-looking urchins"; and prostitution is common in Seville. Graham's familiarity with his foreign scenario is presented thoughtfully and sometimes with sly humour.

Graham enjoyed using Hispanisms. He delights in local place-names and personal names: the Giralda; the Alcázar; Pedro el Justiciero; Triana; and the Calle Sierpes, "the main artery and chief bazaar". He mentions the 'espada' (sword, and by implication swordsman, i.e. the bullfighter); "selling lemonade, Horchata, Agraz..."; " 'bandurrias,' a cross between a mandolin and a guitar"; "drinking their manzanilla in little tumblers of the thickness of a piece of sugar-cane..."; "his instrument well 'requintado'"; and " 'vivas' and 'vayas' rend the air". In most of the Hispanisms there is usually a smoothly arranged context or explanation.

Graham, an accomplished horseman, was besotted with the world of the horse. In "Aurora La Cuijñi" he describes the suffering of the horses abused in the bullring thus: "Hungry and ragged, they had trodden on their entrails, received their wounds without a groan, without a tear, without a murmur, faithful to the end; had borne their riders out of danger, fallen upon the bloody sand at last with quivering tails, and, biting their poor, parched and bleeding tongues, had died just as the martyrs at Lyons or in Rome, as dumb and brave as they." This extraordinary empathy with the horse will surface in many future pieces set in the horse-riding cultures of Mexico and South America.

Aged 45-46 in 1898 Graham had campaigned long and fearlessly for radical change — as an orator, as a Member of Parliament and in regular articles in major journals. He often carries his combative style into his sketches and tales. His deeply-felt mistrust of Victorian progress and capitalism is seen in: "The shops were full of all those unconsidered trifles which in Spain alone can find a market, cheap and abominably nasty, making one think that our manufactories must be kept running with a view to furnish idiots or blind men with things they do not want."

This critical view of late Victorian values occasionally darkens into a bitter view of the whole human condition: the bullfighter's assistants "escaped as usual with their worthless lives, for fortune, Providence, or the great motive but ill-regulated power which some think rules the world comes to the assistance of the strong, invariably"; and "… the horses, all of which had done more service to mankind than any fifty men, and each of which had as much right, by every law of logic and anatomy, to have a soul, if souls exist, as have the wisest of philosophers, had suffered martyrdom".

Only after an older gypsy recalls the mastery of dance of a long-dead girl called 'Aurora La Cujiñi' does the unnamed girl rise to perform. Graham presents her as "dressed in a somewhat older fashion than the others, her hair brought low upon her forehead and straying on her shoulders in the style of 1840…" For Graham the dancer's curiously bent fingers may hint at ancient and certainly pre-Christian cults. On that evening in the 'Burero', the young dancer taking "… a brief and fleeting reincarnation to breathe once more the air of Seville, heavy with perfume of spring flowers mixed with the scent of blood" dances wildly and drives the spectators into orgasm. Through the young ghost dancer, invested with almost supernatural power, Graham romantically calls up an older world which may occasionally surface in present times to remind us of a way of life and a culture that was different from and in some ways better than our present mode of living. Graham's liking for the costumbrist sketch — the depiction of types and times either disappearing or past — suggests that in essence he was a nostalgic.

Not everything in Graham is easy reading. Not all his sketches and tales will be as tightly drafted as "Aurora La Cujiñi". Occasionally a Biblical or Classical reference will test today's reader. He can unfold a long sentence laden with commas, subordinate clauses and parentheses. His foreign-language references are wide-ranging. He can be a careless proof-reader, even of his beloved Spanish. Generally, though, Graham sustains a coherent descriptive or narrative voice, brimming with energy, excitement, insight and commitment.

In 1894 Graham's good friend, W. H. Hudson — born and brought up on the Argentine pampa, a superb naturalist and himself a considerable writer — encouraged Graham to study the vignettes of pampa life published by the French engineer Alfred Ébélot in *La Pampa, Costumbres argentinas* (1890): Hudson wanted Graham to move away from long historical studies towards shorter pieces based on Graham's direct experience. Graham persisted with a longer format in the 1896 title story "Father Archangel of Scotland" and in his reviews of Heriberto Frías' 1892 novel *Tomóchic* (in *Progress* in 1905) and of

Tschiffely's Ride (in *Writ in Sand* in 1932); and in 1901 he will publish *A Vanished Arcadia*, the hefty study of the Jesuit Missions in colonial South America, the first of eleven long studies of aspects of South American history.

"Aurora La Cujiñi", however, generated an extremely positive response from some of Graham's closest and most valued literary associates. Cedric Watts in his 1983 biography of Graham (page 45) reports Arthur Symons, leading light of the Aesthetic and Symbolist movements, showering praise on "Aurora La Cujiñi". The influential critic and editor Edward Garnett wrote: "Only an 'impression' you will say. Yes, but something that transfers the intoxication *to us*: you infect us with the snaky poison of that woman, the delicious madness. Admirably seen, admirably felt, admirably described!" Graham's great friend, the novelist Joseph Conrad, commented: "C'est, tout simplement, magnifique.... This seems the most finished piece of work you've ever done." Graham with "Aurora La Cujiñi" was settling very comfortably into the shorter format of the 3,000-word sketch recommended to him by Hudson.

So "Aurora La Cujiñi" shows: careful introductory scene-setting; a well-ordered narrative line; a motif that through careful repetition deepens the surface narration; realistic detail adding conviction to the text; deft deployment of knowledge and experience of foreign cultures; measured use of the local language to add authenticity; empathy with horses; a dark and sardonic view of the human condition; and a profound nostalgia for the past. Almost every sketch or tale after "Aurora La Cujiñi" is likely to show one, two or several of the features manifested so fluently in "Aurora La Cujiñi".

More broadly, the period 1896 to January 1899 can be seen as crucial in Graham's development. Graham had included in *Father Archangel of Scotland, and Other Essays* (1896) and in *The Ipané* (1899) four pieces on the pampa, the gauchos, the lasso and the gaucho throwing-weapon: these pieces are closer to the essay than the sketch. On the other hand, his remaining seven sketches in *Father Archangel of Scotland, and Other Essays* the independently published single sketch "Aurora La Cujiñi" (1898) and within months thirteen other sketches in *The Ipané* — set in Paraguay, the Mexico-U.S. borderlands, on the pampa, in West African waters, the Atlantic coastal desert, Tangier, Scotland, Iceland and England — show a Graham who is confidently exploring a very wide variety of settings within the format of the sketch. Taken together, the collection *Father Archangel of Scotland, and Other Essays*, "Aurora La

Cujiñi" and the collection *The Ipané* mark a significant step forward in Graham's accelerating definition of his narrative persona.

Speculation

García Lorca's 1930s lecture on *el duende* — artistic inspiration — depicts a scenario in Cádiz where the great singer 'La Niña de los Peines' ['The Girl with the Combs'] utterly failed to impress an audience of flamenco sophisticates. Stung by a sarcastic comment of "¡Viva París!", 'La Niña' sings again — but this time with *duende*. There is a curious similarity between Graham's and Lorca's flamenco scenarios and their depiction of an almost divine moment of creative inspiration that through the live performer shakes the audience to the core of its being. Might Lorca have read Graham's "Aurora La Cujiñi"?

John C. McIntyre

Note - A new colour image of the Aurora lithograph can be viewed on screen in the electronic journal TEJUELO:

http://iesgtballester.juntaextremadura.net/web/profesores/tejuelo/vinculos/articulos/r11/08.pdf

Index of Stories in Volume 1

At Torfaieh	299
Batuecas, The	171
Bolas, The	227
Bristol Fashion	243
De Heretico Comburendo	111
El Babor	141
Father Archangel of Scotland	83
Heather Jock	265
Horses of the Pampas, The	149
In a Garden	181
In the Tarumensian Woods	117
Ipané, The	199
Jesuit, A	129
La Vera de Plasencia	177
Lazo, The	221
Niggers	291
Notes on the District of Menteith	15
Preface, *Father Archangel of Scotland*	81
Preface, *Notes on the District of Menteith*	13
Preface, *The Ipané*	197
Ras Doura	135
S.S. "Atlas"	233
Salvagia	271
Snaekoll's Saga	277
Survival, A	257
Tanger La Blanca	251
Un Angelito	215
Un Pelado	209
Vanishing Race, A	157
Will, A	101
With the North-West Wind	285
Yuste	165

Lightning Source UK Ltd.
Milton Keynes UK
UKOW04f1427081117

312394UK00003B/635/P

9 781849 211000